REBECCA,

NOT BECKY

Rebecca, Not Becky

a novel

CHRISTINE PLATT AND
CATHERINE WIGGINTON GREENE

AMISTAD

An Imprint of HarperCollins*Publishers*

REBECCA, NOT BECKY. Copyright © 2023 by Christine Platt and Catherine Wigginton Greene. All rights reserved. Printed in the United States of America. No part of this book may be used or reproduced in any manner whatsoever without written permission except in the case of brief quotations embodied in critical articles and reviews. For information, address HarperCollins Publishers, 195 Broadway, New York, NY 10007.

HarperCollins books may be purchased for educational, business, or sales promotional use. For information, please email the Special Markets Department at SPsales@harpercollins.com.

FIRST EDITION

Designed by Janet Evans-Scanlon

Art credits:
Pages 27, 71, 73, 74, 75, 76, 82, 83, 164, 182, 216, 226 (heart eyes and heart), 227, 310 (laughing emoji; clapping hands), 322, 323, 377 (heart eyes), 378, 383, 406: © Cali6ro/Shutterstock
Pages 28, 163, 310 (eyes): © orbitoclast/Shutterstock
Page 79: © flower travelin man/Shutterstock
Page 149: © Larryneu77/Shutterstock
Page 226 (skull): © Denis Gorelkin/Shutterstock
Page 377 (cookie): © M_Videous/Shutterstock

Library of Congress Cataloging-in-Publication Data has been applied for.

ISBN 978-0-06-321358-6 (paperback)
ISBN 978-0-06-321359-3 (hardcover)

23 24 25 26 27 LBC 5 4 3 2 1

For everyone on their respective journeys—
remember to choose the paths less chosen, cackle
just as much as (if not more than) you cry, have
unwavering courage to embrace the unknown,
and extend grace and forgiveness to others as well
as yourself. We're all just trying to figure it out.
—Christine

For Nanny, who always had a jar full of cookies,
prayed at her front door whenever an ambulance
passed, and rooted for each *Wheel of Fortune* player
to win a little bit of money. —Catherine

ONE

De'Andrea

Even though De'Andrea Whitman was woefully behind schedule, she continued rearranging the fragrant long-stemmed lilies she'd purchased for the first summer soiree she *didn't* want to host. From the black linen place cards resting on elegant mini easels to the gold-rimmed china, everything De'Andrea envisioned for her and Malik's "Farewell, Friends" gathering was perfect. Well, everything was perfect except having to say farewell. She still couldn't believe they were leaving Atlanta in three weeks.

How was that all the time they had left?

Only three more weeks in the Black oasis of Buckhead before they moved to the whiter-than-white suburb of Rolling Hills? Before Malik had to transfer to his consulting firm's Northern Virginia office where he'd be the only Black executive? And to accept that their five-year-old daughter, Nina, wouldn't be a kindergartner at a Montessori school of Black excellence? Now their sweet girl had to attend Magnolia Country Day School—some not-as-progressive-as-it-thought-it-was private school that paled in comparison, literally and figuratively. And what kind of name for a town was Rolling Hills? *Like, hills don't even roll!*

"Only three more weeks of being Black and bougie with my

besties!" De'Andrea wailed. "Then I'll be living among the whites, and be stuck dealing with Karens and Beckys and all their caucacity!"

Inhale.

She fanned her face with her hands to keep her tears at bay.

Exhale.

"Waitaminute." De'Andrea squinted at two of the six place settings.

How was the spacing between Toni and Craig *still* off? And maybe the two married couples *should* sit across from each other instead of next to each other. Hadn't she read somewhere that any hostess who knew how to do the mostest made it easy for partners to make eye contact?

Inhale. Exhale.

"Dear God!" She sighed. "Let me just put things back the way I had them before."

Determined this would be her last switcheroo, De'Andrea tightened the belt around her tan cashmere robe and quickly descended the steps into the sunken dining room. As soon as her Gucci shearling-lined slippers hit the hardwood floors, she made a beeline for the nearest place setting.

Damn, Dee!

Her reflection in the large picture window overlooking the garden was unforgiving, and she frowned at her chunky, unparted braids before giving them a few reassuring pats with her palm.

"Just make these changes, then you can go get ready and stop looking like Celie in *The Color Purple*," she encouraged herself.

While switching Toni's name card to the mini easel across from Craig's for the umpteenth time, De'Andrea noticed something floating in the water of the floral centerpiece.

Don't do it! No one is going to even see that little leaf. You're being ridiculous.

"What's the point anyway?" she asked herself as she began removing lilies from the vase. It wasn't like there was some magical configuration that would make tonight's dinner feel more celebratory or change the inevitable. After she got this leaf out of the water and stopped playing musical chairs with the guest list, they'd still have to relocate to Rolling Hills.

"Moving to a new city is a new chapter in my blessed life." According to her therapist, repeating the relocation mantra would help calm her nerves whenever she felt anxious. But how many times did De'Andrea have to say the words before she actually believed them?

It wasn't that she doubted God's plans for her life. He was omnipotent, after all. But she *was* starting to wonder if her guardian angel had quietly quit.

Because this was supposed to be *her* year!

Once Nina started kindergarten, De'Andrea had planned to do some real soul-searching. Because there had to be more to life than being Malik's wife and Nina's mother. Not that she regretted holding either of those titles or her decision to leave BigLaw so she'd actually have time to spend with her little family. But damn if she wasn't ready to reclaim those precious hours between 8:00 a.m. and 3:00 p.m. to do something other than pick up Malik's dry cleaning and mothering her daughter. She needed some time to mother herself!

That's what she was supposed to be doing in three weeks— discovering and embracing the next chapter of her life—not moving to raggedy-ass Rolling Hills!

Who knows what she would have done or who she might have

become if they weren't leaving Atlanta? Maybe she would have returned to BigLaw. Not as a full-time attorney, of course. She already knew that billable-hours life was akin to indentured servitude. But maybe she could have worked as a part-time associate. There was also her homegirl's offer to teach a seminar at Emory Law School. And if she discovered she loved teaching, maybe she would have gotten a tenure-track gig. Or perhaps she might have just learned to embrace life as a kept woman. It wasn't like being a homemaker was the worst job in the world. Hell, she might have even allowed herself to be poked and prodded in the hopes of having another baby. Or as the fertility specialist would say, "Another geriatric pregnancy." Sure, being forty-two was *older*, but it wasn't *geriatric*! Geez! Did she even have any eggs left?

So much for the houseful of babies you thought you'd have one day!

De'Andrea sighed as she placed the last lily back in the floral centerpiece. Whatever she might have done or become, she'd never know. Because her life had been rocked to the core ever since her mother-in-law's Alzheimer's diagnosis. Mama Whitman's disappearance, the excruciating wait during the Silver Alert, and everything that followed had forever changed what being "close to family" meant for her and Malik. Mama Whitman was the reason—the *only* reason—they were moving to Rolling Hills.

"This is your reminder the caterers will arrive in . . . one hour," Alexa's monotone robotic voice called out from the kitchen.

De'Andrea glanced at her Cartier Tank as if Alexa were lying.

"How is it six o'clock already?"

Hell, perhaps she *was* geriatric. Because it didn't matter how hideous that damn silicone band was—she had to start wearing her Apple Watch again. She really needed those buzzing wrist notifications.

"Shit!"

"'Shittles,' babe." Malik's deep voice gently chastised as he walked into the dining room.

Shit! I really gotta memorize that kid-friendly swear chart. "Right. Right. Shittles."

"Shittles. 'Shiitake mushrooms.' Anything but 'shit.' Nina's all ears these days, remember?" He slid his arms around De'Andrea's waist and nuzzled his face against her neck.

She turned to kiss him and smiled. With his long locs pulled into a messy man bun, Malik seemed even taller than his six-foot-four-inch frame. De'Andrea gave him a quick once-over. The subtle scent of Le Labo Santal 33. Freshly shaven salt-and-pepper goatee. Classic Burberry polo paired with crisp navy slacks and his beloved house shoes that looked like leather loafers. Very Zaddy. Very *GQ*.

I mean, of course you look good. Since you weren't down here helping prep for our *goodbye party. And this party was your idea!*

Malik eyed the dining arrangements in sincere awe. "You never cease to amaze me."

"I never cease to amaze myself, either," De'Andrea said, straight-faced.

"Wait a second." Malik removed his hands from around her waist.

"Hmmm?" She slid the mini easel with Toni's name card on it one-fourth of an inch to the left. Then she moved it half an inch to the right. "Wait a second, what?"

"Dee, why is the table set for six? Isn't it just us, Toni, Craig, and Simone?" He looked over De'Andrea's shoulder and read the name card. "So Toni is sitting here—"

"Wait!" De'Andrea rushed over to the other side of the table. "Now don't go touching stuff. Let me explain."

"What's there to explain?" Malik followed her calmly. "Dee, who else is coming?"

"See, what had happened was . . ." She stood in front of one of the place settings like a bodyguard.

Slightly amused, Malik stood in front of her and crossed his arms. "You know I can pick you up with one hand, right?" His ink-black eyes stared playfully into hers. "So, are we gonna do this the hard way or nah?"

"Fine." De'Andrea conceded, throwing her hands in the air as she stepped aside. "Fine!"

He's gon lose his shiitake mushrooms in three, two . . .

"Oh, hell nawl!" Malik stared at the name written in gold calligraphy in disbelief. Then he snatched the card off the easel, held it up to his face for a closer look, and repeated, "Hell nawl!"

"Leek!" De'Andrea giggled, failing miserably at trying to suppress her amusement. "You know how much Simone loves LL Cool J. He's like *family*!"

"You and Simone get on my *damn* nerves with that *damn* dog!" Malik tossed the name card at De'Andrea and rolled his eyes when she caught it.

Probably not the best time to remind him to say "dagnabbit" instead of "damn."

Shortly after De'Andrea wed Malik, her childhood bestie, Simone, had found her own life partner—a mini Jack Russell terrier. She promptly named him after her favorite rapper, LL Cool J, and none of their lives had been the same since.

Although he'd been an adorable puppy, under Simone's doting-but-not-so-disciplined eye, LL had quickly grown into a ten-pound fur-ball of terror. And like anyone blinded by love, Simone only made excuses for his problematic behavior. Even after the last dog trainer quit, declaring that LL was not a Jack Russell but was, in fact, Satan's spawn, Simone's rationale was "All these wack-ass trainers want to do is break LL's spirit and then get mad when they can't. My li'l Cool J is like a peacock. I gotta let him fly!"

Malik let out a heavy sigh especially reserved for Simone and LL's shenanigans.

"It's not like we're gonna have a dog *at the table*," De'Andrea continued to plead her case. "You know Simone is going to have him in that little luxury doggy bag, and she can just place it right here on the chair. I still can't believe she spent all that money on a *Louis Vuitton* carrier. Anyway, you know if he's not right next to her, he's gonna be doing all that howling and whimpering, and then she's gonna be getting up to check on him every five seconds. And—"

"Do you hear how ridiculous you sound?" Malik asked. "Seriously."

"Yes." De'Andrea nodded, acquiescing. "Yes, I *do* hear how ridiculous I sound. But you know it's the truth anyhow. And I'm already stressed. I don't have the bandwidth to be dealing with all LL's annoying doggy shiiii . . . shiitake mushroom-ish."

"Cool. Then he can sit closer to you." Malik reached for LL's name card. "Let's just switch these . . ."

De'Andrea smacked his hand away. "Uh-uh, I want my bestie closest to me. Not that dog."

"But you want me to—"

"Leek!" This time, she smacked his butt. "C'mon! I've been decorating and working on these seating arrangements for *hours*! You've got Craig on your left and LL can be to your right. All the homies can sit together."

"Whoa now, that dog is *not* my homie—"

"This is your reminder that the caterers are arriving in . . . forty-five minutes," Alexa announced.

"Oh, shiitake," Malik quipped. "Look at the time. You should really go upstairs and get ready, Dee. Don't worry, I won't touch *anything* while you're gone."

"Leek. Do not." She gave her meanest mean-mug as she backed out of the dining room. "And I'm so serious."

Malik smiled as he pretended to reach for LL's name card. "See you soon!"

God, I love and hate that man so much.

After a quick shower, De'Andrea slipped into a plush robe and turned on her "Hot Girl Summer" playlist. Dancing around her walk-in closet, she unbraided her hair while trying to decide what to wear. And before she knew it, she was fluffing her curls and popping her booty while singing "I'm too classy for this world. Forever I'm that girl!" She *stayed* waiting for a reason to live out her dream as one of Beyoncé's backup dancers! And thankfully, her forty-two-year-old geriatric knees hadn't failed her yet.

Normally, De'Andrea was always down to have a reason to get glammed up. But tonight felt less like a dinner party and more like a funeral.

Dearly beloved, we are gathered here today to say goodbye to De'Andrea, Malik, and Nina as they prepare to move to Rolling Hills, a white suburb in no-man's-land Virginia. A place so far from Atlanta it's like driving across God's back.

"Ugh!" Once again, she combed through the black attire in her color-coded closet.

Why did the only state-of-the-art dementia residential facility on the East Coast have to be in Rolling Hills? Why couldn't Memory Village be someplace more reasonable? And Blacker? If it was just a little farther north in Washington, DC, they could have moved to a place with so many Black folks it was called Chocolate City.

Seemed the only "chocolate" in Rolling Hills was white chocolate.

And De'Andrea had never been a fan of white chocolate.

One peek in the window of the town's only yoga studio was enough for De'Andrea to know it could never replace Atlanta's Beats & Bends classes. She couldn't even remember the last time she'd practiced yoga with a bunch of white women. Must have been when she was a student at Ole Miss Law School trying to relieve some stress. Gosh, had it really been that long since she'd been annoyed by stick-thin Beckys' not-so-subtle gawking in disbelief that her thick thighs and fat ass could fold into a king pigeon pose?

"Namaste. Or whatever." De'Andrea rolled her eyes. *"Nah, Imma stay* getting my vinyasa flow on to trap music."

Rather than continue to waste time deciding on an outfit, she walked over to her vanity and pulled out her makeup bag. She wasn't planning on doing too much, just a light beat. Motherhood had helped her establish a five-minute "drab to fab" routine—a dusting of powder foundation, blush, several coats of waterproof mascara, and a bold red lip.

Yassssss! You serving face, hunty!

Raising her eyebrows, she leaned in closer to the mirror to

assess her handiwork. Well, she *tried* to raise her eyebrows. Because her forehead stayed smooth as a few laugh lines gathered at the corners of her eyes. That was Dr. German's secret—she didn't freeze a client's *whole* face.

De'Andrea tried to raise her eyebrows again just to marvel at the fact that she couldn't. "The Botox is still Botoxing, baby!"

Waitaminute. Who's gonna do my Botox once we move to Rolling Hills?

"Mommy! Mommy!" Nina squealed as she ran down the hallway.

"Stop running, Nina Bear." *Too late!* De'Andrea cringed at the sound of falling cardboard boxes.

"Sorry, Mr. Moving Box! And you too, Mrs. Moving Box." Nina apologized to each carton as she restacked them. "I hope I didn't hurt you!"

"I'm sure the moving boxes weren't injured," De'Andrea reasoned. "And if, by chance, one *did* get a little scrape or bruise, I'm sure it will forgive you." She laughed. "Come here, sweet girl."

Nina rounded the corner, twirling in a pink and white tulle dress. Aside from inheriting her mother's almond complexion, she'd stolen her father's whole face. Giving her best impression of a ballerina, Nina tapped her heels together and gave an impressive plié. This seemed to be her thing as of late, especially when De'Andrea styled her hair into a topknot. Maybe it was time to look into dance lessons.

"Hi, Mommy!" Nina wrapped her arms around De'Andrea's legs and gave them a big hug.

"Hey, sunshine! You look so pretty, my little rainbow baby." She kissed Nina's dimpled cheeks obsessively, which caused them both to giggle uncontrollably.

"Thank you, Mommy. You look pretty, too, even though you're not dressed yet. Tonight's going to be the best party ever! Auntie Toni is coming, and Uncle Craig, and my friends Jasmine and Junior, and Auntie Simone . . ." Nina rattled off the guest list like a sports announcer as she continued to twirl and marvel at layers of white-trimmed ruffles fanning out around her.

As De'Andrea slipped into her favorite black strapless sundress, she was taken aback by her mirrored reflection. *Was that a smile?* It was a weak one, but a smile nonetheless. She'd take it. Nina's youthful optimism about their dreaded "Farewell, Friends" dinner was almost contagious.

Almost.

Saying that she felt like she was at the Last Supper might have been a bit dramatic, but this *was* De'Andrea's last taste of Coleman's Southern goodness until she returned for a visit. So De'Andrea savored every bite of jerk salmon, smoked Gouda mac-and-cheese, and candied yams. If Rolling Hills' restaurants were anything like that yoga studio she saw, their restaurant options were bound to be what Malik called "milk-toast." As in as plain as plain could be. She'd howled with laughter when he explained the meaning, but damn if she hadn't used milk-toast to describe white folks' stuff ever since.

Between reminiscing about their early years in Atlanta, LL barking back whenever Simone chimed in, and the hilarious commentary from the nearby kids' table, De'Andrea couldn't help but be grateful the evening was filled with more joy than sadness. She aimed her Nikon camera at Craig and Toni mid-argument. "C'mon, y'all, you know the drill."

"Aight aight! Come here, boo. Gimme some suga." Craig grabbed Toni's face in his hands and puckered up to her. "Mwah! Mwah!"

"Stop, fool!" Toni laughed as she leaned backward in an attempt to escape her husband's kisses.

De'Andrea snapped away, smiling at the beautiful images she was capturing. As usual, Craig and Toni were wearing their standard uniforms of black on black, a decision they'd made after welcoming the twins and needing to make as few choices as possible. Jasmine and Junior! The children who'd made De'Andrea an auntie-by-love. The thought of not being able to see them regularly made De'Andrea's eyes water.

Click.

She aimed her camera at Simone, capturing her childhood bestie with her mouth wide open mid-cackle as several of her wild ginger curls fell into her face. What was she going to do without her sounding board and confidant living nearby? Sure, she could (and would) always call Simone. But what about those hard life moments when she needed her bestie to hold her while she cried like a baby? What was she going to do *then*? LL looked up at De'Andrea sweetly, and for a moment she forgot that his wide brown eyes were portals to hell. God, she was even gon' miss the damn dog! Surely, hopefully, they'd meet other Black folks in Rolling Hills, but De'Andrea knew she'd never be able to replace this crew. Nor did she want to.

Once the kids were finally set up in Nina's playroom with enough snacks to feed a small army while they watched Disney, it was grown folks' party time. De'Andrea took the first slice of what she knew would be many thin slices of Coleman's infamous seven-layer red velvet cake. Sure, she could just take one large hunk. But where was the fun in that?

"So, how is Mama Whitman?" Toni filled her wineglass with Riesling. "Is she all settled in?"

"She is." Malik popped the cork on another bottle. "Mama's doing great. I mean, she even *sounds* happier."

"Yeah, Memory Village is everything," De'Andrea chimed in. "I mean, disguising a residential medical facility as a small town is just genius. There's a library where she can check out books and take classes and whatnot. There's even a little strip called Main Street where they have boutiques and shops.

"Mama has no idea that everyone in *town*"—De'Andrea made air quotes—"are other dementia patients, medical staff, security, etcetera. She thinks they're all her neighbors!"

"Wow." Toni shook her head in disbelief. "That's brilliant on so many levels. Of course, the only downside is that it's in the middle of nowhere."

"Right. That part." De'Andrea took a long swig from her glass.

"Wait. Mama Whitman can go shopping?" Simone asked. "How does *that* work?"

"It's no-currency shopping," De'Andrea explained as she poured herself another half glass of wine. That was the best part about hosting—not having to worry about being too drunk to drive home. "So whenever Mama goes into any of the shops in Memory Village, the boutiques, grocery store, whatever, she swipes this little card. It looks like a debit card, but it's not linked to her bank account or anything. Just another part of Memory Village's approach to holistic care. It helps Mama maintain a sense of normalcy—"

Malik interrupted. "And, more importantly, her dignity, because that's what truly matters with this type of care. Elder care in general really . . ."

Ah, Malik the mansplainer. Repeating my words yet again. De'Andrea chugged her wine and put the glass down forcefully on the table. *What you should be telling them is that if it wasn't for me, ya momma would be living in some random facility somewhere!*

"Gonna grab more wine," she mouthed to Malik as he continued to rattle off the facts and statistics about holistic dementia care that *she* taught him.

As usual, she'd done everything. The research on Mama's diagnosis. The pros and cons of in-home versus residential care. She'd searched for the best long-term dementia care facilities on the East Coast and found Memory Village. *And* sacrificed her perfect life in Atlanta to move to Rolling Hills so they could live a short drive away from his mama.

And, as usual, Malik had the nerve to take all the credit.

De'Andrea had a lot of feelings about all of it—feels that caused her to think the most awful thoughts, some of which she was even too afraid to share with her therapist. Because she didn't *really* want to smother Malik with a pillow while he was sleeping, did she?

After spending a few minutes alone in the kitchen composing herself, she grabbed a bottle from the wine fridge and took a deep breath before returning to the dining room.

Throughout the evening, De'Andrea continued to snap candids chronicling the last dinner party in what she had thought would be their forever home. Her obsession with photography used to annoy her friends, but as the years passed, they'd come to appreciate her as the archivist of their lives. She glanced at her watch and waved to get Malik's attention.

"It's time." De'Andrea smiled.

He nodded and tapped the side of his wineglass. "My people, my people. Y'all already know how we feel about this move. Of course, we're grateful to have found the perfect place for Mama in Memory Village. But unfortunately, that means leaving *our* village. Over the years, we've all become more than friends. We're family. And my beautiful and amazing wife prepared something special to remind us of that."

De'Andrea walked over to dim the crystal chandelier before lowering the theater screen and turning on the projector. Then she synced her phone and opened the digital file labeled "Not a Goodbye." Instantly, one of her favorite quotes appeared on the screen.

"This is not a goodbye, my darling, this is a thank you."— Nicholas Sparks

"Oh Lawd, I'm finna cry." Toni picked up her dinner napkin, which was already stained with brown concealer from wiping away her tears throughout the evening.

"Ummm, I think there'll be more laughing than crying," Malik promised as the rhythmic beats of Too $hort's "Blow the Whistle" began blaring through the speakers.

"Aye!" Simone jumped out of her chair and did a li'l twerk two-step. "That's my *joint*! And Too $hort can still get it!" LL barked violently and Simone patted his carrier. "Don't worry, bookie bear. I'm not serious. You know you're the only man in my life!"

The music transitioned to '90s R&B classics as a photo of Simone and De'Andrea in their late twenties appeared on the screen. Wearing baggy jeans, crop tops, and shell-toe Adidas, the two friends stood arms crossed in their best B-boy stances under a "Welcome to Atlanta" sign outside a crowded club that no longer existed.

"Okay, I cannot take this cuteness!" Toni squealed as more youthful images of the friends followed. "Look at baby Dee Dee and baby Moni! I hadn't even met y'all yet!"

De'Andrea had not only been Simone's first friend, but there were also many seasons in life when she'd been her *only* friend. Fair-skinned and lanky, Simone's appearance hadn't changed much since their coming-of-age years. Only now, instead of dyeing her hair black to avoid being ridiculed, she embraced her naturally red curls. Growing up in the ghettos of Mississippi as a redbone with red hair hadn't been easy.

"We scrimped and scraped all our pennies together to move to Atlanta. The big city!" Simone laughed.

"So big!" De'Andrea laughed at the memory. Traveling to Georgia was their first time outside of Mississippi and, as far as the two friends were concerned, they might as well have been moving to Paris.

"Remember how excited I was when I got that art scholarship?" Simone asked. "But then I still got that good financial aid so we could live off those interest-free student loans while you studied for the bar? Because you wanted to be a big-time lawyer so you could be rich-rich? But it just ended up making you tired-tired?"

"Do I!" De'Andrea laughed. "God, we were the original 'young and the restless'—and reckless!"

When De'Andrea passed the bar exam on her first try, the two friends had celebrated with Krystal mini burgers and boxed wine. Their celebratory tradition continued even after De'Andrea started earning a six-figure salary at a prestigious law firm and celebrities were buying Simone's Afrofuturistic art faster than she could paint the images on canvases. Soon, the little burgers and boxed wine became the friends' litmus test to see if someone was too bougie to join their clique.

Given her Black generational wealth pedigree, they hadn't expected De'Andrea's legal peer, Toni, to devour a stack of ten cheesy sliders and wash them down with red cups filled with cheap wine without a single complaint. De'Andrea and Simone had been instantly smitten. Toni was the reason their "besties" group chat would ultimately be renamed "the girls."

The three women screamed with laughter when a photo of Toni pre–Craig and the twins popped up on the screen. She was sleeping on a sofa in De'Andrea and Simone's first apartment, mouth agape in a Krystal-and-boxed-wine-induced coma.

"Umph umph umph." Craig feigned disappointment. "I can't believe I married that woman."

"Excuse me? *That* woman is the best thing that ever happened to you, sir." Toni playfully waved her fist in front of his face. "Say I ain't. I dare you!"

"You is, Toni." Craig grabbed her fist and kissed it. "You is smart. You is kind. You is . . ."

For the next twenty minutes, the slideshow took the friends down memory lane. De'Andrea and Simone in their first luxury apartment in Midtown. Simone kissing the futuristic-looking painting of the Obamas that launched her career from struggling artist to in-demand artisan. De'Andrea and Toni standing in front of the law firm where they'd met, their sleek shoulder-length bobs, black suits, and matching pumps making them look more like clones than colleagues. Malik and Craig sitting on the steps of their Morehouse dorm, looking barely old enough to drive. Toni hugging her then-boyfriend, Craig, wearing a hot pink bikini at what still reigned as one of Atlanta's most epic early 2000s pool parties. De'Andrea and Malik on a blind date after being set up by Toni. Simone side-eyeing Malik as De'Andrea looked up at him lovingly. Malik side-eyeing Simone as she looked down at her new fur baby, LL, strapped to her chest in a BabyBjörn carrier.

Engagement and wedding photos. Housewarming parties and couples' getaways. Milestone "Dirty Thirty" birthday parties followed by the births of their children. And more recent "Forty & Fabulous" celebrations and family vacations. When the slideshow ended with a photo of De'Andrea at her most recent birthday party surrounded by dozens of their neighbors and friends, the girlfriends didn't even try to hold back their tears. They hugged tightly as they wept, promising to call and text daily, FaceTime weekly, and not let too much time pass between visits.

De'Andrea's life partnership with Simone spanned over thirty-six years. Toni had not only introduced her to Malik but also supported her evolution as they both transitioned from partner-track-driven young associates to stay-at-home wives and mothers. How was De'Andrea ever going to do life without them? She was the woman she was because of them.

This is not a goodbye, my darlings, this is a thank you.

And De'Andrea *was* thankful. Because she knew her girlfriends would honor their promises to keep in touch and visit. More than anything, she just wished they didn't have to.

TWO

Rebecca

R ebecca Myland loved vacations.

Scratch that.

She loved *planning* vacations.

Once she was on them, however, she didn't quite know what to do with herself. Even now, with all the elements present for a picture-perfect late summer escape: a vivid blue sky with not a single cloud, a light northeast breeze keeping the temperature just right, and a luxury rental home with a heated saltwater pool that could entertain her kids when she didn't feel like making the schlep to the beach. If only she could figure out how to sit still.

Her family didn't have this same problem, of course. Why would they? She had everything covered. Her husband Todd was currently still sleeping in. His brother Jack and wife Tina probably were, too. Child-free and carefree, they could do whatever they wanted. But Rebecca had been watching her daughters play in the pool since practically the crack of dawn. At what age would *they* start sleeping in? Not that it mattered. Rebecca couldn't stay in bed past 6 a.m. anyway.

Having finished arranging the to-do list categories in her latest organization app, Don't Let Me Forget, Rebecca side-eyed the book on the small table next to her lounger. She felt like the cover was judging her: *Woke Yet? Wake Up! Understanding the History of Race & Racism.* She hadn't cracked it open, which she felt bad about. But every time she'd get ready to pick it up, the girls would summon her with another "Watch how many mermaid twists I can do!" or "Do a Boomerang of us jumping in!"

She *would* read the book on this trip, though. Or at least *start* it. She had already emailed the other moms, encouraging them to finish it before school started in a few weeks. "Our first book club meeting of the year will be upon us before we know it, ladies!" She knew she needed to take her own advice.

But first, a little bit of Instagram.

August on the East Coast meant everyone was on vacation. And *everyone* seemed to be doing it better than Rebecca, judging from all the "Hello from . . ." beach and poolside selfies on her feed that morning.

"Really, Harita?"

A reel on Rebecca's timeline showed a series of photos and videos of Harita Garrison and her family being greeted by resort staff, running toward the ocean in slow motion, on a boat ride, snorkeling, at least five different dinner plates filled with colorful, gourmet meals, and then, finally, a video of her children crashed in their hotel bed snoring with the caption, "We did allllll the things! Thank you, Turks & Caicos!"

Rebecca took a screenshot of the last frame and texted it to her girlfriends with the message, "Is she on vacation or working for the Board of Tourism?" She felt satisfied with their immediate reactions—a stream of eye rolling, laughing, and face-palm emojis.

Rebecca opened her camera app. "You're not the only one living your best life, Miss Harita."

Arm extended, she tilted her head down and to the left to show her good side. She lifted her phone at a forty-five-degree angle, capturing her defined shoulders in the frame, as well as her white halter bikini top and a tasteful peek of cleavage. She pushed her tongue to the roof of her mouth, trying the red-carpet hack she'd learned for showing more cheekbone.

Snap. Snap. Snap.

She brought her phone down and examined the results.

Ugh. What the hell?

Whatever happened in the seconds between posing for the selfie and *snapping* the selfie was a goddamn mystery to her because she swore she looked good in the camera frame. But these were awful. She kept trying and swiped again to check out the next round.

In one, her face was too dark, shadowed by her oversized wide-brimmed sun hat. In another, she'd lifted her hat so she could see her face, but her hair was sweaty and matted down. In the next one, she had tried for a pensive, into-the-distance gaze, but she ended up looking confused. And this last one . . . *Yuck. Where did that double chin come from?* She used her phone as a mirror to see if that was for real or just a bad angle.

"Stop scrutinizing your face. You're flawless." Tina stepped out onto the pool deck *actually* looking flawless. This woman was vacation-ready with a straw beach tote slung over her shoulder, a large pitcher filled with something pink and sparkling in one hand, and two upside-down champagne flutes in the other. Her sheer black full-length swim cover-up grazed the limestone tiles as she approached the lounger next to Rebecca.

"I don't know about that. I think I'm getting turkey neck."

Rebecca continued eyeing herself in her phone. She slapped the bottom of her chin with the back of her hand. "Do *you* think I'm getting turkey neck?"

"Rebecca. Your neck looks as taut as ever. There's no use worrying about it right now anyway. When the time comes, there are surgical remedies for that. Right now, mimosas!"

Rebecca checked the time on her phone. "It's ten-thirty in the morning."

"Oh, come on. It's fine!" Tina's aviator sunglasses slipped down her nose as she placed the flutes down on the side table and poured.

"It's twelve o'clock somewhere, amirite?"

Rebecca gave Tina and her corniness a barely audible courtesy chuckle. She eyed the drink mixture. It did look refreshing. She wasn't worried so much about alcohol in the morning as she was about calories before noon. That would interrupt her intermittent fasting schedule.

Tina, apparently sensing this was the heart of Rebecca's reluctance, added, "These are *grapefruit* mimosas, Bec. Practically health food!"

Eh, what the hell. Rebecca accepted the drink. "Cheers," both ladies said in unison, producing a flat clink with their plastic flutes.

Tina settled into her lounger and pulled her own book out of her beach bag: *Choose YOU: Every. Damn. Time.*

What the hell does that even mean? Rebecca wanted to ask but decided to keep to herself. At least Tina was reading.

Giving up on the selfie for good, Rebecca flipped the camera's direction and switched to portrait mode to take a photo of her drink in her hand next to her bent knees, the swimming pool and her daughters who were playing in it blurred in the background. She uploaded it to Instagram with the caption "Mimosas on Martha's Vineyard," and she added a beach umbrella emoji. Yes, the bare-knees-on-vacation pose was cliché, but there was no way she was going to post any of the selfies she'd taken. What else could she do? Not post at all?

"Here," Rebecca said, surrendering her phone to Tina. "Please take this and save me from myself."

But as soon as Tina reached for Rebecca's phone, the alarm sounded with the reminder, "SKIN!"

"Girls! Sunscreen!" she called out to Lyla and Isabella. They ignored her and went headfirst underwater for a handstand contest.

Rebecca locked eyes with Tina, giving her the "Help me out, please" look.

When her nieces came up for air, Tina summoned them. "Lyla-bean! Izzy-bear! Come on out for a minute to get some more sunscreen!"

Leaving a trail of wet footprints, the girls ran to Tina, who wrapped each of them in giant beach towels. She helped Isabella dry off while Lyla made a beeline for the picnic table and its daily spread of pastries, fruit salad, and an ice bucket with sparkling waters. Ever since turning ten years old last spring, Lyla had become downright ravenous as she went through her most recent growth spurt. Rebecca was certain she had grown a few inches in the past week alone.

"Aunt Tina, will you get in the pool with us?" Isabella asked between coughs and gags as Rebecca sprayed her with sunscreen.

"Oh, sorry, hon," Tina replied, not sounding the least bit sorry. "I'm reading. " She held up her book, took another sip of her mimosa, and returned to her lounging position.

Choose you, Tina.

Rebecca instantly felt bad about her snarky thought. *Ugh, be nice.* At least she hadn't said it out loud. She'd been working on that ever since she overheard Lyla judging one of Isabella's dress-up outfits by commenting, "Well, *that's* an interesting choice."

Rebecca's first reaction had been, *Dear God, she sounds like my mother.* And then, *Oh fuck, she sounds like me.*

Even if Rebecca had let her "judginess" slip, it wouldn't have made a difference to Tina. She didn't appear to feel any guilt at all about turning down her adorable little niece in her ruffly purple tankini.

A disappointed Isabella furrowed her brow. "Mommy? What about you? Will you get in with us?"

Unlike Tina, Rebecca *did* feel guilt. But not enough to get in the water. At five years old, Isabella was finally able to swim on her own, and this was the first summer Rebecca didn't have to be in the pool with her. Some developmental milestones enveloped Rebecca in nostalgia. But freedom from being a jungle gym-slash-lifeguard in the pool all day, with her swimsuit getting pulled in all directions so that she was constantly at risk of flashing her boobs, was not something she'd ever miss.

Brushing croissant flakes off her lips, Lyla joined them and assumed the sunscreen application stance as if Rebecca were scanning her with a security wand at the airport.

While spraying Lyla, Rebecca answered Isabella. "Izzy, sweetie,

Mommy's going to relax a little bit, but I promise I'll play in the pool with you later."

Before Isabella could go into a full-on pout, she was interrupted by the sound of the sliding glass door banging open and Todd and Jack charging out onto the pool deck as if they were back in college at a frat party.

"Cannonballlllll!" they yelled in unison.

"Daddy! Uncle Jack!" Isabella squealed and followed them in with her own cannonball.

Rebecca brushed water off her arm from all the splashing and smiled as she shook her head at the man-child behavior that emerged whenever her husband and his brother were together.

"And now there are *four* children in the pool," Rebecca joked, looking in Tina's direction.

Tina looked up from her book long enough to wipe her legs off where the splash had reached her and replied, "Right," without a hint of amusement.

What is going on with them?

Ever since Jack and Tina had arrived, they'd been prickly with each other, which was unusual. The night before, during dinner, Jack had made a passive-aggressive comment about how many girls' getaway trips Tina had taken in the past year. "Who else am I going to travel with, Jack? You never want to go anywhere," Tina shot back. If it hadn't been for Isabella chiming in to start listing all the countries *she* wanted to visit someday, the awkwardness would have lingered.

Jack and Tina were never one of those annoying lovey-dovey couples, but they had always been good-natured toward each other, and Rebecca envied how effortless their relationship had seemed—the result, Rebecca was certain, of deciding not to have kids. Pre-kids, Todd's and her marriage had been easy, too. And they *had* been one of those annoying lovey-dovey couples.

"Mom! Hurry up—I wanna get back in the pool!" Lyla interrupted Rebecca's thoughts. She hadn't even realized she'd stopped applying sunscreen. She swiped a zinc stick on Lyla's freckled nose and cheeks before Lyla bolted to join her sister, dad, and uncle.

Now that Todd and Jack were in the pool, Rebecca knew her daughters wouldn't need her again until they were hungry for lunch. She thought about asking Tina quietly what was up with her and Jack, but Tina was in a deep trance "choosing herself."

Oof, that was judgy again.

Rebecca checked herself and realized she should instead take inspiration from Tina for reading. She reached for *Woke Yet?* and then her phone buzzed. More messages from her mom squad group chat.

Today, 10:58 AM
Victoria
Greetings from Vermont! Hope everyone is loving their
vacays! Check out what I spotted yesterday on my way out
of town . . .

Victoria added a photo to the thread: a real estate sign marked "sold" in front of the Millers' old house on the cul-de-sac in her development, just a few miles down from Rebecca's.

Today, 11:01 AM
Jenny Q
Shit, that sold fast! Oh, and hello from Nantucket!

Jenny sent a selfie from the beach, which, of course, looked perfect. Her shiny black hair was blowing in the wind, but in a glamorous, not messy, way—like she was in a *Sports Illustrated* shoot. Victoria hearted the photo and sent the Shaquille O'Neal shoulder-shimmy GIF.

Today, 11:02 AM

Rebecca

OMG, you look exactly like Brenda Song. SLAY.

Jenny Q

First of all, thank you. Second of all . . . Rebecca, I told you to stop telling me I look like random Asian women. Last week, you said I looked like Chrissy Teigen. Now you're saying Brenda Song, who is Thai and Hmong btw. I look nothing like her.

Oh shit. Jenny *did* tell her that. She didn't totally get what was wrong with telling Jenny she looked like gorgeous celebrities. Wasn't that a compliment? Either way, Rebecca didn't want to annoy her friend. She switched over to Don't Let Me Forget and set a daily reminder: "Count to three before replying to text messages." Then she added another: "Look up Hmong."

Today, 11:05 AM

Rebecca

I'm sorry! 😔

What I meant is . . . YOU look AMAZING. Like YOU always do.

Rebecca followed her text with a GIF of The Rock doing his signature eyebrow raise. She'd seen a headline somewhere that said GIFs were so Boomer, but she couldn't quit them. Besides being funny, they were so efficient.

Today, 11:09 AM
Victoria
I'm much less glamorous up here in Vermont.

Victoria sent a photo of herself with no makeup, her red and gray-streaked curly mane covered by an army green hiking hat, and a waterfall in the background. While her daughter Cassie was in the Bahamas with her dad and his new girlfriend, Victoria had sent herself away on a solo retreat in the mountains. She looked tired, but happy. Everyone hearted her photo, too.

Today, 11:12 AM
Jenny Q
Anyway . . . back to the house. Do we know who bought it? Anyone know a realtor who's willing to be slightly unprofessional and give us the deets? 👀

Rebecca
On it!

Rebecca copied the photo Victoria had sent and left her school moms group chat to compose a new message to Sandra Weathers, one of Rebecca's former clients from back in her pre-motherhood days as a publicist. Sandra dominated the gated community real estate scene in Virginia, and while she wasn't the listed agent on the Millers' house, she could most likely get intel. Rebecca sent the "sold" sign photo to Sandra and got right to the point.

Today, 11:15 AM
Rebecca
25 Oakview Lane. What do you know?

Three dots in a bubble appeared immediately.

Today, 11:16 AM
Sandra
Hey! Gimme a sec . . .

Today, 11:19 AM
Sandra
Looks like it sold before it even went on the market! AND it looks like the buyers came with cash. They weren't playing around.

Rebecca took a screenshot of Sandra's text and sent it to the moms' chat. She switched back to Sandra.

Today, 11:20 AM
Rebecca
What can you find out about the buyers? Inquiring minds want to know!

Sandra
Justine is the listing agent! Hold on, she'll tell me everything. Gimme a sec to see what else I can find out.

Rebecca stared at her phone, completely unfazed by the splashing and the alternating shouts of "Marco!" and "Polo!" going on in the pool.

Today, 11:27 AM

Sandra

Okay, here's what I've got. The buyers are Black. Or African American. Which am I supposed to say? Anyway! Not being racist. Just saying they are. Last name Whitman. Justine says they're a gorgeous little family. Moving from Atlanta.

Rebecca switched over to the moms group chat.

Today, 11:28 AM

Rebecca

Oh my God! They're BLACK!

Jenny Q.

Really???

Victoria

Seriously?!

She checked to see if Sandra had added any additional info.

Rebecca

I know, right?! Hold on, Sandra's still typing.

Then she switched back to her conversation with Sandra.

Today, 11:31 AM

Sandra

Oh you're gonna love this. Apparently, they have a daughter entering kindergarten. AND she's going to Magnolia Country Day.

Oh, this was good information.

Magnolia Country Day was the most prestigious independent school in their area. It was also Lyla and Isabella's school *and* Isabella was going into kindergarten, too.

Rebecca felt like hugging her phone. This was *big news*. She could count on one hand the number of Black people she'd seen in Rolling Hills. She literally squealed and then felt her cheeks flush. She glanced self-consciously over at Tina, who had just dog-eared a page in her book and didn't even notice Rebecca's excitement.

Rebecca had to get back to the moms. She thanked Sandra for the info and told her she'd reach out about getting together in September.

Today, 11:35 AM

Rebecca

Ladies! One more big detail for you . . . the buyers will be a new Magnolia Country Day family! Their little girl will be a kindergartner, too!

She looked over at the pool. Lyla was on Todd's shoulders, fighting Jack and Isabella in a game of chicken. She'd tell Todd the exciting news later—that after nearly three years of running the parent diversity committee, they'd finally have a Black family at the school. Under Rebecca's leadership, the committee had organized an annual multicultural festival at the school, brought in famous diversity and inclusion speakers, and they had the antiracist book club that met four times a year.

Still, Rebecca hadn't made any significant progress on the recruiting front. Magnolia Country Day remained lily white, and Rebecca hated it. She had put pressure on the head of the school to create a Director of Diversity position, but the woman he hired stayed less than a year after she got a more lucrative job offer at an all-girls school in DC that was already really diverse.

Rebecca had a good feeling about the Whitmans. A *really good* feeling. This was going to be the beginning of building the beautifully diverse school she'd always wanted for her girls.

Even more exciting: the Whitmans were moving to a house only a five-minute drive away from the Mylands. Rebecca dared to admit another quiet wish to herself.

Maybe we'll even become friends.

THREE

De'Andrea

As De'Andrea approached the entrance to the Preserve at Rolling Hills subdivision, she reached for the security remote clipped to her truck's sun visor. When she pressed the red button to open the residents' gate, her Apple Watch vibrated softly against her David Yurman bracelets.

"Eight *fifty*?" she screamed at the notification. How was she going to make it to therapy in ten minutes? "Shit! I mean, shittles!"

She tightened her grip on the steering wheel as the wrought-iron gates opened in slow motion. "Come *on*!" she pleaded, continuing to inch her custom bronze Range Rover forward until there was just enough space to safely pass through. But instead of peeling off, which was what she *wanted* to do, De'Andrea began the excruciating five-miles-per-hour journey toward home.

That slow-ass-opening gate and the slower-than-slow community traffic restriction were just two of many on her laundry list of things she hated about Rolling Hills.

"God, it's so hard out here," she groaned. "Fix it, Jesus!"

Tempted as always, De'Andrea refused to drive above the ridiculous speed limit. Not even one extra mile per hour. Even on days like today when there were no other cars on the oak-tree-canopied streets. Even though she didn't see anyone walking or pushing one of those expensive made-for-Instagram-not-really-for-jogging strollers. Because someone might be watching. No, someone was *definitely* watching. And she didn't want to give anyone a reason to complain about the Preserve's newest Black homeowners.

The Preserve's only *Black homeowners*, she reminded herself.

During last night's "Sacred Sundays" Zoom chat with her girlfriends, all hell broke loose as soon as Toni asked the same question she'd been asking for the past several weeks: Had they *seen* any Black folks yet? At least she'd stopped asking if they'd *met* any other Black folks yet. And when De'Andrea said they hadn't, her friends were convinced there weren't any other Black people in their subdivision—and perhaps, in all of Rolling Hills.

"Nah, it's Black folks out here. We saw a few when we were checking out the neighborhood," De'Andrea recalled.

She and Malik had also been checking to see whether any houses were proudly displaying a Confederate flag or those sambo-looking lawn jockey figurines she hated so much.

"Oh, and there was also that Black family we saw at that weird-looking strip-mall-town-center place," she said. "Their daughter was the cutest! I'll never forget because she was around Nina's age. She was so brown and chocolate and yummy with her little braided pigtails." De'Andrea had only recently let go of her pipe dream of the two girls meeting and becoming besties.

And for some reason, sharing that remembrance made Simone go off the rails.

"Listen, white folks who have enough money to stage their entire house just to sell it? Ma'am. You know damn well they got extra coins to stage the neighborhood, too! Think about what you just said, Dee . . ." Simone squinted as she leaned in closer to her computer's camera. "A random Black family just *happens* to be roaming around a strip mall with a little girl who just *happens* to be around the same age as Nina. On the same day y'all just *happen* to be in town looking for a house. And y'all ain't seen them Negroes since? That don't sound staged to you?"

"They weren't *randomly roaming*." De'Andrea felt herself get defensive. "They were *shopping*, Simone. They had bags—"

"You know what was in those shopping bags? All the money they got paid to pretend like they lived in Rolling Hills." Simone laughed. "C'mon, Dee Dee. It's been two months since y'all moved. *Sixty-four days, to be exact*! You would have seen them again by now."

Toni took a sip of wine. "I mean, it does sound . . . a little suspect. And cray-cray."

"Negroes-for-Hire." Simone shook her head shamefully. "That's what's wrong with the world. People will do anything for money."

"Right, and all skin folk ain't kinfolk," Toni said. "But Black folks getting paid to hang out in white neighborhoods so that other unsuspecting Black folks feel comfortable buying property? That's a new level of low."

"Just putting their own brothers and sisters in harm's way." Simone continued her sermon. "Because you buy the house thinking. 'Okay, it ain't gon' be that bad out here. At least I got a Black neighbor or two.' Then, next thing you know, *bam*! You find out you're the only Black family and now y'all starring in *Get Out* part two."

LL barked violently in agreement. "That's the only thing that makes sense, right, bunny boo sweet boy? Those Negroes-for-Hire set our friends up, didn't they?" Simone picked up LL and held his furry face up to the camera while she continued her baby talk. "Tell Auntie Dee Dee. Say, 'Get. Out!'"

On cue, LL barked twice, which made the friends cackle.

De'Andrea knew Simone and Toni were just joking, but . . . what if they were right? What if Negroes-for-Hire was a real thing? Because where *were* the other Black folks?

The more De'Andrea thought about it, the Preserve was kind of like those perfect communities in horror movies. With its beautiful lavish estates where every lawn bristles with aggressive greenness, and everyone feels so comfortable and safe they leave their curtains wide open and lights on . . . *at night*. Probably keep their doors unlocked, too! Everything seems so pristine, so peaceful . . . but in reality, there's a serial killer lurking right around the damn corner.

Had she and Malik been bamboozled by their real estate agent *and* Negroes-for-Hire?

Nestled on one of the resort-style community's coveted lots overlooking acres of open meadows and a winding creek, the Sotheby's listing agent had declared the Whitmans' new residence "a dream, the definition of a new generation of luxury." However, he forgot to tell them a few things. Like how it might feel like a nightmare given the eerie silence save for crickets and God-knows-what-else chirping out there in those damn open meadows.

De'Andrea's wrist vibrated again as she approached Oakview Lane. "Aight, five minutes until therapy. You got this, Dee. You can make it!" Pressing down on the accelerator, she risked it all by going ten miles per hour as she made a right turn onto their street.

Damn, she felt like she was flying!

Across the cul-de-sac, their neighbor Heidi was standing where she stood most mornings, leaning against one of the grand columns of the elevated porch with a coffee cup in hand. Between sips, she encouraged and cooed at her toddler, Charlotte, as she crawled around exploring their front yard. Heidi seemed to have an affinity for wearing bohemian dresses under chunky cardigans, even though it wasn't cold outside. It was like a leveled-up basic white girl uniform one might find at Free People. With her jet-black pixie cut, Heidi reminded De'Andrea of an emo fairy, the cousin Tinkerbell might gossip about for being too edgy 'round these open meadows.

Heidi waved and smiled. De'Andrea waved back, and when Charlotte opened and closed her little hand to wave "hello," both women squealed. It seemed like only yesterday De'Andrea was helicopter-mothering Nina and teaching her how to wave hello and goodbye. How was she already in kindergarten?

Nina is fine. It's not even a full day. It's orientation, for goodness' sakes. Do not go back to that school until it's time to pick her up!

Two white women decked out in all black Lululemon gear jogged toward her driveway, and De'Andrea double-panicked, slamming on the brakes. "Y'all stays running," she muttered under her breath. "And y'all love running 'round my damn cul-de-sac. And taking your sweet time with it, too!"

C'mon, Beckys. If you gon' run, RUN! I need to get to therapy!

"Show-offs!" She watched the women's blond ponytails swing in unison as they passed by. There had to be a special place in hell for people who could run *and* talk at the same time.

"You've got three minutes, girl. You can still make it!" De'Andrea turned and raced up the driveway. But she misjudged how much space she had, and the truck's bumper nicked their blue recycling bin.

"Nooooooo!" she wailed. "Come on!"

She had a brief moment of hopefulness while watching the receptacle slowly wobble in her rearview mirror . . . until it tipped over, and paper and plastic scattered across the driveway.

"Son of a biscuit eater!" Now this kid-friendly swear *had* grown on her. Perhaps because the thought of someone's mother being obsessed with eating biscuits actually sounded a *little* more problematic than being the son of a bitch.

After turning off the ignition, De'Andrea unbuckled her seat belt and took a deep, calming breath that did not deliver on its promise. Therapy started in two minutes, and their driveway was littered with recyclables.

What to do? What to do!

The thought of receiving a "Dear Mr. and Mrs. Whitman" violation letter from the homeowners' association won over being late, so she grabbed her tote bag and slung it over her shoulder before opening the car door.

"She's a runner, she's a track star!" De'Andrea sang as she sprinted down the driveway, righted the bin, and hurriedly stuffed the recyclables back inside.

While running into the garage, she angrily tapped her watch to turn off the 9:00 a.m. alarm.

I know, I know. I'm late!

Hopping from one foot to the other in the mudroom, she unwound the black leather bands around her ankles and questioned why she'd even worn strappy sandals knowing she'd be pressed for time. Feeling more like a contestant on *American Ninja Warrior* than a woman just trying to get to therapy,

De'Andrea rushed into the kitchen, grabbed her laptop from the breakfast nook, and placed it on the quartz island. By the time she logged on, slid in her earbuds, and entered Dr. Jones's virtual meeting room, it was already five minutes past the hour.

Woosah.

Just looking at Dr. Jones's face had a way of calming De'Andrea. She was a manifestation of the older Black woman De'Andrea aspired to be: unbothered and on top of her game. Today her therapist's salt-and-pepper curls were brushed into a slick, chin-length bob, and she was wearing those purple oversized glasses De'Andrea loved.

I aspire. One day. I'm gon be fabulous and have my shit together again, too.

"Good morning. Sorry I'm late. Malik's red-eye got delayed. Twice. Which meant I had to manage his stress *and* Nina's disappointment that Daddy wasn't coming with us to kindergarten orientation. Even though I tried to explain to them both that today is just orientation and not the official first day! But they were both beside themselves, which made me beside *myself*..."

Of course, Malik had found a way to make her managing kindergarten orientation alone *his* problem. God, he could be such a man-child sometimes! Then she had to deal with her child-child, who'd sulked the entire ride to school. De'Andrea didn't even want to look at the high-res photos she'd taken on her Nikon. Even with bribes and promises, Nina refused to smile. It was barely 9:00 a.m., and De'Andrea already needed a nap.

Thankfully, she didn't look as run-down and haggard as she felt. Natural light flooded the kitchen, camouflaging the dark circles under her eyes and adding a sun-kissed glow to her complexion. De'Andrea took the hair band off her wrist and gathered her curls into a messy ponytail. Before getting married and having Nina, she used to manage her days in six-minute increments to stay aligned with her billable-hours structure. Now she couldn't even make it to her standing therapy appointment on time.

"No worries," Dr. Jones said. "Things happen. What's most important is that you're here."

De'Andrea wondered how it felt to be so damn cool, calm, and collected. And what exactly was the cheat code to get there as quickly as possible, because she stayed feeling like a hot mess. "Thank you for understanding, Dr. Jones."

Her therapist nodded, ready to move on. "So, kindergarten orientation. I still cannot believe Nina is starting elementary school. I know the morning started off a little bumpy, but how are you feeling overall? You've been both dreading and looking forward to this day for a while now."

"Well, I was only looking forward to it when we were still in Atlanta." De'Andrea sighed. "But yeah, the dreaded day is here. Orientation is just a few hours, though, not a full day. I'm picking Nina up at noon."

"Okay, that's a nice soft launch for both of you."

"Soft launch," De'Andrea repeated. "It's definitely something."

Something she hadn't been prepared for.

Like seeing Nina walk into the auditorium in a single-file line . . . without her mommy. And Nina sitting with the other almost-official kindergartners . . . instead of sitting next to her mommy. The hardest part was hearing the room assignments where, just as De'Andrea suspected, Nina ended up being the only Black student in her class. There weren't even any *brown* kids! Who was Nina going to play with?

"Did you get to talk to her teacher?" Dr. Jones asked. "I know you had some concerns."

"Yeah, she got Ms. Heather, the teacher I was hoping for. But I'm still stressed about her being the only Black kid in her class."

At least Nina had been assigned to Magnolia Country Day School's newest kindergarten teacher, Ms. Heather. The other teachers were older white women who didn't even try to hide their strong Karen vibes. Despite having little experience as a recent college grad, Ms. Heather was a soft-spoken brunette with a sunny disposition who had a lot of enthusiasm for creating inclusive learning environments. And as far as De'Andrea was concerned, a win was a win.

She decided not to tell Dr. Jones that she was among those parents the administration had politely escorted outside after overstaying the time allotted to take pictures of the kids in their classrooms. Or that she had seriously considered waiting in the parking lot with other parents who were in disbelief that their babies were now school-age children.

"I still need a minute to process." De'Andrea sighed. "Lots of minutes."

"Understandable." Dr. Jones picked up a green file folder and glanced briefly at the notes inside. "We can come back to it whenever you're ready. Do you want to talk about the move? How are you feeling about Rolling Hills since we spoke last week? Better?"

"Meh. Still meh." De'Andrea felt a twinge of caffeine-envy as her therapist sipped from a Spelman College mug. "You know what? Let me just finish talking about this little PWI elementary school. I mean, I know there weren't a lot of options. It was literally between Rolling Hills' predominantly white elementary school, A, and even whiter elementary school, B. But what am I doing, Dr. Jones? Am I making a mistake? How did I let Malik convince me this experience is going to help prepare Nina for the real world? As if a five-year-old needs to start preparing for *that*."

Dr. Jones adjusted her glasses as she flipped through her previous notes. "De'Andrea, you were the one who said you couldn't homeschool, remember? That's a direct quote."

Right.

She just didn't have the patience or the discipline to be Nina's teacher. One frustrating lesson and it would be nap time. For both of them!

"Yeah, I did say that. Because it's true. I can't. But maybe I could have found an online program or something. Am I about to ruin Nina's life? Is she going to have identity issues? Why am I not homeschooling?"

Jesus! Wasn't parenting supposed to get easier after the newborn and toddler years? She'd take a screaming infant and sassy two-year-old over having to decide her five-year-old's academic fate any day!

De'Andrea reached into her tote and fished around the bottom of the large bag. Having a vape pen that resembled an actual ballpoint pen was cleverly discreet but also cumbersome to search for.

Gotcha.

As soon as she clicked on the button to start warming the cartridge, Dr. Jones gave her an unreadable glance.

Does she know I just turned on my vape? She stifled a giggle at the voice in her head repeating the viral clip: *"How could she know? Nobody's going to know."*

But when Dr. Jones opened her desk drawer and took out a protein bar, De'Andrea felt a pang of guilt.

Okay, she knows. Look at her trying to model healthy habits. Great.

Dr. Jones unwrapped the protein bar and took a bite. "I've said it before and I'll say it again. The best and perhaps only way to ensure that Nina has a positive experience is to get involved."

"I will," De'Andrea promised. She eyed the vape pen and silently pleaded with the cartridge to hurry up and warm.

"And even though Malik's schedule is a little cray right now, I know he'll get involved, too."

And you'll get stuck doing all the work while he gets all the shine. Because marriage is teamwork!

"How is Malik doing?" Dr. Jones asked.

"Malik is . . . Maliking." De'Andrea chose her words carefully so she wouldn't sound as salty as she felt. "I mean, you know, he's mastered the art of doing just enough, stepping up and stepping in at the last minute, and continuing to get on my damn nerves. That being said, I still love him. Or whatever."

"Got it." Dr. Jones smiled.

De'Andrea snuck a look at her vape. Why was it taking so damn long to heat up?

"So aside from being an alright-of-a-husband, Malik is good," she continued. "Of course, he's so much happier now that we're closer to Mama. He still misses his Black coworkers in Atlanta. He still travels too much for work, but what else is new. And our libidos are . . . still libidoing."

Even though Malik got on her last nerve, and even with the Preserve's eerie horror-movie-silence, they still had a healthy sex life. That was the one thing Malik *always* did right. They'd be the ones to get got by Freddy Krueger because they were too busy humping like teenagers.

"Glad y'all are doing well. And how is Mama Whitman?" Dr. Jones took the last bite of her protein bar. "Any updates?"

"Everything is just about the same health-wise, which I guess is all we can ask for these days. And she seems happier, too. Memory Village has reawakened her spunk. You know those concerts I told you about? The ones they host on family visitation days?"

Dr. Jones nodded.

"Yeah, well, this past weekend, they had this go-go band from DC. And you couldn't tell Mama she wasn't one of Chuck Brown's backup dancers. That woman is living her *best* life."

"I love that for her." Dr. Jones grinned. "Now what are we going to do to make sure you're living *your* best life?"

Well, damn, Dr. Jones!

De'Andrea knew it was a fair question. What *was* she going to do besides be a devoted wife, mother, and daughter-in-law? She eyed one of the few things helping her live her best life and was pleased to see her vape pen's "status" light had changed from red to green. *Finally!*

"Soooo . . . I'm just not sure what we can do about me living my best life in *Rolling Hills*," she began. "I don't think it's possible."

Dr. Jones crossed her arms and sighed with her whole chest.

"Now hear me out," De'Andrea said defensively. "Wait until I tell you what happened last week. Listen, it's hard out here." She grimaced and elongated the "a" in "hard" for dramatic effect.

"Alright, I'm listening."

"So, last week, I took Nina to our community park. Because I'm trying to do what you said, I'm trying to get out more and get to know people. Anyway, this little white boy was instantly smitten with Nina. He was grinning in her face, offering her rocks and blades of grass and whatnot. But his mama? When I tell you Becky was traumatized? Because—"

"So you introduced yourself?" Dr. Jones asked. "Is Becky one of your neighbors?"

De'Andrea hated whenever she couldn't tell whether her therapist was being condescending. "Noooo, I called her Becky because she was well . . . a Becky."

"Hmmm, I see. Continue."

Thank you! Because Becky is not the most important part of this story.

"So Becky is in her feelings, watching her son fawning over Nina. Especially when they started playing tag and he was clearly *letting* Nina catch him. Becky was sick! It was like she'd fast-forwarded time, the kids were in their twenties, and she was *this close* to having a Black daughter-in-law. And Becky does not want a Black daughter-in-law, mkay?" De'Andrea laughed out loud at the memory.

"Anyway, that night, I had a dream that the same little boy and Nina were back at the playground. Only this time, he'd arranged for a bunch of his little white buddies to be there, too. No other parents in sight, by the way. Just me. And all these little white boys start chasing after Nina. And she's screaming as they chase her around the playground, out of the playground, and down the street until I lose sight of her. I woke up having a full-on panic attack! Those little boys were, like, mini David Dukes or something! I mean, statistically, a lot of white boys *do* grow up to be—"

"De'Andrea!" Dr. Jones reprimanded sharply. "That is an *awful* thing to say."

"I know, I know. That's why I said statistically—"

"You can't view everything in life statistically," Dr. Jones continued. "Especially people. Or you'll always make broad and often incorrect assumptions. For example, statistically, one of every twenty-five people is a sociopath. But that doesn't mean—"

"Wait, what?" De'Andrea grabbed her vape pen. "All these damn white folks out here in Rolling Hills and you're telling me that one in twenty-five is a *sociopath*? Jesus!"

"No, not just white people," Dr. Jones clarified. "That statistic is irrespective of race and gender."

"But there *are* more white sociopaths than Black ones, right? Pretty sure I read that somewhere." De'Andrea took a long pull from her vape and exhaled before realizing she hadn't turned off her camera.

Shit. I mean, shittles. Nope, I mean shit.

"Don't worry, I'm not vaping as much as I used to," De'Andrea said between coughs. She waved her hand to clear the smoke. "I've switched to edibles. It's just that they take so long to kick in. But Toni told me about these fast-acting ones, they're made just for stressed-out moms. So I ordered some. I'm just waiting for them to get here. But I gotta keep vaping until they get here 'cause—"

"De'Andrea—"

"Like I said, it's hard out here, okay? Being around all these sociopathic white folks and whatnot. I need something to calm my nerves!"

Again, Dr. Jones sighed with her whole chest. "In the same way you don't want Black people to be considered as a monolith, you have to stop thinking that all white people are some big racist collective. Every white woman isn't a 'Becky' or the next 'Karen gone wild.' And every little white boy isn't destined to be a member of the Klan. As hard as it may be for you to believe, there *are* good white people in this world."

"Where?" De'Andrea put a hand to her brow like an explorer, squinting her eyes as she dramatically looked around the kitchen. "Where they at?"

"Well, perhaps if you stopped prejudging everyone you meet in Rolling Hills, you'd actually find some good ones. In fact, I think you should," Dr. Jones challenged.

"Find *who* how? And what do you mean by"—she bunny-eared her fingers and made air quotes—"you think I should?"

Dr. Jones leaned forward and looked straight into the camera. "I want you to commit to making a friend in Rolling Hills. Someone you can learn to rely on and trust. And yes, I want this person to be a white woman."

"You cannot be serious." De'Andrea balked. "This is a joke, right?"

"More like a prescription. Doctor's orders."

"No, Dr. Jones. Please," De'Andrea pleaded. "Make a white *friend*? I mean, how? And where—"

"What about Heidi?" Dr. Jones suggested. "You're neighbors. You're both mothers. Maybe you can even take your kids on a walk together—"

"I don't know that emo fairy woman!" De'Andrea shouted.

"Emo fairy?" Dr. Jones looked genuinely confused.

"Heidi rocks this blue-black pixie cut," De'Andrea began to explain. "Whatever. I'm just saying, yes, we're friendly, but I don't know her like that."

Dr. Jones shrugged. "Well, then, get to know her. And get to know some of the moms at Nina's school, too. Join the PTA.

Volunteer. Put yourself in places and spaces with like-minded white women. Just put in some real effort and you might find out—"

"Find out what? That I've befriended the one Becky in twenty-five who's a sociopath?" De'Andrea rolled her eyes, and somehow that activated the marijuana because she started feeling dizzy.

"Just try, that's all I ask. It's great that you keep in touch with your girlfriends, I love that you all connect and catch up every Sunday. But you need folks who are local. People you can meet up with in person for support and to have fun."

What Black woman in her right mind would meet up with a white woman for fun?

De'Andrea's shoulders slumped. "Alright alright. I'll talk to Heidi more. And I'll meet some white mamas or whatever."

"Just try," Dr. Jones encouraged. "That's all I'm asking is that you try."

"Fine. Fine! I will *try* to make a white friend."

Liar, an inner medicinal robot voice said. *There is no try. Only do. And you will not do it.*

Whew! She was hiiiiiiiiiiigh.

"You got this, De'Andrea." Dr. Jones held up her hands in the shape of a heart, their unprofessional yet endearing way of signing off after ten-plus years of therapy sessions.

"I got this! Yaaaaaaay!" She tried to sound upbeat as she returned the hand gesture before signing off.

De'Andrea sighed as she closed her laptop and thought about Dr. Jones's ridiculous challenge.

Make a white girlfriend? That don't even sound right!

FOUR

Rebecca

Five minutes before her alarm went off, Rebecca's eyes popped open. It was that dream again.

There was a scroll of lined paper, ribbon-like almost, that reminded her of Santa's Naughty and Nice list. Except this was a *to-do* list and somehow she was the pen writing out each task, line by line. She wanted so badly to mark something as "done" but could never get enough control to do it. And each time she wrote out a new item, the paper unscrolled farther, revealing more space for more tasks.

Panicked that she'd missed something on her real-life list, she picked up her phone and opened the Don't Let Me Forget app. Oddly relieved that the list was still as long as ever, she continued lying in the dark, trying to calm her heart rate. She turned off her alarm before the sound of wind chimes could wake Todd in case he felt in the mood for morning head. This was not a regular favor she performed, but she'd surprised him with an early morning blow job on vacation for his birthday, which had been enough to give him hope that maybe it would become a *thing*.

It wasn't going to be a thing.

Especially not today.

It was the first day of the new school year and she'd carved out the next thirty minutes for herself. She quietly slipped out of bed, changed into the sky blue yoga pants and matching crop top she'd laid out the night before, then crept up to her new meditation room in the attic, or "Mommy's playroom," as Todd had taken to calling it, cracking himself up as usual.

Standing in the center of the room, she stared at her reflection in the floor-length mirror. She pinched about a half inch of skin peeking out from over her waistband. *These pants are just tight from washing*, she tried to convince herself instead of obsessing over possible weight gain. She leaned in closer to the mirror and raised her eyebrows. No movement whatsoever on her forehead. Exactly the way she wanted it. The Botox injection from a few days earlier was kicking in.

Wait. Was that a scuff on the wall? It must have happened when the delivery guys leaned the mirror's nickel-colored steel frame against it.

After Rebecca's favorite yoga instructor, Serena, had given a workshop on the importance of de-stressing, Rebecca hired her to create the perfect refuge within the Myland home. "Higher cortisol means more wrinkles, ladies. And don't get me started on the damage it does to your gut health."

Serena had insisted on a minimalist décor. Rebecca loved how pristine the room looked, but now that it was finally ready for her to use, she wasn't really sure what to *do*. Sure, she'd been taking yoga classes for years, but that was about maintaining her lean physique. Plus, it was social.

Meditating was so . . . quiet. So *slow*. And Rebecca's most comfortable speed was "warp."

Still, she needed to try. Feeling somewhat self-conscious, as if there were a hidden camera somewhere with Serena judging her in real time, Rebecca sat on the meditation cushion and folded her legs into lotus pose. She lit her hand-rolled incense, watching the fragrant blend of sandalwood and patchouli slowly rise toward the attic's exposed wooden beams. She placed the incense on the curved ceramic dish to collect the ashes, which she planned to mix with rosemary and then bury near the front door to invite tranquility into the home—another suggestion from Serena. She opened the MindDiscovery app on her phone and hit play on "No More Manic Monday Mornings."

Inhaling deeply through her nose, Rebecca softened her gaze and lifted her hands to her heart center.

"Ahhhhh," she exhaled in one long, continuous breath, begging for peace to descend.

"Oh, shit!" Her giant exhale had sent ashes across her handwoven chakra carpet and all over her pants.

Rebecca brushed it off, blending the dust into the rug with her fingers until she could no longer see any trace.

She sighed. And not a yoga sigh, either. She was good at everything else she had ever tried in her life; she could certainly figure this out. It was either that or get a prescription for Xanax, which was what most of her girlfriends were doing. She wasn't ready to take that step, though. She'd heard too many stories about loss of sex drive as a side effect; she barely had any of that left anyway. On top of everything else, when on earth would she have time to see a psychiatrist? At least she could do this at home and fit it in before her family woke up.

Preparing to try again, Rebecca straightened her posture. She was about to close her eyes but that mark on the wall . . . it was staring at her. She hopped up off the floor to grab a cleansing wipe from the basket in the corner, thinking maybe she could clean it.

As she wiped, the scuff faded and spread, leaving a gray film more noticeable than what had been there before. If she could move the mirror enough to cover up the mess, she'd be able to focus again.

She stretched her arms as wide as they'd go and hooked a hand on each side, tilting it away from the wall, back toward her. She let out a grunt, summoning all her strength to slide the mirror a few inches.

There. Much better.

Now, *that* was getting shit done. She stepped back to admire her work.

As soon as she sat back down on her cushion, she checked her phone. At the most, there were ten minutes left of quiet.

Let's try again.

Rebecca returned to lotus pose, closed her eyes, and once again drew in a deep breath.

"Moooooom!" her daughters called up from the bottom of the attic stairs.

The next giant exhale she let out was in exasperation. More ashes flew from the incense dish. *Dammit*. She should have started earlier. The first day of school was one of only a few days in the year when she didn't have to nag Lyla and Isabella out of bed.

"I'll be right down, loves," she called out before dictating to her iPhone, "Hey, Siri. Remind me to ask Sylvia to hand-wash the chakra rug today."

Feeling defeated, Rebecca stood up and scanned the room one last time before shutting off the light and heading downstairs to switch into mom mode.

There's always tomorrow, she thought.

In the time it took Rebecca to shower, pull on a pair of jeans and a tank top, slick her hair back into a low bun, and even apply some tinted moisturizer and blush, her family had accomplished . . . nothing.

She entered the kitchen to find Todd and the girls paused like characters in a video game, waiting for her to set the morning in motion by pressing play.

Both girls were still in their pj's, Lyla doing that thing where she held the refrigerator door open and stared inside, while Isabella sat on the floor, putting high heels on one of her Barbies.

Todd was at least dressed for work, but he wasn't doing anything to move the girls along. Instead, he was leaning against the marble countertop, thumbs rapidly tapping his phone.

Even more concerning, she didn't smell any coffee; she couldn't hear it brewing, either. She could have sworn she had set the timer the night before.

"Uh, good morning!" Hands at her temples, she went to the coffeemaker and asked no one in particular, "What is happening here?"

"Morning, babe." Todd's fingers and eyes never left his phone, even while he craned his neck to kiss Rebecca on the cheek. "There was no coffee this morning. I think something's wrong with that thing."

Rebecca pressed the on button, and the machine emitted a comforting gurgling sound. She cleared her throat. Todd looked at her, then at the machine.

"I swear I tried, babe," he said with a shrug.

"Honey, you promised the girls you'd make pancakes for the first day of school."

"Mm-hmm. One . . . more . . . second. I should have sent this to Dana last night."

She grabbed a spatula and gave him a little spank with it before holding it in front of him.

"Todd, come on! You'll be at work in an hour."

"Just a sec. Aaaaand done!" Todd put his phone down on the counter with a sense of accomplishment disproportionate to what he'd completed: hitting send on an email to his assistant. He grabbed the spatula and returned the spank. "I'm on it."

Rebecca switched focus to her daughters.

"Girls! Time to get dressed! Let's see who can get back down here faster. First one ready gets an extra pancake!"

Lyla and Isabella bolted upstairs.

Todd tied on his Best Dad Ever apron the girls had given him last Father's Day and rolled up the sleeves on his dress shirt, a pale yellow button-down that popped against his skin, still tan from vacation. *He was cute like this*, Rebecca thought, gazing at her six-foot, sporty, C-suite husband trying to be domestic. She poured them each a cup of the freshly brewed coffee and placed the apron's matching Best Dad Ever mug next to Todd while he squinted at the back-of-the-box instructions to find the correct measurements.

Seriously? It's a "Just Add Water" mix, Rebecca noted, proud for having kept that comment internal. No need to give Todd a hard time. He was at least putting in some effort on the home front, unlike a lot of the other dads in their circle. She *did* wish he felt a little less thrilled with himself about it, though.

She pulled two pink notecards and a pen out of the kitchen drawer and wrote:

Happy first day of school, Isabella! I know this will be the best year ever. I love you so much! Love, Mommy.

She wrote out a second one. Except for addressing it to Lyla and signing it "Mom," she took great care to make the notes look nearly identical. Otherwise, she could almost hear them saying, "Why did you write *hers* with bigger letters?"

At last taking a sip of her coffee, Rebecca winced at the bitterness. She was trying to give up creamer and still hadn't gotten used to the taste without it. Still, it was caffeine.

"It's not supposed to rain later today, is it?" Todd asked, whisking the pancake mix. He tossed his head back after a section of his sandy blond hair flopped down on his forehead, covering his eyes. Rebecca typed into Don't Let Me Forget: "Sched Todd haircut."

"I don't think it's supposed to rain again until later this week," Rebecca said. "But let's double-check." She grabbed the remote and turned on the TV mounted above the fireplace in the family room adjacent to the kitchen. It was already set to the station airing *Good Morning Today.*

"It's the first day of school for millions of children across the country. Coming up after the break, we'll have ideas for healthy *and* delicious lunches that your kids will actually want to eat."

"Oooh, nice!" Rebecca set the remote down on the coffee table. "I always want new ideas!"

"You know kids swap. That's the best part about lunch," Todd said.

"Not *our* girls! They love my lunches." Rebecca pulled the two stainless steel Bentgo boxes out of the fridge that she'd packed the night before with sunflower seed butter, banana, and honey sandwiches, baby carrots and hummus, and one dark chocolate-dipped strawberry for dessert. She taped each of her daughter's notes to the inside of their lunch boxes, grabbed her phone, and snapped a photo. She'd include these in an Instagram post later.

Rebecca took the lunch boxes over to the mudroom, placed them in the girls' backpacks, and pulled her new dark brown monogrammed leather-bound On Time All the Time planner out of her handbag. She placed it on the kitchen counter to cross-check with her phone.

"How many calendars do you need?" Todd teased.

"Do *you* want to keep this all straight?" Rebecca jabbed back. She had read somewhere that physically writing things down made it easier to remember them. And after recently bringing Lyla over to a friend's house for a playdate *a day early*, an ad for this planner popped up on her timeline, a phenomenon she found disturbing yet helpful.

"Well, with school starting, you'll have some extra time to yourself, right?"

Rebecca looked up, mouth agape. She glared at him. "I can't tell if you're joking right now."

Todd was no dummy. Even if he hadn't been joking, he now understood he needed to be.

"Of course, babe. I know you're busy! Whaddya have slated for today?"

Rebecca leaned forward on the kitchen island to read through her planner and go through all the day's tasks out loud. "Let's see . . . after drop-off, I'll head to Nana's. Oh, wait. That's gonna be a short visit today. Stu is meeting me here at eleven to show me the landscaping designs. Then I've got the pool guy, the cable guy, and the windows guy all coming between twelve and three. Then it'll be time to pick the girls up and take them to soccer."

She looked up at Todd. "See all that extra time in there *for me*?"

Todd shrugged his shoulders apologetically, probably because he wasn't sure what else he could say, and got back to breakfast-making.

"Babe, check this out." He scooped a pancake off the griddle, flipped it into the air, and caught it on the plate in his opposite hand. "Bam! THAT'S how you make a pancake."

"Very impressive, Bobby Crocker."

"These really may be my best pancakes ever." He arranged fresh blueberries into smiley faces on the pancakes and waved them in front of Rebecca. "You know you want one."

Rebecca took a whiff, the smell alone torturing her. She hadn't eaten a pancake since her birthday in July and was nervous about what just one could do to the post-forty-year-old body she worked so hard to maintain. She wasn't about to test it.

"You've really outdone yourself this time." Rebecca put her hand on Todd's back and gave him a light pat. "I'll stick with my coffee."

As soon as the pancakes were done, Todd was back on his phone, which meant Rebecca would be serving breakfast. To make the first day of school feel extra special, she set the table like she would for one of her dinner parties, with white porcelain plates, forks and knives from the silver Todd's mother had gifted them for their wedding, and crystal wineglasses for the girls' orange juice. One final touch: she'd folded the burgundy-colored cloth napkins into swan shapes—a trick she'd learned while working for the campus catering company to help pay her way through college.

"I win!" Lyla shouted, winded. She ran into the kitchen with her arms raised in victory.

"You did NOT, Lyla!" Isabella cried out from behind her big sister, her blond curls shaking as she protested. "Mom! I was done getting dressed way before she was. But then she locked me out of my side of the bathroom and spent a *million* years in there!"

Lyla held her hands up, absolving herself of any blame. "Hey, I told you to use the other bathroom."

For the love of God, we have more bathrooms than people in this house, and they are still fighting about the freaking bathroom!

"That's enough." Rebecca did not want to lose her temper this morning and declared a tie. "You each get an extra pancake."

She took a step back from her daughters to take in the full view. "Now, let's talk about how incredibly gorgeous you two look!"

Isabella had on an embroidered jean skirt, knee-high argyle socks (August humidity be damned), brand-new sparkly sneakers, and a T-shirt with sequins in the shape of a rainbow that could be flipped up and down to change the rainbow's colors. At five years old, she still had squeezable rosy cheeks and a cute little potbelly. Rebecca hadn't meant for her girls to be five years apart, but that was how long it had taken her to have another full-term pregnancy. Devastated at the time, she now felt relieved to have a little girl for a few more years. Rebecca wanted to freeze her in time like this, knowing it wouldn't last much longer.

As soon as Lyla had turned six, her squishiness disappeared and now, as a ten-year-old, she was coming into that awkward stage where some days she looked like a little girl trying to grow up too fast, while other days she looked like a girl who was a little too old to be playing with dolls. More recently, there were days she'd show a glimpse of the beautiful teenager she'd become in only a few years. Today was one of those days.

"I look good, right, Mom?"

Lyla had picked out a pair of high-waisted light-wash distressed jeans, white Converse high-tops, and a white boxed tee with the *Friends* logo on it (even though Rebecca didn't let her watch the show). She had decided to wear her hair down for the first day of school, instead of the usual soccer-friendly French braid or ponytail, and her glimmering blond hair reached the middle of her back with a level of volume adult women killed for.

"Magnolia Country Day School, watch out!" Todd said. He lifted his phone up to take a candid shot of the girls.

"Dad! I wasn't ready for a photo!" Lyla held up her hand to shield her face, but she was too late.

Todd smiled at the picture he'd taken. "Those are always the best ones." He gave Lyla and Isabella a kiss on the top of each of their heads.

"Plenty of time for more photos after breakfast, everyone," Rebecca said. "Let's FaceTime Uncle Jack and Aunt Tina really quick so they can see these amazing outfits and wish you a happy first day."

Lyla grabbed Rebecca's phone. "Let me do it!"

She took the phone into the living room with Isabella chasing behind her. "Lyla! Wait for me!"

Once they were out of earshot, Todd said, "Lyla uses your phone like it's hers. Maybe it's time to get her one?"

"She's ten, Todd. That's way too young," Rebecca said. "Besides, Jenny and Vic and I agreed we'd wait until all the girls were twelve before they got their own phones."

Before Todd could respond, the girls came back into the kitchen.

"That was fast!" Rebecca and Todd said at the same time.

"Aunt Tina wasn't there, so we just talked to Uncle Jack." Lyla had opened a game app on Rebecca's phone and was sliding her thumb around Rebecca's screen. Isabella was on her tiptoes trying to see what her big sister was doing.

"Lyla, get out of that game. Give me my phone back." Rebecca held out her hand, but Lyla ignored her.

"Lyla!"

"Okay, okay. Geez, Mom. Relax."

As Lyla relinquished the phone, Rebecca asked, "Did Uncle Jack say where Aunt Tina was?"

"No." Lyla shook her head.

Isabella added, "He said he loved our outfits and to have a good day and then said he didn't want to make us late."

No Tina? That's weird.

Rebecca raised her eyebrows and looked over at Todd. He shook his head slightly, as if to say, *Don't read too much into this.*

"Why do you guys always look at each other with weird faces and not say anything?" Lyla asked.

"Mom and I have been together a long time, sweetie," Todd explained. "We have a secret language."

What Rebecca was saying in their secret language was *First, Jack and Tina bicker the entire vacation, and now she's not at their house first thing in the morning?*

But Todd had been adamant about not prying and said that if Jack wanted to talk about it, he would. Todd also made Rebecca promise not to ask Tina. "You don't have to fix everything, hon."

She wasn't trying to fix everything. Just this one thing. But she'd agreed to stay out of it, so she would. For now.

She checked the time. "Yikes! We need to keep things moving. Time for breakfast! Sit down, sit down."

Todd, in an exaggerated gesture of chivalry, pulled a chair out for each of his daughters to sit at the table.

"Whoa, Mom! This is so fancy!" Lyla remarked. Without needing to be reminded, she placed her napkin on her lap, and Rebecca felt a pang of both pride and heartbreak about how fast her firstborn was growing up.

"It's so pretty, Mommy!" Isabella said, beaming. She joined her sister at the table and *did* need to be reminded about her napkin, which Lyla was more than happy to do.

Todd fixed himself a plate of pancakes and, still wearing his apron, sat down to eat with his daughters. Rebecca remained standing and monitored the girls as they poured syrup. They would drown their pancakes if she let them.

"Not too much!" Rebecca had been the same way as a kid, only her mom never stopped her. She still had memories of Dave Simpson calling her chubby in the fifth grade.

While the rest of the family ate, Rebecca battled with Isabella's curls.

"Ow, Mommy! You're pulling too hard!"

"Almost done, love." Rebecca put her little girl's hair into a ponytail and tied ribbons matching the school colors, one red and one white, into a bow.

Rebecca inspected Lyla and noticed a small tangle in the back of her hair.

"Lyla, honey, you did a great job with your hair! But can I run the brush through it one more time for you?"

Lyla rolled her eyes. Rebecca wondered how her little girl could go from sweet to surly within minutes. "Fine, Mom."

"Now, tell me," Rebecca said as she worked through the knot in Lyla's hair and tried to remain upbeat. "What are you girls most excited about this school year?"

"Mommy!" Isabella shouted, pointing toward the TV. "You said no screens while we're eating!"

Rebecca looked over and realized *Good Morning Today* was still on. Once the girls had come back downstairs, it had become mere background noise and she'd stopped listening. Had she missed the school lunches segment? "You're right! Sorry! Daddy and I were just trying to get the weather forecast. Honey, where did I put the remote—"

"Another day, another viral video," the TV blared. "In cell phone footage posted to Twitter early this morning, a white woman walking her dog in a suburb outside of Denver can be seen yelling at a Black woman in her car, stopped at a stop sign. Here's a clip. And a note to viewers, this video contains racialized language."

Click.

Geesh, couldn't turn that off fast enough.

Rebecca shook her head at the TV. "How can people still act like that? It's absolutely shameful." She tossed the remote onto the sofa and returned to the kitchen table to continue brushing Lyla's hair.

"What's shameful?" Isabella asked.

Todd, with his mouth full, replied quickly, "Don't worry about it. It's nothing."

Neither of them wanted the news to dampen the morning, but

Rebecca had read enough parenting blogs to know she shouldn't dismiss her girls' inquiries altogether.

"Well, it wasn't *nothing*. But we don't need to worry about it right now."

She put the brush down and ran her fingers through Lyla's detangled hair. "All done." She walked over to the microwave to warm up her coffee.

Lyla gathered her hair and pulled it all to one side in front of her shoulder, and said to Isabella, "They were talking about a white woman being racist against a Black woman, Izzy." This caught Rebecca off guard. She assumed the girls hadn't really paid attention to the details.

"What's being racist?" Isabella asked before taking a sip of her juice.

Todd got up from the table and fumbled, grabbing his plate of pancakes. "Who wants another one?" His attempt to change the subject had so little finesse, Rebecca felt like he was delivering a punch line in a hokey family sitcom. Lyla, however, took him up on his offer and handed him her plate.

"It's when you don't like people because of the color of their skin," Lyla said, repeating verbatim what Rebecca had explained to her over the years.

"Why would anyone be like that?" Isabella asked, her brow furrowed and head tilted.

"Because they're idiots," her big sister answered through a bite of her pancake.

"Lyla, we don't use that word. And don't talk with your mouth full!" Rebecca scolded, then reconsidered. "Although, I guess in this case, maybe 'idiot' is the right word to use."

"Why are they being idiots?" Isabella asked.

I don't know! Stop asking me all these questions!

Rebecca drew in a deep breath.

"Normalize the conversation" and "Don't make race a taboo topic." Isn't that what all the experts say?

She just wished she didn't have to answer all these questions right now, especially since she wasn't certain what the answers were. Grabbing her coffee mug from the microwave, Rebecca sat down at the table across from her daughters. She took a sip to give herself a few more seconds to find the right words, or as right as she could get.

"The reason the white woman was being racist is she probably lives in a neighborhood that doesn't have many Black people in it, and so she saw this woman driving and thought she didn't belong. This kind of thing happens with people who don't value racial diversity."

"What's racial diversity?" asked Isabella.

"Having lots of people with all different skin colors," Lyla answered before Rebecca could. "But racial diversity isn't important here," she added.

Rebecca almost spit out her coffee.

"Yes, it *is*, honey! Racial diversity is *very* important here!" Rebecca tilted her head in her husband's direction, saying to him with her eyes, *Want to help me out?*

His response was another shrug of his shoulders and sip of his own coffee, as if to say, *You've got this one, babe.*

Why did the hard stuff always have to fall on her? On all moms? It infuriated Rebecca, but at the same time she knew she didn't really trust her husband to handle it responsibly anyway. Todd never read anything—not about parenting or about race, and he certainly never read anything about parenting *and* race. Of course, she could have pushed him to educate himself; and they could have talked about how they, together, would approach these conversations with their children. But that sounded like even more work than taking care of it all herself.

"Why don't we know any Black people then?" Lyla countered.

"We *do* know Black people!" Rebecca started a count with her fingers. "There's Sean at the front gate. There's his backup . . . Todd, you know, the guard from over at The Preserve who fills in for Sean. . . ."

"James." Todd finally said something helpful.

"Right, there's Sean and James. And there's a new Black family joining your school. Remember, Isabella? Nina is going to be in your class. You met her at orientation."

Thank God for the Whitmans.

"Oh yeah—Nina! We're gonna be friends!"

Rebecca beamed at Isabella.

Always good-natured and welcoming, Izzy would be a great friend to Nina, like she naturally was to all kids. She wouldn't mess things up like Rebecca had when she was a kid.

"But we don't actually *know* them yet," Lyla said. She cocked her head and looked satisfied that she was winning an argument. Lately, she was always trying to win arguments . . . with everyone.

"Why are they called 'Black'?" Isabella asked. "Nina's skin is brown. So is Sean's."

Rebecca believed these were all good questions. Truly. But she hadn't planned on taking a deep dive into the topic of race on the first day of school. She also still didn't know if it was going to rain later in the day. Did *Good Morning Today* even report on the fucking weather anymore?

Todd still wasn't bothered and was clearly moving on with *his* day. He grabbed his navy sport coat and slid his laptop into his bag.

It was time for *everyone* to go.

"Girls, we can talk about this later. I promise," Rebecca said. "Plates to the sink. Get your backpacks. We need to get out front to take pictures!"

While Lyla and Isabella followed orders, Rebecca grabbed her own bag, dropped her planner back in it, and shepherded everyone out the door. "Thanks for your help," she whispered to Todd as she closed the door behind them.

"Bec, you're the one who kept the conversation going. I was trying to keep things light."

As was their tradition on the first day of school, Rebecca positioned the girls in front of the sweetbay magnolia tree she and Todd had planted in the front yard when they purchased their "forever home." With each year's photograph, Lyla and Isabella grew taller, their outfits less frilly, and their facial expressions transformed from the smile-on-command-for-Mommy look to reflections of their increasingly distinct personalities. And always in the background was the tree, also growing a bit taller, branches extending and more blooms sprouting at a seemingly unnoticeable pace until Rebecca would look back at the previous year's first-day photos.

Rebecca handed Isabella and Lyla the signs she'd decorated the night before using glitter markers to write, "First Day of Kindergarten!" and "First Day of 5th Grade!"

The moment she centered her girls on her phone's camera,

there was an issue. "Oh, dang it! I can see the edge of the big hole in the lawn." Stu had broken ground the previous week on what would eventually be a koi pond, another one of her tranquil home projects. "Todd, honey, move them about six inches to the right."

Todd took each girl by the shoulder and shuffled them over while Rebecca framed the perfect photo. "That's it! Right there. Nobody move!"

Todd froze, his arms up in the air as if he'd been told to "stick 'em up." This made the girls giggle. "Daaaaad! Not you!"

Once he moved out of the way, Rebecca started snapping, asking the girls to pose for at least a dozen photos—with the two of them together, separately, at different angles, and some in portrait mode. Rebecca checked the pictures.

"Mom! Let's go already!" Lyla said.

"Bec—" Todd pointed to his watch.

"Just one more," Rebecca insisted. Ten minutes and many photos later—most including an increasingly frowny Lyla—she realized how late it was getting.

Todd scooped up Isabella in one arm and hugged Lyla with the other. "Have an amazing day, girls!" He gave each girl a kiss on the cheek and Rebecca a quick peck before getting into his black Mercedes SUV.

Rebecca ushered the girls into her silver Range Rover. While they buckled themselves in, she quickly swiped through the photos she'd taken and hearted a few favorites. She opened Instagram and posted the best two of the girls with their first-day-of-school signs, plus a shot of their homemade lunches. #FirstDayOfSchool #MomLife #LunchboxesOfInstagram.

"Mooooom!"

"Okay, okay!" The rev of the engine sent them on their way.

FIVE

De'Andrea

Malik sat motionless in the driver's seat of his black Escalade, his large hands clutching the steering wheel even though he hadn't turned the car on yet. In his navy pinstriped suit and crisp white button-down, he looked like a businessman at the starting line of the Daytona 500: Consultant Edition. De'Andrea reclined her seat and leaned back into the buttery-soft leather with an exasperated sigh. Their heads turned to face each other, their expressions conveying both shock and sympathy as they sat in the school's parking lot.

Just like that, their baby girl was officially a kindergartner.

"You alright, Dee?" Malik pressed the ignition button, then he placed his right hand on her thigh and squeezed twice to offer a bit of encouragement.

"Nope! Not alright." She buckled her seat belt as Malik began reversing and the dark safety straps tightened across her shoulder and tummy.

Damn, even the car knew she needed a hug.

"It's okay to cry, you know." Malik waved "thank you" to the driver waiting patiently for him to back out of his parking spot. "Nothing wrong with shedding a few thug tears. Hell, I might even shed a few myself on my way to the office."

She gave a dry chuckle and it sounded as forced as it felt. "Honestly, I'm surprised I'm not bawling. Guess I'm still in denial? Babe, how is Nina in *kindergarten*?"

"I have no . . . *whoa!*" Malik slammed on the brakes.

The tall blond woman who'd darted out didn't even look in his direction. She smiled as she continued running toward her mom friends, seemingly oblivious that she'd narrowly avoided being hit. A short redhead woman opened her arms wide and the tall blond woman fell into her embrace as a brunette rushed over to join them in a group hug. They were all wearing variations of basic white girl high-end athleisure—not Heidi's Free People ensemble. These women weren't emo-fairy cool enough for that.

De'Andrea kissed her teeth as Malik drove by the friend trio. "It's giving 'Stop Sign Karen' energy."

"Yooooooo! Stop Sign Karen was *wilding*!" Malik's booming laugh was contagious, and De'Andrea couldn't help but join in.

"She really was doing the most." De'Andrea shook her head as she snickered. "And for no reason at all. And the internet! That song!"

"Right?" Malik cleared his throat before he started singing, "Oh, you were gonna hit us. You were gonna hit us—"

"You look like a Black lady *who doesn't like to stop*!" De'Andrea sang along with Malik as they both erupted in laughter.

When De'Andrea had woken up and seen #StopSignKaren trending, she'd braced herself for the worst. But it was actually the type of social media shenanigans that De'Andrea and Malik were *always* down for watching: white people caught on camera white peopling.

The latest viral incident involved a white woman walking her dog who *assumed* the Black woman driving toward her wasn't going to stop. Much to the internet's delight, the Black woman was a broker who just happened to be recording a property listing so she'd captured the entire hilarious encounter on her cell phone—from the white woman yelling as her car approached to how she'd already come to a complete stop well before she'd reached the crosswalk. The Black woman alternated the camera between her unbothered expression and the white woman's hysterical ranting, all while she sat in her car with a bright red stop sign in plain view.

"Just who do you think you are, Black lady?" Malik sang out as he continued making his way through the back-to-school congestion.

"Did you hear the latest remix? It's fire." De'Andrea hummed a bit of the hook.

"No, I haven't. Pull it up! You know how much I love a compilation for the culture."

Within a few seconds, they were cracking up listening to the latest auto-tuned remix of Stop Sign Karen's shrill voice over a tight beat.

"Just who . . . just who . . . just who do you think you are?" De'Andrea sang along to the catchy hook. "Just who do you think you are, *Black lady*?" She bounced her shoulders up and down to the rhythmic baseline drumming. "It's a bop, right?"

Malik agreed. "Fire. I love my people."

Traffic thinned as they moved farther away from the town's school zones. De'Andrea tried to take in the beauty of the tall oaks flanking the two-lane roadway and selected a jazz essentials playlist for the short ride home. She tried to imagine Thelonious Monk sitting at a baby grand piano—anything not to think about how Nina must be feeling as the only Black child in her class.

De'Andrea's phone lit up in her hand. Damn, she'd forgotten it was still on silent. Her banner notifications showed missed texts in The Girls' group chat. "Here they go!"

"Who?" Malik asked as he switched lanes.

"Who else?" De'Andrea pretended to be annoyed, but few things brought her more joy than hearing from her girlfriends. She missed them terribly and quickly entered her passcode to unlock the latest text thread.

Today, 8:29 AM

Toni

Well, De'Andrea. Today is the first day of the rest of our lives. We's free now! 😂 But also 😭

Simone

Freedom ain't free! Y'ALL DID THAT! My godbabies are amazing because of all the hard work Y'ALL put in. Congratulations to both of you! 🥹 And LL says congratulations too!

De'Andrea tapped the picture Simone had attached. LL was grinning like he knew it was the kids' first day of kindergarten. She chuckled and kept scrolling.

Today, 8:31 AM

Toni

I just can't believe Jasmine and Junior are in kindergarten y'all. KINDERGARTEN! The house just feels so empty without them. And it's so quiet. And I just love it so much! 😵

Simone

Alright Mamas. Drop them first day of school pics. Let's see the babies looking so fresh and so clean!

Toni

Here you go! I mean, look at them! 🥹

De'Andrea tapped the picture to enlarge it.

Junior and Jasmine were holding hands standing side by side in front of a yellow school bus, both clad in green and white uniforms, matching mid-calf socks, and brown loafers. With freshly faded curls and sharp edge lines around his temples, Junior was the spitting image of Craig. And his sister looked like a little doll! De'Andrea tried not to get emotional seeing Jasmine rocking her first silky press, her straightened hair draped over her shoulders, giving a glimpse of preteen.

She held up her phone near Malik's face. "Look at the twins! If Junior ain't Craig two-point-o!"

He glanced over at her screen. "Aye! I see you, homie. Little man looking like money today!"

"He's so stinkin' cute!" De'Andrea continued scrolling through the thread. "And I cannot with Jasmine. She looks like such a big girl! I wasn't ready."

If they still lived in Atlanta, the kids would have taken first-day-of-school pics together. And De'Andrea could have spent the rest of the day crying and drinking White Claws with Toni and Simone.

Today, 8:37 AM

De'Andrea

Hey hey, y'all. Sorry I'm late to the party. Nina's all settled in at her little PWI. And I have feels! I wish I was there so y'all could hold me! 😭

Toni and Simone reacted to her message with heart emojis.

Today, 8:38 AM
Toni
Awww, Dee. We miss you too. SO much, sunshine.

Simone
For reals, Dee Dee. We love you.

De'Andrea
Love y'all more.

God, she missed them. Especially on days like today.

Today, 8:39 AM
De'Andrea
Okay, the moment you've been waiting for. Check out Miss Nina Bear. The kindergartner!

Of course, the best photos were on her real camera. Still, she sent two photos she'd taken with her camera phone. First, a headshot of Nina standing on their deck, smiling sweetly with her boxed braids draped over her shoulders. The second image was full-length and showcased the adorable ensemble Nina had picked out for her big day: an embroidered jean skirt, knee-high argyle socks, her favorite sparkly sneakers, and a flippy rainbow T-shirt. De'Andrea had done the most by color-coordinating the beads at the bottom of Nina's braids with her outfit . . . and she had no regrets.

Several heart emojis and celebratory reactions from Toni and Simone popped up.

Today, 8:40 AM
Simone
I can't deal! Too cute and too cool for school! 😎

Toni
Look at my Nina Pumpkin Sweets! Dis tew much! 🥲

De'Andrea
I know! Like I said FEELS! I'm just praying she has a great day and I don't have to fight somebody.

She laughed at her friends' "ha ha" reaction bubbles.

Today, 8:41 AM
Toni
You won't have to fight anybody. She's gonna have a great day. You'll see! 😃

Simone
Exactly. And if she doesn't, I'll just fly up there and fight the whites. They better not mess with my Nina!

And De'Andrea knew Simone was serious.

Today, 8:43 AM
Toni
I know today is supposed to be all about the babies but . . . look at me, y'all. Look at meeeeeeeeeeeee!

De'Andrea double tapped Toni's selfie. Clad in a white bathrobe with a pale green mask on her face, she smiled at the camera while balancing an elaborate half-eaten charcuterie spread on her lap. Her free hand was holding a raised champagne flute.

Today, 8:44 AM

De'Andrea

That mimosa is looking real light! Might need to add some more juice, ma'am.

Simone

😄 For real! How much orange juice did you put in there? A teaspoon?

Toni

👆 Whatever. I'm winning, bitches. This is the first time I've been home alone for real for real in five MF years. I'm finna have my mimosa with a thimble full of juice, eat my char-coochie board, and celebrate!

De'Andrea

Awww, you know you miss those cuties.

Toni

Actually, no. No, I don't. 😄

Simone

What about you, Dee? How you celebrating your first day as an elementary empty nester?

De'Andrea

Not sure yet. Malik is driving us home now. We're almost there.

Toni

Oh shit, girl! Malik's not at work? Well, that's how you're about to be celebrating. He's about to blow your back out!

Simone

😄 Oh yeah. We know EXACTLY how you're about to be celebrating! First time having morning sex in five years!

Oh honey, you don't even know how it goes down over here!

"Oh, we have plenty of morning sex. Trust!" De'Andrea said each word as she typed. Then she added a tongue and eggplant emojis before pressing send.

"Morning sex? Yes, please!" Malik reached over and playfully ran his fingers up her thigh.

She grabbed his hand and put it back on the steering wheel. "Aht aht! Sir, might I remind you that *you* need to leave for work soon?"

"Quickie?"

"Nope! That's a setup because you do not know the meaning of 'quickie,'" she reminded him.

"I mean, I can be late." Malik grinned, slowing the truck to a stop. "I'll just blame it on all this traffic."

Several deer crossed the roadway, their legs moving elegantly in sync as they walked into the woods.

De'Andrea shuddered. "Why do they do that?"

"Do what?" Malik asked. "Live here? C'mon now, Dee. This was their home first, before all the construction and—"

"No, fool. All that staring with those wide, deranged-looking eyes. It's so creepy. Gives me the heebie-jeebies!" She quivered again.

Malik laughed as he drove toward the gated entrance. "Are you serious? Didn't you watch *Bambi* as a kid? You know deer are more afraid of us than we are of them, right?"

"Not me! I am definitely more afraid of them." She looked out her window, straining her neck to see if more deer were nearby. "And that was not cute li'l Bambi and friends. Those things were huge!"

"Oh snap, James is here." Malik honked his horn twice as he bypassed the residents' entrance, veered right, and headed to the visitors' security booth.

A young Black man stepped out of the wooden shed and waved. His white-collared uniform shirt was tucked neatly into his black slacks, but he did an extra tuck for good measure as the Whitmans approached.

Malik let down his driver's-side window and the two men fist-dapped. "Mr. J-Boogie. What's good, youngblood? We ain't seen you in a minute."

"Yeah, I took some time off after my summer exams," James said. "Fall semester starts next week. Only one more year to go! Then I'll be out here flexin' like you." He tapped the side of Malik's truck and let out a low whistle. "This shit is sweet, man." Which was immediately followed by "Sorry for the language, Mrs. Whitman. Good morning."

She looked up briefly from her chat with Toni and Simone. There wasn't a trace of facial hair on the young man's smooth brown skin. "Morning, James. No worries. And senior year, huh? Big big congrats! Hopefully it's light work these last two semesters. Either way, you got this! We'll certainly be praying for you."

"Thank you, thank you." James cupped his hands and peered

through the rear window. "Hey, where's the fresh princess of Rolling Hills?

"In kindergarten," Malik said proudly. "Today's her first day."

"Whaaaaat? Tell my little buddy I said congrats!" James looked up as another vehicle approached. He quickly stepped inside the security booth and opened the visitors' gate for Malik. "Back to the grind. Man, it was good to see y'all. Be easy."

"Always. You too." Malik fist-bumped James once more before he drove off. "He's good people."

"Such a sweet kid," De'Andrea agreed as they began the slow commute home.

Ingrid, their next-door neighbor who seemed to only venture outside to collect her mail and tend to her garden, was watering her flower beds. She was somewhat of a recluse. And definitely on Rolling Hills' one in twenty-five sociopaths list. In fact, the only reason De'Andrea even knew the older woman's name was because Heidi had told her. "She's . . . interesting," Heidi had said. "And that's all I'm going to say about that."

Ingrid raised her head, using one hand to shield her eyes as she squinted in their direction. But when Malik turned into their driveway and waved, she pretended not to see him.

"I don't even know why you try." De'Andrea shook her head. "Ol' stank face Miss Ingrid has made it real clear she ain't happy her new neighbors are Black."

"All the more reason for me to keep saying hi!" Malik laughed as he pulled into the garage.

Today, 9:01 AM
De'Andrea
Home!

Simone

Yay! Have fun! 😈 Call us later.

Toni

Yeah, have a GOOD morning! LOL

But sex was the last thing on her mind.

How was Nina doing? What was Nina doing? And what in the hell was De'Andrea going to do with herself once Malik left for work and she was "alone alone"?

As soon as they walked into the house, Malik headed toward the kitchen and sat at the island. His laptop was right where he'd left it earlier, still flipped open waiting for him to get back to work. "Just need to send off a few emails . . ." His voice trailed off as he entered his password.

"All good. I'm just glad you could reschedule your meetings and be with Nina this morning."

Malik looked up, surprised. "C'mon, babe. You know I wouldn't have missed Nina's first day of kindergarten for anything."

She wanted to believe him, but she wasn't so sure. Work seemed to take precedent over everything lately, and De'Andrea was all-too familiar with escapism.

"Dee."

She jumped, startled that he was standing right behind her. "God, Malik! You scared me. I was just going to make you some coffee for the road." She opened the cabinet to get a to-go mug but Malik closed it and held his palm against the door to keep it shut.

"You didn't really think I'd miss Nina's first day, did you?"

She could hear the hurt in his voice, and rather than cut into his feelings deeper she simply said, "No, of course not. I was just saying I was glad things worked out."

"You're a terrible liar, you know that?" Malik grabbed her by the waist and gently turned her to face him. "I know I've been busy with work lately. Busier than usual. But it's just . . ."

"It's just what?"

Malik continued to stare into her eyes for a moment. Then he looked away as he said, "It's just . . . this is a new office, a new team. And I'm hyper-visible because I'm the only Black guy. I don't know. I just feel like I need to prove myself is all."

De'Andrea knew *that* feeling well, too. She took his face in her hands and kissed him softly. "You don't need to prove anything to anyone. You're brilliant, Malik. You know that. And they know that, too."

"I know but—"

"No 'buts.'" She kissed him again, this time more passionately, and he leaned into her embrace. "Leek, you're going to be late for work," she mumbled between their locked lips.

"So?"

A chorus of birds chirped outside De'Andrea's bedroom window, slowly awakening her with their cheerful melodies. She stretched, grateful for her morning not-so-quickie with Malik *and* for her midmorning nap. As the birds continued to sing, she had to admit, being so close to nature did have its benefits.

"Except those damn deer," she muttered. "They can have all that."

De'Andrea checked the time. *Eleven forty-five?* God, it was still early. She didn't need to pick up Nina from school until 2:35 p.m.! And God only knew what time Malik would get home, especially with him going into the office so late. Maybe that's where the phrase "kept woman" came from—women who kept checking to see how much longer until reuniting with their loved ones.

Now she regretted rescheduling her Monday therapy session. It had seemed like the best thing to do, since De'Andrea didn't know if she'd feel like talking about Nina's first day of kindergarten *on* Nina's first day of kindergarten. She also didn't want Dr. Jones to ask for updates about her li'l Make-a-White-Friend challenge. Didn't her therapist get it? She was Team No New Friends, especially in Rolling Hills!

Not that she hadn't tried. Because she wanted to be able to tell Dr. Jones she'd truly tried. Okay, "tried" was reaching. But she had made small talk with Heidi over the weekend while both of their daughters were playing outside. She was nice enough (for a white lady) but that didn't mean De'Andrea wanted or needed to be her friend. Her *friends* were in Atlanta.

And Nina's friends were there, too.

Nina Bear.

De'Andrea eyed her tote perched on the bench at the foot of the bed.

Really? You're that lazy?

"Yes, yes, I am," she answered herself as she inched down rather than getting out of bed to retrieve it. Once she'd propped herself back up against the pillows, she reached inside the bag and pulled out her camera. Misty-eyed, she clicked through the photos chronicling Nina's first day. The images were stunning, magazine-worthy really. Maybe she wasn't supposed to be a lawyer. Maybe she'd missed her true calling. Didn't people always say "Do what you love"?

But I only like taking pictures of people I love so . . . how's that going to work?

De'Andrea's phone chimed and she reached over to grab it off the nightstand, grateful to have something to do.

Today, 11:58 AM
Malik
Hey you. How you feeling?

She went to type "meh" but then thought better of it. There was no need to make Malik more worried about her than he already was.

Today, 11:59 AM
De'Andrea
Good! Just waking up from a nap. Because someone put me to sleep. 😴 About to get into this ridiculously huge bathtub that we never use.

It wasn't a complete lie. She had been thinking about taking a bath. If she could just bring herself to get out of bed.

Today, 12:00 PM
Malik
Send pics pls! 😏 About to hop on this Zoom. Check in w/ you after. Love you!

De'Andrea
Love you too, babe 🖤

The birds had stopped singing and De'Andrea realized just how quiet the house was—too quiet—and she wondered if she'd ever be able to settle into the eerie stillness. If she'd woken up from her nap a little earlier, she might have had time for a quick visit with Mama. But she didn't want to risk driving to Memory Village, especially because if something caused a delay, there was no one to pick up Nina in an emergency.

All you've got is yourself, girl.

And that truth was a tough pill to swallow.

Determined to take a leisurely soak (more so she could *tell* Malik that she had), De'Andrea got out of bed and went into their massive en suite bathroom. "Jo Malone. Orange Blossom. Scent candle. Bougie parfumée." She giggled at the descriptive label on her favorite candle as she lit the wick. "Perfect for a bougie bath in this bougie bathtub."

It seemed to take forever to fill the gorgeous porcelain claw-foot tub, but once De'Andrea eased into the lavender and Epsom salt-infused warm water, she had to admit it was worth the wait. She submerged herself up to her neck and stared at the cloudless blue heavens through the skylight overhead. And she stayed that way until her fingertips were shriveled like raisins.

⁓

Between chatting with Toni and Simone and incorporating Nina's aggressive school calendar into the family schedule, the early afternoon had gone by much faster than De'Andrea imagined it would. Still, it wasn't fast enough, and she'd been thrilled when it was time to go pick up Nina.

"Hello! And who are you signing out today?" the stunning young woman standing outside the gated area asked cheerfully. Her name badge read "Hi! I'm Mrs. Kay!" but the massive diamond ring on her left hand screamed "I'm here because I want to work, not because I have to work."

"Hi, Mrs. Kay. Signing out Nina Whitman. I'm her mom. Obviously." She smiled so Mrs. Kay knew the "obviously" was in jest. Even though it *was* obvious who she'd come to pick up. De'Andrea and Nina were the only two Black people in the schoolyard.

"*Obviously.*" Mrs. Kay returned the humor. "Nina! Nina Whitman!"

Upon hearing her name, Nina turned around. And when she saw her mother, she squealed and ran toward her. "Mommy, Mommy! Hi, Mommy!"

"Hey, Nina Bear!" De'Andrea crouched to hug her favorite little person. "Did you have a good first day of kindergarten?"

"I did, Mommy! I did!" Nina began rambling about her day, giggling as she shared the highlights in no particular order.

God, I missed you so much today. How in the hell am I going to do this for the next twelve years?

An adorable little girl had followed Nina like a shadow. De'Andrea smiled at her messy, curly blond ponytail, evidence of how much fun she'd had on the first day of the school year. She looked up with the widest, most innocent blue eyes and said, "Hi, Nina's Mommy."

"Well, hello there." De'Andrea noticed that the little girl and

Nina were dressed alike, right down to their flippy shirts and sparkling sneakers.

"Isabella, you have to stay inside the gate," Mrs. Kay reprimanded kindly. "Your mother hasn't signed you out yet."

"But I can see my mommy. She's standing right there." Isabella pointed to three women standing under a tree, deep in conversation.

"Yes, that *is* your mommy, but your mommy hasn't signed you out yet. So, you cannot leave the playground. But you're more than welcome to stand right here and wait for her, okay?"

De'Andrea was impressed. Mrs. Kay sounded like she had the patience of Job.

"Mommy!" Isabella screamed. "Come sign me out. Pleeaaaaaaaaseeee!"

"Isabella is my new best friend." Nina opened her arms wide, and Isabella leaned in for a heartwarming embrace.

Okay, this is giving Gap-commercial cuteness. I can't!

"Hi, Kay." One of the women from the trio Isabella had pointed at was now standing at the gate. "Sorry! I lost track of time. Izzy, c'mon honey. We need to get to soccer practice."

De'Andrea silently sized her up. Pretty—she had the same sky-blue eyes and thick blond hair as Isabella, only hers was brushed into a neat bun. And her outfit was fire—the gladiator sandals, skinny jeans, and silk cami were a whole vibe. But her energy was frantic.

The woman crouched next to Isabella. "Where's Lyla?" she asked after giving her daughter a kiss on the cheek.

"I don't know!" Isabella sang as she wiggled out of her mother's embrace and grabbed Nina by the hands. "That's Nina's mommy," she explained as the two girls began twirling in circles. "Mommy, say hi to Nina's Mommy."

"Hiiiiiiii, Nina's Mommy!" Isabella's mother said excitedly.

Much too excitedly.

De'Andrea nodded. "Hi, I'm De'Andrea. De'Andrea Whitman. Or . . . you can call me Nina's Mommy. That works too."

"I know, right? Do mothers even have names?" The woman chuckled. "I'm Isabella's Mommy, and I've been dying to meet you. Welcome to the Cardinals family, Dee-*ann*-dree-ah!"

She sounded out her name as if she were at a spelling bee.

"Actually, it's Dee-*on*-dree-ah."

Isabella's mom's cheeks flushed. "Oh, sorry! Dee-*on*-dree-ah." She elongated and added extra emphasis to the *on*. "Did I say it right that time?"

"Yup," De'Andrea replied dryly before remembering her promise to Dr. Jones that she'd play nicely with the other moms at Nina's school. She dug deep. "You said it perfectly."

"Yessssssssss!" Isabella's mom pumped her fist in the air.

Why are you so surprised and pleased with yourself? I literally told you how to say it.

Isabella absentmindedly toyed with the pockets of her mother's jeans. "Isn't Nina so pretty? I like her hair. Can I wear my hair like that? I'm so happy she's in my class. Remember what Lyla said this morning at breakfast? Now we know Sean and James and—"

"Isabella!" her mother quickly interrupted. "Go get your backpack, find your sister, and hurry up. Please!"

"I'll come with you," Nina offered. "I'll help you find her."

No, don't leave me! De'Andrea silently screamed.

"Yay! Let's go!" Isabella grabbed Nina's hand, and they ran toward a cluster of preteen girls.

"So Dee-*on*-dree-ah. Like I was saying earlier, welcome to the Cardinals family. And welcome to Rolling Hills. You're going to love our little close-knit community! We've lived here for years. My husband grew up here actually. He's a Rolling Hillsian. That's what they call folks who were born and raised here. Isn't that a hoot? Anyway—" She paused for a moment, her cheeks flushed with embarrassment. "Oh. My. God! I just realized I told you that I'm Isabella's mommy but I never told you *my* name. I'm Rebecca. Rebecca Myland." Smiling, she extended her arm for a handshake.

Rebecca. De'Andrea held in a cackle as she briefly shook the woman's sweaty palm. *Of course your name is Becky!*

SIX

Rebecca

O nly three days into the school year and Rebecca had already returned to the grind as if summer break hadn't happened at all. Thank God for Wednesday mornings when she and her girlfriends met up for yoga and then went back to her place to catch up on all the things they couldn't, or shouldn't, cover in the group chat.

Rebecca turned into the lot on Chancellor Avenue, parked, and downed the rest of her coffee. *Blech*. Her hot pink "Mom Fuel" travel mug was supposed to keep drinks hot. It did not.

She checked her watch. Thanks to a smooth morning getting the girls out the door (which she realized wouldn't last into week two of the school year), she had about fifteen minutes to kill before yoga. None of the Chance Ave stores were open yet except for the Rolling Bean. More coffee was probably a bad idea. Maybe a stroll would be nice. She placed her forehead against the car window to peer at the sky. There was some cloud cover, which meant the temp might be pleasant. Even better, barely anyone was out and about yet so she wouldn't get sucked into any neighborly small talk.

Walking from the parking lot down the block of matching redbrick storefronts, Rebecca felt like she was on a Main Street

America set on a Hollywood studio lot. That's how perfect every-thing was. In fact, when she and Todd first moved to Rolling Hills, it felt *too* perfect. *Is this even real?* she remembered asking herself while annoying Todd with *Stepford Wives* references. She now blamed the initial resistance on insecurity, a feeling that she didn't really belong in this life. That at any moment, everyone else might figure that out, too, and send her back to the working-class Ohio town where she'd grown up. Those fears never disappeared completely, but they had faded over time. Even if Rolling Hills wasn't quite right, it now felt more like "home" than "back home" did. Even more important, it was all her daughters knew. Plus, who wouldn't become accustomed to how quaint, convenient, and *clean* it all was? What was so bad about perfect anyway?

She passed the local Italian restaurant La Roma and noticed a new menu posted on the door; she backtracked to take a closer look.

Yes!

Chef Paolo had added the gluten-free pasta she'd been ask-ing for.

"Make resy for date night," she typed into her phone.

A few more steps brought her to Hilltop, the women's clothing boutique Victoria owned (as a hobby), then the organic grocer, the pharmacy, the high-end stationery shop, and, finally, the small public seating area with bistro tables and chairs encircled by raised flower beds filled with black-eyed Susans in full bloom.

She sat down and scanned all the flyers pinned to the public bulletin board next to the tables. There were the usual notices for events like the monthly town council meeting, weekly story time at the library, and Chance Ave Fridays, when the street was closed off to cars and live bands would play cover songs while kids danced in the street and parents drank wine and local craft beers. Rebecca spotted an announcement she'd not seen before.

She stood up to get a closer look. "Justice in Parks (JIP): Calling for the Removal of All Confederate Monuments."

Huh? Haven't those all been torn down by now?

She kept reading:

"Join us as we rally to remove the Rolling Hills Park statue of Confederate Lieutenant General James Longstreet!"

Wait, what?

In the center of the flyer was a grainy black-and-white photograph of a soldier atop a horse, one arm holding a rifled musket triumphantly. His other arm appeared to be missing. Rebecca couldn't tell if the arm had fallen off the statue or if the man didn't have an arm. Either way . . . a Confederate statue in Rolling Hills Park? No way. Between playground playdates, long runs on weekends, and the girls' soccer practices, Rebecca spent as much time at that park as she did her own home, and she'd never seen this statue. At the bottom of the page was an invitation to join the JIP Rolling Hills Facebook group. Rebecca snapped a photo so she could look it up later.

She returned to the bench and opened up her phone to scroll through the bleak roller coaster that was her newsfeed. Inflation was high, stocks were low; crime was up, jobs were down; water levels were rising, consumer confidence was dropping. After only a few minutes in, she realized she'd gone full zombie.

Her thumb kept swiping up, her eyes staring at the screen, but she had stopped *reading* anything. It was all so depressing, and all the same as the day before. And the day before that.

Having sufficiently arrived at the mental intersection of informed, outraged, depressed, and helpless, she switched over to the "Trending" tab, a potential salve. Number one was #Happy-HumpDay, which had nothing of interest. But number two trending was Barack Obama's new goatee that had debuted on network TV during an interview he gave to Oprah the night before and had immediately caused people to lose their damn minds. Someone had even started an account for his goatee.

How does he look better now than when he was president?

She took a screenshot of one of the memes—a close-up of Obama's mouth and a speech bubble with the Luther Vandross lyrics "You're my first, my last, my everything"—and texted it to Todd.

Also trending was a call from a prominent feminist writer asking women to share the first time they remembered being called a "bitch." She read through a few stories before her own came to mind. It was freshman year of high school. Archie Baker called her a stuck-up bitch after she turned him down when he asked her to homecoming. She and Archie had been friends since kindergarten, but Ethan Armstrong, a junior and the football team star running back, had already asked her. Archie had told her to have fun with all her new rich friends and stopped talking to her after that. That had been a theme in high school—old neighborhood friends starting to call her stuck-up and a rich-girl wannabe.

Rebecca pushed the memory away. No point in dwelling on stuff like that.

She scrolled some more and winced when she saw that #Stop-SignKaren was no longer trending because she'd been replaced by #StopSignBecky. It hadn't taken long for internet sleuths to zoom in on the viral video and discover a white woman in the background just standing there watching while the Karen harassed the Black real estate agent. Within a couple hours, they'd revealed her identity (her actual name was Carolyn Adams), address, and employer. And after being put on administrative leave, Ms. Adams had hired the infamous publicist-to-the-racists Margie Barber to run damage control. The latest tweetstorm was a reaction to her cable news interview that morning.

Do I even want to watch this? No, don't do it. Don't—

Rebecca hit play on the video anyway. She turned up the volume on her phone as the anchor asked, "Tell me, Ms. Adams. What is it you want people to know about you?"

"Well, I want them to know that I am NOT a racist," Carolyn replied, her voice shaking. "My parents raised me to treat everyone the same regardless of skin color. I don't care if you're Black, white, orange, or purple—we're all human. I don't understand why *I'm* being made out to be the bad guy here when I wasn't the one attacking anyone."

There were hundreds of comments on the video.

"Another fake apology from another average Becky."

"She made a mistake! Enough with Cancel Culture!"

"Can people stop saying shit like this??? THERE ARE NO ORANGE AND PURPLE PEOPLE!"

"At least we know where #StopSignKaren stands. I'm telling y'all, #StopSignBecky is worse. And I said what I said."

And, of course, there were plenty of trolls and bots spewing explicitly hateful comments about the Black woman behind the wheel.

Rebecca shook her head. A few years ago, she'd have joined in, but now . . . what was the point? No one's mind ever changed anyway.

What is wrong with people? What is wrong with white *people?*

Sometimes it was just so embarrassing being white. Even worse, white women, in particular, were now considered more problematic than white men. How the hell did that happen? And now people were saying #StopSignBecky was worse than #StopSignKaren? That couldn't be true.

God! What did they want Becky . . . I mean, this poor woman to do?

Whether it was the tears or calling the manager or the police, or—now, not doing *anything*—Rebecca couldn't take another "Becky" in the news. She wasn't anything like those other ladies. Rebecca was *not* a Becky.

She scrolled farther and stopped on a tweet that read, "Why are all the whites so shocked?" There were more than two hundred comments.

Don't keep getting sucked in!

But she couldn't resist. She tapped to read the whole thread, prepared to witness a digital flogging.

@TheRightFight: Y'all woke up after #MountainTop and then went back to sleep. #JamalWashington #BlackLivesStillMatter

@ThePeopleUnited: Black squares plus white tears equals no change. #JamalWashington #MountainTop #SameAsItEverWas

@RadicalLove: Cue the cable news diversity talking heads in 3 . . . 2 . . .

Rebecca's cheeks flushed and her heart pounded. Intellectually, she knew they weren't talking about her specifically. Why, then, did it still feel that way?

It was true that before the whole Mountain Top incident, Rebecca hadn't really been paying attention to the state of race relations in America. She'd been in a bubble focused on making a life with Todd and her kids. But, like the rest of the world, she had been horrified when she watched the leaked dashcam footage of police brutalizing Jamal Washington. He was just being a Good Samaritan when he stopped to help a stranded white woman motorist in the suburban Salt Lake town of Mountain Top.

Rebecca hadn't been sure exactly what she could do to help, but she knew she had to do something. Besides hate herself, of course—which she did—for being so clueless. First, she reached out to her childhood best friend, Tasha, to let her know she was thinking about her during the difficult time and asked Tasha if she wanted to talk. Tasha made it clear she did not want to talk. *Ever.*

Tasha's response had been brutal, but it convinced Rebecca she should spring into action in ways she *could* control. She followed every antiracist influencer she could find on social media and bought every book listed on the Antiracist Syllabus that had gone viral.

One call to action she saw repeatedly challenged white moms to step up and raise better white kids. So Rebecca bought a stack of board books for Isabella, including *All the Babies of the Rainbow* and *Ally Baby*. She sat down with Lyla, seven at the time, to watch a *Sesame Street* special about race. And—what she was most proud of—she formed the parent diversity committee at school.

I do more than anyone else I know—I am woke, not asleep!

But then Rebecca thought back to what Lyla said earlier that week—that their family didn't care about diversity. It was one thing to feel like random people online were attacking her; it *really* stung that her own daughter wasn't seeing her efforts. She'd never planned for her girls to grow up in such a white bubble. And yet here they were, despite all of Rebecca's diversity efforts. She had truly planned to follow up on Monday's breakfast conversation, but by the time she picked her daughters up from school that day, they'd forgotten all about it. There had been so many other more fun things to talk about, like Lyla deciding to run for student council and Isabella hitting it off with Nina Whitman.

Rebecca had been so excited to meet Nina's mom, though she had to admit that she felt a little uneasy about their interaction. First off, she had said De'Andrea's name incorrectly. De'Andrea had *said it was fine,* but Rebecca still had this nagging sense that maybe it wasn't. She knew that getting Black people's names wrong was a microaggression. Had she committed a microaggression? *Dammit.*

Rebecca's phone buzzed her out of her thoughts.

Oh crap.

Only five minutes until yoga. Serena hated when people were late. Rebecca tossed her phone into her bag and jogged back down the block to the studio.

The door to Trust Flow Yoga jingled as Rebecca entered. She paused for a moment to inhale the lavender incense. Over the soft harp music, a bubbly, twenty-ish-year-old white woman wearing a camo cropped tee emblazoned with "Namaste In My Feelings and Out of Your Business" was stationed at the front desk. She looked up from the computer monitor.

"Good morning!" She tapped the sign-in tablet to wake up the screen. "Let's get you checked in real quick. You must be Becky!"

Oh, come ON. Not today.

"Morning. You're new, aren't you?" Rebecca said with a bit more bite than she intended. "It's *Rebecca*, not Becky, actually."

"Oh, right!" The girl fiddled with a strand of hair from her messy bun. "Serena told me about that."

Was it Rebecca's imagination, or was she being mocked? She slipped off her shoes and kicked them into a cubby. Of course, it wasn't this girl's fault that she'd called Rebecca by her old nickname. But she might have had more patience for it on a day when another "Becky" wasn't trending.

She hated that this bugged her so much and could hear Todd's voice in her head trying to reassure her. "I really don't think anyone but you hears the name 'Becky' and thinks 'horrible white woman.'"

But Rebecca knew that wasn't true. She had the same thought when she met *other* white women named Becky. At least she had been able to revert to her full name. Karens weren't so lucky.

She turned back to the new girl—Jenna, according to her name tag.

"Yeah, it's this weird thing that keeps happening to my account. Serena suggested I delete the old account and create a new one, but then I'll lose my class count from all these years. That probably sounds a little obsessive, but I'm so close to a thousand!"

"Oh, I get it, girl. I'd do the same thing," Jenna said, turning the tablet back around. "Alright, you're all set. Hurry on in before Serena shuts the door!"

"Thanks, Jenna." Rebecca softened. "And congrats on the job here. It's a really special place."

Stepping into the studio, she gave Serena an apologetic smile for being the last to arrive, sent air-kisses to Jenny and Victoria, and claimed the spot in the front row they had saved for her.

Serena chimed the Tingsha bells, and Rebecca dropped her shoulders for what felt like the first time that morning.

⁓

"What is UP, Sean?!" Rebecca rolled down her window as she pulled up to the Magnolia Country Estates security checkpoint and held out the Rolling Bean coffee cup. "I brought you your favorite. Extra-large double mocha latte!"

"What is UP, Miss Rebecca?!" Sean flashed his contagious smile. As he walked up to Rebecca's window to receive the drink, she admired how ripped his biceps were through his white button-down. Sean's kids were adults with kids of their own so Rebecca figured he was at least sixty years old, yet he was still in amazing shape.

She knew she wasn't supposed to say it out loud, but all she could think about whenever she saw him was what she'd heard Black people say: "Black *really* don't crack."

Rebecca did wish Sean would call her by her first name. The "Miss" was just so . . . *Gone With the Wind*. Especially since their Northern Virginia gated community used to be called Magnolia Plantation. Thank God the homeowners' association had officially changed the name after the whole Mountain Top reckoning—thanks to a campaign led by Rebecca, of course. Now if she could get the staff to drop all the formality, the community might one day stop feeling so Southern.

"Thank you so much." Sean accepted the cup and took a sip. "But listen, my wife is getting on me about drinking these. She made me promise I'd cut down so I think this better be the last one for a while."

"Now, that's a smart woman who loves you. Next time I'll bring you a green smoothie."

Sean laughed. "You know I appreciate you, Miss Rebecca, but let's not take this too far."

"Like I tell the girls: 'You don't know if you like it 'til you try it,'" Rebecca said in a singsongy tone. "Anyway, you see my friends coming in the two cars behind me, right?"

"Yes, ma'am! Stretch and Sip Wednesday with the ladies."

"Thank you, Sean! Have a great day!"

Rebecca drove from the gate and past her neighbors' homes, each on ten-thousand-square-foot lots, distinguishable only by faintly different shades of white or gray exterior paint and varied flowers and shrubbery lining their vibrant green lawns. She pulled up to her pale gray brick colonial and parked right behind Stu's truck and trailer on the cobblestone half-moon driveway lined with blue and white hydrangea bushes.

Stu was standing near the big hole in the front lawn in his usual army green cargo pants and double-XL T-shirt that made his already stocky frame look even more compact. Rebecca could see sweat running down the side of his sunburned face as he talked with one of his younger guys and pointed to something on a clipboard. He looked up as Rebecca stepped out of her car.

She waved, then gestured to Jenny and Victoria to park right behind her.

"Top of the morning to you, Mrs. Myland!"

"Top of the morning." Rebecca returned Stu's standard greeting, even though she felt goofy saying it; she was pretty sure he wasn't Irish. "How's everything going with the pond?"

"You're gonna love it, Mrs. Myland. We were just going over the designs. Want to take a look?"

"Definitely tomorrow," Rebecca called back as she entered her house, followed by Jenny and Victoria.

Inside, Rebecca inhaled to take in her favorite smell: clean, in the form of hibiscus organic cleaning solution. Sylvia arrived every morning to tackle different sections of the house, but she cleaned the kitchen every day after breakfast, and she knew on Wednesdays to straighten up the entire main level so everything looked perfect for Rebecca's friends' visit. And it did, right down to the shining mosaic marble floor and magazine-ready freshly fluffed black-and-white sofa accent pillows.

"What's with the big hole out there?" Jenny asked as she stepped out of her black Havaianas and left them by the door. She grabbed a rose-colored pullover cover out of her yoga bag and wrapped it around her five-foot-two frame. "And why is the A/C up so high? Brrr!"

Rebecca answered the second question first. "Oh, the HVAC guy was here yesterday and told us to crank it for a couple of days to make sure everything was working okay."

"It feels glorious in here!" Victoria kicked off her white sneakers at the door. "You two will know what I'm talking about in about five years."

Victoria was nearly fifty and, for the past several months, constantly complained about feeling too hot. Despite having told her friends how much she hated her bulging "menopause middle," she took off her shirt, peeling down to her sports bra before taking a seat at one of the leather kitchen island stools.

Rebecca grabbed a bottle of prosecco out of the fridge and began filling their flutes. Jenny walked from the foyer, through the kitchen, and took a little spin before ending up at the sliding glass doors that led out to the back patio. Jenny always did this little inspection through everyone's houses so she could get design ideas. "I'm making my own mental Pinterest board!" she would say.

"Rebecca didn't tell you about her latest outdoor project, Jenny?" Victoria asked.

"No, tell me!" Jenny joined her friends at the kitchen island. Rebecca handed them their drinks.

"Cheers, ladies! To another school year!"

Victoria continued. "Our friend here is convinced some Japanese fish are going to help calm her nerves."

"Oh! Are you getting a koi pond? I've been thinking about getting one, too, to add a little something to our front yard. Our next-door neighbors just built one. It's a bit too big, though." Jenny pulled out a stool to sit down. "I'll wait to see how yours turns out. If it looks okay, then I'll hire your guy."

"You should follow *Slow Life* on Instagram. That's where I got the idea," Rebecca told her.

Victoria smirked. "Hold up. You read *Slow Life Magazine*?"

"Oh, it's an actual magazine? I need to subscribe then." Rebecca pulled out her phone and typed "Order Slow Life" into Don't Let Me Forget.

"Listen, speaking of water projects, have either of you heard the latest on Carl and Laura Jensen?" Jenny's face lit up when Rebecca and Victoria looked at one another and both shook their heads. "Okay, this is a whole lot. You better top us off."

Rebecca obliged and Jenny continued. "So. You know that waterfall that Carl and Laura added to their pool about a year ago?"

"How could I forget?" Victoria said. "That's all the woman talked about for an entire school year."

"Exactly." Jenny leaned in close to her friends, as if she needed to whisper. "Well, back then I heard that Carl never wanted that thing and had only said yes because he was feeling guilty about all his . . . well . . . *extracurricular* activities—"

"You mean the twenty-year-old he was fucking on business trips?" Victoria interrupted.

Rebecca had already known about all that drama back when it happened but definitely wanted to hear what else Jenny had found out.

"Right. You could *also* put it that way," Jenny said. "Anyway, fast-forward to this summer and apparently their contractor had been coming over to the house quite a bit since Carl moved out to, *ahem*, 'check on the waterfall.'" Jenny made air quotes.

Victoria's jaw dropped. "*What*?!"

"Oh. My. God!" Rebecca put her glass down so she wouldn't spill.

"Well, during one of those waterfall checkups, Carl came by the house for whatever reason—probably snooping, the asshole. He saw the contractor's truck, let himself in, and walked in on Laura having *sex* with the waterfall guy right there in the *family room*!"

"Good for her!" Victoria raised her flute to toast the air. "Serves him right. Wish I could have gotten back at Rob like that."

"Well, listen! It took a really nasty turn last week," Jenny continued. "Because now Carl is trying to use this in the custody fight, saying that Laura is acting irresponsibly and that the kids aren't safe in the house."

"No way! What an asshole." Rebecca shook her head. "He can't get away with that! Laura *literally* has the receipts proving his affair."

"You're right," Victoria said. "But this is gonna give her an even bigger headache with all the court stuff. Rob knew better than to pull any shit like that on me. I would have cut his dick off."

Victoria tossed back her remaining prosecco in one gulp.

Geesh, Vic. Thank God I chilled two bottles.

While Rebecca refilled glasses, Jenny grabbed Victoria's hand. "Vic, I'm sorry, hon. Is this bringing up too much stuff for you?"

"Oh, it's fine. I know I sound angry, but we all know Rob did me a favor. I'll tell you what, though. I *would* like to find a waterfall guy for myself. You think Laura's could introduce me to any of his friends?"

The three ladies continued chatting, laughing, and covering subjects that ranged from how their kids all seemed to be doing back at school to who among the school moms looked like they had gotten work done over the summer. Jenny and Victoria asked Rebecca about how her mother-in-law was doing, and, like always, she said everything was fine. Even though it wasn't.

As often happened, their conversation turned toward current events.

"Did you catch the Stop Sign Becky stuff?" Victoria asked, rolling her eyes.

"Ouch!" She rubbed her arm and glared at Jenny, who had elbowed her. "Sorry, Rebecca, but that *is* what they're calling her."

"Oh, believe me, I've noticed." Rebecca sighed. She told her friends about the questions she had to field with Lyla and Isabella before school on Monday. "And Lyla all but called me a racist!" She raised her hands up in exasperation, spilling some of her drink on the countertop.

Victoria was closest to the roll of paper towels and tore one off to wipe up the mess.

"Yikes," she said. "Can't Lyla just slam the door on you like tweens did in the good old days?"

"She actually called you a racist?" Jenny asked.

"Well, I mean, not in so many words. But she said we didn't care about Black people," Rebecca said in a tone of disbelief.

"Why would she say that?" Victoria asked. "I mean, hello?!— diversity committee!"

"So she didn't actually call you a racist," Jenny interjected.

"Her point, I guess," Rebecca said admittedly, "was that we don't have any Black friends."

"What did Todd say?" Victoria asked.

Rebecca tilted her head and gave Victoria a "Really?" look that required no further explanation.

She refilled Victoria's glass again and before she could do the same for Jenny, Jenny placed her hand over the top of her glass.

"I gotta slow down."

"Gotcha," Rebecca said. She pulled three glasses from the cupboard and filled them with water. "I found myself trying to argue with her, and like a total dumbass, I started tallying up all the Black people we know. But the thing is, I get why Lyla would say what she did. I mean, she's not wrong. We don't know a lot of Black people. And we obviously don't have any Black friends. And I freaking hate that."

Jenny furrowed her brow and looked down at the counter. Rebecca knew this was her way of deciding whether she should say something or not.

"Jenny, what? Just tell me what you're thinking."

"Well, I see what you're saying about wanting more diversity. Believe me, I do, too. But I guess I'm wondering . . . well . . . what did you expect when you moved to Rolling Hills?"

"I guess I expected things to have changed by the time the girls were old enough to pay attention."

"Kids do pick up on this stuff sooner than we think they will," Jenny said. "Remember when Chloe asked me out of nowhere why my mom and dad weren't Korean like me? She was four years old!"

"But at least she didn't call you a racist!" Victoria laughed.

"Ha. Ha. Very funny," Rebecca said, not laughing. "You know, it's not just that Lyla has *noticed* how white it is around here. It's that she sees it and has decided that means we don't *care*. All I know is that it felt like divine intervention after school on Monday when Isabella came skipping up to me with Nina Whitman."

"Speaking of divine . . . I spotted *Mister* Whitman at drop-off on the first day. That is a good-looking man." Victoria let out a whistle.

"Easy, Cougar," Jenny said. "His wife is gorgeous, too. I saw her at pickup yesterday looking fierce in an amazing white jogger tracksuit I *must* have. I didn't have the guts to ask her where she got it from, though."

"Why not?" Victoria asked.

Jenny shrugged. "I don't know. You know I get all weird when I meet new people."

"Um, you could try saying 'hi,' you know." Victoria got up from her stool and started stretching, pulling her right arm across her chest. "Has *anyone* talked to her yet?"

"I did!" Rebecca was so eager she straightened up immediately. "At pickup on Monday. Oh, and did I tell you our girls were wearing nearly the exact same outfit? I almost died. I mean, what are the chances? I introduced myself, I told her how excited we all are that they've joined the school, and I told her we *must* do a playdate soon. I meant to tell her about the diversity committee meeting, too, but I was rushing to get the girls to soccer. I'll be sure to send her the email, though." Rebecca paused and realized she was nearly out of breath. She got like that sometimes (well, a lot of the time), talking with such a high level of energy she might as well have been at the gym.

"When are we having our first meeting, by the way?" Victoria asked. "First week of school and the activities are already piling up. Remind me why I agreed to voice lessons for Cassie?"

"You know what, let's figure that out right now," Rebecca said. And on cue, they all pulled out their iPhones.

"How's next Wednesday afternoon right before pickup look?" Rebecca asked.

"I think I can make that work," said Victoria. "I'll make sure Kylie can cover the store for me that afternoon."

"Sorry, that won't work for me," Jenny responded. "We're having one of Gabe's clients and his wife over for dinner, and I need to be home for the caterers."

"Okay, how about Friday morning after drop-off? That's usually when I visit Todd's mom, but I could push that to later in the day," Rebecca said.

"Nope, can't." Victoria shook her head. "I finally got an appointment with that acupuncturist who specializes in menopause, which is on the horizon. At least I can stop talking about perimenopause."

"Oh, that's great, Vic. Gabe's sister loves her," Jenny said. "What about Wednesday morning?"

"Shoot, that doesn't work, either. I've got a facial," said Rebecca. "How about Thursday after drop-off? I really want this to happen next week before everyone's schedules get out of control."

"Works for me," Jenny and Victoria said in unison.

"Great! I'll send the email out to the parent listserv tonight," Rebecca said. She pulled out another bottle of prosecco from the wine chiller. "Look at us being productive. This calls for more bubbles!"

SEVEN

De'Andrea

Driving to Memory Village had quickly become one of De'Andrea's favorite pastimes. Less than thirty minutes from door to door, the winding roadway that led to the facility was dotted with sycamores, and she loved catching glimpses of the bell tower between the lofty greenery. Even though she hadn't made much progress on Dr. Jones's Make-a-White-Friend challenge (although she and Heidi were certainly becoming more *friendly*), she had followed her therapist's orders to establish a weekly visitation routine. Instead of randomly dropping by, she now visited Mama on Tuesdays and Thursdays, and Malik and Nina joined her for Family Day every Saturday. Well, Malik did on those Saturdays when he wasn't traveling for work.

Thank God she truly loved his mama.

No one could ever replace the woman who'd raised her— De'Andrea's mother had been a saint, making countless sacrifices to ensure her only child wouldn't also live a life of poverty—and when she died, she'd left a void that could never be filled. Still, without overstepping her boundaries, Mama had certainly become a mother figure to help fill some of the gaps. Before her Alzheimer's diagnosis, she'd been De'Andrea's shopping buddy, an eager and excited on-demand babysitter, and even a confidante in her toughest motherhood-marriage moments.

De'Andrea missed that woman—Nina's sweet and witty "Glam-Ma"—who once embodied Golden Girl goals. And she was grateful Memory Village had reawakened some of Mama's spunk, that dementia hadn't taken more from their family than it already had.

As she did on most weekday visits, De'Andrea arrived shortly after dropping off Nina at school. Melodic chiming rang out from the bell tower announcing the hour as she drove toward the security entrance. After greeting the guard and signing in, she waited patiently for the short beep—the "you've been granted access" beep. "Welcome to Memory Village," De'Andrea sang in unison with the cheery prerecorded greeting as the gate slowly opened.

Driving through the main thoroughfare, she couldn't help but feel a twinge of guilt. The meticulous landscaping. The ornate faux-front buildings, replicas of post–World War II architecture designed to evoke nostalgia. The award-winning personalized programming and one-on-one services that she now knew were such important components of dementia care. And the exorbitant six-figure price tag that allowed Mama to receive the quality services that *everyone* with dementia deserved.

Given her upbringing, De'Andrea knew just how fortunate they were to have the means not only to pay for Mama's care but to also relocate to Rolling Hills so they could visit as often as they wished. On Family Days, it wasn't uncommon to see the overflow parking lot with cars bearing license plates from as far south as Florida and as far north as Canada. Even though it felt like it at times, the Whitmans weren't the only family who had a loved one with dementia. There were patients at Memory Village whose families were local and visited weekly and monthly. But there were many more whose families could only afford to visit semiannually or, even harder to accept, once a year.

"I'm grateful," De'Andrea said aloud as she headed toward the parking garage. "Lord knows I am."

She pulled into Mama's designated parking spot and smiled at the sign embossed with purple and green windmills. The whimsical feature appeared throughout the award-winning facility to honor its Dutch prototype, Dementia Village. It was still hard to believe that a YouTube video about a magical little town in the Netherlands had led to her discovering there were nursing homes disguised to look like small communities.

And now, here they were.

De'Andrea felt herself getting emotional as she turned off the ignition and unbuckled her seat belt, so she did a bit of breath work to compose herself.

God, I really need to get back to my daily yoga and meditation practice.

She hadn't been consistent since the move. And even though Dr. Jones told her not to be too hard on herself about it, De'Andrea felt so out of touch with the woman she once was. With Nina in school, she now had all the time in the world to do all the things she *claimed* motherhood was preventing her from doing. But truth be told, she hadn't done much of anything.

Closing her eyes, De'Andrea envisioned her mother-in-law's heart-shaped face and warm brown eyes. She inhaled a deep, centering breath and held it for a few seconds before releasing a long, controlled exhale and whispering a compassionate Buddhist meditation. "Mama, may you be happy. May you be well. And may you be thankful for this time we have together."

Following a few more meditative inhales and exhales, De'Andrea opened her eyes, flipped down the sun visor, and stared at her reflection in the lighted vanity mirror.

Yikes!

Frowning at the puffy dark circles under her eyes, she silently cursed them for divulging the truth about her stress. She raised her eyebrows and recoiled when a faint wrinkle appeared on her forehead. She needed whatever Botox was remaining to "hold the line," literally and figuratively. Lord only knew when she'd have time to visit Atlanta and hit up her aesthetician for another dose of forehead crack.

De'Andrea grabbed her tote bag, tossed it over her shoulder, and opened the driver's-side door. A warm breeze moved lazily through the garage, and the smell of fresh country air reminded her of years spent playing outside in the backwoods of Mississippi until the streetlights came on. She closed her eyes and took a final deep, centering inhale-exhale. Then she walked toward the ivy-covered arches framing the visitors' entrance, encouraging herself. "May *I* be happy. May *I* be well. May *I* be thankful for this time with Mama."

Like every patient's living quarters in the East End, the entrance to Mama's residence was reminiscent of whimsical gingerbread cottages on Martha's Vineyard. The white-wood siding was standard, but families were allowed to pick from a selection of paint colors for the trim. Of course, Mama had chosen purple—her and

Nina's favorite color. The groundskeeper had recently planted plum-colored geraniums in Mama's window boxes and the flowers were the perfect accompanying fall annual. De'Andrea smiled as she rang the doorbell and waited.

"Dee! Come in, come in!" Mama opened the door and pulled her daughter-in-law into a warm embrace.

"Hey, Mama!" She followed her inside as did the scent of Chanel No. 5.

I really need a signature scent, De'Andrea thought. Wait, didn't she used to have one back in her heyday at the law firm? Was it Donna Karan's Cashmere Mist?

Patients were allowed to bring a few personal furnishings to decorate their new homes to help aid in transitioning to their new environment, and Mama had brought a few mementos from her former home in Atlanta. Lately, instead of making De'Andrea feel melancholy, she'd come to love and appreciate the little touches of familiarity. She placed her tote next to one of the throw pillows on Mama's plush dark green sofa and smiled at the horrible stitching and memories from their first and last "So, Atlanta, You Can Sew!" crafting class.

Still can't believe you kept that, Mama. After taking pictures and cackling about the experience with her girlfriends, De'Andrea had donated her hideous pillow cover. Now she wished she hadn't.

"You remember my art teacher, Yolanda." Mama gestured to the young Black woman seated at the dining room table wearing denim overalls and a white T-shirt covered with paint splotches. *Strategically placed* bright red, blue, and green paint splotches to help Mama remember the day's activity. De'Andrea had been insistent that, as much as it was reasonably possible, Mama's medical caretakers were Black folks. And Memory Village continued to exceed her expectations.

"Hi, Ms. Whitman. Great to see you again. Pull up a chair." Yolanda tossed her braids over her shoulder before she reached for an old issue of *Essence* magazine.

Most of the tabletop was covered with magazines and newspaper clippings. Mama slid one of the dining chairs closer to her and patted the seat. "Here, baby. Sit down and join us. You're gonna love what we're doing."

"Yes, ma'am." De'Andrea did as instructed and surveyed the scene.

The large white poster board in front of Mama had several images of old Black Hollywood royalty pasted on its surface. Mama picked up one of the glue sticks on the table and swiped the back of a magazine clipping of a young Sidney Poitier.

"Whew, that was a beautiful man, I tell you." Mama smiled as she stuck the image to the poster board, adding it to a cluster of the heartthrob in his younger years.

"And I got Harry Belafonte right here." She pointed to a small pile of magazine clippings.

"We're just getting started on her collage for the annual art exhibition," Yolanda explained. "When she's finished, it will be framed and hung in the art gallery at the community center."

"Oh wow!" De'Andrea was genuinely surprised. "When does the show open?"

"Next month," Yolanda said. "It's the entire month of October. You'll even be able to bid on and purchase some of the pieces. All of the proceeds go towards our Residents Fund."

Which De'Andrea knew was code for "families who need aid."

Mama began humming as she sorted through Yolanda's latest clippings to see if any were worthy of gracing her collage. "Not sure yet if I'm selling mine. I mean if I do, it's only for sale to family and friends," she said matter-of-factly.

"There's still plenty of time for you to decide," Yolanda reminded her.

Mama stopped evaluating the images, turned to De'Andrea, and asked, "You're going to come to the art exhibit, aren't you, Dee? And Malik and Nina, too?"

"Of course! We wouldn't miss it."

Yolanda exchanged a hopeful glance with De'Andrea as she handed her a smaller poster board. "Here you go. Feel free to make your own collage," she suggested. "Yours won't be a part of the art exhibit, of course. But I can still have it framed."

"Oh, that would be wonderful!" Mama said excitedly. "Then I can hang it in the living room. I know just the spot."

"Awww, that's sweet of you." De'Andrea gave Mama a hug. "Let me get started. I mean, if there's anything left. 'Cause you got all the Hollywood cuties on your collage," she teased.

"Hey, Alexa, play Harry Belafonte's Greatest Hits," Mama called out without looking up from the image she was carefully cutting from an issue of *Jet* with sultry Eartha Kitt on the cover.

"Playing Harry Belafonte's Greatest Hits. On Amazon Music." Alexa complied.

De'Andrea tilted her head to the side as she playfully snatched at the air. "Okay, Mama! I see you telling Alexa how to get us moving and grooving up in here!"

"She's a nice lady, that Alexa." Mama frowned, shaking her head from side to side in disapproval. "Such a shame they make her live in that little circle."

De'Andrea and Yolanda exchanged worried expressions.

Mama let out a whoop as she grabbed her belly, clearly tickled. "I'm just teasing, y'all! I might be old, but I do know a thing or two about technology." She winked as the intro chords to a Harry Belafonte classic filled the room. "Oh, this is my favorite!" She shimmied in her seat before belting out, "Day-o, me say day-o. Daylight come and we want go home."

Most weekday visits involved spending time with Mama during her morning activities followed by lunch and a little shopping on Main Street. Sometimes, they went to the cinema to watch a classic film like *The Seven Year Itch* or to the library for an afternoon reading session.

Other times, particularly if Mama was having a tough day, they'd forgo venturing out and instead spend the afternoon looking through the elder's memory box. She and Malik had worked with Yolanda to curate the small ebony chest, and it was filled with familiar items and photos that gave Mama a sense of comfort while she reflected on her past.

"What do you have planned for us today, Mama?" De'Andrea asked shortly after Yolanda left.

"Well, now, let's see." Mama cocked her head to one side. "It's Thursday and I just finished my art class, so . . . so . . ."

These were the moments when De'Andrea was reminded that her mother-in-law had early-onset Alzheimer's . . . and also that they'd missed the warning signs.

According to the specialists, there'd been no way for De'Andrea and Malik to know when Mama was in the early stages of the disease. Assessing the difference between normal-age forgetfulness and dementia in people under age sixty-five was even difficult for professionals. Mama's illness had been detected at Stage 3—the most common stage of diagnosis—and even though De'Andrea knew she was hovering right on the cusp of Stage 4, watching Mama struggle to remember *anything* was difficult. It took everything in her not to finish Mama's sentence or remind her of their routine plans.

"You can tell me later," De'Andrea encouraged. "No rush."

"Lunch!" Mama said excitedly. "It's lunchtime. And I'm sho'nuff ready to eat."

"Me too." De'Andrea laughed.

"Look at my sweet little Nina." Mama picked up one of the many framed photographs of her only grandchild. "After lunch, we're going shopping so I can get her something special, right?"

"Absolutely," De'Andrea agreed. "But let's call Malik before we head out."

"Yes, let's call my first baby *first*." Mama chuckled, pleased with her wordplay.

De'Andrea sent a text to see if Malik was available for a quick chat.

"Malik had to give a big presentation at work this morning," De'Andrea shared as she turned toward the front window to make sure they'd have the best lighting. "I know he rocked it, of course. But I also know he's glad it's over. So when he answers the phone, let's give him a big ol' 'congratulations,' okay? You ready?"

"Ready!" Mama grinned, always down for a surprise.

De'Andrea rang Malik, and as soon as his face appeared on the screen, the two women screamed, "Congratulations!"

Malik let out a bellowing laugh, clearly startled and pleasantly surprised.

"I just know you did a great job on your presentation," Mama said. "You always worked hard, always did your best. *More* than your best. Never gave me and Paul any trouble. I'm just so proud of you, son. I know Daddy is looking down from heaven and he's proud, too."

Malik looked sheepish, like a little boy hearing his mother congratulate him on winning first prize. "Aww, thank you, Mama. Did Dee tell you how I couldn't have done it without her?"

"Well now, she didn't. But I'm not surprised about that, either. A man can't go too far in this world without a good woman by his side. And you got yourself a good one right here. Told you that the first time I met her." Mama turned to look at De'Andrea. "Did Malik ever tell you what I said the first time I met you?"

"No, ma'am," she lied. It was a story she'd heard plenty of times, mostly from Mama herself. And it was among those memories she never got tired of hearing.

"I told him, I said 'Malik, that's a good woman right there. You best marry her before another man does. Don't know what you waiting on, son!'" She leaned in closer to the phone screen and asked, "Remember when I said that?"

"Yes, Mama, I do." Malik's eyes met De'Andrea's with a look that made her stomach flutter.

"And aren't you glad you listened?" Mama asked.

"Yes, Mama, I am."

The eldest Whitman smiled, pleased with herself. "Then, y'all got married and blessed me with that beautiful grandbaby of mine."

"Beautiful like her momma." Malik winked at De'Andrea. "Me and Nina can't wait to give you a big hug on Saturday. Especially Nina."

Mama's eyes lit up with excitement. "What a swell time we had dancing with the band last Saturday. Wasn't that a good time?"

De'Andrea remained amazed at how Nina continued to be an important piece in Mama's memory puzzle. The person she'd known the least amount of time had the most power—Nina seemed to always be able to awaken those parts of Mama's mind that were tied to her heart.

"Sorry, y'all. I gotta run. Need to get to my next meeting," Malik said. "But I'll see you soon, okay, Mama? And don't do too much damage while y'all are out shopping today."

De'Andrea smiled at his joke, knowing good and well Mama's credit card swipes were just another cognitive exercise.

"Oh, don't worry. We won't spend too much of *our* money. Just yours!" She laughed as she waved goodbye at the screen. "See you soon, son. Love you!"

"Love you, Mama. And love you, too, Dee."

After lunch, they walked through the botanical gardens, and De'Andrea found herself fascinated at how Mama could identify and remember the names of flowers. Then they headed to Main Street where they visited their favorite boutiques. Soon, it was time to head back to the house for Mama's late afternoon nap. Before Nina started kindergarten, all three Whitman girls would snuggle in bed together before De'Andrea and Nina headed home. As tempting as it was, De'Andrea didn't want to take the risk of not waking up in time to pick up Nina. So she read Mama passages from Maya Angelou's *I Know Why the Caged Bird Sings* until she was lulled into a peaceful slumber.

De'Andrea toyed with Mama's favorite woven weighted blanket, repeatedly tucking her into and under its softness. It was always hard to leave, and she always found reasons to linger before saying goodbye. She waited until her mother-in-law was snoring softly before kissing her forehead goodbye and whispering, "Mama, may you be happy. May you be well. And may you be thankful for this time we have together."

De'Andrea opened her living room curtains just enough so she could peek through without being seen. Instead of her everyday emo-fairy-bohemian ensemble, Heidi was dressed in a blue dress with a hem barely long enough to hide her Golden Goose sneakers. *Okay! Okay! I see you! Loving the look, Heidi. Yes, ma'am!* Rocking high-end kicks with dresses had also become one of De'Andrea's go-to motherhood uniforms. The thing was, Heidi only wore some variation of this dressy-but-with-sneakers attire on Mondays, Wednesdays, and Fridays. In fact, those weekdays seemed to be the only times she left the house to go anywhere. She ain't even go grocery shopping! Anything and everything that could be delivered came right to Heidi's doorstep.

Heidi flung her diaper bag into the front seat. Then she struggled to buckle Charlotte's child safety straps, clearly frustrated.

"Where y'all going?" De'Andrea wondered aloud. "Because it's too late in the morning for you to drop her at day care and too early in the day for a playdate. And I know it's not a doctor's appointment because you've told me everything about that child from her birth time to her favorite foods so you certainly would have mentioned if she had a medical condition."

Perhaps I missed my calling. Maybe that's what I should consider for this next stage of my life—a whole new career change. And being an undercover detective would work so well with my photography skills . . .

After closing the car door, Heidi's exasperated expression was one that moms knew all too well. As Charlotte flailed her arms in the back seat, De'Andrea heard the faint sound of what she knew was loud crocodile tears wailing.

"Girl, whatever you left in the house, just run back inside and get it. Let her keep right on hollering. She'll be alright in that car by herself for five seconds." De'Andrea chuckled as Heidi sprinted into the garage and returned less than a minute later carrying a very official-looking black leather folio.

Now, that's what I really want to know—what the hell is in that folio file!

Because aside from Charlotte's diaper bag, it was the only thing Heidi took with her on these weekday secret meetings. She was always gone for just a few hours. And she never returned with a single thing . . . except Charlotte, that diaper bag, and that damn folio that she carried like it held the codes to unleash nuclear weapons.

Are y'all in the witness protection program? Or are you front- ing like you a regular ol' housewife . . . but you really over there running a whole drug cartel?

See? This is why Heidi couldn't be her white friend. Who knows what the hell kinda secret life she had going on!

Once Heidi pulled off, De'Andrea returned to her own regu- lar ol' housewife life. And as always, she started with the most daunting task: checking her email.

Not that the chore itself was difficult. It was more so depress- ing. Yet another reminder of how mundane her life had become. And that she still hadn't figured out what was next in order to change that.

Years before, her inbox had been a constant flurry of requests, reminders, and really kind notes from partners and clients singing her praises. She'd tagged every communication and organized them in e-folders with color-coded labels, which her secretary and paralegal had greatly appreciated. But there was no need for such meticulousness now. These days, De'Andrea's inbox was filled with school updates, shipping notifications, and semiannual sale announcements that seemed to happen weekly as opposed to twice a year.

"Let's see what foolishness awaits me today." De'Andrea spoke with an air of British aristocracy. "What do the peasants want *now*? And how do they continue to find me even though I've repeatedly unsubscribed? It's just . . . disrespectful, really."

Filtering the messages from oldest to newest, she began to skim the subject lines to denote levels of importance.

Subject: Your Amazon.com order #117-9872808-5972250 . . .

"I know, I know. Because it's saved in my orders. On Amazon." *Why do they send these follow-up emails? So unnecessary. Delete.*

Subject: Get 50% off at the Children's Place! Hurry! Sale ends soon!

"Girl, don't even look." The last thing Nina needed was more cute clothing. "Delete."

Subject: Lululemon: We Made Too Much! (Aren't You Lucky . . .)

"Uh-uh! It's a setup. I don't need another Lululemon anything."

More sales adverts. More shipping notifications. More mass deletions. And then it was time to sort through the plethora of messages from Nina's school. Within a week of signing up for the Cardinal parents' listserv, De'Andrea regretted her decision. She skimmed through the latest updates to see if any of them were applicable to Nina.

Subject: Hey Cardinals! Let's Get Ready for Fall Sports!

"Let's not." Delete.

Subject: Hey Cardinals! New After-School & Evening Enrichment Activities

Delete.

"Hey, Cardinals," De'Andrea mocked. "Why don't you just stop with all these emails? Wait, what?" She reread the subject line just to make sure she wasn't seeing things.

Subject: The Cardinals Parents Diversity Committee: De'Andrea, We Want YOU!

A parent diversity committee? At a school with no diversity? What in the whole hell!

⁓

Back when they were young lovers, De'Andrea and Malik had a courtship ritual of taking their evening showers together. Some nights they'd lather each other in silence, quietly washing away the unseen burdens of being Black in corporate America from each other's shoulders. Other times, they'd talk and gossip about their colleagues until the water ran cold, which was merely another reason for them to warm each other up.

De'Andrea missed that beautiful season of their lives.

Of course, she'd known the honeymoon stage wouldn't last forever. Lord knew, they'd had plenty of hellish times during those first few years of their marriage. Things weren't perfect. But they'd at least had some semblance of balance. At least they had before Mama's diagnosis. But this move coupled with Malik having to relocate to his consulting firm's Virginia office had thrown off the work-life balance schedule they'd fought so hard to cultivate.

These days, Malik spent much of his time traveling with his newest and most problematic client, the infamous and insanely wealthy Chris Calhoun. The more stories Malik shared about the eccentric billionaire, the more De'Andrea understood how he'd earned the nickname "Tycoon Calhoun." Because that was all he did—wear her husband out with his ideas and plans for how to make more money. And when Malik wasn't traveling and hustling for Tycoon Calhoun, he was rushing home, trying to make it in time for dinner or at least, to read a story to Nina before tucking her into bed.

Malik's schedule had been particularly grueling the past few weeks, which was why she'd been so surprised when Malik arrived home early enough not only to have dinner with his little family but also, to help her prepare it! They listened to Kidz Bop Radio while dancing around the kitchen, the only reasonable compromise so Nina could jam along to R&B's latest hits. Nina'd so enjoyed the playful moment with her parents, and De'Andrea couldn't remember the last time they'd had such fun on a week night. It was most certainly their first time doing so in Rolling Hills. And she made certain to sneak some candid photos throughout the evening to capture the memory.

Bedtime with Nina had been a breeze. After reading several of her favorite books, she'd hugged Malik tightly and said, "I love when you're home before it gets dark, Daddy. It makes me so happy! I love you sooooo much." De'Andrea seriously thought his heart might burst.

As Malik headed to take a shower, De'Andrea felt an urge she hadn't felt in quite some time.

And when she stepped into the warm steam to join him, Malik

didn't hide his surprise. "Oh my! To what do I owe this honor?" He kissed her softly and then turned on the second rain shower-head. "Here, let me get the temp just right. I know you like it scalding hot."

"Thanks, babe." *Two showerheads. Wow.* They'd come a long way from a handheld nozzle with multi-modes, none of which had enough pressure to give a proper massage. In retrospect, that had been part of what made the time together joyful—the fact that they were making it work.

"Can't remember the last time I showered with you, beautiful." Malik lathered up a loofah sponge and began gently scrubbing her back.

Oh my goodness gracious alive! This is what I neeeeeeeed! De'Andrea immediately dropped her shoulders and closed her eyes.

"Feel good?" Malik kissed her neck while he continued scrubbing her back. "You like that?"

"I love it," she whispered. "What a perfect way to end a not-so-perfect day."

"What happened? Is Mama alright?"

"Of course she is. You know I'd tell you if she wasn't. Yolanda told me she's closer to stage four now, which usually lasts several years. But she'll still have a relatively good quality of life, just like she does now."

God, she sounded just like one of Mama's specialists. "Usually" and "relatively" were words the medical community used to not make any promises.

De'Andrea turned to the right so he could get to scrubbing her shoulders and arms. The hell if she wasn't going to take advantage of this moment!

"So what's up? What happened today?"

De'Andrea sighed. "Well, for starters, I still don't know what I'm doing with my life—"

"Nor do you have to continue to pressure yourself to figure that out," Malik interrupted to remind her.

"I know, I'm just saying. Would be nice to be making some progress so I can start carrying my weight around here."

"Oh, you carryin' your weight juuuuuust fine." Malik playfully palmed her butt.

"Ha ha." De'Andrea smiled. "But I'm serious. I know there's no pressure but I *feel* pressured. Like, what am I supposed to be doing? I need a job. A career. A hobby. Something!"

"Don't worry, babe," Malik encouraged. "You'll figure it out in due time. You always do!"

"Yeah, yeah, yeah, I know. Well, I'm hoping that due time is sooner rather than later." De'Andrea grabbed Malik's loofah sponge, lathered it, and began to return the favor.

"Oh, damn!" Malik moaned as she scrubbed his lower back.

"I know, right?" De'Andrea laughed. "So yeah, there's me not knowing what the hell I'm doing with this next chapter of my professional life. Because I can't be no professional homemaker. Tried it. Hated it!"

Malik chuckled. "I know, babe. I know."

"Then, Dr. Jones keeps asking me if I've made any white friends. I keep telling her I'm trying!"

"You have been trying," Malik said playfully. "And Heidi seems pretty cool. What's her husband's name again?"

"I don't know. She told me but I forgot. I just call him 'Heidi's husband who works a lot.'"

"And is that what you call me?" Malik turned around and she ran her hands over his toned chest down to his chiseled six-pack.

Good Lordt, you so fine!

She leaned in to kiss him. "No. I call you 'Malik, my fine-ass husband who works a lot.'"

"I'll be that." He looked into her eyes and raised his eyebrows slightly. "I'll be that and whatever else you want and need me to be."

"Is that right?" De'Andrea smiled coyly. "So you'll go to the parent diversity committee meeting so I don't have to? I mean, the invite said that they want *me* but I'm sure either of Nina's Black parents will do."

Malik squinted. "Wait? Are you serious?"

"Serious!" De'Andrea sang out. "Magnolia Country Day School got a whole parent diversity committee . . . even though they don't have any diversity. Wild, right?"

"Nah, it sounds about white," Malik joked. "Guess things haven't changed that much since I was a PWI kid. So. You going?"

"Well, I *was* going to go. But now I don't have to! Because you said you'd be whatever I wanted and needed you to be—"

Malik shook his head. "Uh-uh, you know I can't, babe. With all this traveling I have to do for work and—"

"Mm-hmm." She rolled her eyes. "Whatever!"

"But I do think *you* should do it. Go to the meeting, Dee. See what they talkin' about."

"Are you serious?" De'Andrea frowned. "That 'we want you' is giving 'we need a Black representative' vibes."

"Sooooo, be the Black representative, then," Malik encouraged. "I mean, the only kid you'll be representing is Nina!" He laughed at his play on words but De'Andrea wasn't amused.

"Leek, you know I am not in the business of wasting my time trying to convince a bunch of white folks of anything. And

I'm especially not interested in taking on the emotional labor of making them feel comfortable about their whiteness and privilege and whatnot."

"I know. And you don't have to do all that. Just go. Sit there and listen and eat up all their snacks. Whatever." Malik took her face in his hands, and she wanted to both kiss and smack the boyish grin off his face. "Seriously, think about it this way. You'll be able to tell Dr. Jones you've gotten involved in Nina's school *and* you've really been trying to make a white friend—"

"I *have* really been trying," De'Andrea cut in. "I talk to Heidi all the time. And not just wave. Like, I actually put on my big-girl panties and walk across the street to have conversations with that white lady!"

"Okay," Malik conceded. "Well, this can be like something extra that you're doing. You're going above and beyond the Make-a-White-Friend challenge!"

"Seriously?"

"For real, Dee. Think about how you'll be able to help . . . not help like that. I mean, like inform them. Let them know what it really means to 'do the work.' They have to hear you out."

"And why is that?" De'Andrea challenged. "Since you so damn smart and think this li'l parent diversity committee is the greatest thing ever. Why on earth would *these white folks* listen to *me*?"

"Because you are my beautiful, brilliant, Black, bad-ass wife." Malik gently pushed her back against the shower wall as he kissed each word aloud. "*And* you're all the diversity this parent committee got!"

EIGHT

Rebecca

ntruder! Intruder!"

"Goddammit." Rebecca was sitting cross-legged on their king-size, four-poster canopied bed, her lower back propped up by pillows and her face glowing from the open MacBook she'd been typing on. She reached for her phone, knowing the alarm company would be calling within seconds to confirm there were not, in fact, burglars.

Just my tipsy husband. The security operator didn't care about the specific circumstances, of course, so Rebecca simply told him the security code and—"Intruder, intru—"

Ahhh, silence.

Rebecca looked down the hallway and held still, willing the girls to stay asleep. Once enough time had elapsed, she got back to playing around with font sizes and text placement on her PowerPoint deck, wondering how long it would take Todd to make his way up the stairs to their bedroom.

From downstairs, she heard keys drop, the sound of peeing, the toilet flushing, and water running—Todd had needed a pit stop in the guest bathroom. A couple minutes later, he appeared. By the way he swayed in the doorway, she was surprised he'd made it all the way up to their bedroom at all.

She offered him her best evil eye.

"You are so lucky you didn't wake the girls."

"Hey, babe." He kissed Rebecca on the cheek. "Sorry about the alarm."

"Bourbon tonight, huh?" She waved her hand in front of her nose. "Tell me you took an Uber home."

"I only had a couple!" He removed his jacket, tossed it on the bed, and unbuttoned his dress shirt. "But yeah, I took an Uber. I left the car at the office."

"Good. But listen, I can't give you a ride to work tomorrow. You'll have to Uber again. Jenny's driving carpool so I can get to school early and set up for our committee meeting."

Rebecca picked Todd's jacket up from the bed, handed it to him, and gestured toward the closet. "Okay so tell me. How was Jack?"

"He was good," Todd replied as he followed Rebecca's orders to hang up his clothes.

"Aaaand?"

"And what?"

"Would you care to say a little more?" Rebecca closed her laptop. She wasn't sure if Todd was *failing* to elaborate (which was typical) or refusing. "Did he say anything about Tina?"

"You know, he didn't really want to talk about it much, Bec," Todd replied. "So I tried to keep things light."

Oh, come ON, Todd. There was a time in Rebecca's life when her husband's "keep things light" approach functioned as a much-needed balance to her constant state of worry. But as their life together had grown more complicated, "keeping things light" was beginning to feel dismissive and downright delusional. She wanted to scream, *Jack and Tina splitting up is HEAVY!*

She could see from the deeper-than-usual creases between Todd's eyebrows that he'd probably been worrying about Jack more than he wanted to let on. She decided it was best not to press him too hard, though she couldn't understand how these two brothers, who were also best friends, wouldn't have talked at least a little about Jack's marital crisis. Were men incapable of processing any emotions at all together? Yes, the answer was obviously yes. But it still irked Rebecca, especially because she wanted details and Todd was clearly not going to be a source.

"So, what did you two talk about then?"

"Oh, you know, the usual: Mom, work, sports . . . stuff like that. Pretty much anything except Tina."

"Well, I texted Tina to see if we could have lunch next week, so maybe I can find out more from her." Rebecca had texted Tina *twice*, not that she was counting, and still hadn't heard back.

"I really don't think we should get in the middle of this." Todd sat down on the dark blue velvet bench at the foot of the bed to take off his shoes and slip his pants off. With his "two" bourbons leaving him moving pretty slowly, Rebecca realized he could use some help. She hopped off the bed to retrieve his shoes and pants and take them to his side of their walk-in closet.

"Thanks, babe." Todd looked up at Rebecca with a goofy sideways smile.

She squeezed his shoulders. "Don't worry. I'm not getting in the middle of anything. But they've been married ten years. Tina is like a sister to me, and I'm concerned. I'm sure this will all blow over, but maybe I can help it blow over a little faster."

"Sounds like getting in the middle of it to me," Todd said. He reached up to Rebecca, who pulled him to a standing position, and he went straight for her lips. Rebecca returned the kiss but couldn't stop herself from wincing. His breath still reeked of bourbon.

"Okay, okay, I get it! I'm brushing my teeth now."

With Todd in the en suite bathroom, Rebecca returned to her laptop, this time getting under the covers to continue working.

"How was *your* day, babe?" Todd called out from the bathroom.

"*So* busy." Without looking up from her computer, she gave him a rundown of all the errands, house projects, and chauffeuring from school to extracurriculars.

"Oh, and Isabella will not stop begging for a sleepover with Nina."

"Nina?" Todd spit out the toothpaste and popped his head out of the bathroom with a confused expression on his face. "Who's Nina?"

"Yes, honey. Nina Whitman. The new girl. The one Isabella declared was her best friend on the very first day of school?"

"Oh, right! The new Black family!"

Rebecca cringed. "Well, that wouldn't be the first thing I'd say to describe them."

"That's how *you* described them!"

"That was different," Rebecca said. "I was getting ambushed by Lyla and trying to point out that we actually knew Black people."

"Babe, we don't really know that many Black people."

"I realize that, Todd." Rebecca rolled her eyes at both him and herself. "But she took me by surprise. And honestly, you know I feel kind of shitty about it."

"What are you going to do, Bec? Go out and find Black people to be friends with? Besides, not having Black friends doesn't make us racist or anything. It just so happens there aren't very many Black people who live out here."

"I know. But I think it *does* make us a little bit racist. Don't you think this is a problem at all? I mean, all the work I've done in the past three years with the diversity committee, and my own child thinks we don't care about diversity."

"Bec, she's ten. It's fine," Todd said.

"I don't think it's fine. And I clearly need to be doing more. Maybe you could reach out to Nina's dad, hon. Invite him to play golf?"

"Do we even know if he plays golf?"

"Every man out here plays golf. Tell me you aren't assuming he doesn't play golf because he's Black?"

"Jesus. You know I didn't mean it like that. As soon as I have a chance to meet the guy, I'll invite him to play a round with us."

"Perfect. With our girls being new best friends, I'm sure you'll be meeting him soon." Rebecca returned to her PowerPoint and Todd emerged from the bathroom.

With fresh breath and undressed down to his boxers, he pulled the covers back on his side of the bed, climbed in, and leaned into Rebecca, resting his head on her shoulder and batting his eyelashes. "Whatcha workin' on?"

Those eyelashes. Why couldn't hers be as full and luscious?

"These are my slides for the diversity committee meeting tomorrow morning," she replied as she centered a text box on the screen. "I'm almost done."

He stroked her leg up her thigh and leaned in to kiss her nape. "Good thing, because you promised me a little action tonight. Remember?"

She caught the laptop as it started to slip off her lap. "Yes, babe. I remember. Give me a few more minutes."

"I guess I can wait a *few* more minutes." Todd straightened back up to give Rebecca some space and glanced at her screen. "You spelled 'privilege' wrong."

"What? No I didn't!" Rebecca leaned in to look. "Oh, geez. I did. Obviously, I know it doesn't have a 'd' in it."

Underneath the Welcome slide's header, "Our Mission," Rebecca corrected her spelling in the third bullet point that read, "To use our privilege for the greater good."

Todd shook his head slightly as he slid away back to his side of the bed.

"What?" Rebecca asked.

Todd hesitated. "Well, it's funny. Jack had this diversity thing at work he was telling me about tonight. He was saying how much he hates that word. I realized how annoying I think it is, too."

"What word?" Rebecca asked.

"Privilege," Todd replied.

"What's wrong with it?"

"It's, like, thrown in our faces all the time. I swear a day doesn't go by that I don't hear one of the Gen Zers at the office mention 'white male privilege.' It's getting old."

"But you do know you *have* white male privilege, right?" Rebecca asked. "Take a look around. We have a ten-thousand-square-foot house in the nicest development in Northern Virginia. You make more money in one month than my parents ever made in a whole year."

"Yes, babe. We are incredibly privileged. But are we supposed to feel bad about that? We have all of this because of how hard

I've worked, not because I'm a white male. They don't randomly give out houses to white men."

Didn't they, though? Rebecca said to herself, but not out loud because, for one, she wasn't really sure who "they" were but also because Todd *did* work hard. That was one hundred percent true. But it was also true that a lot of things in life *had* kind of been given to him. Unlike Rebecca, Todd grew up rich. Both his parents had come from money, a Southern aristocratic family whose first names sounded like last names and whose last names were also street names and building names.

According to Todd, his parents emerged from that high society without too much pretension, but they still had a lot of money, and Todd's dad then built a successful sales career in his own right. In addition to having so much wealth, Todd and Jack were tall, handsome, and good at sports—a jackpot trifecta for popularity. Todd wasn't just *good* at sports, though. He was the type of kid who excelled at any sport he tried, ultimately settling on baseball in high school. He'd even been drafted right out of high school by the Orioles to play for one of their minor league teams. But then right before he was all set to report to training camp, his father died in a plane crash—a small Cessna being flown by a friend who'd recently gotten his pilot's license. Todd quit baseball altogether.

Rebecca hadn't known all of this when she met Todd in an Intro to Marketing course during her third year at the University of Virginia. There were a lot of hot guys in the Comm School, but to Rebecca, Todd was the cutest. They got put into a small group project together, and Rebecca assumed he was yet another rich and entitled bro who would push all the work off onto her. But she'd been wrong. It was the first time she'd ever worked with a guy who pitched in on a group project. Unlike all the other preppy Fortune 500 wannabes, he took school and his future career seriously, rather than simply relying on failing up through the corporate ranks.

Turned out, that was a major turn-on. Plus, he was funny and immediately put Rebecca at ease, even on days she'd felt embarrassed about showing up to group study sessions in her work uniform.

Eventually, he told her about his dad's death and how devastating it had been for him. He also shared that even though his dad had supported his baseball dream, Todd couldn't imagine playing anymore without his dad cheering and recording his stats in the stands. That's why he decided to enroll in his dad's alma mater and study business.

So, no . . . not everything *had* been easy for Todd, and Rebecca didn't want to ignore that he, too, had suffered. But that didn't mean he didn't have privilege. She still couldn't figure out how to convince him of this. Usually, it was easier to back off.

Which was what she chose to do in this moment.

"Well, my slide doesn't say 'white male privilege,'" she finally said. "Anyone who comes to this meeting will know what I mean. And if it makes them uncomfortable, well . . ." Rebecca cleared her throat, remembering a quote she often saw on social media. "They will need to get comfortable being uncomfortable."

"Okay, babe. Whatever you say." Todd's voice was muffled as he kissed Rebecca's neck. "All I know is I wanna get comfortable with *you* right now."

"Okay, okay! Hold on, cowboy."

Rebecca made a point to have sex with her husband at least once a week and, after turning him down the previous two nights, tonight was the night. Otherwise, he'd start complaining, and she wanted to avoid that more than she didn't want to have sex.

She wasn't sure when, exactly, sex had become another item on her to-do list, but, if she was being honest with herself, that's what it was. It wasn't that she disliked it, but she couldn't remember the last time she *wanted* it; she was just so damn tired by the end of the day. She knew that a couple minutes in, she could start enjoying it—as long as it didn't take too long.

So, she clicked "save," closed her laptop, and took a final swig of wine. She switched off the lamp on the bedside table and turned toward Todd, pinning him down by his shoulders and straddling him.

Just this one last thing and then I can go to sleep.

"Good morning, Mrs. Myland." The matronly Diane Hammil greeted Rebecca as she entered Magnolia Country Day. Mrs. Hammil had been Todd's and Jack's English teacher back when they were students. Now in her seventies, she had "retired" to serve as the school's receptionist.

"Good morning, Mrs. Hammil!" Rebecca dropped her phone into her handbag and abruptly straightened her posture, as if Mrs. Hammil had been her teacher, too. "Thanks for letting me in early."

"You're welcome, my dear." Mrs. Hammil unlocked the front door and walked in first as Rebecca held the door open for her. "You know the way!"

Rebecca ascended the grand staircase from the school lobby, made her way down the hallway lined with antique gold–colored framed portraits of white man after white man, all former heads of school, until she reached the Letcher Meeting Room—her favorite space on the entire campus. This had been the formal dining room in the centuries-old Georgian-style mansion that had been restored to serve as Magnolia Country Day's first building. The school had worked to maintain the original décor, keeping the wood-paneled walls, restoring the stone fireplace surrounded by intricate marble carvings, and acquiring Renaissance-era paintings and an antique Persian rug. She loved the feeling this room gave her of stepping back in time.

As the school expanded over the years, the building was preserved but also modernized. Rebecca picked up a remote off the fireplace mantel, pointed it at the portrait of John Letcher (whoever he was—she had never bothered to ask), and clicked. A white screen slowly lowered over the portrait. Rebecca set up a dozen folding chairs in two rows facing the screen and rolled the projector cart to the center of the room. She took out her laptop and set it on the cart and fiddled with various cables before finding the right one so she could test her PowerPoint.

She clicked through the slides:

Welcome & Introductions

Event Calendar

Action Items

She also included some inspirational quotes, photos from last year's programs, plus a final slide with a graphic and a definition of diversity she'd found online the night before that she absolutely loved.

"Good moooorning! Your children are safely in the building!" Jenny Q. walked in wearing a sleeveless pink halter blouse with white cropped designer jeans. Despite her four-inch wedge sandals, she effortlessly balanced an oversized handbag, a grocery bag filled with napkins and paper plates, *and* a catering tray.

"Morning!" Satisfied everything with her deck was working perfectly, Rebecca clicked back to the cover slide. "Thanks for driving today. And for taking care of breakfast."

"No problem. We did our own version of Carpool Karaoke. I was impressed Lyla knew all the lyrics to that new Sauce Gang single." Jenny dropped her handbag on one of the folding chairs, handed Rebecca the grocery bag, and took the food tray over to the nineteenth-century dining table in the back corner of the room that had been repurposed for refreshments and meeting materials.

"That's my girl." Rebecca followed and began stacking the plates and napkins at one end of the table. Jenny removed the cover from the food tray to reveal an assortment of croissants, muffins, and scones.

"Wow." Rebecca cringed. "That's a lot of carbs."

"What are *you* worried about? You're not going to eat anyway!" Victoria interjected as she appeared in the doorway with a box of coffee and all the accoutrements. She joined them at the table and started setting up the coffee station.

"I'm not going to eat any of this, either, but what were you expecting, an omelet station?" Jenny asked.

"Okay, okay, point taken. Thank you, my dear," Rebecca said. "By the way, those jeans make your ass look amazing."

"You're welcome, and thank you," Jenny replied, then turned toward Victoria. Looking her up and down, she gushed, "I *love* that jumpsuit, Vic."

"Cute, right? And check this out—it has pockets!" Victoria put her hands in both pockets and twirled, showing off a black racer-back jumpsuit with a drawstring waist. She'd dressed it up with a chunky turquoise-beaded necklace, silver hoop earrings, and black peep-toe boots. "Also comes in navy. I ordered a few for the store."

"Ahem?" Rebecca kicked up a red-bottomed heel.

"Whaaat?! You got new Louboutins!" Jenny said.

"Damn right I did. Why should our kids be the only ones who get to do back-to-school shopping? I'm here almost as much as they are." Rebecca checked her watch and nearly jumped. "It's almost nine!"

While her friends poured themselves cups of coffee, Rebecca returned to the projector cart to double-check her setup. She placed her remote clicker in her pocket and looked up to see Jenny Stanton arrive and immediately walk over to the other Jenny so they could do their usual greeting.

"Hey, Jenny S."

"Hey, Jenny Q."

They huddled and started chatting as Jenny S. poured herself a cup of coffee. Rebecca turned back toward the door to see "the Power Couple" make their entrance. That's what Rebecca and her friends called Lisa Johnson and Megan Randall. On point as usual, they wore perfectly tailored pantsuits—Lisa in all black and Megan in navy pinstripes—black kitten heels, and matching navy and black leather work totes. Partners at Top 100 law firms in downtown DC, they were also white moms to second graders, biracial twin boys Jayden and Quentin, and showed up to every school event. Rebecca had no idea how the hell they made it all work. She greeted them as they headed over to the corner of the room to join the Jennys and Vic for coffee and pastries.

More of her mom friends arrived—Amy, Sara, Julie . . . and Laura Jensen. *Yikes, she looks tired.* Was that from the custody battle with Carl or all the action she was getting from the waterfall guy? Rebecca hoped it was the latter. She gave them all a quick wave and then a trio of young moms arrived who Rebecca didn't recognize. They looked as if they'd called each other the night before to coordinate their looks. All three had blond highlighted hair, parted in the middle, that fell right below their shoulders. They were also quite short, probably about the same height as Jenny when she wasn't wearing heels. While they didn't look particularly fit, they all wore workout leggings, cover-up tops, and sneakers.

Classic preschool moms, Rebecca thought. *Bless their hearts. They'll learn soon enough that we don't do athleisure here.*

But damn, their faces looked good with all that natural collagen. Rebecca introduced herself. As soon as they told her their names, she forgot them and felt bad about it. She'd get name tags for next time.

She took a head count. Numbers-wise, this wasn't so bad. But . . . ugh . . . everyone except Jenny Q. was white. Where was De'Andrea Whitman?

"Hello, Rebecca."

She knew that voice and braced herself as she turned around. It was Harita Garrison, still tan from the Turks and Caicos vacation Rebecca had hate-watched on Instagram stories. Calm and carefree, she wore a maxi dress that was whiter than white against her dark brown skin, her thick black hair in a loose braid.

Okay, we should have more moms of color. But . . . ugh . . . Harita?

Rebecca bit the inside of her cheek, scolding herself for having that thought. It was just that she and Harita always butted heads with planning any kind of school functions. The two had barely spoken after their disagreement about whether to bring in a live cover band or hire a DJ for last spring's school auction. Rebecca had won that argument (everyone had *loved* the band, of course), and she figured Harita would no longer want to be part of anything Rebecca was leading.

"Harita! I didn't know you were coming." Rebecca smiled, willing herself to be polite.

"Why wouldn't I?" Harita had a smirk on her face. Rebecca sensed she was trying to provoke another argument.

"Well, I thought that after the auction . . ."

"Oh, please, Rebecca," Harita interrupted. "I've moved on. I'm not going to let our little difference of opinion prevent me from repping for the South Asian contingency at this school. And by contingency, I mean my kids and me."

Before Rebecca could respond, Harita added, "Anyway, I'm getting coffee!" And she made her way to the refreshments table.

Rebecca pulled out her phone and opened her group chat with Victoria and Jenny.

Today, 9:10 AM

Rebecca

Remind me to tell you about convo with Harita.

She dropped her phone back into her pocket and scanned the room again. Was this everyone? Should she start? If De'Andrea was going to come, Rebecca didn't want her to miss introductions. Maybe she should wait a few more minutes. But before she had to delay any longer, De'Andrea Whitman arrived.

Yay!

Rebecca felt giddy and was sure something had shifted in the room. What was this new feeling? Credibility? Legitimacy? Now that a Black mom had arrived, it was as if the committee was finally complete.

De'Andrea must have been a model at some point, Rebecca thought. She was a little taller than her, maybe five-foot-ten or so, and she wasn't wearing anything *particularly* fabulous—a crisp white button-down with dark-wash distressed jeans and black strappy sandals—but her vibe oozed "catwalk."

Okay, get her name right.

"De—ON—drea! So good to see you!" Rebecca nearly opened her arms out wide but caught herself. A hug would have been *really* weird. Instead, she contained her energy by clasping her hands together. "All Isabella talks about is 'Nina this, Nina that,' and she's been begging me for a sleepover! It's so sweet what fast friends they've become. I told her I'm fine with a sleepover, but I'd need to talk with Nina's mommy first, of course. And here you are!"

Pump the brakes!

Rebecca knew she talked in overdrive when she was nervous. Why was she so nervous?

"Good morning," De'Andrea replied with a polite smile. And as if trying to slow Rebecca down, she added calmly, "Nina has been talking a lot about Isabella, too." De'Andrea placed one hand in her pocket while she clutched her handbag at her shoulder with the other. She looked down at the floor for a moment before returning eye contact with Rebecca. "I'm not sure about a sleepover just yet."

"Oh yes. I mean, I would never let my daughters sleep at a

complete stranger's house, either, obviously. And I know that's essentially what we are to you—"

De'Andrea looked over at the coffee table, and Rebecca realized she was rambling again.

This time, she interrupted herself. "Oh gosh, you probably want a cup of coffee. I'm so sorry! Anyway, all I'm trying to say is I understand. Let's find a time to talk after the meeting. Maybe we can have you *and* Nina over."

"Sure, that sounds fine. And, yes, I think I will grab some coffee, thanks."

"Welcome—again!—to the school!" she called out to De'Andrea's back.

Rebecca smoothed out her dress pants, checked the back of her waistband to make sure her silk blouse was still tucked in, and mentally rehearsed her welcome remarks. This was the committee's fourth year and Rebecca had it running like clockwork, so she didn't necessarily have any reason to be nervous, but something about De'Andrea's presence had her on edge. She knew it was silly, but she really wanted to impress her.

"Good morning, everyone!" Rebecca clapped her hands a few times to get everyone's attention. "Let's get started, shall we?"

Taking her position at the front of the room, Rebecca stood to the side of the projector screen and pulled the clicker out of her pocket. Her mom crew filled up one entire row; the preschool moms huddled together in the second row right next to De'Andrea; and Harita took a seat next to her on the other side.

Rebecca paused and waited for the chatter to die down to address the group. "I can't tell you how thrilled I am that you're all here this morning."

She clicked to her first slide. "I'd like to start by sharing a quote from Maya Angelou: 'It is time for parents to teach young people early on that in diversity, there is beauty, and there is strength.'"

She waited a few beats to let the message sink in, then clicked on her welcome slide.

"It really is up to us to teach our children how important diversity is here at school and out in the world. Thank you for all being here today. Welcome to the first diversity committee meeting of the school year. And a special welcome to our newest Cardinal, De'Andrea Whitman, mom to Nina, who is in kindergarten." Rebecca nodded toward De'Andrea, who smiled in response as the other women clapped. Not a big smile, though, Rebecca noticed. It was a closed-lip, polite kind of smile.

Rebecca noticed the preschool moms making eye contact and one of them looked straight at her and cleared her throat. *Oh, shit! What is wrong with me?* Rebecca prided herself on being welcoming. She couldn't believe she'd completely ignored these sweet, young moms.

"And of course, we have some new moms here whose little ones have started school for the first time." Rebecca gestured to them and invited each to share their and their children's names. While they did that, Rebecca eyed De'Andrea, whose face showed no affect whatsoever.

Is she annoyed? Probably nervous, Rebecca decided. *It must feel weird being the only Black mom, right? Gosh, I hope she feels welcome.*

The preschool moms wrapped up and everyone looked back at Rebecca. There was no more time to ruminate.

"Great, thank you! Everyone else, be sure to introduce yourselves to all our new moms after the meeting. Let's keep things moving, shall we?"

Rebecca continued with a series of slides with photographs from the previous year's "We Are All Cardinals" multicultural festival that had included a step dance performance from a high school in DC, a mariachi band, a gallery of flags painted by the lower-school kids, a demonstration from the Rolling Hills Tae Kwon Do Studio, and country presentations from the upper-school students. The other moms' reactions to the photos— "Awww, so cute!" and "Oh, that was the best!"—calmed Rebecca's nerves, and she regained her usual confidence.

She talked about a few of the highest-profile speakers the committee had brought in over the past few years—including her favorite, Mariana Myers, author of *Stretch Your Way to Antiracism*, who led community members through a yoga class designed to "free themselves from their racist bones."

"And this year"—Rebecca clasped her hands together with excitement—"we may even get Braxton Walsh to give a talk."

The news that the bestselling author of their next book club pick—*Woke Yet?*—might visit their school created a buzz in the room. The trio of preschool moms looked at one another and squealed. Even Harita appeared impressed, raising an eyebrow and nodding approvingly toward Rebecca. De'Andrea looked around at the others' reactions, but Rebecca couldn't tell from her facial expression what she might be thinking.

How can she be so calm? Was Braxton Walsh not a good choice?

No, that's not it. He's THE leading antiracist thinker.

Then why isn't she reacting? Oh my God, she must know him! Of course she's playing this cool, then.

She waited for the women to quiet down and continued with her presentation, reviewing the calendar—"Better start thinking about what dishes you'll bring to the multicultural fest this year!"—

and encouraging all the women to sign up to help with various planning tasks. "Check your inboxes for the SignMeUp lists I'll be sending around. We need everyone's help!" She reminded them they only had four more weeks to read the book before they met for their meeting to discuss it at her house.

Rebecca then clicked to the last slide—her favorite one: "Diversity is one big party where everyone deserves the right to dance like no one's watching."

Beaming, she now felt a combination of pride and relief that the meeting had gone so well.

"Here's to another great year, ladies!"

NINE

De'Andrea

Somehow, by the grace of God, she'd made it out of her first (and last) parent diversity committee meeting without being designated as the unofficial spokesperson for Black folks. Actually, De'Andrea knew *exactly* how she'd gotten through the gathering of well-meaning white and might-as-well-be-white parents and their incessant chattering about a whole lot of nothing. As usual, Toni had been right. Forget that slow-to-heat vape pen—those fast-acting "Mama Needs a Break" edibles were the real MVP.

De'Andrea had only taken one-third, just a bite of a gummy bear's head, because she wanted to be somewhat present and not a total zombie. It had been more than enough. Because for the last hour, she'd had the wherewithal to observe all the parent diversity committee meeting's shenanigans without speaking, or even worse, losing her mind.

God, she couldn't get Becky's smug satisfactory smile out of her head. It was clear all she cared about was having THE De'Andrea Whitman, new Black mama extraordinaire, attend her little diversity get-together. Because it wasn't *really* a committee. More like a gathering of Rebecca and her well-meaning white mom friends who thought "doing the work" meant selecting a book about racism from the *New York Times* bestsellers list.

Her Apple Watch buzzed with a reminder that Malik's flight was leaving in fifteen minutes. She knew he was on standby waiting for her to call with an update. But she needed to talk to someone who would corroborate her foolishness, not someone who wouldn't condone it. Besides, Malik's perspective was skewed. He'd attended these same types of highfalutin schools growing up so he didn't understand. But De'Andrea knew exactly who would.

Simone.

"Girl," she groaned as she drove by the young mommy-friend trio huddled in front of a pale pink Mercedes sedan. They were clearly having their own parent diversity meeting recap. She threw up her hand to give them a weak wave as she passed.

"*Girl!*" Simone laughed. "You know I've been over here waiting for this tea all morning. You know I likes my gossip piping hot!"

"Moni! That meeting was so ridiculous. Seriously, I don't even know where to start."

"Let's start with why that white-ass school even got a diversity committee," Simone joked. "I mean, besides you, were there even any *diverse* parents there?"

"Well, there was this one Asian woman. Her and Becky seem pretty tight, actually. And—"

"Uh-uh," Simone interrupted. "They don't count."

"Who doesn't count?"

"Asian folks," Simone explained. "They don't count as people of color."

De'Andrea sighed. She loved her bestie but damn, she could be problematic at times. "Girl! What is wrong with you? Of course, Asian people count."

"Well, not as far as I'm concerned," Simone reasoned. "Seems like they're people of color only when it's convenient for them. You know, like for scholarships and stuff."

"Moni, you are dead wrong for saying that. First of all, Asian encompasses so many different types of people. And ain't none of 'em considered white! Girl, stop with this nonsense. And I'm serious."

"Aight, calm down, president of the POC committee," Simone conceded. "Continue. So, it's you, the not-white Asian lady. And who else was there?"

"Well, there was this Indian woman too. Gorgeous. Like drop-dead gorgeous—"

"Wait," Simone paused. "Is she Indigenous Indian or like, Indian Indian?"

Jesus!

"Indian. As like she's from the country of India, fool." De'Andrea sighed. "See, this is why I hate trying to tell you stuff because—"

"I just be wanting all the details! It's like painting a picture of the story, you know? Keep going. I'm just gon listen. Well, I'll try my best." Simone giggled. "Sorry, but you know white folks and white adjacent lives are so damn fascinating to me! Now *that* is a reality TV show I would watch. *The Secret Lives of White People . . . and People Who Want to Be White.*"

"Moni!"

"Okay, for real for real. Continue." LL started whining and Simone shushed him. "We gots to be quiet so your Auntie Dee Dee can finish giving us the tea. Because I heard nothing about any other Black parents being there. Did you?" LL barked once. "Same. Me either, boo. Me either."

"No, there weren't any other Black parents there," De'Andrea admitted sadly.

"Of course not. Because Negroes-for-Hire. Keep going."

De'Andrea shook her head. "I think that was it. Just the Asian and Indian ladies. Everybody else was white."

"Or passing," Simone deadpanned. "Did you look at folks' noses? You know the noses never lie."

Beep.

Malik! Shit!

"Girl, this is Malik. Let me give him a quick update before he gets on his flight."

"Ugh!" Simone wailed. "You were supposed to be *my* heterosexual life partner. Then this Negro came along and ruined everything!"

"Moni."

"Alright, call me back. And tell Malik I said hi . . . or whatever."

De'Andrea chuckled as she clicked over. "Hey, you. Sorry, was just wrapping up with Simone."

"All good," Malik shouted over the airline announcements in the background. "Just wanted to check in to see how the meeting went before we start boarding. Sooooo, how did it go?"

"It went just as I suspected. Didn't I tell you I would be the *only* Black person there? I told you those pictures on the admissions brochure are old as hell. Those Black kids are probably good and grown with kids of their own!"

"Pretty sure my high school still uses some of my pics in their brochure." Malik laughed. "I am kinda shocked we're the only Black family, though. There's usually two or three."

There's usually two or three? Really? Wow.

"Well, what is the committee going to do this school year?" Malik continued. "Did y'all come up with any plans?"

"Well, first of all, I haven't committed to joining said committee. Because it seems like the only goal they have in mind is to treat diversity like a big party where everyone deserves the right to dance like no one's watching." De'Andrea rolled her eyes as she remembered the quote on Becky's last slide. "Aside from that, the only other thing they're doing is having a book club. You'll never guess what—"

"Sorry, babe," Malik interrupted. "Calhoun needs me to send him some data right quick. You can finish telling me all about it when I get home in a few hours. Love you!"

"Love you too, Leek."

Not only had Tycoon Calhoun become Malik's most demanding client, but he'd also quickly taken De'Andrea's spot as the most demanding and needy person in her husband's life. All she knew was that Malik had better make partner. All this traveling and being unavailable had better be worth it. Because Calhoun had her feeling like a side chick for real.

At least Malik was boarding soon. He'd surprised her with an entire day of pampering at Eau Rolling Hills Spa—a full-body massage, a microdermabrasion facial, and a deluxe mani-pedi as well as lunch at the Eau Cafè. He'd even rearranged his schedule to be on pickup duty so De'Andrea wouldn't feel rushed. It was truly such a thoughtful gesture.

So why didn't she feel supported and loved?

Today, 10:23 AM
Simone
Stop playing and call me back! 😟

I'm calling, girl. I'm calling!

"Seriously, Moni, I don't know what's wrong with me," De'Andrea confessed as she drove around Chance Ave looking for parking. "Like, I have no idea what I'm doing with my life. Remember when I was a mess trying to decide between going to law school or getting my master's? That's how I feel. Only worse because at least back then I had options, least I was struggling to make a *choice*. Presently, I ain't got a damn clue and Malik certainly ain't got time to help me figure it out."

"First of all, there's nothing wrong with taking as much time as you need to, especially with all you got going on with caring for Mama Whitman, mothering Nina, and wifing that man," Simone encouraged. "Seriously, figuring out what you want to do with the rest of your life shouldn't be a rushed decision. Ain't that right, LL?"

Her fur nephew barked in agreement and De'Andrea couldn't help but smile. "Waitaminute? Why is he home? I thought LL started doggy day care?"

"Girl, he did. I dropped him off early this morning. But then I had to go pick him up because they *claimed* he started a fight. Like, that don't even sound like him! I'm thinking about keeping him home for the rest of the week. Just on general principle, you know? Because they love posting pics of LL on social media to promote they li'l doggy day care. But as soon as my sweet baby—"

"Moni, stop it. He did not get expelled for fighting. I cannot!" She burst out laughing. "Well, one thing is for sure. Like mother like child. Apple don't fall far from the tree!"

"First of all, my li'l sweets was not *expelled*," Simone explained. "He was suspended. And only for twenty-four hours. I bet he's missing all his friends. Aren't you, boo boo? I know you didn't start that fight. No, you didn't! No, you didn't!" Which was followed by barking and smooching.

De'Andrea continued to listen and laugh at her bestie's she-nanigans until it was time for her appointment. She had no idea if Eau Rolling Hills Spa would live up to all the hype, but she knew it would have nothing on her favorite masseuse back in Atlanta. Angel had been just that: an angel. Someone who De'Andrea could confide in as her magic hands kneaded and hot-stoned away the stress knots in her back until she felt like Jell-O.

Although she became a bit more hopeful when she opened the upscale spa's large glass doors and was greeted by the fragrant aroma of essential oils and calming meditative music. Large slabs of marble flooring served as the perfect complement to the minimalist decor, abundance of indoor plants, and skylights that drenched the serene space with natural light.

Oh, okay, you fancy, uh?

After signing in, a kind and soft-spoken concierge member gave her a tour that ended in the ladies' lounge. De'Andrea slipped into one of the plush terry cloth robes and Turkish spa slippers. Then, for the first time since Mama's Silver Alert, she turned off her cell phone and committed to only being responsible for herself for the next few hours.

From her extended Swedish massage to the aptly named Morning After Glow facial, every service that De'Andrea received had been impeccable. Thankfully, Malik's flight home had been on time and he'd been able to surprise Nina by picking her up from school. She checked her messages after her manicure and smiled at the "ussie" Malik snapped of him and Nina. He looked beyond pleased with himself and Nina was grinning like a Cheshire cat.

Life in Rolling Hills wasn't great. And it wasn't exactly good. But it was certainly getting better.

During her late lunch at Eau Cafè, De'Andrea found herself reminiscing about those years she'd been single and untethered by familial obligations. Back when life was as simple or as complicated as *she* made it. Perhaps that's what she'd been doing—complicating things. Perhaps everyone was right. Maybe she was being too hard on herself when it came to figuring out the next chapter of her life.

Perhaps, like always, life would have a way of figuring itself out.

The Eau's Amethyst Crystal Salt Room delivered on its promise to relieve her stress and bring deep inner peace. So much so that her moment of relaxation turned into an extended afternoon nap. But even after exploring the spa's saunas and therapy rooms, it was still too early for De'Andrea to go home.

She was eager to see her little family, even though she knew Nina wasn't missing her at all. Not after her daddy surprised her in the carpool line *and* took her out for a daddy-daughter-dinner-date. But De'Andrea wanted to give Malik that precious time alone with his favorite girl. She knew how important it was for both of them. So she continued to linger and window-shop along Chance Ave until she knew Nina was fast asleep with a big ol' smile on her face.

She dialed Malik on her way home. "Hey, you."

"Hey, you," he replied. "Feeling good?"

"Very. Thank you again, Leek. A spa day was just what I needed."

"You're welcome, Dee. I know it's been a lot lately. And it's been lately for a good minute now, especially with Mama." Malik's voice cracked. "I just wanted to do something so you know how much I appreciate you. Because I do."

"I know you do, Leek." What was that weird feeling in her stomach? Were those . . . butterflies?

They continued to exchange pleasantries, recapping their highlights from the day. Just as De'Andrea knew she would, Nina had lost her mind when she saw her daddy waiting for her. And apparently, her excitement was contagious. "I'm telling you, I got a taste of what it must feel like to be Barack Obama." Malik laughed. "Because every woman on that playground was staring at me like they could sop me up with a biscuit!"

Well, that *was* one bonus about living in Rolling Hills. There weren't any Black women who might cause Malik's eyes to wander or his heart to stray. In Atlanta, she hadn't been as confident. And for good reason.

"So finish telling me about the diversity committee meeting," Malik said. "Think it will be helpful?"

"I mean, you already know what it was. A bunch of white folks with hopes, wishes, and dreams that won't go further than their hearts and minds. And a dollop of love and light and, voilà! The Cardinals parent diversity committee meeting is hereby adjourned!"

"Gotcha. Well, at least they're trying."

"Yeah, I guess," De'Andrea said dryly. "You're the lone magical Negro in your Virginia office so I'm sure they'll be trying soon enough, too. Can't wait for you to be asked to launch *and* lead their diversity initiative. Just gotta wait for the next tragedy to make national news. Watch what I say. I'm telling you!"

"And I'm telling *you* that I ain't doing it," Malik promised. "Managing Calhoun has my plate more than full."

"Now, Leek, you know damn well white folks don't care nothing about your plate being full, especially when it comes to diversity and whatnot. They stay wanting Black folks to *do* the work. They just like *saying* they're doing the work."

"I mean, white folks gotta do the work, Dee!"

"Oh, *the work*!"

They both laughed.

"Remember that antiracist yoga book that came out a while back?" De'Andrea asked. "The parent diversity committee read that. And they loved it, of course. God, the Black internets had me *dying* with those reenactments!"

The week that *Stretch Your Way to Antiracism* debuted, social media had been filled with remixed videos of Black folks stretching alongside white folks who genuinely believed there was a vinyasa flow sequence that could make them antiracist. De'Andrea and her girlfriends had laughed so much they'd literally cried. She made a mental note to revisit #antiracistyoga for a good giggle.

"Want to know what they decided to read this year?" De'Andrea asked.

"Probably not." Malik laughed. "But let's hear it."

"*Woke Yet?* by the award-winning antiracist grifter himself, Dr. Braxton Walsh Jr."

"Ask yourself"—Malik cleared his throat before continuing in a serious monotone voice—"are *you* woke yet?"

"Because if you're not, it's time to wake uuuuuuuppppppp!" De'Andrea screamed.

"That dude . . . I just don't understand how folks get so caught up believing his bullshit."

"C'mon, Leek. He's such a palatable Negro for white folks."

De'Andrea scoffed. "So educated *and* soft-spoken. And he doesn't challenge them to do *anything*. They can 'do the work' by buying his damn books. I just hope Becky doesn't try to bring him in as a speaker because she said they do that sometimes—ask the authors to come for a talk. Hopefully, he'll be too busy with some other well-meaning white folks' cause—"

"Or too expensive," Malik reasoned. "After what happened to Jamal Washington at Mountain Top went viral, Craig told me that his firm tried to get Dr. Junior Braxton to come for a talk—"

"Braxton Walsh *Junior*," De'Andrea corrected him.

"Whatever," Malik said dismissively. "Dude's speaker's fee was twenty-five thousand. Firm's budget was only—"

"*Twenty-five thousand dollars!*" De'Andrea demanded. "For what? To talk about his book and what else? What else is he doing for the people to charge twenty-five grand? Stripping?"

"Antiracist Only Fans," Malik suggested. "Now, *there's* a market that hasn't been explored."

"I think you mean exploited," De'Andrea quipped. "I just hate it all so much. Hopefully, we'll just read his wack-ass book and that'll be that."

"Oh! So you're actually gonna join the committee and read the book?" Malik asked. "Look at you, Dee. I'm impressed!"

"You know damn well I ain't reading that man's book. 'Cause I *been* woke. All the Beckys and Bobbies and the Notorious POC seem really excited to read it, though."

"The Notorious . . . POC?" Malik asked, confused.

"Oh, that's what I'm calling the handful of colored folks on the diversity committee," De'Andrea explained. "Because the diversity is really just me, this Indian woman—and like South Asian Indian, not Indigenous Indian. There's also this Asian woman, but I think she's Becky's friend so I'm still feeling her out. Anyway, together we're the Notorious *People of Color*. Get it?"

Silence.

"Malik? You there?"

"Shhhhh!" he whispered.

De'Andrea looked at the time.

Oh, I know that's not Nina giggling.

"Why is she still up?"

"C'mon, Dee." Malik laughed. "I let her stay up a little bit later. I haven't seen her all week."

"So?" How was that *her* problem? Didn't he know tired children were like smaller versions of drunkards—absolutely ridiculous and impossible to manage? "You know I like to keep her on a schedule. Since I'm the one who has to do everything around here while you're flying everywhere doing everything for Tycoon Calhoun. God, Nina is going to be a menace in the morning! Well, so much for this relaxing spa day. Back to the day-to-day stress and—"

"Got it." Malik cut her off. "I'll put her to bed right now. C'mon, Nina. It's bedtime, sweets!"

"Just five more minutes, Daddy? Pleeaaaassseee?" Nina began to cry, and De'Andrea felt a pang of guilt. "Leek—"

"All good. She'll be in bed and asleep by the time you get home." But his heavy sigh let her know that all was *not* good.

"Listen, I—"

Click.

De'Andrea called back twice, but Malik's phone just rang until it went to voicemail.

"Shiitak . . ." *Ah, why even bother?* "Shit, shit, shit!"

God, why did she have to be such a bitch sometimes? Or rather, why did Malik have a way of bringing out the bitch in her?

Now here she was yet again finding herself preparing to apologize when he was the one who did something wrong.

She tried calling again and this time, Malik picked up.

"Hey." She hadn't thought about what she would say if he answered.

Silence.

"Look, today's spa day was amazing. Thank you again. And I'm sorry about Nina's bedtime and all. I—"

"Nah, I get it, De'Andrea."

She knew *that* tone. And he used her government name? *Uh-oh.*

"Seriously, babe." She tried again. "Sorry for being so snippy. I'm just tired and—"

"Oh, and you think I'm *not* tired of being at the beck and call of this rich white dude?" Malik shot back. "And that I'm not tired of you *telling* me about Nina's day or giving me updates about Mama because I'm not around to spend time with them myself? You act like I *want* to be away, like I enjoy the grind. But I don't. I'm not like you."

Waitaminute. What now?

"I'm sorry, but what do you mean 'you're not like me'?" De'Andrea demanded.

"You know what I mean."

"No, I don't, actually," she pressed. "So if you want to say something, you just need to go on ahead and say it."

"I'm not trying to fight tonight, Dee—"

"Nah, nigga!" she yelled. "Don't knuck if you ain't ready to buck. What did you mean by that, Malik?"

"You know I hate that word."

Yeah, I know. That's exactly why I said it.

"I asked you a question, Malik. You gon answer it or not? Because—"

"I'm not doing this with you, De'Andrea." He cut her off. "It's been a long week. I'm just getting back in town and—"

"Riiiiiiiiiiiight. Because you're always just getting back in town."

"And you're always complaining about it," Malik shouted. "But then again, you always complained when you were working, too. Trying to balance being a lawyer and a mother was too much. So I quit a job that I loved so I could do a job I hate . . . just so I could make a shit ton of money so you could stay at home. Now you're at home and you hate it. *And* you hate that I have to be gone for work so much just so you can sit at home and hate it. So who knows what the hell you want to do. I'm damned if I do, damned if I don't."

"Fuck you, Malik! How dare you? I don't just 'sit at home and hate it.' I do everything around here. Everything! For you, ya mama, for Nina—"

"And it's just killing you, isn't it?" Malik asked. "Being my wife and Nina's mother and caring for Mama. Worst thing that ever happened to you, uh? You hate working unless it comes with a fancy title and some prestige. You hate working unless it's the work *you* want to do.

"That's what I meant earlier, by the way. When I said I'm not like you? Because even when it sucks, I don't mind working hard for my family. Being whoever y'all need me to be and doing whatever y'all need me to do. Anything! I'll do *anything* if it means y'all will be good. Even let this white dude treat me like Fonz Bentley if that means y'all can have the best life. But you? You'd rather work for someone else. Anyone else but your own damn family! Billable hours? Bring 'em on! You'll work yourself to the bone. Taking care of home? Caring for your family? Shit is the worst for you, huh?"

De'Andrea was stunned, literally speechless. Malik was always so nonchalant, so nonconfrontational. She couldn't remember the last time they had an argument that went this far. She would have said she was sorry, he would have said sorry, and they'd have make-up sex later that night.

"Just remember, *you* were the one who decided to stop practicing law," Malik continued. "*You* said you wanted to focus on being a wife and mother. *You* asked me to support you and I did. I have. But these past five years. Man! Aside from a few joyful moments here and there, as far as I can tell, you've hated every minute of it. And I'm tired of you taking your shit out on me."

"That's not true. I—"

"Hey, I need to take this call. We can finish talking when you get home. Or not. Whatever."

It took a few seconds before De'Andrea realized Malik had hung up without even saying goodbye.

Fully caffeinated and clad in her favorite oversized sweatshirt dress, De'Andrea realized she was forever indebted to Dr. Jones. Over the past decade, she'd lost count of how many emergency sessions her therapist had made room in her schedule to squeeze her in for. Today would be part two of being counseled on making amends with Malik. Even though the energy between them was different and they were in a better place, they still had a long way to go. And every time De'Andrea said that, she found herself wondering, *A long way to go* where *exactly*?

The last time she'd doubted whether her and Malik's marriage would survive was in the first year. But that seemingly tumultuous season now seemed like child's play. After following Dr. Jones's advice to "spend some time not just hearing what Malik is saying but also processing," De'Andrea knew there was some truth to what he'd said. But damn! Did he have to say it like *that*?

It wasn't that she hadn't tried to settle into being a housewife. But being *just* a housewife had quickly become mundane and monotonous, especially as Nina grew older. Attending work functions with Malik had long since become stressful because there was always someone who asked, "So, what do you do?" And De'Andrea would find herself talking more about what she used to do before she became a stay-at-home mother.

She checked the time.

"Fifteen minutes!" She hadn't been early to a therapy session since they left Atlanta.

Fifteen minutes. Dammit, she started to feel that itch. Like Pookie in *New Jack City*, she was feening to engage in a pastime that, since the move to Rolling Hills had become somewhat of an obsession.

"Just five minutes," she promised herself as she prepared to snoop on LinkedIn to see who among her mediocre peers had "made it" simply because they hadn't quit . . . like she had.

Normally, she skipped over her professional profile, preferring not to see that she hadn't updated her e-résumé in over five years. But today, perhaps because her emotions were still raw from everything Malik had said, she paused to read her once-impressive credentials. Remembering what a trailblazer she'd been made her proud.

"You were such a bad-ass back then, Dee!"

Then she checked her notifications. As usual, she'd received several requests to join her network. She rolled her eyes at the message from a spammer asking if she'd be interested in learning more about his legal marketing services.

"Nope, I don't!" She hit the "ignore" button.

Ah! An aspiring law school grad who obviously hadn't looked at her profile closely enough to see that she was no longer practicing.

"You're never gonna make it in these legal streets if you don't read the fine print, child." De'Andrea accepted the invitation out of common courtesy. She couldn't help *anyone* get their foot in the door *anywhere* anymore. And as soon as this BigLaw hopeful realized that, they'd unfollow her just like countless others had done.

Once she cleared her notifications and inbox, De'Andrea rubbed her hands together like Birdman before she started scrolling through her network. It was showtime!

Unfortunately, it was a slow day for BigLaw news. And the more she scrolled through trying-to-be-modest boastful shares about recent publications and guest speakers on high-profile panels, the more annoyed she became. De'Andrea was going to have to do a deeper dive into the legal gossip waters.

Who haven't I checked on in a while?

"Molly O'Shea." She grinned while typing her former colleague-in-crime's name into the search bar. "Let's see what you've been up to these days, shall we?"

Seconds later, her screen was filled with a stunning profile picture of a woman with blond hair, piercing blue eyes, and a wide, sincere smile. Molly hadn't aged a bit. De'Andrea scrolled down and read her latest post, which was populated with hundreds of reactions and over three hundred comments.

Oh, I know damn well—

De'Andrea leaned in closer to her screen.

Partner? Partner!

"Oh, I know damn well Molly ain't a PARTNER!" she screamed at the screen.

They'd met as junior associates at the firm where De'Andrea thought one day she'd become partner, and Molly had ridden her coattails on nearly every project they'd been assigned together. She was beautiful and hilarious, and the latter made it especially difficult for De'Andrea to address her "I'm doing the bare minimum" work ethic, but it always came back to haunt De'Andrea during review time. *They* had done an outstanding job on the case. *They* had done great work securing a new client. *They* were always awarded as a team.

Once they were both associates on the partnership track, however, Molly became a machine. They'd worked long hours with Toni occasionally joining them to "Bill & Chill" in their offices. Fully aware of and quite proud of her pretty privilege, Molly leveraged what God gave her without shame. And because De'Andrea was her ride-or-die, she was the Black person who often reaped the rewards of being in proximity to white shenanigans.

De'Andrea laughed out loud remembering the first time she'd seen Molly shed her white woman's tears on demand. They'd missed a filing deadline, plain and simple. An oversight that was going to cost their very pissed client tens of thousands of dollars. And when they were called to the managing partner's office, De'Andrea tried to reason that they should own up to their mistake to mitigate the damage already done.

But Molly was indignant. "We're not owning *shit*. If we weren't working 'round the clock, we wouldn't miss these little deadlines. The other day, when I calculated our salaries based on the amount of hours we work, you know what? We *should* be earning six figures. And you know why? Because we're putting in the hours of two full-time goddamn jobs!"

"But Molly, the client—"

"I don't care." Molly tossed her blond hair like she was auditioning for a shampoo commercial. "Technically, the client is the firm's problem, not ours. Like, I honestly don't give a fuck. They're just gonna write it off anyway.

"Just let me handle it," Molly whispered on the way to meet with the partner for their scathing critique. "If things get really bad, I'll start crying and we'll be fine. Trust me."

And it *had* worked. Several times. Some of De'Andrea's fondest BigLaw memories were of Molly sobbing while De'Andrea hung her head, not in shame but to hide her smile. Yet somehow, this was the woman who'd garnered the coveted title of partner?

She picked up her phone and messaged Toni.

Today, 8:53 AM

De'Andrea

Sis. You not gon believe this, but guess who made partner? Just guess!

Toni

Who? 👀

De'Andrea

Molly MF O'Shea!

Toni

Oh shit! That's amazing! Congratulations to your old work-wife!

Several loud pops sounded as colorful confetti dropped from the top of the screen.

Yeah, congrats. Or whatever.

As she reminisced with Toni about their past BigLaw lives, De'Andrea fought back tears. Would she have made partner, too? *Could* she have made partner if she'd just stuck out the demands of trying to have a work-life balance and seen it through?

Today, 8:58 AM

De'Andrea

Gotta run, love. Time for another much-needed therapy session!

Toni

Heal, baby. Heal! 🖤

Right.

De'Andrea clicked on the link for Dr. Jones's virtual meeting room.

She had to let it go. That chapter of her life was over. Hell, that entire book was closed! Who would rehire the former Black woman superstar who abandoned partner track to raise her child? Even if she were still in Atlanta where a few folks in the legal community might remember her name, she'd be a tough sell.

"Well, hello there. Surprised to see me on time?" She grinned when Dr. Jones looked up, clearly startled.

"I am indeed! Good morning." Dr. Jones picked up De'Andrea's file and read a few notes before setting it aside. "So, now that you and Malik are doing better . . . You *are* doing better, right?"

"Yeah, we're alright," De'Andrea replied. "I mean, I guess I'll keep him. For now."

Not like she had a choice. That was the other side of being a kept woman—it kept you from being independent and jumping ship. And in a way that only her therapist could, after nearly an hour of complaining and confessing, Dr. Jones convinced her to remain on board. Her marriage, their marriage, was worth saving.

"Since we have a few minutes before we end today, how are things going with making new friends?" Dr. Jones asked. "I know you were on the fence about attending the diversity committee's next meeting."

"Oh yeah, right. The book club." *Woke Yet?* was still sitting in her Amazon cart. "I'm not sure. Do I really want to be talking to these white folks about waking up to racism? Not quite sure that's how I want to spend a wild Friday night in Rolling Hills."

"De'Andrea—" Dr. Jones began.

"Alright alright. I'll go. I mean, the host is the mother of Nina's new li'l bestie, so I probably should find out more about the folks raising her."

"Yes, you should." Dr. Jones smiled. "And you know you can call this woman by her name. 'Mother of Nina's bestie' is a mouthful."

You so petty, Dr. Jones!

She sat up, straightened her back, and pretended to have an air about her. "You're right. I shall go to Becky's house and—"

"De'Andrea," Dr. Jones chided. "Her name is Rebecca."

"No, her name is Becky," she countered. "I've heard people call her that. *And* she's also a certified Becky. Isn't that the best?"

Dr. Jones shook her head. "Well, I hope you, Becky, and the rest of the diversity committee have a wonderful book club discussion. I look forward to hearing how it goes. And what book are you reading again?" She looked at her notes. "Did I miss the name?"

"Nah, I didn't mention it. It's so cliché. And annoying." De'Andrea rolled her eyes. "It's called *Woke Yet?*. It's only a *New York Times* bestseller because the cover is so Instagrammable. White folks post about it on social media all the time.

"*Woke Yet?* The book that everyone purchased but no one has read! Wake up and get your copy today! Only nineteen ninety-nine plus shipping and handling." De'Andrea quickened her infomercial spiel when it was time for the disclaimer. "Results of whether you'll actually become less racist may vary. But who cares!"

Dr. Jones shook her head and smiled. "Well, again, I'm certainly looking forward to hearing how this goes."

"Yeah, me too," De'Andrea said dryly as she popped an entire "Mama Needs a Break" gummy bear into her mouth.

God, I hope there's a special place in hell for those Negroes-for-Hire who tricked us into believing there were Black folks in Rolling Hills.

TEN

Rebecca

A s soon as Rebecca closed her driver's-side door, she flipped down the sun visor and slid the mirror open to admire her eyelashes. *Not bad.* She'd calculated the benefit of falsies once to justify the cost to herself. Five more minutes a day that weren't spent curling her eyelashes and applying mascara. Thirty-five minutes per week, more than two hours per month, nearly thirty hours a year—*so* worth it. And this way, she could bat her eyelashes right back at Todd.

She opened her Don't Let Me Forget app.

Todd's dry cleaning. "Check!"

Toy drive drop-off. "Check!"

Catering order confirmation. "Check!"

Eyelashes. "Aaaand, check!"

Was there anything better than crossing off a to-do list? Not for Rebecca. Plus, the app gamified tasks, and she was on a twelve-day streak earning the daily "Go-Getter Medal."

Visit Elaine. That was the next stop.

Pay Stu. This one she could delegate.

"Call Todd," she dictated to the car as she maneuvered over speed bumps on her way out of the spa's parking lot.

"Hi. You've reached Todd Myland . . ." Straight to voicemail.

Perfect. Leave a message. Keep things moving.

"Hey, babe, it's me. Listen, I need you to—"

Beep, beep.

Grr. That was Todd calling right back. *Please let me finish the damn voicemail!*

"Todd . . ." Rebecca answered, annoyed.

"Hey, babe, sorry," Todd said, sounding cheerful. "I was just getting off another call. What's up?"

"Can you stop and get cash on your way home tonight? We need to pay Stu tomorrow for the next phase on the pond and I don't have time. I'm headed to your mom's and then I need to get back home to prep for book club."

And I still haven't read the freaking book. She hadn't put that "to-do" in her app; she convinced herself (sort of) that was okay because the app was only really meant for the daily, quick-win stuff anyway.

Todd was silent on the other end.

"Hello? You still there?" Rebecca asked.

"I'm good, thanks. Having a great day, how are you?"

Rebecca rolled her eyes and sighed. Todd had told her last week he felt like she was treating him like another one of her contractors. At first, she thought he had been joking. Wasn't this their agreement? He worked outside of the house while she kept everything (and everyone) inside and around the house working. "I have a lot to manage, Todd," she told him, feeling defensive. "What am I supposed to do? Not ask you to chip in at all because you're making all the money?"

"Of course that's not what I mean. I'll help anytime I can," Todd had said. "But could you at least ask a little nicer?"

She realized he had a point, though it was clearly going to be an adjustment for her, which was why leaving a voicemail with her request would've been a hell of a lot easier.

"I'm sorry," she conceded, relieved they were on the phone so he couldn't see how much this hurt her face. "How's your day going, hon?"

"Therrrrre you go! That's not so hard. No problem about the cash." She could tell he was smiling. "Why do we pay Stu in cash again?"

"I think that's how he pays some of his guys. Best not to ask questions."

"Gotcha. The girls and I will swing by the ATM after our daddy-daughter-diner-dinner-date."

"Cute. Have you been practicing that?"

"I have, in fact! I'm gonna make it a thing."

"They'll love it," Rebecca said. "Oh, and *please* don't forget—Laney and Lucy's mom said they need to leave their house at five-thirty sharp, so you need to pick the girls up from their playdate on time."

"Yes, babe, I got it," Todd said with total confidence, and Rebecca detected maybe a hint of irritation.

"Todd. That means you *have to* leave work early. No later than five." She could hear herself and knew she was acting like she couldn't trust him to get it right, but . . . she wasn't sure she could trust him to get it right. The last time she asked him to pick the girls up, it was for piano lessons. He didn't leave his office in time, and they waited in Mrs. Shelby's living room for thirty minutes.

"I will leave the office at four fifty-five p.m. How about that?"

"Even better." She relaxed a bit. "The girls are super excited. Hey, I just got to your mom's. I'll see you later tonight, okay?"

"Give her a hug for me," he said. And Rebecca instantly regretted having felt annoyed with him. Even though Todd wouldn't say it, Rebecca knew his heart hurt a little more each day at the thought of his mother. He'd lost his dad so abruptly. Losing his mom had become agonizingly gradual. Rebecca wasn't sure which was worse.

"Of course," she said, wishing she could hug him. "I love you."

As Rebecca approached Nana's room, she paused for a moment to steel herself. Though she would never compare her sadness to Todd's, Rebecca was hurting, too. Not only because she shouldered most of the caretaking burden, but because she loved her mother-in-law nearly as much as she loved her own mother. It was more than that, really. She'd been a role model and mentor to Rebecca. Elaine Myland had been larger-than-life. And now . . . well, she was disappearing. These visits had been getting harder in recent weeks. Nana's moments of lucidity were so rare that Rebecca could no longer predict whether her mother-in-law would recognize her, and she'd all but given up on her asking about Lyla and Isabella. It was as if her memories were liquid, stored in a giant measuring cup with a reverse timeline of the years of her life marked on the side, starting with "Present" at the top. Only, the measuring cup was leaking, and each week, another year drained from Nana's memory. She'd reached the point where her grandchildren had never existed.

Rebecca lightly knocked on the door and mustered up all the cheer she could find. "Good morning, Elaine!" She stood in the doorway to give her mother-in-law a chance to adjust to having a visitor.

The room mimicked a tasteful condo with a beautiful view of the facility's five wooded acres. It mercifully looked nothing like a regular nursing home room, but Nana could no longer have a kitchen, so instead of it feeling like a home, she seemed to think she was staying in a hotel—a perpetual loop of vacation. There were worse scenarios, Rebecca supposed, except that on Nana's really bad days, she complained about the service. She could barely remember her family, but what she would never forget, it seemed, was what a five-star hotel should feel like.

"Oh, hello." Nana turned toward Rebecca and smiled. She was sitting in a dark brown leather armchair, her hands folded in her lap. She had on navy dress pants, a silk blouse with tiny purple and pink flowers, and her signature pearls. Not a hair in her heavily sprayed strawberry blonde coif was out of place. Her makeup was tasteful today—a light foundation and a touch of blush—a relief, given the beautician's previous visit when Elaine had taken one look in the mirror and chided her, "You've made me look like a floozy!"

Nana continued grinning at Rebecca without recognition and asked, "What can I help you with?"

"I'm Rebecca, your son Todd's wife."

"Oh yes! Of course, Becky, dear. How are you? Why don't you come in? Have a seat. Would you like some tea?"

"No, thank you. May I give you a hug?"

"Yes, of course, dear. You're so sweet."

Rebecca bent down to hug Nana, who remained seated. She couldn't embrace her like she wanted to, afraid she'd break the fragile bones of the former towering woman.

Maybe today will be a good day, Rebecca thought. Remembering her as "Becky" was better than not remembering her at all.

"So, Elaine, your birthday is coming up. I thought we'd all go out for a nice lunch. How does that sound?"

"That sounds lovely, dear. Will Jack and Tina be joining us?"

"Yes, we will all be there." That was a lie, of course. What would be the point in telling her Tina had moved out? She'd be inconsolable for a few minutes, then forget, and then Rebecca would . . . what? Imprison them both in an endless loop of breaking the news? *No way.* Lying was the better, *more compassionate* choice. Besides, Rebecca wouldn't be able to answer a single follow-up question. Jack still hadn't disclosed anything to Todd, and Tina hadn't returned any of Rebecca's calls or texts.

"Do me a favor and don't tell anyone—including me—how old I am."

"My lips are sealed!" Rebecca sat down on the antique love seat next to Elaine, the same one she sat on when Todd first brought her home to meet his mother. Rebecca remembered how nervous she'd been to sit on something that looked so expensive. But Elaine had been so kind and funny—an unexpected, irreverent funny—that Rebecca quickly felt at ease. The two became fast friends. Todd had often joked that if they ever broke up, his mom would choose Rebecca.

"Tell me, dear, how's work going for you?"

"It's going great, Elaine. It's very busy, but I'm enjoying it." The Memory Village staff coached all the residents' family members to agree with whatever their loved ones said, *entering* their world, instead of *correcting* it.

"Wonderful. You're so ambitious. I always tell Todd I admire that in you. I was too old for the women's lib movement, you know."

Nana placed her hands on Rebecca's and inched closer to her.

"Now, listen. You don't have to give in to anyone's pressures about having children if you don't want to."

Leaning back in her chair, she added, "Though I wouldn't mind having a grandchild or two." And then winked at Rebecca.

"Thanks, Elaine, we'll see about that." Rebecca felt a warm kind of heartache, moved by all that remained of who her mother-in-law was and saddened by all that was lost.

Nana looked at Rebecca as if she'd already forgotten what they had been talking about and turned her gaze out the window, entranced by a pair of American goldfinches pecking at the feeder hanging from one of the nearby trees. Rebecca typed into her phone, "Order binoculars." After a few minutes, Nana turned back toward Rebecca with an expression that revealed they'd starting the visit over again.

"Oh, hello! Can I help you?"

"Hello, Elaine. Good to see you. It's me, Rebecca," she said, wondering if their exchange would be the same or completely different this round.

"I don't think we've met. Aren't you pretty! You know, I have two very handsome sons," she said to Rebecca. "They're what we call Irish twins, only eleven months apart."

"Well, with such a beautiful mother, I'm sure they *are* handsome. Would you like to show me some pictures?"

Rebecca had organized photos of Todd and Jack at various ages into small albums so she could quickly pull one off the shelf that corresponded to where in time Nana was at any given moment. She handed Nana the one labeled "High School," and together they looked through the pages while Nana told stories Rebecca had heard hundreds of times.

"I love this one," Nana said as she pointed to a photo of Todd and Jack with their dad. Both boys had on black dress pants with pleats, button-down shirts that looked about a half-size too big, and neckties. Their dad, in light-wash jeans—also pleated—and a pastel green polo shirt, stood between them beaming, with one arm around each of his sons' shoulders. Rebecca loved this photo, too. It was taken right before the boys left the house to pick up their homecoming dates. Todd and Jack, awkward lanky frames and braces notwithstanding, looked like teen heartthrobs. Rebecca would have crushed on them in high school. And now, they both looked exactly like their dad did in this picture.

Nana continued. "Graham had to tie their ties for them that day. He teased them about it, but I know he was glad to do it." She stared at the photo for a few more seconds. Rebecca noticed teardrops welling at the corners of her eyes and wondered if they were the nostalgic they-grow-up-so-fast kind or if she was remembering Graham was no longer with them.

After turning a few more pages, Nana stopped on one of both boys in their baseball uniforms after a game. She looked up from the photo and said to Rebecca, "They're both great athletes, especially my older one. He's also *very* smart, and they both have such a great sense of humor. Which they get from me, of course. I know either of them would adore you. You could take your pick." She gave Rebecca a sly look.

If you only knew, Elaine.

Back in college, before Todd and Rebecca had gotten serious enough to meet each other's family, Jack had approached Rebecca at a party and asked for her number. As cute as he was, he still had some dribble on his lip after shotgunning a beer, and his buddies were all *so* loud and *so* drunk—even for a party. When she turned him down, her friends thought she was nuts for blowing him off. "*He's too hot to give up. Get him to ask* me *out then*," her roommate had only sort of joked.

When Todd eventually introduced them, neither spoke up about having met before. Jack probably hadn't remembered. Rebecca wasn't sure why she never mentioned anything to Todd. It wasn't like he was the jealous type or anything. But the longer she waited to confess, the weirder it became. She decided it was best to let it go. Instead, it lingered as a fun little secret she protected about a time when she was desired, when her every waking hour wasn't spent holding other people's lives together.

"They sound wonderful," Rebecca said. "I can't wait to meet them both."

They flipped through the photo album and talked a little while longer until Nana's personal attendant, Joanne, arrived.

"Hello, Mrs. Myland! Ready to go see the community art exhibit?" As Joanne eased Nana into her wheelchair, Rebecca returned the photo album to the bookshelf and fluffed up the sofa cushions.

"I'll see you soon, okay, Elaine?" Rebecca knelt to give her mother-in-law a hug but stopped when she saw Nana look back at her blankly, as if they hadn't spent the past forty-five minutes together.

"That sounds nice," Nana replied, then tilted her head and added, "What's your name, dear? You're so pretty."

The drive back home from Memory Village was Rebecca's chance to blow off steam and transition from dutiful daughter-in-law to hostess. She pulled up the new Taylor Swift/50 Cent collab on her phone to sync to Bluetooth and played it on repeat. She was singing along to the hook when she pulled up to the security gates and rolled down her window.

"Good afternoon, Miss Rebecca!" Sean waved from his booth.

"Hey, Sean! Have you heard this song yet? It's my new jam!" Rebecca lifted her arms and bopped them back and forth, a little seat dance that would have made Isabella giggle and Lyla cringe.

Sean laughed and shook his head. "Alright, Miss Rebecca, I see you with the moves! I like that song, too. You have a blessed rest of your day."

"Thanks, Sean!"

As Rebecca harmonized with Taylor Swift, she approached her house slowly. From a distance, she could see a pile of debris in the front yard. "For fuck's sake!" She smacked the steering wheel with one hand while she reached to grab her cell phone with the other. She took a photo of the gaping hole in the front yard filled with black liner and piles of rocks, texted it to Stu, and typed:

Today, 4:00 PM

Rebecca

Hi, Stu. I'm a little confused by the state of things in the front yard. I have guests coming tonight. Any chance you can come back in the next hour or so and tidy this up?

Inside the house, the situation was much better. *Thank God.* Sylvia had laid out everything: the white linens, red and white wineglasses, cocktail-size plates, tiered silver serving trays for the meze that would be delivered later from Dabir's Restaurant, and charcuterie boards waiting for Victoria to do her thing. The house was sparkling, and the best part was that it would stay that way until her guests arrived since Todd and the girls wouldn't be home until after dinner.

She looked over at the coffee table, eyeing the book, and checked the time. Two hours before Victoria would be there.

I only need about fifteen minutes to touch up my hair and makeup. That leaves plenty of time to skim it.

She grabbed a water bottle out of the fridge and settled into the couch to read. As soon as she put her feet up, her phone buzzed on the counter.

Today, 4:12 PM

Stu

Hi, Mrs. Myland! Me and my guys will be back tomorrow to install the water pump. You're gonna love it! Have a great night!

Rebecca groaned. She liked Stu. She really did. But he didn't answer her question.

Excellent. Now everyone's going to see my yard looking like shit.

At least everything else would be perfect.

She returned to the couch, this time with her phone. Maybe a quick social media scan before getting focused on the book. She opened Instagram.

@HilltopFashion: <image: dancing sweaters with orange and red leaves falling> Ladies! It's almost time for sweat-a weath-a! Stop in the store this week to see our new fall arrivals.

Rebecca double-tapped and swiped up, scrolling through ads, pausing on photos of friends' kids long enough to double-tap and add a heart-face emoji or a "they're so big!" comment.

@TeachersForAntiRacistSchools: <image: classroom bookshelf with a dozen spines displaying multicultural and antiracism book titles> **What's on your bookshelf?**

Feeling directly scolded by the post, Rebecca put the phone down and picked her book back up. She went straight to the introduction and read the first sentence.

"If you're reading this, you know we have a race problem in America."

"Damn straight," Rebecca said to herself.

She continued reading. "And if you know that we have a race problem in America, then you know it is the result of centuries of systematic wrongdoing."

"Yes, exactly!" Rebecca called out as if she were at a rally.

"This book aims to be a complete retelling of how we got to where we are today. But a history lesson isn't enough. We all need to take action, which is why I also include a step-by-step guide for how we must do better."

Oh, this is good, Rebecca thought. *Crap. I really should have started reading sooner.*

She was trying not to beat herself up but . . . Dammit, why hadn't she read the book? It was easy to come up with excuses: Todd, his mom, the girls, the house projects. But even with all that she had to manage, she still could have squeezed in a few pages a day. She used to be able to read for long stretches of time. What the hell had happened to her attention span? Was this an age thing? Stress? She picked up her phone to google "Women in their forties and attention span," and then stopped herself.

How 'bout you READ the book instead of reading about why you can't read? This is what she would have said to literally anyone else.

She scanned the table of contents, hoping to skip directly to something that would give her enough information to at least be able to talk about the book with the other moms.

Part I: In 1492, Columbus Sailed the Ocean Blue? Time to Learn America's History Anew

Nope. No need to go that far back in history. Also, why the rhyming? And anyway, she had watched part of a documentary on PBS a few years ago that sounded like the same thing.

Part II: Laws, Loopholes, and Longevity: Designing the American Dream

Racism is institutional. Got it. She knew enough on that front to be able to join in the discussion if any of that came up tonight.

Part III: Are You Awake Yet? Let's Get Woke

Yesssss! *This.* Why couldn't more of these books focus on actually telling people what to do? Rebecca flipped to the first chapter in Part III and read aloud:

"'Congratulations! You've made it this far, which means you are committed to this work. You also know by this point what I'm going to tell you, but it's worth repeating: I can't give you a list of things you can do to end racism.'"

What the fuck. You literally said in the introduction you'd be giving us a step-by-step guide.

She shook her head but tried to keep reading until her phone rang from an unknown number. She silenced it and waited to see if there'd be a voicemail. Seconds later, there was an automated message from the dentist's office with a reminder to schedule biannual cleanings for the whole family.

You know what, let me knock this out now. She grabbed her planner from her handbag and tapped call on her phone.

Making appointments with the dentist led Rebecca to schedule a whole slew of other appointments, and before she knew it, she'd booked annual physicals for both Todd and herself; a bikini wax, haircut and highlights, and a laser neck lift; and a personal training session for Todd, followed by a call to the on-site restaurant at Memory Village to make a reservation for the whole family for a birthday lunch with Nana. And finally, she ordered the binoculars for Nana's emerging bird-watching interest.

Whew! Getting all that done felt good. And then it didn't. *Shit!* Victoria would be there in fifteen minutes. Rebecca opened and shut the book several times and dog-eared a dozen or so pages to make it look a little more read than it was as she continued to rebuke herself.

Why am I like this?!

She felt a pit in her stomach, but what else could she do at this point? She left the book open, face down on the couch, and hurried upstairs to get ready.

As Rebecca applied her lipstick, she heard the doorbell ring. She did one last close-up inspection in the mirror. Pretty good for such a quick turnaround, though she had hoped to run her ends through the curling iron once more. It would be fine, she reassured herself.

Don't look like you're trying too hard to look good.

Especially when you should have tried harder to read the damn book.

The doorbell rang again, interrupting her real-talk self-talk.

"Coming, coming!" she called out, as if Victoria could hear her.

"Helloooooo!" One of the Country Farms Organic bags slipped off Victoria's shoulder as she greeted Rebecca with an air-kiss. "Nice big hole out there still, huh?"

"Don't even get me started." Rebecca rolled her eyes.

"Gotcha." Victoria stopped in the middle of the foyer and looked around the house. "Oh my God, it's so quiet!"

"I know, right? It would've been nice if I could have had time to enjoy the house to myself."

"What's wrong?" Victoria asked as they walked into the kitchen and started unpacking the meats and cheeses. "You look . . . *off.*"

"Gee, thanks."

"Sorry. Let me rephrase: You *look* amazing, as usual. Love the white jeans, especially, as you know I've never been a fan of the Labor Day rule. But I am sensing you may be *feeling* a bit off. There, how's that?"

Rebecca sighed. "I'm fine. But I didn't get through the whole book. I had planned to finish it this afternoon, but things got so busy."

"Oh please, don't worry about it. Everyone knows the hostess doesn't read the book. It's too much!" Victoria made the sign of the cross in Rebecca's direction. "I hereby absolve you of all guilt."

"Thanks. I'll go say some Hail Marys." Rebecca bit down on her lip before asking Victoria, "Soooo . . . did *you* finish it?"

"Yeah. Last week. Well, the audiobook. I listened when the

store was slow while taking inventory," Victoria said, washing her hands. She put them up to her nose and sniffed. "Mmm, this soap smells so good."

Rebecca always believed listening to a book didn't count as reading, like it was cheating. But that would have been better than nothing. She would probably be the only one who hadn't read it. *Shit.*

"And? How was it? What did you think?"

"I mean, it was pretty interesting. Dense, though. A lot of history. A lot about modern-day race stuff, too. I'm still processing it, I guess. I do wish it had more information about what to *do* about racism."

"Yes! Exactly!" Rebecca shouted. "Please, somebody just tell us what to do!"

"Oh, I almost forgot." Victoria pulled out a padded shipping envelope from her handbag. "This was on your driveway when I got here. Why don't delivery guys bring packages up to the door anymore?"

"Oh, yay!" Rebecca ripped open the package to pull out custom-printed bookmarks that read, "Cardinals Parents ♥ Diversity." I ordered these last week and put a rush on them but wasn't sure they'd make it. What timing!"

She fanned them out on the dining table that would serve as a buffet for the evening and placed them next to a stack of name tags and a gold Sharpie, which she'd put out specifically for the preschool moms whose names she could not remember.

A few minutes later, the food was delivered, and she and Victoria got to work.

"Alexa, play nineties pop," Rebecca commanded.

"Oh, baby, baby . . ." Victoria and Rebecca sang along with

Britney while they arranged the food, set out two charcuterie boards—one in the kitchen and one on the family room coffee table—and then Rebecca opened four bottles of wine—two red, two white—and placed the whites in stainless steel chiller buckets.

Rebecca moved the book—spine sufficiently cracked—from the couch to a console table and fell into the family room armchair.

"Now we wait!"

"Now we drink!" Victoria corrected, already pouring sauvignon blanc into two glasses. She brought a glass over to Rebecca and joined her in the family room.

"Cheers!" She clinked Rebecca's glass.

"Cheers!" Rebecca took a sip and leaned back.

If only she could do this, and only this, for the rest of the evening.

Ding-dong.

Nope, break's over.

Rebecca willed herself out of the chair and back into hostess mode.

"Alexa, play John Legend Radio, level two."

First to arrive was the trio of preschool moms. They traveled in a pack, and not only did they dress alike, they were beginning to look alike, too. Tonight, they each had pin-straight blond hair, distressed skinny ankle jeans, silk tank tops, jean jackets of various shades, which they all opted to leave on, and Rothy's flats. At least they had moved on from the workout clothes. She directed them straight to the name tags and hoped Victoria would make sure the other moms wore name tags, too, so the young moms wouldn't feel singled out.

Next to arrive were Sara, Amy, and Jenny S., and right behind them was Megan. No Laura tonight; she'd texted Rebecca earlier saying it was her week with the kids while Carl was doing who-knows-what.

"Lisa wanted to be here, too," Megan explained, taking off her black leather moto jacket so Rebecca could hang it in the coat closet. "But our nanny couldn't stay late tonight."

"We will certainly miss her," Rebecca replied, and she meant it. She had been so excited to have the couple over. "We'll have you both, and your boys, over for dinner soon. I'm so glad *you* could be here, though. Please help yourself to some food and wine, and don't forget a name tag!"

Rebecca turned back toward the door to see Jenny Q. rushing in.

"Hey," she said, practically breathless. "Sorry I couldn't come earlier to help. I had to wait for Gabe to take over with Miles and Chloe."

"No worries! I'm glad you're here now. Here, give me your coat. Go on back to the kitchen. Almost everyone is here."

Rebecca closed the front door and looked at her watch. She had asked her guests to arrive between 6:15 and 6:30 and they'd all been so prompt that even though it was only 6:25, she was beginning to worry that De'Andrea wouldn't show.

And then the doorbell rang.

"Oh, hi! De'Andrea!" Rebecca heard herself squeal as she opened the door. What was it about being in De'Andrea's presence that made her voice jump up three octaves? "I wasn't sure you'd be able to make it."

"Didn't you receive my RSVP?"

"Yes, but you know how these things go. Finding time for anything extra is so hard for all of us. I'm glad you're here." Rebecca gestured for De'Andrea to come in. "Let me take your jacket."

Except De'Andrea hadn't worn a jacket—though she did look

elegant, as usual, in a black midi-length cashmere sweater dress and boots.

Stop being so awkward!

De'Andrea laughed, then stopped for a moment, surveying all that she could see from the foyer. Rebecca didn't know De'Andrea very well, but she did know what it looked like when another mom sized up her home. Rebecca didn't blame her; she did the same thing herself. And she was proud of her home.

"Oh, I brought you this." De'Andrea handed her a bottle of wine. "Thank you for hosting."

Rebecca looked at the label. It was a Cabernet Monte Bello from 2015.

Good taste. The woman continues to be perfect.

"Wow! This was so thoughtful of you! My husband and I went to this vineyard a few years ago. This is amazing. I *love* wine. But who doesn't, right? I'll add it to the table so we can all enjoy. Shall I pour you a glass?"

Good Lord, Rebecca. A simple "thank you" would have sufficed.

"I'll go pour myself a glass of whatever is open," said De'Andrea.

Rebecca checked the time again. It was now 6:30. Was that everyone?

No. She was missing someone. She knew it.

Ding-dong.

Rebecca opened the door.

"Harita!" Of course. *Harita.* "What a surprise. You made it!"

Why? Why did you make it?

"Sorry I didn't RSVP," Harita said as she walked in, also handing a bottle of wine to Rebecca, now double-fisted. "I wasn't sure I'd be able to get here. This week has been nuts with the kids' sports, music lessons, and everything."

Yeah, we're all busy. Rebecca pursed her lips to keep the thought safe inside her mind.

She was annoyed, though. Harita's mom lived with her family and helped her out all the time. How nuts could life be with an extra set of hands?

"It's fine. Glad you're here. Go on to the family room. I'm sure you remember the way."

Rebecca closed the front door with the back of her heel and returned to the family room to find her glass and mingle with the guests. Each comment she received about how fun the bookmarks were or how delicious the food was or how beautiful the house looked helped her feel increasingly better about not having read the book. Everyone appeared to be relaxed and enjoying themselves. Rebecca laughed at herself for having gotten so stressed for nothing. After about fifteen more minutes of small talk, she clinked her glass to get everyone's attention.

"I'd like to welcome you all to our very first book club gathering of the year. And I'm so happy to see our newest community members have joined us tonight!" Rebecca said, making eye contact with the preschool moms and then De'Andrea. She raised her glass.

"Hear, hear!" Victoria said. She and the others exchanged *cheers* with whoever was closest.

"We're here to talk about this book, right? Why don't we get started?" said Harita.

"Yes, of course, let's all take a seat," said Rebecca.

As everyone sat down with their books, Rebecca took a bottle of red in one hand and a bottle of white in another and refilled her guests' wine. Finally, she took a seat and noticed how quiet it had gotten. She looked around at everyone, and they were all looking back at her.

No one is talking. Why is no one talking? Shit, they're waiting for me to get things started.

"Okay . . . Well, as everyone knows, we read *Woke Yet?* So powerful. I'm still waiting to hear back from Dr. Walsh's agent, but fingers crossed he'll be part of our speaker series! Anyway, I'm so looking forward to tonight's discussion. So . . . what did everyone think?" Rebecca waited. And waited. She saw bodies shifting in seats, and she could hear one person—she thought it might be Victoria—trying to swallow a belch. She had expected this to flow a bit more . . . organically.

Except for Harita, Jenny Q., and De'Andrea, everyone was looking down at their books, avoiding eye contact. Even Victoria, who was *never* quiet. Rebecca glared at Victoria, willing her to look up at her. They locked eyes and she raised her eyebrows as a signal for help.

But it was Jenny Q. who spoke first.

"I guess I'll get us started." She set the book down on the side table next to her and wiped her palms on her jeans. "A big take-away for me, *personally*, is that I realized how challenging it has been, *for me*, to determine where I fit in conversations about race. I am Korean, obviously. But my parents are white. And, honestly, I always kind of thought of myself as white and was surprised every time I looked in a mirror." Jenny paused and grabbed her book again, bending it back and forth.

She kept going. "I grew up with economic privilege and, in many ways, I think, racial privilege, too. At least while I still lived with my parents. But at the same time, I knew people had expectations of me because I am Asian, and those expectations never felt fair to me, but I never had the words to talk about why."

Harita nodded. Not the polite "yes, I am listening" type of

nodding, but rather, the kind where she might hurt her neck from agreeing so hard.

"What type of expectations?" asked Megan.

"All kinds. Like, for example, that I should be really smart or have some kind of genius aptitude for math or music. Or that I do martial arts," Jenny said. She placed her book on her lap and reached for her glass of wine.

"But those are all really positive expectations," said Amy. "I *wish* people assumed I was smart. They see my blond hair and assume I'm a ditz."

"It doesn't matter if they're positive," said Harita, who was leaning forward so much she practically risked falling off the couch. "They're stereotypes. And think about what happens when you're *not* good at those things that people expect of you. Or that you're not interested in them. That can make you feel really ashamed. I still fight that feeling sometimes."

"Exactly," Jenny said. "Shame. That's exactly it."

Rebecca scrunched her eyes. She felt unsteady and maybe a little bit duped. It was as if Jenny Q. was taking a mask off after all these years she'd known her. Jenny had never said any of this to her before. And to hear Harita—the queen of no-fucks-to-give—talk about feeling shame was unsettling. She had never thought about any of this.

A preschool mom spoke next.

Looking over at De'Andrea with a sympathetic expression, she said, "You know, listening to Jenny and Harita, I was just thinking . . . if they feel this way about positive stereotypes, I can't even imagine what it's like for *you*, De'Andrea, when people must have so many negative expectations of you because you're a Black woman."

A surge of affirmations followed.

"Oh, yes, of course!"

"I cannot imagine!"

"It's awful!"

Rebecca squinted to read the mom's name tag. "Ema." Was that like "Emma" with only one "m" or more like "Emu" but with an "a"? She regretted not doing one of those name games she'd learned when she was the room mom during Isabella's and Lyla's preschool years.

De'Andrea had cocked her head to the side and waited patiently to respond. Was she taken aback by the pointed comment? Comforted that someone made this point? Rebecca couldn't tell.

Jenny's face turned red and Rebecca suspected it wasn't from the wine.

Jenny looked at De'Andrea and said, "I'm so sorry. I didn't mean to suggest that—"

De'Andrea smiled. "Don't worry. I know you weren't comparing your experience to mine. I'm not sure why this suddenly became about me. To be honest, I hadn't ever thought about what you and Harita were saying. So I was listening and trying to learn."

Phew! De'Andrea didn't know any of that stuff, either.

"Can we go back to something else Jenny was saying?" asked another of the preschool moms. She had draped a giant burgundy scarf around her shoulders and arms, hiding her name tag.

Dammit. I need to memorize their names.

All the moms shifted in their seats to look toward Preschool Mom #2.

"What you were saying about thinking you were white really resonated with me."

Rebecca nervously glanced around at everyone and wondered where she could possibly be going with this. Obviously, the part about being white resonated. This woman was white. But if Jenny felt confused, she wasn't showing it. She remained quiet as the younger mom continued.

"My mother is from Mexico. She met my dad in college and after they got married, they moved to Maine for my dad's job. You all probably know it's, like, *super* white there. And, as you all can see"—she shrugged and forced a soft chuckle—"I pretty much look white. My mom only spoke to me in Spanish, and we went to Mexico every year to visit our family there. But by the time I got to middle school, I was tired of having to be both white and Mexican. It just felt easier to be white, if that makes sense. I got fed up with explaining my background. And even when I did, no one ever believed me anyway. So, I mean, I know it's not the same thing as what you were saying, Jenny, but I wrestle with my identity and expectations, too."

She stopped abruptly and took a deep breath with a look on her face that made Rebecca wonder whether she was regretting all that she had shared.

The two other preschool moms placed their hands atop hers in a comforting gesture.

"Thank you for sharing that with all of us," Preschool Mom #3 said and leaned the side of her head into Ema's.

That was brave, Rebecca thought. And another aspect she hadn't thought about. She didn't really know anything about her ancestry except that she was basically a mutt of Western European countries.

I'm just . . . white. So boring. Then De'Andrea spoke up. "You know, I will say that I had never heard the term 'model minority' before, and I appreciated the author's explanation of that because I didn't know that it was a very intentional strategy to pit Asian folks against Black folks."

"Right?" said Jenny Q. "I appreciated that, too. I mean, I've heard the term before, but I always thought it referred to Asian stereotypes—but not about the part you just mentioned."

"Which kind of goes back to what you were saying earlier, Jenny, about not knowing your place in discussions about race. I've often felt the same," said Harita. "Especially being married to a white man. I mean, I have it *really* good so I have no right to complain. But as soon as I step outside our house and I'm not with Jacob, I am definitely *not* treated like I'm white. And I'm still trying to figure out what this means for my kids."

"Exactly," said Jenny. "Like, I'm not white or Black, but after reading this book, I realized I've been internalizing that white is better. I've been trying to get as close to white as possible." She turned to Preschool Mom #2. "Which is kind of what you were saying, too. Maybe not that white is better, but it is easier."

Rebecca considered that point—that it's easier to be white. It made sense. Maybe that's how she could better explain the "white privilege" thing to Todd.

"Damn," said De'Andrea. "That's pretty deep."

"And it makes me a shitty ally to Black people," Jenny added.

Wow. Rebecca couldn't imagine admitting something like that out loud. She was blown away by the conversation these women were having with one another.

I could literally listen to this all night.

How had this group been meeting for three years and never talked like this before? She had been right: De'Andrea *did* change the dynamic. She couldn't wait to hear what came up next.

A thought popped into her head that maybe she could add a storytelling component to the multicultural festival this year. The school community needed to hear these stories, and this was all way better than reading a book.

As soon as Rebecca finished her last thought and before she could add a note to herself about it in her phone, Harita looked around at Rebecca and the other white moms with a jolt, as if she had been yanked out of the fishbowl they'd been in.

"Hey, I have a question. Did any of you read the book? You're all sitting here gawking at the BIPOC folks like we are here to put on a play for you. We can't be the only ones who got something out of this book."

"Yikes," said Jenny S. "That was a bit harsh."

"What was harsh about that?" Harita asked. "We've shared some pretty intense shit and the only thing most of you are doing is watching us."

"I'm only speaking for myself here," said Rebecca. "But I haven't said anything because I didn't think it was my place."

"But it can't only be people of color talking about race all the time," Harita said.

"For me," Megan added, "if I'm being honest, I don't know what to say. I feel really overwhelmed by all of it. And I feel really guilty."

"I don't get the white guilt thing," Harita said. "Like, what is that about?"

"I feel guilty that as a white mom of biracial boys, I won't be able to protect them. They won't have the same privilege I have. That's what I mean when I talk about guilt."

"Oh, I've got it, too." Victoria finally chimed in. "My therapist says I need to name the feeling to work through the feeling. So, yeah, I feel guilty that I don't have to deal with issues like the ones you all talked about, and I feel guilty about not paying enough attention to race." She grabbed a nearby bottle of wine and refilled her glass. "At least that's what it is for *me*."

"But your guilt doesn't do anything for anyone," Harita said. "I know when *I* feel guilty, I try to figure out what I can *do* to stop feeling guilty."

"Well then, what, exactly, are we supposed to do?" asked Sara.

"I'm not here to answer that for you," Harita responded.

"Why did you come tonight, then?" asked Jenny S. "And I'm not trying to ask that in a rude way, Harita. I'm genuinely curious."

Then the room got quiet again until Rebecca pulled in a deep breath and pushed it back out so that her cheeks puffed up with air. She still didn't really know what she was supposed to say next but felt as if she had to come up with *something*.

"Okay, so . . ." Rebecca clenched her fists after she realized she'd been picking at her nails. "To answer your question, Harita: I didn't have a chance to finish the book. Things got so busy and—"

Harita looked smug at Rebecca's confession.

Fair enough.

"Look, I know that's no excuse. We're all busy." Rebecca felt a lump forming in her throat. She was feeling sad about Jenny Q.— both because of what she'd shared tonight and because she'd never shared it before. And she was embarrassed. She hoped she'd get through the evening without having to admit she hadn't read *Woke Yet?*.

Do NOT cry. Don't be the white woman crying.

This isn't about you. Make it about everyone else.

She took a deep breath and opened her eyes wide so the tears welling at the corners wouldn't find their way out. "But can I just say that I am blown away by everything that has been shared tonight?"

The other moms clapped in response.

Cringe face, as Lyla would say.

Clapping probably wasn't the right response given Harita's earlier comment that they weren't there to put on a play. Rebecca kept going to try to push through the awkwardness and regain some control of the evening.

"I'm really moved by how each and every one of us has shown up tonight. Conversations like this are *so* important and—"

"I don't know about that, Rebecca," Harita interrupted. "I'm tired of talking. When are we actually going to *do* something?"

"You know what, I agree," Megan said. And others began nodding.

Fueled by the group, Harita added in a louder voice, "I mean, how many years now have we been meeting and all we have to show for it is a festival each year?"

"We can't get rid of the festival, though! That's such a highlight of the year!" Sara blurted out, talking for the first time during the entire evening. Rebecca felt grateful for the support.

"We definitely can't! I love your chicken tikka masala dish you bring every year, Harita!" That was Megan again. Rebecca was getting whiplash from Megan's flip-flopping.

"You know that's not really my dish, right? I'm *South* Indian. We didn't grow up eating that. My mom would never cook meat. I only make it because I know that's what all the white people want."

De'Andrea snickered and Harita, looking pleased, laughed, too.

Damn, that sucks. Does she really think white people are so bad that we can't handle the real food she wants to make?

"Anyway, I'm not saying we get rid of the festival," Harita added. "I'm saying we need to do *more*. We need a cause! We need to make change!"

Rebecca was wondering how the hell book club had turned into Harita on the campaign trail. She maintained a smile on her exterior, but internally her heart was pounding from a convergence of embarrassment, defensiveness, guilt, shame for feeling guilty, and irritation with Harita—both for always trying to take over and . . . *dammit* . . . in this case, for being right. Rebecca knew she hadn't been doing enough. Lyla had made that pretty clear.

"What do you suggest, Harita?" Victoria asked.

"Well . . . I'm not really sure." Harita responded in a much quieter voice than before. Apparently, she'd hit the end of her stump speech.

Rebecca searched for an idea. *Anything!* And then she remembered.

"I've got it!" she shouted. She pulled her phone out of her back pocket, opened up her photos app, and swiped until she found what she was looking for. She held the phone out for everyone to see.

"This!"

The other moms leaned in to try and make out what "this" was. It was De'Andrea who asked, "Who is that?"

"It's James Longstreet. He served as some kind of assistant to General Robert E. Lee during the Civil War," Rebecca explained. "This is a statue in Rolling Hills Park. Of a Confederate general! In OUR park!"

"Oh, wait, I know that statue," Victoria said. "It's been there forever. Over by the outdoor theater and the restrooms. Right in the middle of the park."

"I've never noticed it," Jenny said.

"Me either," said the preschool moms in unison.

"Me either," Harita added. "Wait." She leaned in, squinting. "Is he missing an arm?"

"Yeah, I was wondering about that, too," Rebecca replied.

Ema pulled out her own phone and typed. "I'm googling him," she said, reading from her screen. "Says here on this site History-Net that Lee considered him his 'war horse.' Doesn't say anything about his arm, though."

"Either way, we are not the type of community that has a Confederate statue. This is totally unacceptable. What if our committee helps to get it removed? The flyer says there's a Face-book group for Justice in Parks. I'll join, get all the details, and at our next meeting, we can come up with a plan. How does that sound?"

Rebecca and all the other moms looked at Harita, who looked quite satisfied with her new role as the decider.

She waited a few moments for what was clearly only for dramatic effect, then nodded. "I like it," she said. "Let's do it."

With Harita's sign-off, all the other moms except De'Andrea chimed in with yesses and "I'm in!"

"De'Andrea?" As Rebecca addressed De'Andrea, all the other women in the room stopped talking and turned toward her. "Are you in?"

ELEVEN

De'Andrea

In theory, sure, De'Andrea knew everyone was equal in God's eyes. But in *her* eyes, there was also an undeniable truth: Black folks and white folks were just different. What else could explain why Becky and her friends were so excited about removing the statue of a rarely known one-armed Confederate soldier? No one even knew or cared about General Longfellow or whatever his name was!

"Girl, so you know I had to go see this statue they were so pressed about," she'd giggled to Toni. "So I get to the park and honestly, I don't know what I was expecting to see. But I can assure you, *nothing* could have prepared me for what I saw. All I could do was laugh. I mean, I couldn't tell whether this racist lost his arm in the Battle of Rolling Hills or whether it just fell off because the statue was so damn old!"

"I mean, does it matter?" Toni asked. "Either of those scenarios work for me!"

But it wasn't just the group's obsession with the statue that rattled De'Andrea's nerves. Aside from Harita, Jenny, and Ema, it was the lack of awareness, which she still wasn't quite sure was sincere or genuine stupidity.

And the icing on the cake was Becky.

It was clear Isabella's momma was more excited to have a Black woman in her home than to actually talk about Black issues. Hadn't Becky been the one who was all hype about reading *Woke Yet?* Then why the hell didn't she read the book!

At least De'Andrea had had an opportunity to do a bit more reconnaissance on the Mylands. It was clear Nina had no plans on easing up on her demands for a sleepover at Isabella's. And, well, De'Andrea had no plans of even considering her requests until she was certain there were no stuffed animal heads mounted on the walls. Perhaps she had gone a bit far by moving items around in the bathroom and lifting up the toilet seat to make sure Becky hadn't spot cleaned just for appearances. *That* confession had really set Dr. Jones off.

"Do you lift toilet seats when you go to Black people's homes?" Dr. Jones had asked with an expression that made De'Andrea wonder if her behavior would end up on some private "The Wildest Things Therapists Have Heard" online forum.

De'Andrea certainly didn't help her case by admitting that yeah, sure, it was petty to inspect for dust bunnies and random strands of hair, but she'd been relieved to discover that the Mylands' house met her standards of cleanliness. "I don't know how those white folks are living over there" had been her last excuse as to why Nina couldn't have a sleepover with her bestie.

The truth was, she just wasn't sure about her Black daughter attending a sleepover with a white classmate, no matter how clean and orderly her parents kept their home.

Malik certainly wasn't helping by making her the bad cop. Of course, he didn't have nearly as much trepidation about the sleepover. Following Dr. Jones's advice to talk to him about the trauma she'd experienced at her first and only sleepover with a white classmate had been eye-opening, and De'Andrea continued to be surprised by how much she didn't know about her husband.

"You know I was one of the few Black kids in our neighborhood," Malik shared. "So aside from me, my Little League team was all-white, all-American. And there was this one kid, Christian, who I was cool with. We lived on the same street, were in the same class, played together outside of Little League. I'm thinking this is my li'l homie, you know?

"So when he asks me to sleep over, I'm like, 'Bet.' And my folks were cool with it. Told me that if I wanted to come home at any time, they'd come get me or whatever. So I go over there, and it's what you'd imagine a boys' sleepover would be like. Roughhousing in the backyard and playing around. And out of nowhere, Christian's like, 'Want to hear this joke I heard about Black people?'

"Now, keep in mind, I'm like eight or nine years old. I don't know better so, I say, 'Yeah.' And he says, 'I heard the reason Black people are so mad all the time is because they have pubic hair on their heads.'

"And get this. He didn't laugh. It was almost like he was waiting to see if *I* laughed, you know, to give *him* permission to laugh. And before I knew it, I'd punched Christian square in the face. His nose was bleeding and everything. I told him that if he ever said anything like that again, I'd tell everyone he still wet the bed. Aww, man. He was crying and apologizing, telling me that he actually thought my Afro was cool. Said he wasn't even sure why he shared that stupid joke. And that was that."

"Dear God, Malik!" There was just so much to unpack, De'Andrea didn't even know where to start. "So, you just chose violence?"

"Basically. And I bet he never told another person that dumbass joke."

And I bet he did, De'Andrea wanted to say.

She hadn't stopped thinking about Christian. Whether he'd truly been sorry or just scared of getting the brakes beat off him. Whether he'd grown up still angry at how it all went down and made a vow to make Black men pay for what Malik had done. Who had Christian and others like him become? Judges who treated young Black boys like grown men? Police officers who turned traffic stops into death sentences?

Given his own experiences, how could Malik be so cavalier about Nina sleeping over at Isabella's? Instead of being concerned about what could possibly happen, it was as if he was intent on finding the silver lining in every racist cloud.

"If we're going to live in a white supremacy culture, we have to know how to navigate their world," Malik reasoned. "Sure, I had awful experiences going to white boarding schools and PWIs, but those same experiences taught me how to survive corporate America. I know how white folks move, how they lie, what they value, what drives them, what can destroy their sense of confidence and more. It doesn't mean I don't get upset or that I don't see the injustice of it all. I just know how to exist in white spaces. And because I know who so many of them really are at their core, I'm rarely surprised by what they do."

And that was supposed to make De'Andrea feel at peace? Not!

Today, 2:00 PM

Becky

Hi there! Just wanted to follow up to make sure you saw my text earlier in the week. This weekend or next would be perfect for the girls' sleepover! Let me know!

Dear God! Had Becky and Nina made a pact to tag team their sleepover requests until she folded?

"Call Toni," De'Andrea commanded the voice assistant. She needed her voice of reason.

Thankfully, she answered on the second ring. "Hey, Dee Dee? What's good?"

"Nothing much. Just coming from visiting Mama. She's doing good. And . . ."

"Uh-oh," Toni said. "And *what*? Talk to me."

De'Andrea took a deep breath, then let out all the fears she'd been holding close to her chest about Nina sleeping over at Isabella's house. About what could happen, what might happen, and what she would do if something did happen. And how all Malik seemed to focus on was how much fun Nina would have and that, well, if something did go bad, the racist experience would help shape her into a strong Black woman.

"She's a child, Toni! I don't want Nina to have to be a strong Black girl. Just a Black girl. Just a happy little Black girl!"

And much to her surprise, De'Andrea burst into tears.

"Awww, Dee, it's okay, love." Toni tried to comfort her. "And that's a lot to place on this one sleepover. Let's talk it through."

"I know it's a lot." De'Andrea sniffled. "And I know it's because of my own stuff, my own baggage. But I know how these seemingly innocent things can go horribly wrong."

Even though she hadn't thought about her first (and last) sleepover with her first (and last) white childhood friend in years, De'Andrea knew she would forever carry the mistrust and pain from the experience.

She recounted how her seven-year-old childhood friend Ellie had kicked her brother under the table when he said De'Andrea's skin was the color of poop. How her older sister refused to call De'Andrea by her real name and called her De'Blackie. And how Ellie's mother ignored both comments and instead cut De'Andrea a slice of cake that was noticeably smaller than everyone else's dessert.

When Ellie called her siblings "stupid meanies," her father had sent both girls to her room where the two friends cried. De'Andrea had felt powerless, and although she didn't have the words to call the situation what it was, she knew what was happening was wrong. It *felt* wrong, and *she* felt awful. She'd lain awake for hours, continuing to cry long after Ellie had fallen asleep.

When the girls returned to school the following Monday, De'Andrea had learned what it meant when older folks said, "Things went from bad to worse."

"My parents said I can't play with you anymore," Ellie sadly informed her, "because we're different. And they said I can't have friends who are different from me, only friends who are the same."

"Damn, Dee. Guess we all have a story," Toni said.

"Wait, what?" De'Andrea asked. "You too?"

"Yup. I went to this all-girls private school. One of the few Black girls, so you know how that goes. My mom used to style my hair in these cute pigtails, and there was this li'l hating-ass Karen-to-be who sat behind me in class who was just . . . I don't know. Infatuated? Jealous? I mean, I still don't know what her deal was. Anyway, one day, she cut one off—"

"Stop!" De'Andrea shouted. "She did not!"

"Yes, ma'am, she did. Said 'Black girls aren't supposed to have long hair.' And she didn't even get into trouble." Toni sucked her teeth. "Our teacher just picked up my ponytail, threw it in the trash, told *me* to stop causing problems, and kept on teaching."

"See? This is what I'm talking about—" De'Andrea began.

"No, Dee—" Toni interrupted. "This is what we have to *start* talking about. Girl, we went through some shit our kids will never go through. Things are different now. Not the best. But certainly better."

"That's where you and I are just gonna have to agree to disagree."

Toni sighed. "Just hear me out, Dee."

"No," De'Andrea argued. "You hear me out. We're not in Atlanta. We're in *Rolling Hills*. And we're one of a few, if not the only, Black families, here. Some days, I feel like I've time-traveled to the civil rights era. There are white folks here who don't even acknowledge us, who leave the playground when we show up. Our next-door neighbor won't even wave to us, let alone speak! She's that upset that her new neighbors are Black. So maybe in some parts of the country, things are better for Black folks. But there are still plenty of places and spaces where we are not welcomed, and Rolling Hills is one of them."

"But, c'mon, Dee. Not every white person there treats y'all that way."

"Oh my God, you sound like my therapist!" De'Andrea groaned.

"Because me and your therapist know you are tripping!" Toni

said. "Listen, I know it's not easy to look at Becky and not see Ellie's mother. And I know it's hard to not think about Isabella saying or doing something that will break Nina's heart. But look how things have gone so far? The girls have a blast together! And it's not like you haven't been to Becky's house. I mean, she's low-key obsessed with y'all."

"Low-key?" De'Andrea asked. "Ummm, I'd say she's more toeing the line as a certified 'I want a Black friend so bad' stalker."

Toni laughed. "Facts!"

"So, what am I supposed to do?" De'Andrea asked. "Just let Nina go to this sleepover? Knowing damn well that the worst could happen?"

"Yes," Toni said. "But you have to switch your perspective. You have to believe that the best could happen, too."

"But—"

"Do you really think Becky won't be doing the most if you let Nina sleep over? Like she's not going to be doting on her like she's some special Black gift-of-a-child sent from heaven? Girl, this might actually be a come-up for Nina. Becky is gonna treat her like royalty! What we need to be doing is praying for Isabella because her momma might forget all about her!"

De'Andrea burst into giggles. "Becky is so extra!"

"And you know Nina is just like Junior. Damn documentarians, the both of them. She's gonna tell you everything that happened at that sleepover. *Everything.*" Toni let out one of her infamous cackles that made it impossible for De'Andrea not to cackle along with her.

"Okay, okay. I'm going to try to think positive. I'm going to try to think about the best time that Nina could have, not the worst."

"That's all I'm saying. And you know I'm just a plane ticket away if things go crazy. I will take my earrings off and slap some Vaseline on my face so fast. Becky don't want this smoke, trust me."

"Oh, I know she don't," De'Andrea said in agreement. "From either of us."

"And look, make Malik do drop-off. That way, you don't even have to deal with Becky. You can just wait for her to blow your phone up with texts and pictures all night."

"That's a good idea." De'Andrea smiled. "Let me give his ass something to do. Especially since he's all 'let Nina have the sleepover time of her life' and whatnot."

"So you're gonna let her go?" Toni asked hopefully.

De'Andrea inhaled deeply and exhaled loudly. "I am. I guess I am."

TWELVE

Rebecca

The rhythm of the windshield wipers put Rebecca in a trance as she drove through the winding roads on her way to pick up Lyla and Isabella from school. The rain wasn't so heavy that soccer practice would be canceled, though it would have been nice to have a break. This was the kind of day she wished she could snuggle under the covers with her girls and watch a Disney movie. When was the last time they'd done that? Years. Literally years. She let out a long, sad sigh.

She couldn't shake the funk she'd been in for the past couple of weeks. It didn't help that she, Jenny, and Victoria had skipped another Stretch and Sip that morning. Jenny's curt "can't make it" texts this week and last had been the only communication Rebecca had received from her since book club. Hadn't things ended on a high note by the end of the meeting? Everyone had said they were on board with the statue project. But before Jenny left that night, she said to Rebecca, "You always *say* you're so committed to fighting racism, Rebecca. But you couldn't even read the book?"

"She can't possibly still be mad that I didn't read the book, right?" Rebecca lamented to Victoria, who also hadn't heard from Jenny.

"No, this is probably about more than the book. I think she just needs some time, Bec," Victoria had said. "All that stuff she shared that night. We've known her for seven years and she never got that deep. I feel like she makes jokes about being Asian more than anything else."

"Yeah, I was shocked. Honestly, I feel like I've always talked about race more than she ever has. I mean, I guess I'm feeling kind of hurt," Rebecca admitted. "The stuff she was saying to De'Andrea and Harita . . . I mean, we're supposed to be her best friends."

"I think the best thing we can do is give her space," Victoria said.

"Okay, I'll try that. But for exactly one more week *only*," Rebecca said. "If I need to apologize for something, I'd like to know what it is now so I can go ahead and do it and we can move on from this."

One bright spot, Rebecca thought, was that De'Andrea had finally agreed to let Nina sleep over. Maybe De'Andrea was warming up to her?

Aside from all the mom drama, something else had been distracting her, though. She had tried to ignore it, but it felt like a traffic light flashing in her periphery. Earlier in the week, Rebecca had awakened in the middle of the night, and after the Mind-Discovery "Fall Back into Sleep" meditation had the opposite effect, she decided to scroll through Instagram. She was barely reading anything until a white square with bold red font caught her attention.

@YtPersonToYtPerson: Hey, white people: Class is in session. What's your first memory of when you realized race mattered?

Initially, Rebecca wasn't sure what the post meant, but only a few seconds later, a memory popped up for her. Something she'd tried to forget about. The weird thing was she had never thought of it as having anything to do with race until that moment.

It was ninth grade and she and Tasha, her best friend since kindergarten, had scored an invite to a party at Claire Miller's house. Claire and her older sister were the prettiest and most popular girls at Trimble High. Once a year, their parents let them have a coed dance party with a DJ in their basement, which also made them the coolest girls in the school.

Rebecca and Tasha couldn't believe their luck in getting invited as freshmen. They coordinated their outfits, got a ride from Rebecca's mom (Tasha's mom didn't exactly know about the party), and promised to stick together the whole night. Rebecca still remembered the way they walked into the party, arms linked with both shared anticipation and social terror.

It would be the last time they shared anything.

Most of the night was a blur. The girls were separated for a bit as Rebecca got swept up with her volleyball teammates and talked up by a few of the cute boys on the football team. But when the DJ put on Rob Base and DJ E-Z Rock, Rebecca and Tasha found each other on the dance floor. Not that they were going to do their "It Takes Two" dance routine at the party, but they were out there living the high school experience they'd always pictured for themselves. It didn't last long because the next song was the one that had been tormenting Rebecca ever since the single released.

Cursed with the wrong name even back then, Rebecca *loathed* "Baby Got Back" and Sir-Mix-a-Lot after enduring classmates shouting the opening "Oh my God, Becky" line at her every time they passed her in the hall. Tasha knew this, of course, and grabbed Rebecca's hand so they could make their way to the snack table.

But before they could exit the dance floor, they found themselves surrounded by all the other kids at the party, who began acting out the song's opening lines and dancing just like they'd all seen in the music video.

Rebecca never remembered making a conscious choice to stay on the dance floor and go along with what everyone else was doing, but that's what she did—even after locking eyes with Tasha, who made it clear she was opting out. Rebecca couldn't explain why she didn't join Tasha, other than social pressure. That didn't feel like a strong enough reason in retrospect, but was there anything *stronger* than that in the ninth grade? By the time she'd found Tasha a few songs later, it was time to meet Rebecca's mom for their ride home. Instead of spending the night at Rebecca's like she'd planned, Tasha asked to be dropped off at her own house that night.

Their friendship was never the same. Rebecca knew it was dumb that she'd gone along with the other kids, but she didn't understand why Tasha had been so upset by it. She figured things between them would eventually go back to normal, but they never did. All Tasha said to Rebecca was that she obviously liked all her new rich white friends better. Rebecca *did* like the new friends she had made, but not because they were white. They were popular and fun, and she got invited to do things and go places her family never would have been able to afford. But she didn't like them better than Tasha. She had been heartbroken and remembered writing in her diary at the time that she felt sadder about Tasha ending their friendship than she did when her grandma died.

After a while, the friendship breakup stung less. Tasha found a new group of friends—all of them Black—and seemed happy.

Rebecca would bump into her every once in a while at parties during high school and they were cordial but never close again. They had connected on Facebook sometime after college, but Tasha didn't post much so Rebecca knew very little about her life.

When Rebecca reached out to Tasha on Messenger during the whole Mountain Top–Jamal Washington crisis, she figured she'd get a polite, and maybe even gracious, response. But Rebecca was shocked at Tasha's reply: **"Becky, rest assured I have plenty of people in my life I can lean on for support during this and all other difficult times. Perhaps these recent events are prompting you to reckon with systemic racism and your white privilege. If that's the case, I wish you luck, but I do not wish to be part of that process. Regards, Tasha."**

Ouch. It was like their high school breakup all over again. How could Rebecca be a grown-ass woman and still have her feelings hurt in that way? It more than hurt. She had felt pissed, too. So what if Rebecca danced along to that song all those years ago? Why had that been such a big deal? Why was that enough to end a friendship? It was Rebecca's name in the song anyway. But, she had left Tasha alone and forced herself to move on. Only a few weeks later, Rebecca noticed Tasha was no longer on Facebook. Either that, or she'd blocked Rebecca.

Over the past few years since Mountain Top, Rebecca discovered that all those kids she used to hang out with in high school were pretty explicitly racist—so bad, in fact, she'd unfriended most of them after getting into too many dead-end Facebook arguments.

Oh shit! Did Tasha think Rebecca was like the rest of them? She wasn't, was she?

Running all this through her head, she almost didn't notice the stoplight she was approaching. She slammed on the brakes. Once she caught her breath, she grabbed her phone to open up her music app and find the old song.

"Oh my God, Becky, look at her butt . . ." Rebecca winced. She hated every second of it but kept listening.

"She looks like one of those rap guys' girlfriends . . .

I mean, her butt, it's just so big . . .

Look, she's just so . . . Black."

Oh wow. Those lyrics were a lot worse than Rebecca remembered.

A horn honked from behind; the light had turned green. She stopped the music before driving forward and thought back to that night nearly thirty years ago. All those white kids shouting the lyrics and laughing, all around Tasha, the only Black kid at the party. And Rebecca went along with it, thinking *she* was the one who had to suck it up because her name was Becky. What a shitty friend.

But I was only fourteen years old. I'm better than that now.

Maybe she could reach out to Tasha again to apologize for real this time, let her know she got it now. That she had done a lot of work to understand her privilege. If Tasha was still hurt, maybe that would help?

Rebecca hated thinking that she'd harmed anyone, especially Tasha.

These feelings—guilt, shame, confusion—always lived in the margins of her headspace. But in recent weeks, they'd lodged themselves right at the forefront so that every conscious thought first passed through their filter. It had started with Stop Sign Becky and Lyla's comments; then Jenny and the book club mess.

And now, these resurfaced memories of Tasha—magnified and sharpened by the understanding of her grown self—they were adding something else she'd rather live without: regret.

She needed to regain some sense of control.

"Hey, Siri. Call Mom."

The phone rang five times. Rebecca knew her mom was doing one of two things: helping her dad reconnect to the internet so he could keep playing in his online poker rooms, or she was out in the front yard tending to her rosebushes. Rebecca was getting ready to leave a message when her mom picked up.

"Becky!" her mom answered, winded.

"*Mom*," Rebecca replied in a tone reminiscent of her irritated teen years.

"Right, sorry. *Rebecca*." Her mom corrected herself. "I almost didn't make it to the phone in time. I was helping Dad with something on the computer."

"Okay, I'm on my way to pick the girls up from school so I only have a couple of minutes, but I have a random question for you. Do you keep up with Tasha's family at all?"

"Who?"

"Mom, *Tasha*. My best friend from when I was a kid. Tasha Morgan."

"Oh—Taaaaasha! The Morgans. Yes, of course I remember. Such a sweet girl. What about her?"

"Do they still live over on Decatur Street? Do you ever hear anything about Tasha or her brothers?"

"No, honey, they moved to, I think, St. Louis? About ten or fifteen years ago. Such a shame. It was nice having them in town. They were so *refined*. Unlike some of the other families on that block."

Rebecca had to literally visualize gluing her lips together so she would not start an argument with her mother. This was always a risk whenever she called home. She knew her mom's racial code words, but she didn't have the energy today to call her out.

"Why are you asking about the Morgans, honey?"

"Oh, it's nothing major. I was thinking about something from back in high school and wondered what Tasha was up to. Anyway, I'm getting close to school so I better let you go. Tell Dad I say hi."

"Bob! Becky says hi!" Rebecca could picture her mom yelling from the kitchen up to her dad, who was in Rebecca's old bedroom, now his gaming room.

"Hi, honey!" She faintly heard her dad yell back.

"Thanks, Mom, we'll see you for FaceTime on Saturday morning, okay?"

"Give those girls a squeeze from their Grandma Sue!"

⁓

"Hi, Mommy! Look!" Isabella jumped in the back seat and handed Rebecca a sheet of paper with colorful crayon markings, a big black oval, and clumps of blue glitter.

"Hi, sweetie! Wow! This is gorgeous," Rebecca said. *What's it supposed to be?* She knew better than to even try and make a guess and then get it wrong. "Tell me about what you've made here!"

"Since it was raining today we learned about clouds in art class and made these. This is a big dark cloud, and these are the raindrops, and then this is the rainbow that comes out after the rain," Isabella said. "I'm going to bring it to Nana this—"

"MOM!" Lyla opened the door and chucked her book bag into the back-back of the car. "Today was the WORST day."

"Lyla! You interrupted me!"

"Lyla, honey, what's wrong?" Rebecca asked as she pulled out of the school pickup lane.

"First of all, Mrs. Worthingham asked for volunteers to go up to the board and put the decimal points in the right place and when nobody raised their hand, she made *me* go up and do it."

"That's mortifying!" Isabella chimed in, proud of herself for using a new word she'd learned.

"No, it's not! Lyla, that's a compliment. She asked you to go up to the front of the room because you're so good at math!" Rebecca said.

"But when I did what she asked me to, she told me I got it wrong," Lyla answered.

"Well, did you get it wrong?"

"Yes. But she didn't have to say it in front of the whole class! And *then* Kayden said, 'Guess who's not Little Miss Perfect anymore,' and everybody laughed!"

"What a jerk!" Isabella yelled. Rebecca was proud of her for having her big sister's back.

"I'm sorry, honey," Rebecca said, also thinking about what a little jerk Kayden was. "You *are* perfect. Don't listen to anyone."

"Here." Isabella handed Lyla the rainbow creation. "I was going to give this to Nana, but I think you should have it."

Lyla smiled. "Thanks, Izzy, I love it."

Rebecca said, "Oh, girls, remember we aren't seeing Nana this weekend because she has her hairstyling appointment on Saturday. But we still have FaceTime with Grandma Sue."

Rebecca noticed Lyla's face relax. She had become increasingly upset after visits with her paternal grandmother. Unlike Isabella, Lyla had known Nana *before*, when she was still the brilliant, one-bourbon-a-day storyteller everyone fell in love with. Lyla couldn't understand how her grandmother, who had always adored her and treated her with trips to the Kennedy Center and high-tea excursions at the Ritz-Carlton, no longer knew who she was. Rebecca couldn't blame her daughter for feeling relief about missing a Memory Village family day.

"But I wanted to see Nana!" Isabella, on the other hand, loved playing "pretend" with her grandmother since all the other grown-ups were no fun.

"Yes, I know, Izzy, but we'll all see her for her birthday lunch. And Uncle Jack is coming, too!"

"Yaaay!" both girls yelled.

"Is Aunt Tina coming, too?" Isabella asked.

"She's not our aunt anymore, Izzy. They're getting a divorce," Lyla said.

Rebecca sighed. "We don't know if they're getting a divorce, Lyla. And even if they do, she'll always be your Aunt Tina. It won't change how much she loves you." Rebecca could see why the girls were questioning this though. "I'm sure we'll see her soon.

"Anyway, don't forget that Nina is coming to sleep over Saturday night. Lyla, I set up a sleepover for you at Cassie's," Rebecca said, trying to pick the mood back up.

Thankfully, by the time they pulled up to the soccer fields at Rolling Hills Park, the rain had completely stopped.

"Okay, girls, try not to get too muddy!" she shouted in vain, as the girls had already closed their doors and run off toward the fields.

Rebecca checked her email and found a message from the printer: the statue removal posters weren't ready for pickup yet.

Damn. This was the errand she'd planned to do while the girls had practice. She needed those posters! The diversity committee was supposed to meet the next day to hang them up at school and get parents to sign the removal petition during pickup and drop-off. She'd have to reschedule. She texted Harita, now her co-chair on the statue removal subcommittee.

> **Today, 4:22 PM**
> **Rebecca**
> No-go on the posters for tomorrow. Delay at the printers. 😠

> **Today, 4:23 PM**
> **Harita**
> Don't worry about the posters! I'll get the kids to make some tonight. I say we stick to the plan for getting signatures tomorrow.

Rebecca thought about it for a minute. She guessed Harita was right. Things were still prickly between them (for instance, Harita had insisted on being co-chair. Why did she always need to be in charge of *everything*?), but the statue had given them a common enemy.

Now that she didn't have to run to the printer, Rebecca had time to kill. She checked off "posters" on her app, then opened Twitter. She pulled up @WeWoke, the account for *Woke Yet?* author Braxton Walsh. His daily threads were usually pretty informative.

@wewoke: White people! Stop telling people of color's stories for them. Tell your own stories.

@whi.te.man.walking: I thought you didn't want to hear us talk. Which is it?

@ytforblm: @whi.te.man.walking There you go again. Are you actually curious or just here to troll?

@whi.te.man.walking: @ytforblm @wewoke The real question is are you here to actually teach or just try to indoctrinate more sheep into your Woke Culture?

She recognized the @whi.te.man.walking account. That guy was bad news. But—and she'd never admit this publicly—she was sort of wondering the same thing he was. What did "tell your own stories" mean? Why would she talk about being white? What people *really* needed to hear about were all the horrible things happening to people of color. Like racial profiling. And that there were still so many Confederate statues throughout the country!

She went back to Google and typed the question she wasn't sure she wanted an honest answer to: "Can white and Black women really be friends?"

A lot of links turned up. One, in particular, caught her eye:

Top 10 Do's and Don'ts for White Women—From the Black Best Friend You'll Probably Never Have

She clicked on it, hopeful, but also prepared for yet another headline that oversold the contents of the article. She scrolled past the two intro paragraphs to get directly to the list. Okay, these were pretty good. Actual, practical advice. She wasn't seeing anything groundbreaking, but it felt good to get confirmation that she was getting *some* stuff right.

#1 DO: Believe people of color when they say something is
about race. DON'T: Assume all people of color agree.
#2 DO: Listen first in multiracial conversations. DON'T:
Put the burden of your education on people of color.

Check. Check, Rebecca mentally noted for herself as she skimmed. Then, toward the end of the article, she paused.

DO: Speak up when racist incidents occur. DON'T: Share
violent videos.

Rebecca was confused. How was she supposed to speak up about incidents without sharing the videos? Without videos, people never believed these things were happening.

She continued clicking through more articles. In one—"Stop Saying 'But I Have Black Friends'"—terms like "objectification" and "exotification" glared at her. It even mentioned "model minority." *Oh! That's what Jenny was talking about.* She took a couple of screenshots and nearly texted them to Jenny before stopping herself.

Ugh. Rebecca felt an ache somewhere between her heart and her gut. She hated not knowing what she'd done to piss Jenny off, but more importantly, she really missed her. She didn't realize how consistently they were in touch with each other on any given day until they weren't anymore. She saved the screenshots to her photo album. Maybe she could share them with Jenny later, if Jenny started talking to her again.

Another article—"All Are Welcome Here and Other Myths of White Liberal Utopia"—was kind of long and academic-y, so she emailed it to herself to read later and then she went back to Google. She still hadn't found a solid answer to her original question. But then another headline grabbed her attention.

"Black Women Don't Exist to Make You Feel Less Racist."

Rebecca gasped. De'Andrea couldn't possibly think Rebecca was using her like that, could she?

No way.

Did she, though?

Yikes.

Sleepover day had finally arrived, and Rebecca wasn't sure who was more excited, Isabella or her.

"Mommy, look! I made a list of all the things Nina and I are going to do at our sleepover!" Rebecca was crouched down in the dining room looking through the buffet for a serving platter. She stood up and turned to see Isabella wearing a white bonnet and matching gloves stretched up past her elbows. She could still squeeze herself into Lyla's old flower girl dress from Jack and Tina's wedding, a golden gown with a satin and tulle hoop that could be twirled and twirled. It was one of those exquisitely eccentric outfits that only a small child could pull off.

"Look. At. You!" Rebecca said as she pulled her phone from her back pocket. "Let me take a picture." Isabella handed her list over to her mother, then smiled and curtsied, inherently comfortable with everyday photo shoots.

Thank God this day had finally arrived. Rebecca didn't think she could take another "Is it Saturday yet?" from Isabella.

"It looks like you're starting off with going to a ball. Well, you are going to look fabulous for it. Then swinging in the backyard, snacks . . . is this a tea party? And now I see your menu . . . pizza and ice cream. Then a movie with popcorn—"

"Can Daddy make the popcorn?" Isabella interrupted. "I like how he melts the butter on it. Just like at the movies."

"Yes, of course," Rebecca said, happy to off-load a task on Todd. "Daddy makes the best popcorn. You have an amazing night planned, sweetie."

Rebecca returned the list to a beaming Isabella. "Now go finish picking up the playroom while I get things ready down here."

"No fair! Lyla should have to help me," Isabella said.

"Izzy, you and Nina practically get the whole house to yourselves tonight while Lyla spends the night at Cassie's. You can manage picking up on your own. Go on."

As Isabella ran upstairs, Todd walked in the door.

"Hi, Daddy! Did you win at golf today?" she called out to him.

Todd put his hands on his hips. "You know I did, Izzy!"

Rebecca sometimes wished he didn't spend so much time playing golf, but he sure looked handsome in the jacket she'd ordered for him with his pink polo shirt that matched his sun-kissed nose and cheeks.

"Hey, babe!" Todd pecked Rebecca on the cheek.

"Hey, hon." Rebecca returned the gesture with a kiss to the air. "How'd it go today?" she asked, although she didn't really want to know any details.

"Amazing! Weather was perfect. Jack was our fourth because Mike Tanner canceled at the last minute."

Rebecca raised her eyebrows. "And how *was* Jack?"

"I mean, I shot par so he obviously wasn't going to beat me."

"You know I have no idea what you're talking about," Rebecca said. "I mean, how was he *emotionally*?"

"Fine, I guess. He wasn't going to complain about Tina in front of the other guys. He told a lot of jokes. Classic Jack. They loved him. He did have a lot of beers, though."

Rebecca wanted to say, "You and Jack have been drinking a lot of beers these days," but she didn't have time for an argument. So she left it alone and changed the subject.

"Well, I'm glad you had fun," she said. "Isabella is busy getting ready for Nina to come over, and your popcorn-making skills have been requested tonight for the sleepover."

"Daddy's movie theater popcorn!" Todd said, proud of himself.

"And hey, I thought that while the girls watch their movie, we can watch something together tonight, too."

"Ooooh, you mean like a date?" Todd wrapped his arms around Rebecca's waist from behind her as she washed her hands.

"I guess something like that, yeah." Rebecca laughed. She turned around, wrapped her arms around his neck, and gave him a kiss, then excused herself from Todd's hold so she could grab her cheese knife set from one of the kitchen drawers.

"How 'bout we order takeout, too? Dinner and a movie. You know what that means," Todd said, trying his best to sound sexy, but like usual he only sounded corny.

"Seriously? During Izzy's sleepover? That's weird," Rebecca said. "I *will* let you pick up the takeout order, though. I thought we'd share that new salmon entrée from Little Roma."

"Yep, I can pick it up. You can have the salmon all to yourself, though. I'm getting the gnocchi," Todd said.

"You're just gonna eat that right in front of me, huh?"

"I'm happy to share."

Rebecca tapped her phone a few times and said, "Okay, order's in. It'll be ready for pickup in about thirty minutes." She focused on the serving platter again and began arranging a block of Manchego cheese, garlic crostini crisps, and some grapes and olives.

"Yum, this looks good." Todd grabbed a few crisps and stuffed them in his mouth. Rebecca smacked his hand.

"Hey!" Todd said with his mouth full, rubbing the top of his hand as if truly wounded.

"This is for Nina's mom. I'm going to invite her in for a glass of wine." Rebecca arranged the crackers and sliced cheese until she heard the doorbell.

"Oh! They're here!" Rebecca squealed. She grabbed the platter and placed it on the coffee table in the family room. "I'll get the door. Babe, do me a favor and grab a couple of wineglasses out of the hutch?"

"Only two? I'm not invited to have wine with the ladies?"

"Izzy! Come down, sweetie. Nina and her mommy are here!" Rebecca yelled upstairs as she rushed over to the front door.

Rebecca opened the door with an "Oh!" upon seeing Nina's dad with a bedazzled purple overnight bag slung over his shoulder, holding Nina's hand. He had on a white polo shirt, khaki Bermuda shorts, and white sneakers with not even a speck of dirt on them. Victoria was right. Malik was hot. And not hot for a middle-aged dad. And he was so tall.

Had De'Andrea mentioned whether he played basketball?

Should I ask him? No, don't ask! Stereotype!

Worried he might interpret her surprise at seeing him at the door as fear, Rebecca quickly recovered and extended her hand. "Helloooo! You must be Nina's dad. I'm Rebecca. It's wonderful to meet you!"

Malik extended his hand to shake. "Hi, I'm Malik. It's a pleasure to meet you."

Rebecca knelt down to Nina's eye level. "Nina! We are *so happy* to have you spend the night with us tonight."

"Hi, Miss Rebecca," said Nina. Sean always called her "Miss Rebecca," too.

Miss Rebecca. Just like Sean says. Is that a Black thing?

She'd Google that later.

"Nina!" Isabella raced down the stairs and embraced her friend. "Come on, let's go to my room!"

"Isabella! Don't be rude. Say hello to Nina's daddy. *Mister* Malik."

"Hi, Mister Nina's Daddy!"

Malik laughed and said to Rebecca, "Don't worry. 'Nina's Daddy' is a great name. He turned toward Isabella. "Hello Isabella. Don't you look fancy this evening."

"Izzy, say thank you!" Rebecca hated that she had to remind her.

"Thank you!" Isabella said. "Now can we go play, Mommy?"

Nina looked up at her dad, who said, "It's okay, Nina Bear. Give me a big hug and a kiss first." He lifted her up and she hugged him koala style. "I'll miss you, baby. Have fun!"

"Bye, Daddy, love you!" As soon as Nina was back on her own two feet, Isabella grabbed her hand and led her upstairs, telling her all the big plans for the night.

"It's so nice to finally meet you, Malik. Todd, honey! Come out here."

As Todd joined them by the front door, Rebecca said, "Malik, meet my husband, Todd. Todd, this is Nina's dad, Malik."

"Hey, man. Nice to meet you," Todd said, shaking Malik's hand and dropping his voice about two octaves lower than normal. *Why did he always do that when talking with other men?*

"You too," Malik said, in a voice deeper than Todd's, which *he* probably wasn't faking. He smiled, revealing the whitest and most perfect set of teeth Rebecca had ever seen. "Nina talks about Isabella all the time. She's been counting down the days. Thank you so much for having her."

"Izzy talks about Nina all the time, too," Todd said.

"You know what?" Rebecca interrupted. "Why don't I go pick up the dinner order and you two can have a drink?"

Todd turned to Malik. "Can you stay? I've got beer in the cooler, but I've also got a bottle of Glenlivet I've been wanting to open."

"You had me at scotch!" Malik said. "I can stay for that. Let me text De'Andrea to let her know."

"Please give her my best." Rebecca forced a smile and tried to access the most casual and nonchalant tone possible. "You two enjoy your drink. I left out some appetizers, too. Malik, so nice to meet you. We'll be in touch if anything comes up with Nina tonight."

Rebecca grabbed her bag and headed out the door, confused by how embarrassed she felt by that entire encounter. De'Andrea could have texted her to say Malik would drop Nina off. And why didn't Todd ever do drop-offs or send texts when *he* came home later than expected? She felt dumb for spending time setting up the cheese platter and expecting De'Andrea to have a glass of wine with her.

Maybe she *would* have some of Todd's pasta tonight.

THIRTEEN

De'Andrea

As usual, Toni the "voice of reason" was right: Becky had gone above and beyond to make sure that Nina and Isabella had an epic sleepover. From what De'Andrea could gather from the shared photo album, the girls' adventure began in Isabella's playroom with their American Girl dolls. De'Andrea had also visited the Tyson's store too many times to count and likewise had given in to Nina's demands to have matching outfits with her doll. So she wasn't surprised to see the friends and their mini-mes in coordinating rainbow flippy T-shirts and jeans. But the video of the girls making their dolls ride on miniature horses complete with saddles and stirrups? Now, *that* had nearly taken De'Andrea out. Especially when she realized they were making their way across the room to perform at a small-scale theater.

She forwarded a clip of Nina helping her doll play a tiny violin while Isabella sat her doll on a stool in front of a tiny grand piano with ivory keys that made real music. The video ended with the dolls being ushered into a mini pink convertible to drive to an outdoor café where they sat at bistro tables and ate snacks with Nina and Isabella.

Today, 7:42 PM

De'Andrea

Y'all. 💀 😍

Simone

OMG! Can I be an American Girl doll in my next life? This is the CUTEST! 😍

Toni

Dee, your inner child is happy (and healing!) 🖤

Shortly before midnight, De'Andrea received the final update of the evening: a photo of Nina and Isabella snoozing on a king-size air mattress on the playroom floor, snuggled under a fuzzy pink blanket with their dolls tucked in at their sides.

She sent the image to Toni with a sincere message.

Today, 11:47 PM

De'Andrea

Thank you again for encouraging me to make it happen.
Don't know what I'd do without you.

Toni

Of course, girl. That's what friends are for. I'm so happy.
For ALL of you! 🖤

De'Andrea zoomed in on the picture, shaking her head in awe at the girls and their dolls wearing matching sky blue pajamas with twinkling white stars. Several books were scattered nearby, evidence that Nina and Isabella had demanded half a dozen bedtime stories before calling it a night.

Today, 11:49 PM

De'Andrea

Looks like the perfect night! Thank you for making Nina's first sleepover in Rolling Hills one that she'll never forget. 😃

Becky

You are so welcome! Will I see you in the morning for pickup?

Hmmm. She'd planned to put Malik on pickup duty, but as she reflected on the evening, De'Andrea's heart couldn't help but soften. Even though Becky's energy was frenetic at times, most times, she wasn't the worst Becky in Rolling Hills by far (unlike Ingrid, the racist next-door neighbor from hell). Maybe she'd even score some brownie points with Dr. Jones! And it wasn't like she had anything else going on in her still-ain't-figured-out-nothing life.

Today, 11:50 PM

De'Andrea

Sure thing! See you soon. Night!

"Finally decided to stop working, huh?" De'Andrea whispered as Malik climbed into bed. "What time is it?"

"Our time." He kissed her neck and pulled her closer to him.

Although Malik had only planned on dropping off Nina for the sleepover, he'd ended up staying to have a drink with Becky's husband.

"I mean, listen, I'd drink Glenlivet with an enemy," Malik joked when giving De'Andrea a recap of the men's time together. "Seriously. Todd is a cool dude. Reminds me of some of my co-workers. Hella rich. Hella smart. And hella corny."

When Malik finally returned home, he'd gone straight to his office to call Tycoon Calhoun.

The more Malik worked with the eccentric billionaire, the more it seemed like Calhoun had become less of a troublesome client and more like her husband's friend. In an effort to be more "housewifey," De'Andrea had cooked dinner for Malik, made his plate, *and* brought it to his office. Still deep in conversation with his boss, Malik had mouthed "thank you" and gestured to a clutter-free space on his desk for her to place his meal. She'd felt more like Malik's servant than his wife, especially when Malik burst into laughter at some private joke as she left.

Would they ever get back to the place where *she* made him laugh like that?

She turned to face him in bed and, instinctively, he kissed her. First briefly and softly. Then more passionately. Their lovemaking was tender. Afterward, Malik stroked De'Andrea's curls as she rested her head on his chest and listened to his heartbeat.

Things weren't the best between them, but Dr. Jones was right—consistently trying helped make their marriage better day by day.

"Nina looked so happy." Malik's deep, raspy voice interrupted the silence. "If you had just heard all that giggling and squealing." He chuckled. "They were having the time of their lives!"

"Yeah, Becky sent me a couple videos and pics," De'Andrea shared. "I'm just . . . I'm just grateful Nina's experience was different than mine."

"I know it wasn't easy for you to let her go, but I'm glad you did. Aren't you?"

"I am, Leek." De'Andrea snuggled in closer to Malik and closed her eyes. "I really am."

De'Andrea tried to be patient as Nina and Isabella continued to find reasons to extend their sleepover into late morning.

"So, about these donuts." She eyed the large box on Becky's kitchen island. "Because I'm pretty sure I only have about another minute of restraint left in me."

"Ugh!" Becky groaned. "I *know*. They smell so good. I told Todd to only get enough for the girls. I hate having them in the house because they're so tempting. But of course, he ordered a dozen. I want one so bad, too!"

She looked at Becky's nonexistent waist and barely-there thighs that were struggling to fill her slim-fit navy tracksuit.

Ma'am, you can afford to eat a donut. Or three.

"Maybe we can split one?" De'Andrea suggested.

"Deal!" Becky sounded relieved to have a compromise.

There's no way you can eat half a donut, Becky! De'Andrea schemed. *Let this be your gateway to some carb-laden joy.*

"Now for the real question?" Becky lifted the lid and feigned swooning from the sweet aroma. "Which flavor?"

After much consideration, the women settled on an old-fashioned style blueberry donut with a light glaze, laughing at themselves for rationalizing that they'd at least be having a little fruit.

"Want some coffee?" Becky offered. "I mean, if we're going to live dangerously, we might as well do it right!"

"I'm always down for caffeine." De'Andrea nodded.

"Samesies!" Becky walked over to the kitchen cabinet and De'Andrea chuckled to herself when she saw the "Woke Yet?" wording on the two coffee mugs.

"I won them in an IG giveaway," Becky explained, as if reading De'Andrea's mind.

But if you hadn't, you would have bought them. Don't lie!

After the coffee brewed, Becky poured them each a cup. But before handing De'Andrea her mug, she reached into another cabinet and pulled out a small dark bottle.

What the hell is she doing? De'Andrea eyed the bottle in Becky's hand. *Is that wine?*

"Want some tequila in your coffee?"

"Tequila? In *coffee*?" De'Andrea asked. But what she really wanted to say was: *What kinda white people shit is this?!*

"It's coffee-flavored so you won't even taste it. Just a splash," Becky explained as she added one dash to her cup and then another for good measure. "Health gurus swear by it. Seriously, it's so good for your gut. Remember Sara? From the diversity committee? She lost ten pounds just drinking a shot of tequila a day! Tequila is the new kefir!"

Looking rather blissful, Becky closed her eyes and took a long sip. "Ahhhh, so good."

Sure, why the hell not.

"Let me get a little of that." De'Andrea held out her coffee mug for Becky to top her off. She took a sip. *Damn, this is good!*

"Let's go into the sunroom," Becky suggested. "The light is perfect this time of day, and it's so relaxing. I think you'll just love the view of the backyard and—"

She followed behind Becky, hoping the coffee-flavored tequila didn't make her as hyper.

Like the rest of the home, the sunroom was simply furnished with a gorgeous white wicker living room set and a matching coffee table. An abandoned teal yoga mat lay unfolded on the tiled floor.

"Oh, let me get that." Becky put her mug on the coffee table and retrieved the mat. She rolled it up quickly before tucking it into one of the corners. "Sorry about that. I was doing a HIIT yoga video this morning. I have a meditation space and studio upstairs, but I didn't want to be too far from the girls."

"No worries." De'Andrea sat in one of the side chairs, crossed her legs, and continued to savor her tequila-laced coffee. "Do you practice regularly?"

"Well, I try to. Me and my girlfriends take a weekly class at Trust Flow Yoga. Serena's the best teacher there, but there are a few other good ones, too. After class, we all come hang out at my house for a little bubbly. We call it Stretch and Sip. You should join us! Have you ever tried yoga?"

"Yes. Yoga and meditation daily, actually. It's how I stay sane."

Becky looked stunned. "Yoga *and* meditation? Okay, you're my new hero. I've tried to meditate so many times, but my mind just races and—"

"Mommy? Where are you?" Isabella called out.

"And I'm constantly interrupted." Becky winked. "We're in the sunroom, honey!"

"Mommy!" Isabella called out again.

"Sunroom!" Becky shouted. "You know, I never asked. What brought you to Rolling Hills?"

"Well, it's complicated. I mean, we absolutely loved Atlanta. Still do. We'd never really planned to move. But then, Malik's mother was diagnosed with dementia. That's why we moved, to be closer to my mother-in-law. She's a patient at Memory Village."

"Oh my gosh! Todd's mom is there, too. We moved her in about three years ago. I can see why you'd come here, then. It's the most amazing facility. But still . . . I'm really sorry to hear about Malik's mother. It's absolutely devastating. And I'm sorry to say it but the reality is, it doesn't get any easier. It's harder every day. Sorry. Was that too honest? Gosh—"

"All good," De'Andrea said. "It is what it is."

"Mommy! Mommy!" Isabella and Nina walked clumsily into the sunroom, squealing as they both tried to carry the box of donuts from the kitchen.

"Can we have another donut?" Isabella asked. "Please, Mommy? Please?"

"Yes, Isabella, but this is your last one." Becky got up to help the girls place the box on the coffee table. She walked over to the curio and grabbed a roll of paper towels.

Nina looked to De'Andrea for approval. When she nodded, the two girls gleefully grabbed a donut before climbing into their mothers' laps.

"We know what we want to be for Halloween," Nina said between munching, her lips covered with crumbs. De'Andrea resisted the urge to wipe them off, knowing Nina would not want to be treated like a baby in front of her bestie.

"Is that right?" She cuddled Nina closer in her lap.

"Yes!" Isabella shouted.

"Inside voice," Becky said.

"But I'm so excited!"

"Me too!" Nina screamed, which made Isabella burst into giggles.

De'Andrea and Becky looked at each other.

"Well then, I'm excited too!" De'Andrea yelled.

"And me three!" Becky screamed. "Actually, I make four!"

Wired from the sugar and excitement from their sleepover, the girls were soon running in and out of the sunroom, chattering nonstop about their Halloween plans to dress up as Frankie the Kid Reporter from their favorite television show.

Becky walked back over to the open box of donuts. "Okay, seriously, last half."

"Girl, you know I'm game." De'Andrea would eat as many half donuts as Becky would allow.

"More coffee? I'll add a little something extra for our gut health." Then she whispered, "And our sanity!"

"I'll come with you," De'Andrea said, in a desperate attempt to escape the girls' sugar rush.

"Thank you." Rebecca grabbed their mugs. "You know, I actually wanted to talk to you about something."

"What's up?" De'Andrea asked.

"Well, it's about the diversity committee. I mean, honestly, this statue removal is the biggest project we've ever taken on. I really want to help take this thing down, you know?"

No, I don't know. De'Andrea offered a weak smile. "And?"

"Well, I was thinking about making flyers. So . . ." Rebecca paused to choose her words carefully. "I wondered if you might be interested in passing out flyers with me, to help get the word out. Maybe even some businesses will let us post them. And I was thinking . . . like, maybe *we* could make a day of it? You know, maybe meet for coffee in the morning. With a little bit of goodness for our gut." Rebecca winked. "Then we could post the flyers and, after, maybe take a yoga class. And then, I don't know. Maybe we can just see where the day takes us!"

Dang, Becky! Did your therapist task you to make a Black friend? Why are you so pressed? All the time! And I was just starting to like you a little bit!

FOURTEEN

Rebecca

Rebecca stared at her reflection in the pond, rippling from the light breeze. Finally, it felt like fall had arrived for good, and with the temperature starting to cool down, her Saturday morning run felt almost enjoyable. She pulled the bottom of her running tank up to wipe sweat from her forehead, then untied the running fleece from her waist and pulled it over her head. She grasped her right ankle for a quad stretch while she inspected Stu's progress. He had done beautiful work. The pond was surrounded by lilac and juniper bushes, which would look gorgeous come spring, and all sorts of other green shrubs that Rebecca couldn't remember the names of, plus a small, curved wooden bridge. Stu had also built a tiered rock waterfall with some kind of high-tech filtration and stormwater-capturing system that made it good for the environment, too. The only things left to add were two stone benches. And the fish, of course. But it would be at least another few weeks before they arrived because he had ordered premium-grade butterfly koi. It would be perfect. She pulled up her left ankle to stretch the other quad, counted to fifteen, and went inside to get everybody moving for the day.

In the kitchen, Lyla and Isabella sat on the countertop stools in their pj's, eating cereal. Lyla was playing a game on her tablet while Isabella leaned over her shoulder and watched. Todd was still in his pajamas and robe and had his feet up on the couch. He rested his coffee mug on his small but growing paunch while he tapped around on his phone, likely playing a word game.

"Good moooorning!" Rebecca sang. She kissed each of her daughters on the tops of their heads.

"Hi, Mommy," Isabella replied.

"Hi, Mom," said Lyla.

Neither turned her head away from the screen.

Todd at least looked up from his phone to acknowledge her. "Morning, babe. How was your run?"

"Good! Eight miles!" Rebecca grabbed a water bottle from the fridge, still proud of herself. "You wanna get out there, babe? The weather is *literally* perfect and there's plenty of time before we leave for your mom's."

"Nah, I'm good." Noticing his wife's disapproving look, he added, "What? Can't a man enjoy his Saturday morning?"

"Only because I do everything around here," Rebecca said. Todd raised his eyebrows. He was being lighthearted, and she meant to respond similarly, but she realized she sounded kind of salty.

"Umm, is everything alright, babe?"

"Yeah. Sorry." She had been in such a good mood seconds ago. "I don't know where that came from. I meant it as a joke."

"Okaaaay. Why don't you come over here and sit down for a minute? Or maybe go up to the attic?" he said, lightly shimmying his shoulders. "You know, and git yo meditation awwwn?"

Rebecca snickered and rolled her eyes.

Such a dork.

"No, I'm fine. I haven't had my coffee yet," she replied. She wished he hadn't mentioned the attic. All that money and effort to create that space and she couldn't sit quietly up there for even five minutes. Once the koi pond was finished, she'd be able to meditate better outside near the sound of running water. She opened the cupboard and shifted the mugs around to find the one she clearly needed this morning: "Zen AF."

That counts for meditation, right?

She filled the mug with coffee and took a first sip. But what should have felt satisfying was overridden by a foul smell emerging from the mudroom. She set her coffee down to face it.

Oh, gross.

Shit! How had she forgotten? Both girls' soccer bags lay on the floor next to the garage door, still filled with all their sweaty gear. Palm to forehead, she cursed herself for not having cleaned them out sooner. She'd been on the phone when they'd gotten home from practice, begging a town council aide to get her an appointment with the chairman about the Longstreet statue removal petition.

She held her breath and unzipped both bags, dumping out everything that had been sealed up for two days: sweaty socks, cleats, shin guards. And a half-eaten granola bar.

Ew.

Isabella's didn't smell all that bad. But Lyla's . . . good God, how could such a beautiful child produce this ugly stench? She gagged.

"What's wrong, Mom?" Lyla called out from the kitchen.

"Your soccer bag is disgusting! *You* should be doing this, not me," Rebecca called back. She was about to clean it out herself anyway when she heard Todd.

"Lyla! Izzy! Pause the game and help your mother."

"Daaaad." Lyla groaned. "How many times do I have to tell you? You do not *pause* a game."

"Well, turn it off, whatever," Todd replied. Rebecca laughed because the girls said the same thing to her all the time. He corralled them into the mudroom and insisted they take over with the soccer bag cleanup. And they did, because of course they did.

Because *Dad* asked.

"Now you can finish your coffee," Todd said, taking Rebecca's hand and leading her back into the kitchen.

Rebecca was bemused by how helpful Todd was being. He rarely stepped in like this, though she wished he did it more often. She wondered if he was feeling anxious about their visit with his mom. *Or maybe because I was such an asshole a few minutes ago.* Either way, she tried not to resent that the girls never protested his directions and instead feel grateful for the effort. She grabbed his mug, rested it on the counter, gave him a quick kiss on the lips, and leaned in to hug him, relaxing instantly upon feeling the cashmere in his robe.

Todd, a little surprised, squeezed back. "Thanks, babe."

"Sorry for being kinda bitchy earlier." Releasing her arms from around him, she added, "And sorry for the smelly hug. I know I need a shower."

"I'll take a smelly hug anytime," he said. Rebecca knew she needed to be better about showing affection. They'd done the "Love Languages" quiz years ago, and Todd's was physical touch. Hers was a combination of all the categories *except* physical touch.

"Hey, Mom, what are these?" Lyla and Isabella returned from the mudroom, and Lyla was holding a stack of flyers about the Longstreet statue removal.

Rebecca's plan was to drop them off at the shops on Chance Ave. She had hoped De'Andrea would go with her, but she hadn't shown any interest when Rebecca suggested the idea. She couldn't shake the feeling that she'd done something wrong by inviting her.

"Those are for the statue removal project I've been working on. Go ahead and read it," Rebecca encouraged.

Lyla read aloud. "'Join us as we rally to remove the Rolling Hills Park statue of Confederate Lieutenant General James Longstreet.'"

"What's a Confederate statue?" Isabella asked.

"Have you ever seen that statue, sweetie, over by the outdoor theater? It's a soldier on a horse?" Both girls shook their heads. "Well, he fought with the Confederacy in the Civil War."

"What's the Confederacy?" Isabella asked.

Rebecca waited, knowing Lyla would want to answer. "Those were the bad guys in the Civil War," Lyla said. "The ones who wanted to have slaves."

"Remember, honey, it's important to say enslaved people." Rebecca had learned that from the Black History Month speaker last year.

"Why would anyone put up a statue of a bad guy?" Isabella asked.

"I don't really know why, Izzy," Rebecca answered. "But either way, we shouldn't have any Confederate monuments up anywhere."

Isabella and Lyla both looked like they had more questions, but there was no time.

"Look, we can talk about this more later. Go on upstairs and start getting ready. We've got FaceTime with Grandma Sue and Grandpa Bob and then Nana's birthday lunch."

Once the girls were up the stairs and out of earshot, Rebecca asked Todd, "Hey, honey, what do *you* think about this statue thing?" Rebecca realized she had told Todd about what the committee was doing to get the statue down, but he had never expressed any support or even shared an opinion on it.

As Todd rinsed out the coffee mugs and the girls' cereal bowls, Rebecca leaned on the countertop and pointed to the flyers.

"Did you know about that statue before? Had you ever heard of James Longstreet?" Rebecca asked.

"Nope. Never had any idea."

"According to the organizers we've been working with, Longstreet was Robert E. Lee's number two. And there's a historical society festival honoring him every year! You grew up around here! How could you not know about this?"

"I guess I had bigger things to worry about than a statue of some dead soldier?" Todd said, wiping the counters. "I've *never* heard of this guy or any festival. He couldn't have been that big of a deal."

"Well, either way, we can't have a statue of a Confederate general in the park where our children play," Rebecca said. "Don't you care about that? You know I've been working on this, and you haven't said anything about it."

Todd stopped cleaning the countertop, turned around to face Rebecca, drew in a deep breath, and exhaled. "You really want to know what I think, Bec? You're always talking about how busy you are. Why would you take this on, too?"

Rebecca felt that salty feeling returning. They had just had a nice moment together; she hadn't thought this would lead to an argument. "I don't know, Todd. Maybe because it's the right thing to do? How can we have little Nina in our home yet accept that there's a Confederate monument down the street from us? And forget about any other Black families ever wanting to move to the area."

"I don't think it's as big of a deal as you're making it out to be, honey. We didn't even know about any of this until a couple months ago."

"Well, when you know better, you have to do better." Rebecca didn't remember who said that originally, but she'd seen it on Instagram and had screenshot it.

"Look, I understand getting rid of the statues of Lee and Davis. But why bother with this guy? Look at him—he's missing an arm, for God's sake!"

"Okay, now you're being ableist, Todd. It doesn't matter how many arms he has," Rebecca argued. "He used the one he had to fight for slavery. I know you're a Southerner and all, but come on! We can't celebrate these people."

"I'm from *Northern* Virginia. We're not considered *Southerners*, Bec. Look, I'm just wondering where do you draw the line? Are we going to take down all the statues and change all the names of buildings and street signs? What about the Washington Monument? Are we going to take that down because George Washington owned slaves?"

"Why do you care so much about preserving monuments all of a sudden? I never knew you were such a history buff," Rebecca said.

"Well, I don't understand why *you* care so much. His statue was put there for a reason, and it clearly means something to somebody."

"Yeah, it means they're pro-Confederate," Rebecca replied, to which Todd rolled his eyes. "Don't you want to be on the right side of history?"

"History? Something about this strikes me as *anti*-history."

"I don't agree," Rebecca said. "Why can't you just—"

"Agree with everything you say?"

"Yes. Well, no. Not like *that*. I mean, why can't you—"

"Can I have my tablet back now, Mom?" Lyla had returned with Isabella trailing behind. Both girls wore dresses they knew Nana loved. "We're ready to call Grandma and Grandpa."

Rebecca got the girls set up for FaceTime. She and Todd remained for a few minutes, long enough to say hello to Rebecca's parents and engage in a bit of small talk, before heading upstairs to change in silence.

~

"Uncle Jack!!!!" Rebecca was applying concealer to the dark (darker than usual, she noticed) circles under her eyes and could hear the girls squealing all the way downstairs. She had warned them not to bring up Tina. She knew Lyla would comply. Isabella was the wild card, so Rebecca wanted to get downstairs quickly in case she needed to intervene.

She added blush and lipstick to her face and then, careful not to smudge her makeup, changed into a pair of light wool burgundy wide-legged pants and a pale blue blouse. She put on the pearl earrings Nana had given her on her wedding day, took one last look in the mirror, and, with her Gucci booties in hand, went downstairs to join the rest of the family.

"And this is what I made in art class this week," Isabella said to Jack, holding up the Picasso-resemblant self-portrait she painted. The girls were seated back at the kitchen counter and were talking incessantly, competing for their uncle's attention.

"This is beautiful, Izzy-girl." Jack held it up at his eye level to admire. "It looks exactly like you!"

Rebecca tossed her shoes by the front door and entered the kitchen. "Hey, Bec!" Jack said, his beaming smile hiding any signs of heartbreak. He had on slim-fit khaki pants, a blue and white striped button-down shirt, and a navy linen sport coat. Next to him on the counter were two bouquets of flowers.

"Hey, Jack." Rebecca approached him with her cheek turned to one side so he could give her a kiss hello. "Thanks for picking up the flowers. There are so many!"

"He got one for Mom and one for you," Todd said as he joined them in the kitchen. "Always showing me up!"

"Awww, Jack," Rebecca said. Looking straight at Todd, she added, "How *thoughtful*."

Todd picked up his phone and pretended to type while saying aloud, "Note to self: Buy your beautiful wife flowers."

"Don't forget to add an alert for that, babe," Rebecca quipped. She pulled a vase out of a closet in the dining room and put her bouquet in it. She'd trim the stems and arrange them later. "Alright, everyone, let's head out. They only give us two hours in the restaurant."

"Uncle Jack, will you ride in the car with us?" Lyla asked.

"Only if I can sit in the middle!" Jack insisted, putting his hands on his hips.

Rebecca laughed to herself at the thought of Jack's six-foot-two frame crammed in the back seat between the two girls.

She observed him interacting with them, looking for any signs of . . . anything. This was the first time she'd seen him since Tina had moved out, but he looked pretty good. Or at least he was putting on a good show for his nieces. Maybe things weren't as bad as she thought?

Isabella grabbed Jack's hand to drag him to the car. "Come on!"

"Hang on, Izzy. Let me grab these flowers," Jack said. As he reached for them, he stopped and pointed to the statue removal flyer. "What's this?"

"Don't ask," Todd said right away.

"Yeah, don't ask," Rebecca agreed.

Jack raised his eyebrows and looked from Todd to Rebecca and back to Todd again. Todd shook his head.

"Come on, let's go!" Jack said to the girls. "I bet I can get to the car first!"

Rebecca, Lyla, and Isabella stood in the waiting area of the Memory Village Grille while Jack and Todd went to get their mom.

"There they are!" Isabella shouted and pointed as soon as she spotted her Nana. Rebecca could tell Isabella was about to take off running so she placed her hands on her shoulders.

"Let's wait here, honey," Rebecca reminded her. "We don't want to overwhelm her, okay?"

Nana smiled and looked straight ahead while Jack pushed her in a wheelchair, with Todd on her left, down a bamboo-covered promenade that connected the West End to the restaurant in the facility's main building. Nana's blush-colored chiffon tea-length dress had been tailored yet again to fit her shrinking body. Still, she looked elegant as ever.

When they reached the restaurant, the brothers helped their mother out of her wheelchair. She hooked arms with them and began walking slowly toward Rebecca and the girls. Someone on staff was already wheeling the chair out of sight.

"Happy birthday, Nana!" Isabella said as soon as they got close. She handed her the card she'd made.

"Happy birthday, Nana," Lyla said with much less enthusiasm than her little sister. She smiled but then looked toward the floor.

"Hello, Elaine. Do you know who these two are?" Rebecca asked, with her hands placed on the girls' backs.

"Yes, of course I do." Nana smiled so warmly at Lyla and Isabella that Rebecca thought her body on some level must have known they were her granddaughters. "You're Rose Worthington's girls. My goodness, you're getting so big."

Rose Worthington?

That was a new one. Rebecca made eye contact with Todd, then Jack; they both shrugged.

"Let's get seated, shall we?" Jack said.

As the hostess showed them to their table, Elaine walked arm in arm with Jack, gazing up at him, while Todd, Rebecca, and the girls followed behind.

Rebecca quietly asked Todd, "Did she know who you both were today?"

"She knew Jack, not me," Todd said. "She called me Luis. He was our family's landscaper for twenty years."

Ouch.

Rebecca squeezed Todd's arm and grasped his hand. Todd had always joked that Jack had been their mom's favorite, her precious baby. But for her to recognize his brother and not him? Sure, it wasn't personal, but it had to sting.

Lunch went as well as it could have. The restaurant staff

seated them at a round table near the windows overlooking the Village grounds. Jack and Todd flanked Nana and each took turns helping her with the meal—Todd cutting her steak into smaller bites, Jack spotting her each time she reached for her water glass. Rebecca took great care to include both Lyla and Isabella in the conversation and asked Nana to tell stories about her sons. Some were true; others not so much, but everybody went with it. They didn't wince when she transposed phrases, asking the server for a "water of glass," or when she asked repeatedly where her husband was. Those were the moments that used to take them off guard. They still felt gut-wrenching but had, over time, settled into normal, which meant they could laugh, too. Like when Nana gossiped about Deborah being sweet on Jerome. No one in the family was sure whether she was telling a story from her teen years or if the gossip was about Memory Village residents. And, of course, she patted Lyla's and Isabella's skin repeatedly and told them how soft and smooth it was.

But the funniest moment came after the servers had cleared the main entrée dishes and replaced the silverware with clean forks and spoons for coffee and dessert. Lyla and Isabella were telling everyone at the table about the videos they had been watching that morning of a family with ten kids making an ice-skating rink in their own backyard.

Waiting for the inevitable "Can we do that, too?" from one of the girls, Rebecca noticed Nana take a fork from her place setting and slide it into her purse. She looked up and glanced around the restaurant, presumably checking to see if anyone noticed. Then she took her spoon and did the same. Just as she was reaching for Jack's spoon at the place setting next to her, Isabella stopped mid-sentence and gasped, her eyes widening.

"Nana!" Isabella exclaimed. "Are you stealing the spoons?"

"Of course not, young lady! I am making sure no one steals these from *me*!"

At this, Jack and Todd burst out laughing, which then led to everyone else at the table catching a fit of the giggles, too—including Nana. Rebecca noted to herself to let the staff know so she could return the silverware to the kitchen later.

After dessert and a round of singing "Happy Birthday," Nana's aide appeared with the wheelchair to take her back to her room, and they all said their goodbyes. The whole Myland crew joked about Nana's thievery on the car ride home. Rebecca felt relieved that it had been, overall, a good afternoon.

Once they all arrived back at the house, Lyla asked if Jack was staying for dinner.

"Not tonight, Lyla bean," Jack replied. And Rebecca wondered if maybe he had plans to meet up with Tina and that maybe they could reconcile. "I'm gonna hang with your mom and dad for a bit, and then I have to head out."

"But when will we see you again?" Isabella asked, pouting.

"How about this. Why don't we plan another day at that ropes course?" Jack said.

"Oh my God, I *loved* that place," Lyla said. "Okay, when?"

Rebecca jumped in. "Uncle Jack and I will look at the calendar and figure out a day, okay, girls? Why don't you go change out of your dress clothes, and then you can have some screen time for a bit." Rebecca told the girls to do exactly what she wanted to do herself.

"Come give your favorite uncle a big hug," he said, crouching closer to their height.

In unison and as was their routine, they replied, giggling,

"You're our *only* uncle!" and nearly knocked him to the floor as they wrapped their arms around him.

Todd went to the wet bar to make drinks for himself and Jack. "Want anything, Bec? Glass of wine?"

Rebecca thought about it. What she *wanted* was to lie down on the couch and binge the newest season of *The Monarchs*. But she also hoped Jack might open up about the Tina situation. "Sure, I'll have one glass."

With drinks in hand, Todd, Rebecca, and Jack convened around the kitchen island, Rebecca sitting on a stool and the two brothers leaning on the countertop. Rebecca knew Todd would likely tell her later that she shouldn't butt in, but she couldn't hold it in any longer.

"Jack, how *are* you?" She looked at him sympathetically.

Jack sighed. "Listen, Bec. Todd told me you'd probably ask about Tina and me. I really don't feel like talking about it yet. But don't worry about me. I'll be fine." He smiled, and it didn't even look fake.

The Brothers Myland were good at many things, but what they did best was compartmentalize. Put whatever devastation they were going through in a box inside them, lock it up with a broad smile, and wash it down with a bourbon. It could be useful at times, but right now, it was annoying.

"But I don't understand what happened! This came out of nowhere, and Tina won't respond to any of my texts. Think about Lyla and Isabella! Are they going to see their Aunt Tina ever again?" Rebecca's voice got higher with each sentence. She could hear herself and knew she was bordering on unhinged, but what the hell. How could Tina be part of their family for ten years and then . . . not be.

"Honey," Todd intervened.

Don't say it, Todd. Don't say it.

"Calm down."

He said it.

"Todd, did you really just tell me to calm down? Come *on*."

"He said he doesn't want to talk about it. So, please. Leave it alone." Todd rarely lost his temper or gave any kind of directions to Rebecca, but he was glaring at her.

"Guys, it's gonna be okay. Bec—I get it. You want to know what happened. I'm still figuring it out myself. I promise we'll talk about it eventually, okay?"

"Okay." Rebecca's shoulders dropped. "I'm sorry, Jack, that I came at you but also sorry that this is happening."

"Don't sweat it any more, Bec. I'll be good."

"You know what you're not gonna do, though?" Todd asked.

"What's that?" Jack responded, looking somewhat nervous about what Todd would say next.

"You're not gonna take my money on the golf course next weekend."

The men laughed and Rebecca rolled her eyes. The two of them talking about golf was not how she was going to spend the rest of the day.

"Alright, then. I'm going upstairs to watch my show," Rebecca said. She turned toward Todd and said, "*Please*, honey, don't drink too much."

Jack assured her, "It'll only be this one, Bec. Promise. I can't stay much longer anyway."

"Alright, enjoy!" She gave Jack a hug and walked out of the kitchen.

Before she made it to the top of the stairs, she overheard Jack ask, "Is this statue takedown another one of Rebecca's projects? I've heard about what they're trying to do, man. It's messed up."

Rebecca lingered a moment to eavesdrop.

"I mean, where do you draw the line?" Jack added. "What's next—taking down the Washington Monument because George Washington had slaves?"

Oh, for shit's sake. She didn't need to hear that same conversation all over again.

FIFTEEN

De'Andrea

When it came to living the "my Black kid attends a white private school" life, De'Andrea was learning that the decision was more than a notion. Sure, she'd been somewhat prepared for Magnolia Country Day's costly independent school fees being more akin to college tuition than kindergarten. But the exorbitant price tag was only a fraction of families' responsibilities and obligations. And the one that annoyed De'Andrea most was the mandatory parent volunteer hours.

Thirty hours per semester? Per child per family? Where they do that at?!

Magnolia Country Day School, apparently.

As if she wouldn't be involved in Nina's high-priced, highfalutin school on her own accord. As if she'd rather donate their hard-earned coins in lieu of volunteering. A $500 donation to the school's fundraising committee if the Whitmans didn't meet their thirty-hour parents-as-partners fall requirement?

In the words of Randy Jackson, "it's a 'no' from me, dawg."

"What the hell are they even raising funds *for*?" De'Andrea had complained to Malik when she'd read through the short yet ironclad contract at the beginning of the semester. "With all that tuition we're paying? Uh-uh. Magnolia ain't getting another dollar from us. I'm about to be the best li'l parent volunteer they've ever seen!"

Except . . . she wasn't.

De'Andrea didn't even deserve a gold star for trying.

Aside from attending the parent diversity committee meeting and book club, she'd done a whole lotta nothing when it came to volunteering at Nina's school. Unfortunately, showing up for pickup and drop-off didn't count as parents-as-partners work. When it came time to sign the contract for spring semester, she looked forward to unapologetically checking the "I/We will make a $500/semester donation" box and writing a check.

It was only by the grace of God that she found her parents-as-partners calling in late September when Nina's teacher asked her to fill in as a classroom helper.

"Joshua's mom decided to take early maternity leave," Miss Heather explained. "She used to do storytime, which is like, *the* most coveted role when it comes to parent volunteer hours. So I wanted to give you first dibs." She'd whispered that last part to De'Andrea as if there were moms lying in wait to swoop in on the opportunity.

"I'll do it!" De'Andrea had immediately agreed, before adding, "And thank you so much. I had no idea how I was ever going to reach the volunteer requirement." Especially without Malik's help. Of course, *he* hadn't volunteered a single parents-as-partners hour.

As usual, it was all on her.

Luckily, volunteering for storytime was a dream. There was nothing like seeing Nina sitting front and center on the colorful, plush rug with Isabella by her side, beaming with pride as *her* mommy read books to the class. Always down for being extra,

De'Andrea's animated voices and theatrical performances quickly made her a classroom fave. Sometimes, she even hung around after storytime if Miss Heather needed her assistance.

And then there were days like today. When even though she'd known going all out for Halloween-themed storytime would put her slightly behind schedule, De'Andrea couldn't resist doing the absolute most. The students had giggled loudly when she'd entered the classroom dressed as a slice of pepperoni pizza. And they'd given resounding applause at the end of her Oscar-worthy performance of *The Day the Crayons Quit*. Now she was late for her special visit with Mama to the art exhibition. But without a doubt, it had been worth it.

"Mama Sweets!" De'Andrea called out as she knocked on the front door. "I'm here!"

She waited for the door to open, and for Mama to pull her into a Chanel No. 5–laced embrace like always. But she didn't answer. De'Andrea knocked again. After a few more minutes passed and Mama still hadn't come to the door, she began to worry.

She's okay, Dee. Don't start stressing.

There was no way Mama could go missing again. Memory Village had plenty of security measures in place to avoid that happening. But what if she'd fallen? What if Mama needed help?

De'Andrea realized she'd never used her key fob and her hand trembled as she retrieved it from her tote. Caregivers were only supposed to use it to gain access in case of an emergency.

But what if this *was* an emergency?

Chill out, Dee. Mama's probably just taking her sweet ol' time getting ready.

Instead of using her key fob, De'Andrea stepped into the small yard in front of the house. Using the windowsill to steady herself, she placed her hands on either side of the flower box filled with fragrant African violets, stood on her tiptoes, and peeked inside. The house was still and quiet, and nothing seemed out of place.

Besides taking her sweet time getting ready, there was also the very real possibility that Mama was napping. Then, just as De'Andrea prepared to step away from the window, she saw Mama walk across the living room and head toward her bedroom. Within seconds, she was once again out of De'Andrea's sight.

Mama, what is going on with you today?

De'Andrea walked back to the front door. She was tempted to knock once more for good measure but her gut instinct told her to go inside. Quickly, she tapped her fob against the keyless lock. As soon as the dead bolt clicked, she opened the front door and walked inside.

"Mama?" De'Andrea called out as she made a beeline for the bedroom. "I'm here. We're going to the art exhibit today, remember?"

She stood in the bedroom doorway, and when Mama turned toward her, De'Andrea opened her arms wide. But instead of coming in for a hug, Mama walked over and gave a curt "hi" before asking, "Have you seen Paul?"

Paul had been Mama's soulmate, her high school sweetheart and husband for over forty years. He'd died shortly after Nina was born, and everyone believed he held on just to see and hold his first grandbaby. It wasn't uncommon for Mama to mention her late husband. But she'd never asked De'Andrea if she'd *seen* him.

Be gentle. Be kind. Be honest.

"It's so good to see you," De'Andrea said as she pulled Mama into her arms. "He . . . Paul isn't here."

"Well, I can see *that*!" Mama's face contorted in anger as she backed away from De'Andrea. "Where is he? I need him to pick Malik up from school today. I can't do it. I just can't do it! I'm too tired."

"It's okay," De'Andrea said calmly. "You don't have to pick up Malik from school today."

"It is *not* okay!" Mama screamed, her eyes wild. "So, what are you going to do? Just keep standing there looking stupid? Help me find him, you bitch!"

De'Andrea was almost too stunned to speak.

"Let's go for a walk so we can talk about it. I—" But before she could finish her sentence, Mama lunged at her, nearly knocking her off her feet.

"Don't you tell me what to do, missy! You know where he is, don't you? Don't you! Answer me!"

"Calm down, Mama!" De'Andrea pleaded as she regained her balance. "I'm trying to help you."

"Where is he? Where is Paul? You better tell me where he is *right now*!" Mama lunged at her again, scratching De'Andrea's face with her nails as she tried to wrap her frail hands around her daughter-in-law's neck. The elder's grip was weak and De'Andrea easily slipped out of the chokehold, which only added to Mama's anger.

The bathroom. Run to the bathroom. Now!

As De'Andrea ran out of the bedroom and down the hallway, she could hear Mama's slower, heavier footsteps chasing after her.

"Made it!" Breathless, she went to lock the bathroom door.

Shit!

There wasn't one. It was the only way to ensure patients didn't accidentally lock themselves inside or out of the small powder room.

"Is Paul in there? Let me in!" Mama's fists banged against the wooden panels.

Using her body weight, De'Andrea leaned against the door to keep Mama at bay. And then with a shaky hand, she pressed the red button next to the medicine cabinet. Immediately, someone answered through the intercom. "This is Memory Village Emergency Care. Medical staff have been dispatched to your location. I'm Nurse Katie and I'll remain on the line with you until they arrive. What's the emergency? Are you okay?"

"No" was the only word De'Andrea could get out before she began to sob.

———

The week had been a blur of signing consent forms and caregiver documents, and De'Andrea lost track of how many doctors and specialists she'd spoken with about the new challenges awaiting them. Each one tried to explain the seemingly sudden change in Mama's condition. Each one tried to prepare them for what might come next.

"Her mind is time-shifting, and when this happens it's as if she's returned to that period of her life . . ."

"This is why dementia is not only considered a life-altering disease. It's also life-limiting . . ."

"Stage five patients experience decreased independence . . . Under her new treatment plan, Mrs. Whitman will have a live-in dedicated nurse to assist her with daily tasks like bathing and getting dressed . . ."

"When East End patients become a risk to themselves and others, we transition them to Memory Village's West End . . ."

Even though Malik was physically present for the specialists' talks, mentally he might as well have been on another planet. And even though De'Andrea was sympathetic, she was also sick of having to be the glue that held their lives together. Mama had attacked *her*! But between trying to manage Malik's emotions and Mama's move to the West End, De'Andrea had barely had a moment to process how the entire ordeal made her feel.

Of course, she still loved Mama. But something about their relationship was different. And De'Andrea knew she needed to figure out what that *something* was before it became too deeply rooted in her heart.

Not like Malik was any help. Like always, he continued to use work as an excuse to escape reality. When he told De'Andrea last minute that he wouldn't be on hand for Mama's move to the West End, she'd lost it.

"So you'd rather travel with Calhoun instead of helping Mama move to what is most likely her last residence?" De'Andrea yelled. "This is *your* mother, not mine. Can you at least *act* like you love her?"

Those had been fighting words. Although that argument led to Malik staying for Mama's transition to the West End, De'Andrea might as well have been alone. He barely spoke to her on move-in day unless it was absolutely necessary, and even then his responses were curt and dry. As soon as Mama was settled, Malik had promptly left for the airport to catch his flight to join Calhoun in Texas.

And De'Andrea had been heartbroken.

"I'm telling y'all, I don't think we're going to make it," she told Toni and Simone during their Sacred Sunday Zoom chat. "All Malik does is work. And when he ain't working, all we do is fight."

"Y'all are gonna make it, Dee," Toni encouraged. "This is just a really tough season for y'all right now. Every marriage has them. Y'all love each other and—"

"What if love doesn't carry as much weight as we'd like to believe it does," De'Andrea argued. "Also, I should clarify. It's less of a 'we love each other and don't know what to do' and more of a 'I hate him and he hates me' thing that we've got going on over here."

"Stop it," Simone demanded. "You and Malik do not hate each other. Like Toni said, I think this is just a really tough season for y'all. But you will get through it. What's the alternative? Get a divorce and let some hussy reap the benefits of all your hard work to make Malik the man he is today? You trippin'!"

"So I'm just supposed to be unhappy?" De'Andrea shot back. "Just stay married and be unhappy so he can't be booed up with some thot? She can have him! He's probably fucking somebody else anyway. Might even be fucking Calhoun for all we know."

"Oh Dee, don't say that," Toni chimed in. "You don't mean that."

"Oh yes I do," De'Andrea shouted. "Malik stays getting flewed out—"

"For his job," Toni argued. *Stop being so damn extra.*

"Whatever, that's how it starts. It always *starts* at work." De'Andrea air quoted the word "starts." "And then, next thing you know? Your husband tells you he's gay and that he's in love with his boss!"

"You know what? I'm not even entertaining this." Toni rolled her eyes as she took a sip of wine.

"Now wait just one minute." Simone tilted her head and put her fist to her chin in a thinker's pose. "I know Malik is not out here bent over and letting that young billionaire blow his back out. Because if he is, let me tell y'all something. I volunteer as tribute to be the one who takes Malik dooooooowwwwwnnn. And we 'bout to get paid in the process. I'm talking blackmail, baybeeee. Selling the stories to tabloids. Ransom—"

"Ransom, Simone? Really?" Toni shook her head.

"Yes, *ransom*. He's a billionaire. We at least gotta try!"

"Try what?" Toni deadpanned. "To get arrested for kidnapping?"

"See, I need you to think bigger, dream bigger," Simone reasoned. "We like Jada in *Set It Off*. We ain't gon get *caught* for nothing. C'mon, man, we better than that!"

The friends' bickering was a welcome and hilarious momentary distraction from thinking about Malik, and De'Andrea found herself amused. Simone was the only person capable of pushing Toni's buttons. Nothing Simone was saying made any sense, but she continued to stand firm in her foolishness. Which only made Toni continue to argue with her like she was once again a litigator in court.

"So that's the plan." Simone clapped her hands together. "We finna get his ass."

"There is no plan! And if there is, it cannot and will not involve any of the scenarios you've just presented. And I ain't going to jail with you," Toni howled.

"Okay, that's cool." Simone was unbothered. "I don't need you to help me kidnap that man. I can totally take down Calhoun by myself." LL barked loudly. "And with you, sweet baby. I know you'd come with me and together, we gon snatch up Calhoun and hold him hostage. And we won't give Toni any of our ransom money. Only Auntie Dee Dee because—"

"You know Simone is certifiable, right?" Toni lifted a pointer finger to her temple and twirled it around as she mouthed the word "crazy."

"I miss y'all so much." De'Andrea fought back tears. "It's been so hard going through all this without y'all."

"I mean, you want us to come through?" Simone asked excitedly. "We've been giving y'all space, trying to let y'all get settled in. But if you're ready for houseguests, just say the word."

"Oh, I'm ready," De'Andrea said. "So ready. And it doesn't matter whether Malik is ready or not. He's never home!"

"Nah, you know he'll make time to see us," Toni reasoned. "Especially with Craig and the kids coming."

"Maybe Craig can talk some sense into him," De'Andrea said hopefully.

Simone sucked her teeth. "I keep telling y'all, you don't even have to do all that. There's this thing called *blackmail*—"

"Oh my God." Toni buried her face in her hands.

"So, y'all are coming? Like, for real for real?" De'Andrea felt herself getting excited at the thought of it.

"We coming, boo!" Simone promised. LL barked to let her know he was coming, too.

"That's right," Toni agreed. "Sit tight, Dee. Help is on the way."

~

De'Andrea pulled her favorite cashmere cardigan off its hanger and slid her arms into the extra-long sleeves. The elegant piece made her black T-shirt and matching leggings scream "chic" instead of "I've been wearing workout clothes even though I ain't been working out." She pulled her curls into a quick messy bun and took one last look in the mirror before heading downstairs.

After popping a hazelnut pod into the coffee maker and placing a cup under the spout, she checked on the progress of her infamous macaroni and cheese casserole.

Yes, Lawd! She peeked inside the double oven at the melting cheddar nearly bubbling over the sides of the large aluminum pan.

Malik was already outside grilling. After slipping into her house shoes, she pulled her sweater tighter, cocooning herself deeper into its warmth. Then she stepped out onto the redwood wraparound deck.

"This is my last trip to the store," De'Andrea said. "Speak now or forever hold your peace, mister." She kept some distance between them. Although she loved the smell of burning charcoal, she didn't want smokiness lingering in her hair and on her clothes for the rest of the day. She also didn't want to bother Malik because, these days, it seemed her mere presence could annoy him. They were having a peaceful morning and she wanted things to stay that way.

Malik took out one of his wireless earbuds. "What did you say, Dee?"

"I said do you need anything from the store because this is my last run and I promise you that once I get back inside this house I'm not going back out so speak now or forever hold your peace." De'Andrea smirked as she finished her run-on sentence and added, "Respectfully." And she was serious. Hell, if she hadn't forgotten the sour cream for her pound cake, she wouldn't even be going out!

"I don't need anything." Malik shook his head, then put his earbud back in.

"Alright, don't say I didn't ask!" De'Andrea threw her right hand up with the peace sign to let him know she was out.

By the time she returned from the store, Malik was adding his first round of smoky sweet ribs to the double oven to stay warm alongside several trays of her mac and cheese. He took one look at her arms laden with grocery bags and shook his head.

"I'm sensing some judgment," she teased. "And I don't like it."

"No judgment here," Malik said as he took the bags from her arms and set them on the counter. Then, much to her surprise, he reached out to hug her. "I know you're excited the crew is coming. I am too. Thanks for setting this up, Dee. And look, I know I've been—"

"Mommy! Daddy!" Nina interrupted. Upon seeing her parents hugging in a warm embrace, she smiled, blushing. "Hi, Mommy. Hi, Daddy."

"Hi, sunshine." Malik stepped away from De'Andrea and swooped up Nina in his arms. "Mommy and Daddy were just talking about how excited we are to see our friends. Are you excited, too?"

"Yes!" Nina squealed.

As De'Andrea watched Malik loving on his daughter, she couldn't imagine taking such precious moments away from either of them. She grabbed her camera off the kitchen island and snapped a few pics. Even though she'd once said she'd never be *that* woman, she was starting to understand why couples stayed together for their children's sake.

De'Andrea's wrist buzzed with a new notification. "Toni said they're thirty minutes away!"

The house smelled heavenly. De'Andrea couldn't wait for their plates to be stacked with barbecue, mac and cheese, potato salad, baked beans, and cornbread. When the visitors' entrance security guard called to let them know their guests had arrived, De'Andrea, Malik, and Nina went outside to wait for their friends. As soon as

Nina caught a glimpse of Craig's SUV turning onto their cul-de-sac, she squealed, "They're here! They're here!"

Simone got out of the truck first, looking as fashionable as ever wearing an off-white oversized sweater, skinny jeans, and ankle boots. She stretched and then reached into the back seat to grab LL.

I know she ain't have that dog in a car seat! De'Andrea giggled to herself before screaming out, "Moni!"

"Dee!" she cried as she ran over cradling LL in her arms. His tail wagged as De'Andrea made sure she got in her doggy kisses, too. "God, I've missed you, lady."

"Same, Moni," De'Andrea whispered in her ear. "Same." She stepped back, motioning with her forefinger for her to twirl. Simone was more than willing to oblige, slowly turning in a circle and poking out her lips in a sexy pout. "Cute boots. Cute braids," De'Andrea said, playfully flicking one of her friend's ginger box braids.

"Thank you, thank you." Simone tossed her braids over her shoulder. "You know how I do."

As Junior and Jasmine jumped out of the truck and made a beeline for Nina, Toni ran over to join De'Andrea and Simone for a group hug. "Reunited and it feels so gooooooooood," Toni sang out, horribly off-key as usual, which made the friends laugh.

De'Andrea smiled at the kids. With Nina wearing her pink velour sweat suit and rainbow sneakers and Jasmine decked out in a green sweat suit with princess socks and distressed white Converse, the girls looked like mini–AKA sorors.

"That's still Jasmine's favorite outfit, huh?" De'Andrea eyed her goddaughter's too small hoodie and high-water sweatpants.

"Still." Toni shook her head. "And unless we going out in public, it ain't a battle worth fighting."

Junior looked adorable in his dark gray sweatshirt, light-wash jeans, and a brand-new pair of Air Force 1s. The kids giggled as they ran in circles in the driveway, unsure of who was chasing who. And before De'Andrea knew it, they were in Ingrid's yard, dangerously close to her precious flower beds. The kids stopped running and bent down to inspect the hearty orange and yellow mums. "So pretty!" Nina cooed. "I love flowers."

"Me too." Jasmine reached out to touch one of the tiny buds.

"Aht aht!" De'Andrea hissed. "Don't touch that. Get back over here!"

"Junior and Jasmine!" Toni sighed. "Jesus, she loves flowers."

"That's the next-door neighbor who don't like Black folks," De'Andrea whispered through clenched teeth. "The one I'm always telling y'all about!"

"Oh shit!" Simone said as the friends went to retrieve the kids. "Come here, y'all. Get out that—"

Ingrid's front door opened and the three women froze.

God, no! De'Andrea pleaded silently. *They literally just got here.*

The children looked up at Ingrid as she said something too low for their mothers to hear. Then De'Andrea watched in disbelief as Ingrid bent down, plucked three tiny mum buds, and handed one to each of the children. She looked over at De'Andrea and gave a weak smile before going back inside her house. The kids ran back over, their faces beaming as they held their flowers high in the air like trophies.

"Okay, I have no idea what just happened," De'Andrea said. "I swear that woman has never said two words to us! Right, Malik?"

But he'd missed the entire interaction because he was standing next to Craig, staring into the trunk that was packed to capacity.

As the women walked over, they overheard the two men deep in conversation.

"I told them it was too much," Craig said sheepishly, looking like his accountant self with his tortoise-frame glasses and black-on-black sweater, jeans, and loafers. He pulled out one of the kids' colorful rolling suitcases. "But ain't no winning an argument with Esquire Toni."

"Hey, I heard that!" Toni said as she playfully smacked him on the butt before wedging herself between Malik and Craig. "I promise you it didn't look like this much when we were loading it all in," she said sheepishly.

Craig silently mouthed to Malik, "Yes, it did."

"We just wanted to make sure we had everything we needed to cook some of your favorites," Simone said as she tapped one of the two large blue coolers packed underneath several pieces of luggage.

"I mean, I know we're in the sticks," Malik teased, "but we *do* have grocery stores out here."

"But do your grocery stores sell Black people food? And seasoning?" Simone teased as LL wiggled in her arms alternately barking and growling. "Dee, I swear he's been restless ever since we got to these Rolling Hills. His racist radar is on high alert."

What had started as a joke when LL was a puppy had somehow become a self-fulfilling prophecy. It sounded ridiculous to say he only barked at white people, but it was true. Except LL didn't bark at *all* white people, which was why Simone was convinced he had a special and unique gift to sniff out racists.

Simone looked around cautiously and whispered, "They out here."

"Hi, De'Andrea!" Heidi called out from across the cul-de-sac as she prepared to go on a walk with Charlotte. The toddler squealed in her stroller as she waved at Nina.

"There go one right now!" Simone whispered. "Harpo, who dis woman?"

"That's Heidi." De'Andrea laughed. "I told y'all about her. She's cool."

Simone shrugged. "LL, what you say? Is that Heidi lady good white folk or nah?" LL stared at Heidi and Charlotte for a moment. Then he wagged his tail.

"Oh aight, she's good then." Simone gave LL's forehead a smooch.

While the guys unloaded the truck, De'Andrea gave her friends a tour of the house. Now accustomed to their new home, she'd forgotten how obscenely large it was until they reached the third level and Simone sat down on the top step. "Whew, chile! I need a minute."

"For real for real!" Toni exclaimed, pretending to be more winded than she actually was as she sat down beside Simone. "This is the longest house tour I've ever been on in my life. You could have at least told us to pack a snack first."

"I know she said this was a single-family home," Simone chimed in. "But it has to be for two families, right?"

"Definitely," Toni agreed. "This is definitely a two-family home."

"Oh, stop it, y'all." De'Andrea chuckled at their commentary.

After eating a small feast of Southern goodness, the friends lingered on the deck and soon, the sun was starting to set. Malik lit the fire pit as De'Andrea pulled fleece throws from the outdoor basket and passed them around. As if knowing the Whitmans had guests in town, the early evening sky put on a colorful spectacle as late day transitioned to early evening. Everyone stared at the bright yellow and orange sun as it hugged a majestic purple and blue horizon before slowly descending through the meadow's barren trees.

"Gosh, it's beautiful out here." Toni stood at the wooden railing, her husband's arms holding her close as she snuggled deeper into the blanket around her shoulders.

"It really is." De'Andrea looked up at the sky as Malik walked over and stood behind her. Surprised once again by his affection, she allowed herself to be held as he wrapped his arms around her. They stayed that way for a moment, listening to the sound of the burning wood crackling behind them. And in that moment, everything just felt right.

We can make it. We're going to make it. De'Andrea tried to encourage herself.

While the dads got the kids settled in for movie night before retiring to Malik's man cave for a game of pool, De'Andrea and her friends stayed around the firepit. Cuddled under their blankets with wineglasses in hand, they talked and laughed into the night.

"Can you believe we've been friends for *decades*?" Simone asked. "Like, literally since forever."

"I'm just glad I passed the Krystal burgers test." Toni laughed. "I seriously don't know what I'd do without y'all."

"Same. Where would we be without our sisters?" De'Andrea raised her wineglass to initiate a toast. "To friendship and sisterhood. Our chosen family."

The women clinked their glasses together under the fire's golden glow. Then De'Andrea reached into her pocket and pulled out the latest gift she'd purchased for herself—a monogrammed sterling silver and yellow gold bean-shaped pillbox from Tiffany & Co. She'd eyed the coveted Elsa Peretti collaboration for months before forking over the two grand, and she had no regrets.

"Ohhhh, whatchu got there?" Simone leaned in for a closer look.

De'Andrea twisted the clasp to open the pillbox to reveal an assortment of gummy bears. "Here's how I've been getting by." She smiled.

SIXTEEN

Rebecca

Rebecca arrived at Trust Flow early to have a fifteen-minute one-on-one with Serena.

"Your energy's not good." Serena hovered her hands a few inches from Rebecca's shoulders, moving them up toward her head.

Ya think?

There was all the usual stuff with the girls' activities and homework; the never-ending house projects (she needed that damn pond finished); and taking care of Nana. Then there was the statue removal project, and Todd was up for a promotion and working more than ever. He had even missed Lyla and Isabella's soccer games two weekends in a row. Plus, Thanksgiving was around the corner, and then things would be nuts the rest of the year. On top of all that, the check engine light came on in the car on the way to yoga. All this was swirling around in her mind. So, no. Her energy was not good.

"Yeah, there's a lot going on."

"Girl, when do you *not* have a lot going on?" Serena said, walking around the studio lighting candles. Her cocoa-colored yoga jumpsuit had a faint snakeskin pattern and looked like it was custom-designed to match her natural red curls and hazel eyes.

With her sheer cover-up—identical to Rebecca's—she slithered around the room effortlessly. She blew out the flame on the matchstick and watched the smoke rise. Present in every single moment.

How the fuck does she do that?

"I know, I know," Rebecca said, rolling her extra-long royal blue mat out on the floor. "If I can get through these next couple months, I'll be able to slow down a bit."

"Rebecca Myland, you know that's a lie," Serena challenged. "You know what, though? I just learned about something that might help you."

Rebecca now had her legs spread wide in a dancer's stretch, forehead facing the floor, arms out straight with her fingertips reaching for the front of the room. She lifted her head. "What? I'm desperate for anything."

Serena took her phone out of a handwoven basket she kept in the front corner of the studio. "Here, check this out," she said, squatting down next to Rebecca.

Serena's screen displayed a futuristic-looking yoga mat, mostly black but textured with what appeared to be purple embroidery.

"What is this?" Rebecca asked.

"A home sauna mat. It sends electromagnetic pulses of infrared heat all along your body. And it's layered with amethyst crystals, which will be soooo relaxing for you."

"No way! That sounds amazing," Rebecca said, placing her thumb and index finger on Serena's phone to zoom in. "How do they do that?"

"You know, everyone in wellness—including me—used to be so resistant when it came to technology, but this is what it can do for us."

"So what do you *do*, though? Just lie there?" Rebecca asked.

"Yes, or you could do yoga on it. Think of how warm your muscles will be and how calm your mind will feel."

"You know what, you're right. Let me order it right now so I don't forget," Rebecca said, jumping up to get her phone from the cubbies in the lobby. "Do you have one for yourself?"

"No, I haven't had a chance to order yet—"

"Done!" Rebecca said, pleased. "I ordered two."

As she put her phone away, the bells on the entrance jingled as others began arriving for class, including Vic and Jenny. She greeted them both with air-kisses, which was slightly awkward with Jenny. The past few weeks they had been talking again, but it was all pretty surface-level—logistics about playdates, carpooling, committee stuff. But they hadn't yet talked about how Jenny had put their friendship on a break. Victoria insisted they be patient with their friend, that Jenny would come around. And all signs pointed to today being the day because Jenny had asked them if their "sip" after stretch could be coffee at the Rolling Bean instead of prosecco at Rebecca's. *That felt like a "heart-to-heart" type of plan*, Rebecca hoped.

The ladies slipped off their shoes and entered the studio together. Vic rolled out and positioned her mat next to Rebecca's. Jenny did the same on the other side of Rebecca, spraying and wiping her mat down with the lavender-scented cleaner.

The Tingsha bells chimed and Serena called everyone together. "Let's begin."

～

"Half-caf, oat milk, matcha!" the barista called out.

Vic picked up her drink from the counter and joined Rebecca and Jenny at their corner table. She cupped her right shoulder and winced as she tried to roll it forward and backward. "I tweaked something in class. I think I'm nearing the end of my shoulder-stand days."

Rebecca pulled a bottle of ibuprofen from her bag and handed it to Vic.

"Yesss, thank you," Vic said, popping three into her mouth and washing them down with her latte.

"You definitely didn't look like it hurt, Vic. Everything about you is goals," Jenny said.

"What are you thinking about, Bec? You've got kind of a goofy smile on your face."

"I am so, so happy that the three of us are back together doing this again," Rebecca blurted out. Whatever had happened between her and Jenny was now the centerpiece of their little three-top bistro table. "Oh no. Did I make it weird?"

Jenny set her cup down and drew in a deep breath. "It's alright. We can talk about this."

Rebecca and Vic waited for Jenny to keep going, but Jenny also waited.

Rebecca forced herself to speak. "So, I guess, well, I wasn't really ever sure why, exactly, you were upset with me, Jenny. I mean, I know it was messed up that I didn't read the book for book club. And I felt—no, *feel*—really, really bad about that. It was just that things had been so busy with the start of school and getting the committee going for the year and hosting the meeting. But I did start reading the book afterward! And I've been reading other stuff, too—like about the whole model minority thing. Look—" Rebecca reached for her phone to pull up one of the articles she'd read by an Asian American writer.

"Okay, okay," Jenny said, holding her hand up to stop Rebecca. "You're going off the rails. Slow down."

Jenny was right. Rebecca heard herself rambling. She wasn't supposed to force Jenny to talk, but she also wasn't supposed to talk too much . . . *ugh*.

"To be honest, I was surprised by how upset I got at book club. That's part of why I didn't say anything to either of you right away, because I needed to process."

Vic jumped in. "Yes! I said that—I knew you needed to process. I said to Rebecca—didn't I, Bec—'She needs time.'"

Rebecca nodded.

Jenny continued. "It wasn't *only* that you didn't read the book, Rebecca. I mean, I did find that *really* annoying, especially because you're the one who pushed for the book club. But let's be real. How many books have any of us been able to finish since having kids?"

"Oh my God, seriously," Rebecca said with relief. "Not to save my life."

"Right," Jenny said. "So part of what was going on with me is that even though it's hard to find time to finish most books, it wasn't hard to finish *that* book. Like everything in it to me was so eye-opening. But it was also really *emotional* for me. And embarrassing."

"Embarrassing? Why?" Victoria asked.

"Because why the hell didn't I already know all that stuff?"

"Well, you've said before your parents never talked about race."

"Yeah, but I've been a grown woman for a long time. I had plenty of chances to think about all of this on a deeper level. And, I can't explain it, but reading that book . . . well, it was like I was going through all the racist stuff I had to deal with as a kid all over again."

"Like what kind of stuff?"

"All the Asian jokes you can imagine. They're the same everywhere. And then in college there were all the dudes with weird yellow fever. Gross," Jenny said, shaking her head as if that would expel a bad memory.

Yellow fever?

I don't think she's talking about mosquitoes.

Don't ask her about it now.

Google it.

"But that's not really the point," Jenny continued.

"I'm sorry about all of that, Jenny," Rebecca said. "But I still don't know what I did to offend you. If I have ever said anything anti-Asian I am so, so—"

Jenny put her hand up again. "Rebecca, stop. You haven't said anything anti-Asian." Then she paused and appeared to reset. "Or, I don't know, maybe you have. You probably have. Hell, *I* probably have. Again, *not* the point. My point is, you are two of my closest friends, and I've never felt like I could talk about this stuff with you," Jenny said.

Rebecca jolted back and raised her eyebrows. "*Ouch.*"

"Okay, that right there," Jenny said, gesturing toward Rebecca.

"What right there?"

"You said 'ouch' like *you're* the one who is hurt. That's why I don't tell you about this stuff."

"But you didn't even give me a chance!" Rebecca said, raising her voice.

"And it's not only that. I'm also worried you'll make it about *you*, and then *I* will have to make *you* feel better," Jenny said.

"Look, you know how you don't like to tell people about Todd's mom because then they want to talk about their own mother or grandmother's battle with dementia? And it's not that you don't care that they've also had to deal with something similar, but you are kind of dealing with your own shit and don't have a lot of space for theirs. Or they start feeling sorry for you and then you have to spend a bunch of energy trying to assure them you're okay so that *they* feel better?"

"Yes, one hundred percent." Rebecca couldn't nod any harder. It was exhausting. Why had she never thought of it like that before?

"So, you haven't wanted to talk about race with us because you feel you have to make us feel better?" Victoria asked.

"Yeah. Like remember Stop Sign Becky? My first reaction was to worry about *you*, Rebecca, and how you're so sensitive about the name 'Becky.' And then our conversation became all about you and how Lyla might think you're racist and how much you wanted Black friends. Why didn't we talk about how messed up that white woman was or how shitty the whole thing must have been for that Black woman she yelled at?

"And the thing is, at the time, none of this felt problematic to me. I went along with the conversation. It wasn't until I read *Woke Yet?* that I realized I've been kind of brainwashed—or white-washed, I guess you could say. And I didn't think I could process any of this with either of you without having to spend a bunch of time making sure you didn't think I was calling you racists."

The three of them remained silent for a few seconds before Victoria reacted. "Damn," she said. "White women are the worst, amirite?"

Jenny chuckled.

Rebecca was still thinking when Victoria changed her tone and added, "Sorry, Jenny, I shouldn't be making jokes. I'm hearing you. And I'm sorry. I can work on this. We *are* kind of the worst."

Jenny smiled. "Vic, I would be worried if you hadn't made a joke. And, thank you."

Jenny and Victoria both looked at Rebecca, whose thoughts were racing. What Victoria was saying . . . *White women are the worst.* She had been trying so hard to *not* be included in a statement like that. *Other* white women were the worst, but not Rebecca. She wanted to be the exception, the one that Black women—well, any women of color, really—would talk about and say, "Oh, Rebecca? She's one of the good ones." But maybe she was, in fact, the worst. Like all the other Beckys and Karens and whatever other Boomer names would take hold. She wasn't as bad as the white women who called the cops on Black people, though. Right? And she had stopped asking to speak to store managers years ago. Couldn't white women be on a racist spectrum?

Her face must have shown she was spiraling because Victoria snapped her fingers. "Rebecca! Stop spinning out!"

And Rebecca knew she owed Jenny a response. She didn't want to overexplain herself and then say the wrong thing. Was there a right thing to say? Maybe asking a question would be better.

"And all this is why you didn't want to talk to me after book club?"

"Well, it was that plus this vibe I've gotten from you for a few years now that you only care about racism when it happens to Black people. And then when you didn't read the book . . . that was the straw. I felt like you didn't really care."

"Jenny," Rebecca said, feeling her face heat up. *Don't make it about me.* She closed her eyes and took a deep breath. When she'd maintained her composure, she said, "I am really, really sorry I made you feel that way. I *do* care." She placed her hand on Jenny's arm. "You know that, right?"

"I do," Jenny said. "And here's the deal. You're right that I wasn't giving you a chance. I mean, the first few days after book club, I was upset, but then Chloe was asking about Lyla and Cassie and an iPhoto memory popped up on my phone of the three of us at that yoga retreat last year and I realized I was missing you two."

"We missed you too!" Victoria and Rebecca sang out in sappy unison, loud enough that people at other tables looked over, which made the three friends giggle.

Rebecca was grateful for the levity but was also still thinking about Jenny saying she only cared about racism when it happened to Black people. She realized it was true. She felt awful.

Once their laughter subsided, Jenny said, "You know, I'm also realizing that every time I've made a joke in front of you two about being Asian, I was doing it because I felt uncomfortable with it in some way. Did I ever tell either of you that my parents tried to send me to one of those Korean culture summer camps when I was a kid?"

Both Rebecca and Victoria shook their heads no.

"Do you know what I told them?" Jenny winced at the memory. "I told them, 'Why would I want to hang out with a bunch of Koreans? I'm white.'"

Rebecca cringed. Victoria probably did, too, but Rebecca didn't want to turn her head to look.

"Messed up, right?"

Victoria took a deep breath and leaned back in her chair. "Whew! That's a lot."

"But not too much!" Rebecca was quick to add. "We can handle it!"

Jenny smiled. "I know."

"Well," Victoria said, rolling her shoulder again, "my pain is gone. That's a plus."

The three of them talked a little while longer. Vic showed them before-and-after photos of the "no more sad face" filler she got, they caught up on some school gossip, and they returned to the debate over when they would let Cassie, Chloe, and Lyla get their own phones, which the kids were begging for, full-court-press style.

"I think it's a bad idea," Jenny said. "They're too young."

"I agree! Todd is trying to talk me into it, but we have to stay strong!" said Rebecca. "Plus, what if once they get phones they never talk to us again? I like being the only one in the house addicted to a smartphone."

"I don't know," Victoria said. "Think of how convenient it would be. I would love to be able to stay in my car and text Cassie to come outside from wherever I'm picking her up from. Less small talk with other parents."

"Oh, speaking of other parents . . . this reminds me," Rebecca said. "Harita and I printed out a ton more statue flyers. I have a stack to put in all the Chance Ave stores."

At the mention of Harita, Jenny and Victoria both cocked their heads, looked at each other, then back at Rebecca. She knew what cognitive dissonance looked like on these two.

"I know, it's weird how we're working together on this thing. She's still driving me crazy, but it helps to have a common enemy. Thank you, James Longstreet." Rebecca saluted. "Anyway, do you both have time to do this with me now?"

The ladies agreed to join Rebecca, and the three friends chatted and laughed while placing Justice in Parks flyers all up and down Chance Ave. Now even more people could get behind the statue coming down, and Jenny was back. Rebecca's energy was suddenly feeling much better, but she wanted to make sure Jenny felt the same.

She stopped walking and put her hand on Jenny's arm to get her attention. "Hey, so we're good?"

Jenny smiled. "We've been good, Rebecca. We'll always be good." She shrugged and sighed. "I just needed some time to figure out what I was feeling and what I wanted to say."

"Well, I *am* sorry," Rebecca repeated. "And, like Vic said, I can work on this. I *will* work on this."

Jenny squeezed her hand and motioned for them to keep walking. "Oh, I forgot to tell you. I heard from Gabe's sister that her oldest, Chloe's cousin, who is only six months older than Chloe, got her period last weekend. She's not even eleven yet!"

Rebecca wasn't ready for that, either, but she was relieved for the conversation returning to the types of topics they usually covered. She realized race, and how it affected Jenny, would and should be part of their friendship, but they'd taken a big step today and it would take time for it to become comfortable.

I guess this is me getting comfortable being uncomfortable, Rebecca thought. And she recognized the irony.

SEVENTEEN

De'Andrea

Traveling to Atlanta for their annual Malik's-Birthday-Friendsgiving had seemed like a good idea but in retrospect, De'Andrea should have known that it would be a disaster. From forgetting to pack Malik's gift to Nina throwing a tantrum and screaming, "I don't want to go back to Rolling Hills! I want to stay here with my friends!" when it was time to leave, the entire trip had been stressful. And now, somehow she was supposed to get into the holiday spirit and start decorating for Christmas?

Nah. Bah humbug for real.

Because preparing to spend their first Christmas in Rolling Hills was also a sobering reminder that New Year's Eve was right around the corner. And De'Andrea couldn't believe she was about to ring in yet another new year without a "new you" plan. Not that she hadn't put in the work there, either. But just like she kept trying (and failing) to get into the Christmas spirit, De'Andrea wondered if she'd ever get out of struggle mode and figure herself out.

Shortly after Mama's move to the West End, De'Andrea had taken on a home design project to distract herself. Now the smallest of their spare bedrooms was akin to her personal vision board, and as she entered the room, just as she did most Sunday mornings, there was plenty of evidence of her efforts.

De'Andrea bent down to pick up a large pink sticky note and tucked it back into the cluster of inspirational quotes on the wall. Several self-help books lay scattered on the daybed, which had also become her "Read and Nap" spot. In the far corner, a white-board displayed a colorful unfinished mind-mapping diagram. Determined, she walked over and picked up a green dry-erase marker.

"You hold the keys to unlock the door to the life you want and deserve." De'Andrea quoted the mantra from her latest self-transformation read.

The first step of the process required her to write down every-thing she loved doing *and* excelled at. Seeing the lengthy list had been very empowering. Until she moved on to the next step, which required her to pick her top three. The mental gymnastics of trying to whittle down her essence had worn her out—so much so that De'Andrea still hadn't completed the task.

"You good in here?" Malik opened the door wide enough to poke his head inside.

"You know you can come in here, right?" She curled her pointer finger at him, motioning him to enter.

"Just trying to respect your creative process." Malik stepped into the room and looked around.

De'Andrea opened her arms and gestured around the room in a sweeping motion. "Welcome. This is where your wife spends all her free time trying to figure out her life."

"And how's it coming along?" Malik asked. "Anything I can do to help?"

De'Andrea shook her head. "Nah. But I appreciate the support.

I know you want me to figure my life out just as much as I do. So I can stop being such a bi—"

"Dee, don't say that." He walked over to the whiteboard and pulled her into his arms. "Honestly, I just want you to be happy."

She rested her head against his chest. They hadn't had an argument since they'd returned from Atlanta. It had been over a week, which she was certain was a new personal record. And she wanted to keep the streak going.

"What am I going to do, Leek?" she asked. "I miss practicing but don't want the hassle of BigLaw life or billable hours. I'd love to do advocacy work, but there aren't any legal aid clinics around here. And I want to help the less fortunate, but there isn't anyone in this town who's in need of anything.

"What do I miss? What do I love? What do I want to do?" De'Andrea continued thinking aloud as she stared at the mind-mapping prompts on the whiteboard and twirled the green marker between her fingers.

"I miss practicing."

"I love advocacy work."

"I want to help the less fortunate."

Waitaminute!

She wriggled out of Malik's arms and drew green circles around the words "practicing law," "being an advocate," and "helping the less fortunate."

De'Andrea ran over to the daybed and flipped the page of her workbook to read the next step. "Okay. Got it. Got it."

"What, Dee? What have you got?" Malik asked anxiously.

She shushed him as she returned to the whiteboard and looked at the phrases with green circles drawn around them.

These are keys to unlock the "what do I want to do" door.

Suddenly, it all made sense!

This was what that genius man must have felt like in *A Beautiful Mind*!

She put down the green marker and picked up an orange one to write out her personal vision and mission statement. When she was finished, De'Andrea stepped back to read what she'd written like MadLibs.

"I would like to use my legal expertise to do advocacy work that benefits the less fortunate. I live in an abundant community which means there are populations outside of my community that are in need. I understand that I cannot help everyone and so, I will focus on one cause that is closest to my heart: Alzheimer's care. In the new year, I will start a nonprofit organization that allows me to not only do fulfilling work but that also allows me to feel fulfilled."

"Babe." Malik looked at the whiteboard, then at De'Andrea, and then back at the whiteboard. "I don't know what just happened or how it happened, but that was unbelievable. Maybe I need to read this book—"

"Leek!" she interrupted him. "I'm going to form a nonprofit that will help make the type of holistic dementia care Mama receives available to the less fortunate. Imagine every state having its own Memory Village. Dementia care communities that don't cost an arm and a leg because they're funded through grants and donations and whatnot. Isn't this so exciting? Oh my gosh, I need to tell the girls!" She picked up her phone to text Toni and Simone.

"It's amazing, Dee. And seriously, it's the perfect role for you. And there's such a need for affordable health care in general. I never even thought about drilling down to focus on dementia care though. Oh shi—shiitake . . ."

"What?" she demanded. "Whaaaaaaat?"

"Sorry sorry, I just had a thought—"

"I know. And I'm waiting for you to share it. C'mon!" De'Andrea gestured for him to get on with it.

"Calhoun!" Malik said excitedly. "We've been expanding his philanthropic portfolio beyond tech. Finding meaningful projects and innovative partners focused on some of this country's most critical needs—"

God, he sounds just like he's reading from one of his damn PowerPoints.

"Like healthcare." De'Andrea finished his sentence.

"*And* that help the most vulnerable communities."

"Like Black and brown folks," she chimed in. "And the elderly!"

"Right! Dee, I bet Calhoun would love this. Of course, I'll have to tell him you're my wife and recuse myself from the selection committee. But you'd be a top contender even if I didn't work for Calhoun."

"Really?" She felt her cheeks warm. "You think so?"

"Are you kidding me? It's genius! It's the perfect way to—"

"That's what I'm going to call the nonprofit." De'Andrea interrupted him and picked up her trusty green marker.

"What?" Malik asked.

De'Andrea smiled as she wrote the words on the whiteboard. "The Whitman Way."

⌒

The doors to Trust Flow Yoga closed behind De'Andrea as she stepped into the brisk December morning. Despite her initial reluctance, she was glad she'd attended Stretch Away the Holiday

Stress with Becky. She felt invigorated, and even more importantly, inspired.

Thanks to Toni calling in a favor to a former colleague who specialized in all things copyright, patents, and trademarks, De'Andrea had already secured her nonprofit's name. And Simone had surprised her with a beautiful rendering of the Whitman Way logo. During the closing meditation, De'Andrea's mind started racing with ideas and she couldn't wait to get home to update her marketing and financial plans.

"I don't know when I became such a wimp, but I swear, anything below fifty degrees now feels like it's freezing." Becky grabbed the zipper of her puffer coat and pulled it up to the top.

Wearing black-on-black attire save for their tan Uggs, the two women appeared as if they'd coordinated their outfits. And she bet Becky was secretly thrilled they were matching. De'Andrea shivered as she tugged at her zipper as well. "Whew, the hawk is out!"

"There's a hawk? Where?" Becky looked around anxiously. "I don't see it."

"Oh, you missed it."

Oh, Becky! Bless your heart! De'Andrea chuckled to herself. *You have no idea what "the hawk is out" means.*

"So, what did you think of class? Do you feel less stressed? I do. Well, I did. I mean, I think the stress is all flooding back now that we're outside and I see all these people shopping. I saw this article in *Slow Life Magazine* this week—have you heard of it? They have so many good tips. I found them on social. Anyway, they said the best way to get through the holidays without so much stress is to dial back the shopping. Do you and Malik and Nina get each other a lot of gifts? I can't believe how much my kids get. Anyway—class! I was asking you about the class. What'd you think?"

Damn.

De'Andrea felt stressed just listening to Becky. *Let me help her out here and take a breath and slow this all down.*

"So yeah, holiday shopping can be stressful, which is why I don't do a lot of it. And yeah, class was great." She adjusted the straps on her yoga mat bag and slung it over her shoulder. "I'd definitely come to another one."

"And there's always Stretch and Sip at myyyyyyy hooooouse," Becky sang out to her. "You won't regreeeeet iiiiiiiiiiiit!"

De'Andrea laughed. "Maybe I'll drop by one day. In the new year."

"Yes!"

Becky shimmied her shoulders and De'Andrea wasn't sure if she was doing a happy dance or shivering from the cold.

Chance Ave had officially transformed from shopping plaza to a holiday hub. A literal winter wonderland with twinkling lights strung on lampposts, snowflakes randomly shot into the air from a machine that also provided snow for Santa's Rolling Hills Workshop. A real reindeer stood in a gated enclosure waiting for children to pet him or treat him to handfuls of moss.

Becky pointed to a red and white mailbox with a wooden sign labeled "Letters for Santa" with the "s" in Letters purposefully written backward. "Remember, Nina has to drop off her letter by December twentieth. And then, the next day? *Whoa*, let me tell you. Get down here early because that's when the elves arrive."

Say what now?

"Real elves?" De'Andrea asked. "Like, elves elves?"

"Well, I mean, they're hired actors, of course. But yes, real elves. With the pointy-tipped ears and everything," Becky said excitedly. "The kids all gather around to watch the elves put their letters into a big red sack for Santa. It's the cutest thing!"

Hired actor elves. Wow. Just . . . wow.

"It sounds . . . adorable. I know Nina is going to lose her mind." De'Andrea made a mental note to put Malik on elf duty. Hell, she might lose *her* mind if that reindeer somehow got out. She eyed its holding pen suspiciously.

"Oh, Isabella goes bonkers." Becky laughed. "All the older kids know it's a rite of passage and to not ruin the fun. So sometimes they participate, too. It's a Rolling Hills Christmas tradition. You're gonna love it!"

Thank God they'd agreed to wait another year to tell Nina that Santa wasn't real. With the move and Mama's health challenges, it seemed unnecessary to burst her bubble with a lesson on man-made holidays and capitalism.

Suddenly, Becky's phone buzzed. "Jesus, Todd! I've barely been gone an hour." She lifted her phone to her face to unlock her messages. "I swear, our babysitter is lower maintenance than this man when he has our kids."

She read the message quickly and when she looked up, her cheeks flushed with embarrassment. "Well, now I feel bad," she said sheepishly as she held out her phone so De'Andrea could see what was on the screen.

"I mean, the girls are adorable." She laughed as she swiped through the photos Todd sent. "What we can see of them any-way!"

Becky groaned. "Dear God. I need to send him to Instagram Husband Training School."

The women continued to lovingly assess the images, giggling

at blurry photos of their girls with parts of their bodies cropped out of the frames. Becky hearted a few good ones to mark them as favorites. But it was the last photo of the bunch that they agreed was the best.

Whatever Todd used to prop up his phone obscured the bottom of the photo in a reddish blob. He was smiling at the camera, the top of his blond hair cropped out of the frame. Malik was looking away from the lens, his mouth open and his gaze confused as if he were asking Todd a question. And it appeared that Isabella and Nina were about to hold hands, but the timer went off and captured them mid–love fest.

"I mean, it's adorably awful." De'Andrea was near winded from laughing as Becky pointed out each perfect imperfection. "Definitely more adorable than awful, though."

"Oh my God, it's so packed." Becky peeked through the Rolling Bean's front window and waved at the purple-haired barista behind the counter. She smiled and returned the gesture while steaming a cup of milk. "We'll never find a seat in there. Wanna just get our coffees to go and walk around for a bit? The dads seem to have everything under control. Basically."

Uh, no thanks. How much more time do I really need to be spending with Becky?

That was her first thought. But then she questioned herself. She'd gotten so used to saying "no" and trying to keep Becky at a distance but she wasn't having a horrible time. And Nina and Malik seemed happy. Was she making a white friend?

Dammit, Dr. Jones!

"Sure, let's walk," she replied.

Soon, the women were back outside in the cold, warming their hands around their Rolling Bean to-go cups. De'Andrea followed Becky down a well-worn path in the grass.

"This isn't a *real* walking trail," Becky explained as she expertly navigated a small incline. "It's just that so many people walk this way to get a peek at the expansion—well, I guess we've kinda forged our own trail. Get it?"

God, Becky had a way of being hilariously endearing.

"Oh, I get it." De'Andrea smiled. "And what expansion? Are they adding more shops?"

"They're adding more of *everything*!" Becky squealed like Rolling Hills was about to get its first Premium Outlet. "C'mon, I'll show you!"

Still populated with trees and wild shrubbery, the off-the-beaten path was tricky to navigate. De'Andrea unzipped her puffer coat a little as her body heated up from their brisk walk.

"So . . . how are things with Malik's mom?" Becky asked.

De'Andrea noted the compassion in her voice. It was a gentle inquiry, one that she could lean into fully if she needed to unload. Or briefly if she wasn't feeling up to going in depth.

"Mama is doing . . . alright," she answered, choosing the latter. "Thanks for asking."

"Of course."

"And how about Todd's mom?" De'Andrea felt a pang of guilt upon realizing she rarely, if ever, asked Becky how her mother-in-law was doing.

"With Nana, I've just learned to take it day by day, moment by moment." Becky sighed.

"I get it. I mean, it's tough but . . . well, you know that already."

"Yeah," Becky agreed quietly. "Boy, do I know."

They walked in silence for a bit, honoring their shared journeys of having mothers-in-law with dementia. There wasn't anything that really *needed* to be said. It was simply enough knowing that someone else understood.

"Gosh, there's been so much progress since the last time I dropped by." Becky surveyed the open lot where dozens of brick-and-mortar spaces were still under construction. "I can't wait until it's finished. It's going to be amazing. I mean, we've complained about wanting more retailers since *forever*—"

De'Andrea half listened as Becky shared the history of how the long-waited mixed-use expansion came to be. Then, something caught her attention. Something she hadn't even considered until that moment. And she began walking across the dirt road to get a closer look.

Several handwritten dimensions had yet to be cleaned off the recently installed front bay window, so De'Andrea didn't feel too guilty for adding her handprints to the glass as she peered inside from different angles.

The stunning double-glass doors with bronze handles. The sunlit waiting room with a small adjoining room that would be perfect for a kids' reading nook. The two separate rooms on either side of a hallway leading to what appeared to be a larger unfinished space in the back—the perfect size for a dedicated one-person office and, perhaps, another for a colleague once she grew the nonprofit into a fully-staffed organization.

God, it's perfect!

"And over there, in phase three?" Becky pointed to another area under construction a short distance away. "There's going to be the cutest little coffee shop called the Brew Bar. Isn't that such an adorable name? And clearly we need another one since the Rolling Bean has become so popular."

And there'll be a coffee shop right around the corner?

"Hello, hello? Earth to De'Andrea," Becky teased.

De'Andrea snapped out of daydreaming about the Whitman Way logo centered in the front window. "Sorry, I—"

"All good!" Becky said excitedly. "I was the same way the first time I came over here. Just the idea of more stores and places to hang out. I mean, like I said, it's long overdue. Chance Ave has been around since Todd was a kid!"

As recommended in her self-transformation workbook, De'Andrea took a deep breath and dug deep for some courage. "I'm actually looking at this office space because . . ." *Breathe.* "I'm starting a nonprofit."

There. You've said it. The more she shared her dream, the more people would ask her about it and hold her accountable.

"A nonprofit?" Becky questioned. "That's *amazing*! I mean, what's it about? Can you tell me more? I mean, only if you want to, of course."

"Sure." De'Andrea cleared her throat. "I mean, it's still in the early stages of development. But I have a name. And a logo. And most importantly, a mission, a vision."

Becky grinned at her, eager to hear more.

"So, it's called the Whitman Way," De'Andrea continued. "And its mission is to provide affordable holistic dementia care for anyone in need. I'm still working on the services and program offerings. But I guess my wish list would be for every state to have its own version of Memory Village, you know? Because not everyone is as fortunate as we are. Just because the average family can't afford to spend six figures a year on dementia care for their loved ones doesn't mean their loved ones are any less deserving of quality care."

Becky just stared at her.

"I mean, this is my first time telling someone other than Malik and my girlfriends," De'Andrea explained. "I'm definitely going to fine-tune it—"

"No, no, it's great! I mean, it sounds great. And you're great . . ." Becky's voice trailed off as her eyes welled with tears. "Sorry, it just made me so emotional."

"Really?" De'Andrea smiled.

"*Really.*" Becky wiped her eyes. "You're so right. This is so needed. And I love the name. I love it all!"

Becky cupped her hands around her temples and peered through the glass. "Gosh, it's much more spacious than it appears from outside. You definitely need to manifest this as your office space."

"Isn't it perfect?" De'Andrea gushed. "I love that it's off in the cut too."

"In . . . *the cut*? Not sure I understand—"

"Oh, it just means off the beaten path," De'Andrea explained. "Like, there's no reason for anyone to walk all the way down here unless they are looking for me."

"Well, how about *you* look at *this.*" Becky smiled as she pointed to the sign in the bottom corner of the window. The words "Commercial Property Available for Rent" were stamped in bold blue font. Below it, the property management's contact info was listed. "Take a picture of it," she urged. "Call them when you get home!"

De'Andrea opened the camera on her phone and snapped a

picture of the sign. Then she took several other pictures of the space and construction site.

"Okay, now give me your phone and go stand in front of the window," Becky instructed.

De'Andrea started to object, but then had a change of heart. She dug inside her tote to retrieve her power-red lipstick. After swiping it on her lips, she posed. Becky angled the camera to get the perfect frame, held up her hand, and began counting down. "Three, two, one. Say cheeeeeese!"

EIGHTEEN

Rebecca

Rebecca sat with Lyla at the kitchen table trying to help with math homework, though *she* knew, and Lyla knew, that she wasn't being all that helpful.

"What are 'place value disks'?'" Rebecca groaned. "And what do they mean by algorithm division? What happened to long division?" She wasn't good at math when she was in the fifth grade, and she definitely wasn't good at fifth-grade math now.

"Geez, Mom. Calm down. You're more stressed than me."

"Want me to help you?" Isabella asked in earnest. She was kneeling on the floor of the family room, coloring a page full of rainbows on the coffee table with one of the three different art sets she'd gotten for Christmas.

"Uh, thanks, but that's okay." Lyla and Rebecca locked eyes and smiled. "I'll ask Dad when he gets home." Lyla moved on to the next problem and started drawing a bunch of circles on her worksheet in various boxes. Rebecca had no idea what the hell any of it meant. She was having flashbacks of her fifth-grade teacher Mrs. Barnes making her miss recess to work on word problems.

"I'll check on dinner, then," Rebecca said.

She had a sheet pan meal baking in the oven with chicken thighs, onions, and broccolini seasoned with all sorts of spices she had never used before. It smelled delicious. De'Andrea had shared the recipe with her when Rebecca had been whining about running out of dinner ideas. The oven timer showed twenty-two more minutes. Enough time for a glass of wine. *Or two.*

She pulled a bottle of cabernet from the wine cabinet. While opening it, she heard her phone buzz on the kitchen counter. And then it buzzed again. And again. And again.

"Mommy! You need to check your messages!" Isabella brought the phone over to Rebecca. Thirty-two unread messages. All from the diversity committee group chat. And more messages kept coming in. She scrolled to the first new message.

Today, 4:42 PM
Amy
Ummm . . . did you all see what is happening on the Rolling Hills listserv right now?

Victoria
No, what?

Today, 4:44 PM
Megan
WTF, I just opened it up.

Jenny S.
What is happening?

Victoria
These people are nuts.

Megan
We have to do something, right?

Today, 4:47 PM

Jenny Q.

I'm not seeing any emails. What's going on?

Harita

Driving! Can someone send a voice note?

Today, 4:48 PM

Megan

\<Sends link\> "Council Chair Strummond Calls Town Hall to Review Petitions Regarding General Longstreet Statue"

Rebecca couldn't keep up with the flurry of messages coming in all at once like popcorn. Between the text thread, the link Megan sent, Amy's voice note, and the neighborhood listserv, she was piecing together what was happening:

Some group that Rebecca had never heard of, called Supporters United for the Confederate Society, had filed a counterpetition to *block* the removal of the statue on the grounds that it might be a historical landmark.

Bullshit, Rebecca thought. And everyone knew that. Rolling Hills wasn't even founded until the 1960s.

As far as Rebecca could gather from the listserv emails, this pro-statue group had gotten the ear—and maybe the pocketbook?—of someone on the council, and now they were putting the brakes on the whole statue removal process.

Council Chair Harry Strummond.

Rebecca never quite trusted him; she'd seen his lawn signs during the last presidential election.

Council bylaws called for a public town hall whenever there

were petitions and counterpetitions. Rebecca stopped reading as soon as she realized why the text thread and listserv were blowing up.

She typed into her phone:

Today, 4:56 PM

Rebecca
WTF?! They've called an emergency town hall for TONIGHT?!

Amy
That's what I'm trying to tell you all!

The nerve! They were clearly scheduling this at the last minute so it would all slip under the radar. *And less than a week after Martin Luther King Day!*

Rebecca
I'm showing up tonight. As soon as Todd gets home. Let me know who's in.

She texted Todd:

Rebecca
Hi, honey. Last-minute mtg I need to attend. School thing. Please don't be late. Also: Lyla needs help with math homework.

She wasn't about to give him any more details. He might try to talk her out of going. She poured herself the glass of wine and kept texting while she waited for Todd to get home.

"What in the—" Rebecca approached the Rolling Hills Community Center. She had never seen so many cars in the parking lot. That didn't even happen during the rec league championship basketball game, let alone a town hall meeting. An older man wearing an orange vest over a dark gray puffer coat was standing next to the community center marquee that read: "Rolling Hills: Where All Are Welcome!"

Rebecca lowered her window and felt an icy chill on her face. "Is this all for the town hall?"

"Yes, ma'am," said the older gentleman. "You're going to need to follow these cars here back out of this lot and then take a right and another right where you'll see a sign for the overflow lot."

"This is wild!" Rebecca said.

"Yes, ma'am. I was only here tonight to lock up after the meeting ended. But so many people showed up, they have me out here directing traffic."

"Well, be careful out here," Rebecca muttered before driving ahead to take a photo of all the backed-up cars.

She followed the directions to the overflow lot and parked. Before getting out of the car, she checked the diversity committee group chat to see if anyone had responded about joining her. Everyone except De'Andrea and Harita had written back saying they couldn't swing it on such short notice. De'Andrea didn't reply at all, and Harita said she'd be there. Victoria sent everyone a link to the website where the meeting could be live-streamed. Others chimed in that they'd try and watch.

Rebecca texted the photo to the group along with: "Check this out! Overflow parking!" She then texted Harita that she'd arrived.

Since the start of the new year, Rebecca had noticed there was much less snark between the two of them. They still butted heads over logistics, but it wasn't so loaded every time—they were simply disagreeing over one specific decision, rather than years of accumulated resentment and power struggles.

So while the school mom drama was improving, the same could not be said for what was happening outside the community center entrance. As Rebecca approached, she couldn't believe what she was seeing. It was bustling like a county fair. On either side of the walkway tables were set up. One side had SUCS signage— *who called themselves the SUCS?*—the other, JIP's.

Did no one think about the acronyms when naming these groups?

Each side had at least half a dozen people—some with clipboards, others distributing brochures. The ones with clipboards were cajoling people to sign petitions and add their names to email lists. How did they get organized so quickly for a supposedly emergency town hall?

She didn't recognize any of them as Rolling Hillsians. She went to the JIP side of the path and took a brochure.

A young woman sitting at the table looked up and asked Rebecca, "Would you like to sign up for our listserv to get more information about Justice in Parks?"

"Hi, no, I wanted to introduce myself. I'm Rebecca Myland. I run the parent diversity committee at Magnolia Country Day. We've been helping get the word out about the statue removal."

"Yes, Rebecca! I'm the Facebook group moderator. I'm Rainee. I work for JIP's Mid-Atlantic chapter. It's great to meet you in person."

"Oh, I didn't realize you all worked anywhere outside of

Virginia," Rebecca said, realizing how little she knew about this group. She'd been so quick to download all their action plans, send out emails, and print out flyers.

Shit. Why didn't I do any research? Are these people even legit?

"Oh, yes, we are all over the place. A small but mighty crew. We identify unknown monuments in parks and other public lands that have Confederate or colonizer ties. Then we organize with local communities to get them taken down. In Virginia, we have several TFTs—"

Rebecca raised her eyebrows. "TFTs?"

"Targets-for-takedown—that's what we call the monuments. This is our first TFT this far north."

"Well, you've certainly stirred something up," Rebecca said.

Was it weird that they weren't from the area? She had assumed this had been something cooked up by locals. But did it matter if it was the right thing to do?

"That you got involved and didn't even really know about us tells me our tactics are working. We start with identifying the target. Then we plant a few seeds; usually the locals take it from there."

"But does this kind of thing usually happen?" Rebecca asked, gesturing toward the SUCS group.

"In a way, yes. What I mean is, there's always opposition to the monuments coming down. What's unknown is whether that opposition will happen organically among the locals or if SUCS ends up coming in to mobilize folks."

"So they're not from Virginia, either?" Rebecca asked.

"Well, some of them might be. But their headquarters is in Wisconsin," Rainee explained.

"What?!" *Wisconsin?* Rebecca wasn't a US history expert or anything, but . . . Wisconsin?

"Ridiculous, right? Who knew Wisconsin was the seat of the Confederacy?" Rainee shook her head at the stupidity. "Anyway, they have a huge network and a tip line. They track street and building name changes and monument removals all over the country so they can put a stop to all of it. You know, to *preserve* history." Rainee rolled her eyes and then looked over at the SUCS table with disgust.

What is wrong with these people? They have nothing better to do? And who pays for all of this?

Rainee continued. "This Longstreet statue wasn't turning out to be very controversial, so SUCS started a Facebook group— Long Live Longstreet—and stirred the pot among folks here."

"So you're saying that actual Rolling Hills residents have no problem with the statue removal, and this whole thing tonight is because of this SUCS group?"

"Not exactly. Now that SUCS has gotten involved, we are seeing plenty of locals getting fired up. People who never paid any attention to that statue are suddenly outraged about it coming down. I've seen this happen over and over again."

Todd's and Jack's comments over the past few months popped into Rebecca's head. They weren't necessarily *outraged*, but they had both made the "we've got to preserve history" arguments even though they'd never even heard of Longstreet or his statue before Rebecca told them about it. Todd and Jack weren't extreme like all these SUCS people on the other side of the sidewalk, but they weren't on her side, either. She felt a little nauseated.

"I guess I better head inside, then. Will I be seeing you again or are you moving on from Rolling Hills after tonight?"

"Oh, I'll be around! We'll continue organizing on the ground here until we can help build up enough pressure to get the landmark status proposal dropped. That's got no legs. Nothing more than a classic SUCS stall tactic to buy some time while they rile the locals up."

"Wow," Rebecca said, feeling overwhelmed by the scale of all of it. "I suppose I'll see you around, then. I'm looking forward to continuing to help. Thanks for all the info."

Rebecca slid the JIP brochure into her handbag and continued walking toward the community center, falling into a single file line as the entrance got more congested.

Still processing everything Rainee had told her, Rebecca heard someone call out from behind her, "Good evening to you, Mrs. Myland!"

Rebecca turned around. "Stu! Hi!" She let two people pass ahead of her in line so that she could stand next to him. "This is nuts, isn't it?!"

"Sure is," agreed Stu.

"Tell me, you've lived here a long time. Did you know about General Longstreet before all of this?"

"No, ma'am," Stu answered. "But I'll be damned if I let some outsider elites come into our community and tell us what statues we can and can't have." Stu held up a SUCS brochure.

No, not you, Stu! You're such a good guy!

How could he possibly want to keep a Confederate monument?

And doesn't he have Black and brown men working for him?

Surely if he could understand what was going on, he'd side with Rebecca. She didn't want to make him feel bad, but she had to explain.

"Stu," she began. "I need to talk to you about this conversation I just had—"

"Oh, I saw you talking to those JIP-ers over there. I don't need to hear any more about that," he said, literally waving the thought of them off. "The guy *I* was talking to told me all about them. But you don't *agree* with them, do you, Mrs. Myland? They're not even from around here!"

"Oh, but Stu, neither are—" Rebecca could feel her face flushing as she tried to figure out how much she wanted to get into this with her landscaper.

"Rebecca!" Another shout from behind. She turned around to see Harita on her tiptoes in the doorway, waving. People filed in and around, so Rebecca could only see Harita's cashmere-gloved hand stretched high. Rebecca rubbed her hands together to warm them, wishing she'd brought gloves.

"Excuse me, Stu," Rebecca said. "That's my friend I'm meeting here. I'm going to go back there and join her."

"Sure thing, Mrs. Myland," he said, his cheerful demeanor restored.

Rebecca let a few more people pass ahead of her.

"What in the actual fuck?!" Harita said once they linked up.

"I know, right? Did you talk to any of the groups over there?"

"No." Harita held the JIP brochure up in front of her. "But I knew I wanted a brochure from the group that had young people with tattoos and face piercings over those old white dudes."

Rebecca lowered her voice, nervous about who was in front of her and who was behind her and what side they were on. "Let me fill you in."

＿＿＿＿＿＿＿＿＿＿

"Holy shit!" Harita and Rebecca exclaimed at the exact same time once they finally made it inside the council meeting. Standing room only.

They clutched their handbags, shifting them to the front of their bodies as they pushed their way into a spot among the crowd where they could both see.

"Have you ever been to one of these things before?" Harita asked. "Is it always this crowded?"

"Only once. Years ago when there was that petition to add a second speed bump on Chance Ave. There were maybe five people here. And it was boring as hell. Felt like the longest night of my life."

"Well, this most definitely isn't going to be boring," Harita said.

Rebecca figured the crowd must have been close to two hundred. She and Harita tried to point people out as soon as they recognized someone, but it was hard to make out who everyone was by the back of their heads. She did see some Cardinal parents scattered around the room.

"Mrs. Myland!" That was Stu again. He'd snagged one of the last seats in the last row and was shouting over all the chatter, which was nearing a live-concert-volume-level. "Would you like my seat?"

Ugh, don't be so nice! You're on the wrong side of this.

"That's kind of you to offer, but no thanks. I'm all set right here," Rebecca yelled back.

"Suit yourself!" He shrugged and turned back around to face the front of the room.

Up on the dais, the council members had all taken their seats and were compulsively shuffling through stacks of papers set in front of them. Council Chair Harry Strummond looked up from whatever he was reading, took off his spectacles, and picked up the gavel.

"Call to order! Call to order!" He hammered at least five times before the room quieted down. The other four council members looked out toward the crowd.

"They look just as surprised to see all these people as we do," Rebecca said to Harita.

"It's mighty white up there," Harita said.

Geesh. She's right. Why haven't I ever noticed that?

"Maybe I'll run in the next election," Harita added.

Both ladies laughed at the thought. Who would ever want to deal with all this?

The meeting started off as boring as Rebecca had remembered. Someone read the minutes from the previous meeting. Motions were made, seconded, and votes were taken. Then they got to the reason this room was as packed as a Friday night Marvel movie premiere.

"As you all appear to be aware, a petition has been filed to remove the General James Longstreet statue from Rolling Hills Park as part of an ongoing nationwide movement to eliminate Confederate monuments." Council Chair Strummond paused to flip the page he was reading from. "The council was scheduled to vote on that petition next month, but now a counterpetition has been filed to initiate the review process for determining whether the statue qualifies as an historical landmark. If it receives that designation, it cannot, of course, be taken down. The council has called this emergency town hall in order to hear from constituents as we prepare to vote on the historical classification measure."

Now the crowd was perking back up. People were shifting around, whispering to whoever was sitting or standing next to them. Opposite the dais was a small folding table with a microphone and stand and one chair.

"Thank you to all who registered to speak tonight. We have

a list here of all your names. When we call you up, you will take a seat at this table right here and you will have two minutes to deliver your remarks for the public record," Council Chair Strummond explained.

Harita, still staring toward the dais, nudged Rebecca with her elbow and whispered, "We could register to speak? How were we supposed to know?"

Rebecca shook her head, equally confused. "That's what I'm wondering."

"We now invite Chuck Anderson to deliver his remarks," Council Secretary Thurston announced.

Rebecca was pretty sure she'd never seen him before. His pinkish head was covered by only a thin layer of neatly trimmed silver hair. He was of average height, with a slight crooked gait, which gave Rebecca the sense that he might be in his seventies. Plus, his khaki pants were held up pretty high on his waist by a thin brown leather belt, a look she most often saw sported by her dad and his poker buddies.

"Good evening, council members," Chuck began, adjusting his glasses. He unfolded a sheet of paper and read directly from it, not once looking up. "I am here tonight on behalf of the petition to designate the Longstreet statue as a local historical landmark."

He paused to cough, and a woman around his same age sitting nearby handed him a bottle of water. "Thank you, honey." After taking a sip, he continued.

"Before my retirement five years ago, I served as professor of American history at Southern Christian Community College for thirty-five years. I specialized in Confederate history and have published a book and countless articles on lesser-known heroes from the US Civil War. I am here today to ask that this committee does not succumb to pressure to hop on this woke political band-wagon and make a mistake that you cannot undo."

"I hate when old people say 'woke,'" Rebecca whispered to Harita.

"I hate when white people say it," Harita whispered back.

Noted. Stop saying "woke." But wait, what about the book *Woke Yet?* She'd finally finished listening to it over the holidays. She could say the title, right?

The professor continued rambling on about the problem with "disappearing history," and folks were getting restless, whispering among themselves.

Had he really not reached his two minutes yet?

"General Longstreet was among a number of American heroes who gave his life in service, and he deserves to be—"

"In service to losers!" someone shouted from somewhere near the far left corner in the back of the room. At this, the room erupted. A pressure valve had released cheers, whistles, boos, and plenty of "oh-come-on's!"

Everyone craned their necks to see where the outburst came from. Well, everyone except Professor Chuck, who sat unfazed, looking at his sheet of paper, patiently waiting for the room to quiet back down so he could finish.

"Order! Order!" Council Chair Strummond yelled out, banging the gavel repeatedly. But it was too late. What followed was straight out of a movie—or at least one of those viral videos from school board meetings with parents-gone-wild fighting to keep slavery listed as a career choice in high school history textbooks.

Yet here they were, in their very own town—adults shouting over one another, each person convinced their point was going to be the mic drop.

If only anyone would actually use a microphone.

"This is an attempt to erase history!"

"My brother-in-law is a Black man. Trust me, he won't forget that history."

"The statue isn't causing racism. And taking it down won't *end* racism!"

"The Germans don't have statues of Adolf Hitler, do they?"

"Hitler? What does he have to do with this?"

"This is a slippery slope! Are we going to get rid of any little monument to a person who may have hurt someone's feelings at some point?"

Rebecca felt like she was at a tennis match, watching everyone's heads jerk back and forth following the arguments in whatever direction they came from.

"I can't believe how many people here want to keep this statue up. That slippery slope lady lives in my development. She's the president of the homeowners' association!" Harita whispered to Rebecca.

The back-and-forth continued for another thirty minutes before the council members finally shut it all down, admonishing the crowd for being unruly and uncivil. Unlike scolded children, however, some of the most vocal individuals appeared to feel no shame or remorse and instead walked out in defiance. But up front, still sitting quietly at the table in front of the dais, was Professor Chuck Anderson.

As Council Chair Strummond regained order and prepared to end the meeting, Professor Chuck leaned into the microphone, cleared his throat, and said, "But, Harry, I still have forty-five seconds left."

NINETEEN

De'Andrea

De'Andrea couldn't remember the last time the house had been so still and quiet so early in the evening. Normally, weeknights were bustling and loud with Nina talking nonstop from the moment she got picked up from school until she was tucked into bed. But since Nina wasn't feeling well, De'Andrea made her favorite chicken noodle soup and gave her some medicine to help her sleep.

She'd taken Nina's temperature twice, but it was normal, and she suspected Nina was suffering from a broken heart. It had been a few weeks since her last visit with Mama, and De'Andrea hoped to stall her for just one more. Then she could attend the West End's Children's Session where specialists could provide child-appropriate answers to her difficult questions. De'Andrea knew she sounded like a broken record every time she said, "Mama's still not feeling well."

After making herself a quick salad for dinner, De'Andrea settled into the buttery soft leather sofa in their family room. She snuggled under her favorite blanket and prepared to distract herself with the latest docuseries about the royal family. Like the rest of the world, she'd loved Princess Diana and had been heartbroken when she died. But she hadn't given them much thought . . . until Harry married Meghan.

Damn, I hope they have just one more baby.

A boy or a girl . . . didn't matter. So long as Megan's Negro genes kicked in and gave the royal family the little Black heir they so desperately feared!

She was barely into the first episode when her cell phone screen lit up with a notification from the girls group chat.

Today, 7:08 PM
Toni
Ummm, y'all alright out there? 👀

Today, 7:09 PM
Simone
For real. What in the white folks' ruckus is going on in Rolling Hills! 😂

De'Andrea sat up a little and listened. As usual, there was nothing but eerie silence.

Today, 7:10 PM
De'Andrea
All good over here. What y'all know about that I don't know about? 👀

Today, 7:11 PM
Toni
Bih!!!!! Turn 👏 on 👏 the 👏 news 👏 NOW!

De'Andrea tapped on the image that Toni attached and used her forefinger and thumb to zoom in. Toni had drawn a red circle around the blue ticker at the bottom of her television screen that read: "Prestigious Virginia Community Divided on Historic Confederate Monument."

What in the world!

De'Andrea grabbed the remote and changed the channel. "Malik! Come here!"

The door to his office opened, followed by the sound of his heavy footsteps pacing toward the family room.

"What's wrong? Is everything okay?" Malik sat down next to her on the couch and stared at the screen.

Red and blue flashing lights flickered across the reporter's face as he gave a breaking news update. "A tense scene here in Rolling Hills as residents debate whether a Confederate statue should remain as part of the town's legacy or be removed because of its dark historical past.

"I'm here with Melody Montgomery, a longtime resident of Rolling Hills. What are your thoughts on how tonight's town hall went from conversational to adversarial?"

"It's truly unfortunate," Melody said, tossing her shoulder-length brunette waves with an authoritative air. "We'd hoped this would be an opportunity for residents to voice their opinions, to share their thoughts about this very sensitive subject. I don't think anyone expected things to take such an ugly turn."

More white women gathered around Melody, the reporter, and the camera crew. A strawberry blond with a shoulder-length bob frowned. "Well, it took an ugly turn when other people refused to agree with you."

Ever ready to capture newsworthy drama, the cameraman backed up so he could include both women in the frame.

"Oh my God, Daisy." Melody rolled her eyes. "I wasn't asking anyone to agree with me. I just—"

"Oh yes, you did." Daisy looked straight into the camera as if she'd been waiting all her life for her two minutes of fame. "Yes, she *did*, America."

"As I was saying before I was so rudely interrupted—" Melody tried to continue, but Daisy wasn't having it.

"No," she demanded. "You rudely interrupted me all night. Now it's my turn. Tell America how you refuse to even consider how statues can be used as teaching tools. Have you ever even taken just a minute to think and ask yourself, 'Hmmm, you know what? Maybe these statues can be used as history *lessons*?'"

"No, I haven't," Melody answered dryly. "Because history lessons are taught in books—"

"But they don't have to be!" Daisy screamed as her face reddened in anger. "You just hopped on this antiracism bandwagon to tear down Confederate statues—*historical* statues. Just because that's what other cities are doing doesn't mean that Rolling Hills has to do it, too. We should be doing what's best for *our* children!"

The crowd of women positioned themselves around Melody and Daisy to show their allegiance for the respective arguments. The entire situation reminded De'Andrea of an old-school playground argument that would escalate into a fistfight the moment someone called the other a "jive turkey."

One of Daisy's supporters stepped into the camera frame. "She's right. Everyone has to consider their own local history when it comes to these types of things. What are we going to tell future generations when they ask about the history of Rolling Hills?

That we used to have a statue honoring General Longstreet, an important historical figure who ensured this land didn't fall into the hands of the Union Army, but it had to be taken down because this all happened during a time when white people owned slaves or whatever? What are we going to tell *our* children about *their* history, Melody?"

"Nothing, Mary Ellen. She's not going to tell them anything," Daisy said smugly. "Except that she was one of the antiracist crazies who helped make it happen!"

Oh shit!

Melody glared angrily at Daisy and Mary Ellen, her nostrils flaring. She'd just been called the equivalent of a "jive turkey" and all hell was about to break loose.

"I mean, those wouldn't be my exact words, Daisy." Melody's tone was colder than ice. "I'd probably add a little context about the Indigenous tribes who rightfully own this land. Innocent people and communities that were nearly wiped out by white people like General Longstreet because they were so determined to colonize *a new world*. A world that had existed long before Christopher Columbus claimed he discovered it!" She'd air quoted "a new world," which seemed to make Daisy and her supporters even more furious.

Well, damn.

"Oh, give me a break," Mary Ellen retorted. "There were, like, two Indian tribes here, and they weren't wiped out. Indians still exist, you know. They live on *reservations*." She sounded out "reservations" syllable by syllable as if she were speaking to a child.

"Did she just say that on live TV?" Malik asked.

"Sounds about white." De'Andrea rolled her eyes.

Melody continued to go toe-to-toe, tit for tat. "Oh yes! That's right! I'm sure they just *love* living on measly parcels of government-appointed land that only represent *a fraction* of the land that is rightfully theirs. And stop calling them Indians! It's Native or Indigenous people, goddammit!"

Damn! These Beckys were really going *in* about this statue. This was *so much* better than the royals. This was the reality TV De'Andrea needed and deserved! "Is it wrong that I want popcorn?" she asked, half-joking, half-serious.

"Nah, this is wild," Malik said. "And honestly, I would go make you some. Except I can't. You know how much I love to watch white people white peopling."

While the women continued arguing, the reporter turned to the cameraman to conclude his segment. "Emotions remain high here in Rolling Hills after a town hall that was intended to restore peace to a community often lauded as one of the best places to live in America. Stay tuned for more on this developing story."

De'Andrea and Malik looked at each other.

What in the whole caucastic hell?

It hadn't taken long for the internet to assign the town hall fiasco its own hashtag. De'Andrea had shared many laughs about the #TownHallTissyFit with her girlfriends in Atlanta, who'd been highly amused. But De'Andrea could only use the Town Hall as a distraction from Mama's decline for so long.

Initially, De'Andrea had been somewhat reluctant to join the local chapter of the Alzheimer's Association. She was already dealing with her own emotional fatigue from Mama's unexpected decline, and the thought of sitting in a room with other caregivers with similar problems sounded more heavy than helpful. But she'd been wrong. *Very* wrong. Not only was it comforting to hear how others were coping and even finding humor, but every meeting also left her feeling more excited about the Whitman Way.

She'd invited Malik to join her but he'd yet to attend, preferring to listen to her updates and read articles she shared. But the chapter had helped De'Andrea manage her expectations with that as well. Malik's Alzheimer's journey with his mother was *his* journey. When it came to Mama, their paths might never meet in the middle—and that was okay.

The "Rolling Hills' Other AA," as the chapter liked to call themselves, quickly became a healing balm to her emotional worries and wounds. After a few sessions, she found kindred spirits among the members. Mothers from Nina's school who were honest about the challenges of parenting and caretaking. Wives caring for their in-laws who shared worries nearly identical to her own. Only children who questioned why the gods had chosen them for this seemingly impossible-to-pass test of patience. They were all just regular people who were tired, and this was their safe space to complain about it. And the biggest surprise of all? Discovering Heidi among the members.

When De'Andrea walked into her first chapter meeting, both women's eyes had widened. Heidi rushed over and, without even asking, pulled De'Andrea into her arms and gave her a much-needed hug. "Oh my God! What are you doing here?" Heidi exclaimed. "Never mind. Don't answer that. Because obvs."

They'd laughed, the first of many they'd share. It turned out that Heidi the emo fairy who lived across the cul-de-sac was a riot.

"Yet again the older brother and sister are on vacation," Heidi often shared. "And yet again, they can't seem to find time to visit their father. Oh, but trust me, they'll be first in line when it's time to find out how much they've been *bequeathed*."

Heidi couldn't wait to tell her siblings they'd been "bestowed and bequeathed a whole lot of nothing." Because their father, having long-since accepted that his eldest children were assholes, had an ironclad will that split his wealth between Heidi and the North Shore Animal League America.

"Do you know how hard it is for me to sit on this information?" she'd asked De'Andrea one afternoon.

"Torturous, I'm sure." De'Andrea snickered.

"Beyond! Honestly, it's the only reason I eat healthy and work out. I mean, I have to stay alive just to see the looks on their faces."

Heidi was De'Andrea's type of petty.

Recently, the two women had rearranged their visitation schedules so they could ride to Memory Village together and hang out afterward. It was nice having company, especially on those days when spending time with Mama was particularly challenging. And having Charlotte join them was always a joy because babies just made everything better. Being able to decompress before picking up Nina was super helpful, and De'Andrea was pretty certain she'd finally found "the one" for Dr. Jones's Make-a-White-Friend challenge.

Finally.

Even though Heidi was a mother, she reminded De'Andrea of Simone—she'd *chosen* to live an unencumbered life. Their conversations had more depth beyond which restaurants were perfect for date nights or small talk about school events. She pressed De'Andrea to talk about her life beyond caring for Mama, Malik, and Nina. As a woman whose life centered on prioritizing herself, Heidi could easily see and gently point out the ways in which De'Andrea didn't.

"Alright, I need an update," Heidi demanded. "So, what did you find out about being able to practice in Virginia? Do you have to take the bar exam again? Not that it will be a problem if you do. If Kim Kardashian passed the California Bar, certainly you can pass Virigina!"

"Thankfully, I don't have to take it again," De'Andrea said joyfully. "And I started the reciprocity process this week."

"Amazing!" Heidi cheered. As they walked through the botanical gardens, she recognized a plainclothed doctor and waved. "Dr. Patel was my dad's first doctor, back when he was in East End. She's just the best."

"All the staff is really," De'Andrea agreed.

"Which brings me to my next question. Here, let's sit." She gestured to a wrought-iron bench overlooking one of the fountains. "Any update on Calhoun?"

"Nothing yet. But as soon as I hear anything, you'll be one of the first to know." She hadn't wanted to press Malik about it. The plan they'd put together was solid. All De'Andrea could do was hope Calhoun would at least consider it.

Time seemed less linear, days and nights a constant blur of mothering, wife-ing, and caretaking. She still didn't have the heart to tell Nina that things were different in the Village's West End. That they'd never have those carefree moments of joy ever again.

And then, there was Malik.

Her husband had learned the art of forcing a smile and appearing to be a jovial spirit for Nina's sake. When it came to believing her daddy, she was too young to decipher between what was real and fake. But De'Andrea knew, and she couldn't help but wonder if Malik's optimism would be forever clouded by the dark reality of Mama's new normal.

When Mama was a patient in East End, Malik visited much more often. But after her sudden progression required her to move to West End, his visits slowed. And he never spent time with her alone—a decision she initially thought was driven by fear of him being there if Mama had another outburst. But then she realized what was *really* happening—Malik didn't like to *see* Mama's decline. And she couldn't help but shake the feeling that Malik was on the verge of spiraling.

It had been years since she'd seen this darker side of Malik. But she knew, just like everyone, he had it in him, because she *had* seen it before.

And their marriage had barely survived.

"I'm worried, Dr. Jones," she confessed during therapy. "Like, I'm really worried."

"De'Andrea, you have to remember that Malik hasn't done anything to break your trust again," Dr. Jones reminded her. "He's grieving right now. Anticipatory grief. It's the grief that often occurs before an impending loss. And it's natural, especially when a loved one has an incurable illness.

"So you have to remember that—Malik is grieving. And he's doing it in his own way, using work as a distraction. He was so young then; you both were. And despite the first year of marriage rocking your worlds, everything you went through made you both realize love is worth fighting for. You both learned how important it is to communicate, to stay close to each other."

"We're not close like that anymore." De'Andrea blinked away tears. "We haven't been close like that in a long time."

"But you once had that closeness," Dr. Jones encouraged. "Which means you can find your way back there again. At a minimum, you owe it to yourselves to at least try."

De'Andrea felt she *had* tried. But she couldn't make Malik let her in.

He had to let her in.

~

"Nina Whitman!" the carpool coordinator called out.

De'Andrea let down the passenger side window. "Oh, I'm picking up Isabella Myland, too." She held out her phone to show the email Becky sent to the front office.

After weeks of incessant begging, she'd finally agreed to have Isabella over for an afternoon playdate, and Nina was beside herself that her bestie was finally coming to *her* house.

"C'mon." The woman smiled at Isabella, who was so excited she was literally jumping up and down. "Well, aren't you girls lucky." She helped both girls into their booster seats and watched them secure their seat belts. "Have fun!"

Immediately, the back seat resounded with giggles and chatter as the girls recapped their day.

De'Andrea half listened, nodding and adding "Really?" and "Oh, that sounds like fun" whenever there was a brief pause indicating the girls were awaiting her reaction. When she turned out of the school parking lot, she headed downtown. Nina and Isabella were going to lose their minds once they realized they weren't going straight home because they'd be making a fro-yo pit stop.

"Remember when Brian's teddy bear started marching and singing about sharing honey?" Nina asked.

"Yeah, and Brian is right," Isabella said. "Why should Winnie the Pooh get to have more honey than everyone else? It's important to share and he's not a good sharer. He just sticks his big ol' paw in the honey pot and gobble, gobble, gobble!"

The girls laughed hysterically as Isabella pretended to eat a fistful of honey.

"What do we want?" Nina sang out.

"More honey! More honey!" Isabella shouted while raising her right arm and pumping her fist in the air.

"This is a protest!" Nina yelled. "Everyone has the right to protest things that aren't fair—"

"And when things need to change," Isabella added.

"Everyone deserves to have honey," Nina said. "Not just Winnie the Pooh!"

"And we're gonna protest until it happens!"

Huh?

"Now, what's this about a honey protest?" De'Andrea asked while signaling a right-hand turn.

The girls giggled. "Not a *honey* protest, Mommy," Nina explained. "A toy protest!"

"Miss Heather taught us how to do it," Isabella shared. "And it was so much fun! Everybody protested something different. Yeah, my protest was about dessert. Why should kids only be allowed to have treats if we finish eating our dinner? We should get dessert whenever we finish eating breakfast and lunch, too," Isabella reasoned.

"And my protest was about cars," Nina said proudly. "I think they should make cars for kids. So we don't have to wait for our parents to take us to see our friends. We can drive ourselves and see them whenever we want!"

"If we had our own cars, we could see each other every day!" Isabella squealed.

"And then what happened?" De'Andrea asked.

"Our toys made signs," Isabella said. "And then. And then—"

"And then we all marched around the room and protested with our toys. Because protesting is all about trying to make life more fair for everyone," Nina said.

"More fair and more fun!" Isabella added excitedly.

A toy protest, De'Andrea thought. *That's brilliant!*

Kudos to Miss Heather for finding a cute way to teach kids about protesting.

"Well, that toy protest sure sounds like it was fun," De'Andrea said to the girls.

Still in classroom etiquette–mode, Nina raised her hand. "You know what else I learned, Mommy? People can protest about whatever they want. Miss Heather said that everyone doesn't always agree. But we always have to be respectful."

Isabella nodded. "That's right!"

De'Andrea smiled as she turned into a parking spot.

The girls craned their necks to look outside. They'd been so caught up in talking about the toy protest that they hadn't even realized where they were.

"Are we getting fro-yo?" Isabella squealed.

"We are!" De'Andrea matched her enthusiasm.

"Yay!" the girls cheered, unbuckling their seat belts.

A few moments later, Nina and Isabella were sitting side by

side on a bench, beaming as they dipped their spoons into cups of fro-yo. They'd both chosen the seasonal winter wonderland flavor and smiled as De'Andrea snapped pictures with her phone.

> **Today, 3:35 PM**
> **De'Andrea**
> Decided to take the girls for a little treat this afternoon.

She attached the best photo of the girls' sweet faces framed by a perfect cloudless blue sky.

> **Today, 3:36 PM**
> **Becky**
> Oh my God! ADORABLE! 😍

> **Today, 3:37 PM**
> **De'Andrea**
> 🖤

Then she dipped her spoon into her own cup of winter wonderland.

"Mmmmm, so good." She smiled at the girls. "So good, right?"

Nina and Isabella nodded. And when De'Andrea raised her cup for a toast, they raised theirs, too, and bumped their treats together. "Cheers!"

> **Today, 3:40 PM**
> **Becky**
> So, ummm . . . did the girls tell you about the toy protest? 😬

Today, 3:41 PM

De'Andrea

They did! But why the face? What a fun way to introduce kids to citizen participation. I wonder if Miss Heather got a bunch of questions from the kids about that town hall fiasco. Now THAT was 😬.

Today, 3:42 PM

Becky

Check Cardinal listserv when you get a moment . . .

God, that parents' listserv stayed lit!

As soon as she got to the house, De'Andrea got the girls settled into Nina's playroom. Then, she retrieved her laptop and logged into the parents' forum. Becky hadn't lied. There were so many comments on the "Now Toys Are Woke? Seriously?!" thread that it seemed to take forever to scroll to the first post to see how it all began.

She read the first few lines of each post to get a sense of what the fuss was all about.

"Such a disruption to learning . . ."

"How can we trust Miss Heather with our kids? Sneaking racial politics into the classroom under the guise of toys."

"So now we're being FORCED to have uncomfortable conversations with our kids."

"I agree with the other parents. Miss Heather needs to be placed on administrative leave until this is all sorted out."

"How many times do we need to @PrincipalTanner until he joins the chat?"

"I think it's clear this toy protest made some of the children really uncomfortable, not just their parents."

"I had no idea Miss Heather was planning a toy protest. What else does she have planned that we don't know about? This is so ridiculous!"

"Honestly, this is my first time leaving a comment here. What's all this craze with diversity this year? More diverse photos and posters in the classroom. More diverse books in the library. Then there are flyers all over town from the parent diversity committee. I didn't even know we had a parent diversity committee!"

"I just want everyone to know that this toy protest incident was not contained to Miss Heather's classroom. If your kid went to aftercare today, just prepare yourself because they are going to protest about everything from their afternoon snack to taking a bath. Sophia is literally crying as I type this because her protest to not eat kale didn't work. Are you f*cking kidding me?!"

De'Andrea stopped reading. Jesus! It was Black History Month, for crying out loud. Calling for Miss Heather to be placed on administrative leave or, even worse, to be fired was beyond extreme. Oh, this wasn't about toys. This was about something deeper. And De'Andrea had something to say about it.

She clicked the "add comment" button and began typing:

User: @TheWhitmans
Subject: Now Toys Are Woke? Seriously?!
Hi. Many of you may have seen me around campus, but allow me to formally introduce myself. My name is De'Andrea Whitman, and I am the mother of Nina Whitman, one of the few Black children at our school and the only Black child in

this year's kindergarten class. Given the countless acts of racial violence in this country and the protests that often follow, I stand with Miss Heather and her decision to teach students about protests using toys and fun prompts to help them understand what's been happening in this country and, given the recent town hall that made national news, what's happening right here in Rolling Hills.

Periodt. And that's on Mary had a little lamb.

TWENTY

Rebecca

"Holy shit, babe. You have got to see these messages coming in on the parents' listserv. It hasn't slowed down at all since this afternoon." Rebecca brought her laptop over to the sofa where Todd was checking emails on his own laptop.

"What kind of drama do we have today?" Todd placed his computer on the coffee table and took a sip of scotch.

"The latest is that Carl got all bent out of shape about the toy protest. He drafted a letter of complaint to school admin and is asking parents to sign it."

"Oh yeah?" Todd put his feet up on the coffee table, leaned back, and rested his glass on his stomach.

"Let me read you his email *verbatim* because you won't even believe me otherwise.

"'Dear fellow Cardinals. We may all have different viewpoints on the Longstreet statue issue. And I respect that. We must have civil discourse.'"

Rebecca paused to add her own commentary. "Pssht. Civil discourse, my ass!"

She continued reading. "'As far as I know, we are still a democracy. And we are all entitled to our opinions.'

"Ha! Yeah, right. Only the opinions you agree with, Carl." Rebecca was getting worked up, and she was only two sentences in.

"Bec, keep going." Todd looked amused, like all he needed was a bucket of popcorn.

"Okay, okay, back to Carl's screed. 'But what I do not think we should have to tolerate is that this political fight has now seeped into our children's school. We are paying forty-five thousand dollars in tuition for what is supposed to be the most prestigious education in the region so that our children can be competitive in a global economy. What we are NOT paying for is for them to become a bunch of whiny snowflake social justice warriors.'"

Rebecca stopped to take a breath. "Todd, honey, will you please pour me a glass of wine? Like a big glass?"

Todd obliged, grunting a bit as he got up from the couch. "This one, okay?" He held up a bottle of Pinot Noir.

Rebecca nodded and kept reading Carl's email, "'For those who don't know what I am referencing, ask your child to tell you about what the lower school did with Miss Heather today. I've attached a photograph that Laura sent me. Fortunately, she was volunteering in the library. Had she not, we otherwise would never have known this happened. I ask you all, my fellow parents: What educational objective does this serve our children to arrange toys and stuffed animals in a protest? This is indoctrination, plain and simple. In my view, all this does is serve the subversive political agenda of a tiny group of parents at the school who are clearly being aided and abetted by Miss Heather.'"

Todd handed Rebecca her glass of wine and then returned to his spectator position on the sofa. Rebecca took two swigs and continued.

"'For those of you who want to "cancel" me for my opinions, I'd like to see you try. I wholeheartedly reject cancel culture. I am so tired of being silenced. I am prepared to send a letter to Mike Tanner tomorrow calling for Miss Heather to be suspended from her duties while a committee of parents, board members, and school administrators review her fitness to serve in this position. In addition, I plan to call for an overall review of the school's curriculum to make sure we, the parents—who are the experts on our children, after all—have a more direct say in exactly what our students are learning. Please reply to me, directly, to let me know you'd like to sign the letter. Thank you. Carl Jensen.'"

Rebecca picked up her laptop, waved it around, and said, "What a fucking piece of work this guy is! Acting all sanctimonious as if we don't all know he was sleeping with his assistant all those years like a goddamn cliché. And what the hell is Laura doing? Is she on his side now?! And what does he mean, 'a tiny group of parents'? He's acting like there's some kind of conspiracy against him!"

"Wow, okay, Bec." Todd held his hands up. "You gotta take a breath."

"You're right." Rebecca placed her laptop on the coffee table before she knocked over her glass of wine with it. She focused on the breathing exercise Serena had taught her.

Inhale . . . 1 . . . 2 . . . 3 . . . 4

Hold . . . 1 . . . 2 . . . 3 . . . 4 . . . 5 . . . 6 . . . 7

Exhale . . . 1 . . . 2 . . . 3 . . . 4 . . . 5 . . . 6 . . . 7 . . . 8

She repeated this four times. Any more than that and Serena said she'd get dizzy.

"All better?" Todd asked.

"Yeah, sorta," she said and took a sip of her wine, which she hoped would help even more.

"Now, let's talk this through."

"What is there to talk through?"

"Babe, please don't overreact to what I'm about to say." Todd bit the inside of his lip. "But I can *kinda* see Carl's point." He flinched after he finished his sentence, like he needed to shield himself from Rebecca's ire.

What?! Remember what you read on Instagram: Be curious.

She thought she might explode but managed to eke out, "How so?" as calmly as she could.

Todd, looking encouraged that Rebecca hadn't jumped all over him, continued. "We *do* pay a lot of money for our kids to go to *school* there. To learn *academic* things. If families want to talk with their kids about political issues, then they should make that choice themselves. For their own families. I have to tell you . . . when you sent me the photo of the toy protest, I wondered what else is going on at school that we don't know about. I don't want Lyla and Isabella to fall behind."

Isabella had loved the toy protest; it had been the highlight of her day. Lyla had been jealous *her* class hadn't done one. But she tried to understand what Todd was saying.

"Okay, but Carl is going over the top, don't you think? Calling for Miss Heather to be put on leave? Accusing her of having a subversive political agenda?"

"I agree one hundred percent. Carl is a douchebag on every level. He still owes me a hundred bucks from poker night three years ago."

"Babe, you have *got* to let that go. Still, we're not signing this letter, right?" Rebecca asked, glaring at Todd so forcefully that he knew the correct answer.

"No, of course not."

Rebecca swigged the last of her wine and picked up her laptop.

"Oh look!" De'Andrea commented. "I'm so glad she said something. I've been *dying* to know her perspective on this."

As Rebecca read through De'Andrea's message, she could feel guilt surfacing for even considering Todd's point about academics. She got choked up when she read aloud to Todd what De'Andrea wrote about how much she worried every day about her daughter being the only Black child in her class.

"I see her point, too, Bec," Todd said. "But I don't think Carl's wrong."

As she tried to sort out whether both Carl and De'Andrea could be right at the same time, another message popped up in the thread.

Finally, the head of school, Mike Tanner, entered the conversation.

⁓

Mike Tanner's letter to parents read like a well-crafted statement written by a PR firm. Besides offering platitudes like "We are stronger when we come together in community" and "We must ensure that all voices are heard," he invited parents to come into the school after morning drop-off to share concerns and ask questions about the toy protest and other issues raised in Carl's letter. To Rebecca's surprise and extreme frustration, more than 100 parents had signed. All as "Anonymous," however. *What a bunch of fucking chickens*, Rebecca thought. She wondered how many would actually speak up at the Q&A session.

Should I speak up? she wondered as she jogged up the stairs to the Letcher Room. She'd already had one of *those* mornings and was running late, which she *hated*. First, Lyla waited until the last minute to finish her Black History Month diorama project and they were gluing decorations on it during breakfast. Then she had to go back and forth with Stu over text about the goddamn koi fish delivery. He kept saying it was delayed, but she was beginning to think he was fucking with her on account of the Longstreet statue issue.

So she was already irritated when she finally arrived at the meeting and found the room so jam-packed with parents that there were barely any seats left. She scanned the room and saw the preschool moms standing in the back. Right in front of them were Lisa and Megan but they were in the middle of a row with no seats on either side. Victoria had texted that she couldn't make it but wanted a full report. What about Jenny Q? She hadn't replied to the group chat.

And then Rebecca spotted her.

Oh.

She was sitting with Harita and De'Andrea, their heads lowered and whispering to one another. It looked as if they had coordinated plans to attend and sit together. Rebecca's stomach twisted up in a knot. She tried to avoid making eye contact with them and looked to the opposite side of the room to find an empty seat.

"Rebecca!" Jenny called out to her. Harita and De'Andrea looked over, too, and waved, gesturing for her to come over. Harita asked the person sitting next to her to move down one seat to make space. The three ladies slid over so Rebecca could take the aisle seat right next to De'Andrea.

Jenny leaned forward, around De'Andrea, and said, "Sorry, Bec. Meant to text you I was coming, but Gabe's traveling for work and the morning got crazy."

Rebecca's stomach started settling down, and she was overcome with feeling like she was back in high school all over again, getting asked to sit at the popular table in the cafeteria. She willed herself back to confidence. "I'm glad we all made it. I wonder how this is gonna go." Then she turned to De'Andrea and said, "Your message was really moving. Thank you for sending it."

"Thank you for saying that." De'Andrea sounded sincere. "I hope it gets through to others as well."

Rebecca turned toward the front of the room as Mike took his place to address the crowd. The chatter among parents immediately stopped, as if Mike had a remote control hidden in his pocket and had pressed the mute button.

Damn, he can command a room.

Rebecca was among many moms at the school—and, hell, probably some dads, too—who felt a flutter in his presence. He was six-foot-three with a slim build that defied his fifty-five years, a sharp jawline, thick salt-and-pepper hair, and a giant smile that made Rebecca understand what people meant when they described "melting" in someone's presence.

Aside from gawking at his physical appearance, the moms also swooned at how sweet he was with the students. He'd bend down to meet the littlest kids at eye level and raise his arm when he saw the older kids so they could jump up and try to reach his hand for a high five.

Victoria always said, "Every time I see that man talking to Cassie, I can feel my last good egg drop."

But as Mike started speaking, his usual charisma had vanished and he sounded like a call center rep reading from a script. Nothing he said was any different from what he'd sent in his email the night before.

Harita leaned into Jenny, De'Andrea, and Rebecca and whispered to their group, "This is a whole lot of words without saying anything." They all nodded.

When Mike invited parents to ask questions, Carl was the first to stand up. Rebecca and the other ladies all looked at each other and rolled their eyes.

"For those who don't know me, I'm Carl Jensen." He paused for effect as if what he was about to say was groundbreaking. "I wrote the letter—signed by a hundred and thirteen parents, I might add—raising concerns about political agendas making their way into our children's classrooms."

"What is your question or comment, Carl?" Mike interrupted.

"Well, you still haven't really addressed two of our principal demands. The first being: Do you agree to put Miss Heather on administrative leave? And the second being: Do you agree to conduct a transparent review of all curriculum to assure the parent community that the school's focus is on academic subjects only?"

"I think I *have* answered those questions, Carl," Mike said. "Miss Heather is on leave through the end of this week. In addition, I will continue to emphasize that our focus at Magnolia Country Day is always academics."

A few parents grumbled. Even Rebecca could admit that Mike hadn't really answered Carl's second question. The answer was obviously "no," but why wouldn't Mike flat out say that?

Another dad cleared his throat and stood up. Rebecca recognized his face but didn't know him.

"Good morning, everyone. My name is Mitch Brandywine and my son Jacob started in pre-K here this year; we hope to send our daughter here in two years' time. My concern is this: Even though my boy is still quite young and I don't have to worry about this just yet, I do know what it feels like to be bullied into going along with progressive politics. I face it every day, and I don't want my son to have to go through this. But I fear that with things like this toy protest, he's going to be made to feel guilty for being white."

A dozen or so parents clapped.

Jesus Christ, Rebecca thought. This was almost funny. She and the other ladies rolled their eyes again. De'Andrea shifted in her seat.

Another dad stood up, also white. They were all white, of course, but Rebecca was certain they had somehow become *more* white today. She had never seen so many dads show up to a school function. So this is what it took to get them to participate?

"Hi, Mike. Hi, everyone." He turned from left to right to greet the others. "My name is Christopher Newhouse Junior. My son, Christopher the third, is in the tenth grade; and my daughter Jenna graduated last year. We have been a part of this school community for sixteen years. And I have to say that I'm really concerned with what has happened in the past three years with all of this PC-woke-diversity-multicultural stuff.

"Thankfully, our daughter was only subjected to this at the very end of her time here, but our son is literally being brainwashed during a really formative time, and he's got two and a half more years here. Just the other night at dinner, I asked him how things were going in his Algebra II class. He'd been struggling, so we got him a tutor. I was hoping to hear things have been improving.

"Well, you know what he told me they did in class that day? They did some kind of data collection about how many Confederate monuments still exist and when they were erected. In *math* class! And don't get me started about what they've been talking about in US history. He even came home with one of those posters about taking down the Longstreet statue. I don't even recognize my child anymore!"

"He sounds amazing!" Harita whispered. More than a few people sitting nearby stifled giggles.

Three more dads had their hands up to speak. It was getting absurd. Rebecca wanted to speak up. She felt she *should*, as the founder and chair of the parent diversity committee. But she didn't quite know what to say. She still had what Todd said swirling around in her head. And she was afraid she wouldn't be able to explain very well why the toy protest—and lessons like it—were important.

After several more white dads, plus two white moms, echoed versions of comments already made, Rebecca checked the time and saw the meeting was running over an hour. Wasn't anyone going to defend Miss Heather? Or challenge Carl and the other parents? Why wasn't Harita saying anything? Rebecca now knew she wasn't supposed to rely on people of color to teach her about race, but she wasn't supposed to speak for them, either. Was it her place to say anything right now? What would she even say? She could tell Mike was attempting to wrap up the discussion; maybe it wouldn't be any use to say anything at this point. Everyone wanted to leave anyway. Maybe she could craft an email to all parents tonight. It could be a unified statement from the diversity committee.

As Mike thanked everyone for attending De'Andrea stood up. Everyone turned to look at her. The room was so silent that Rebecca thought it might be possible for others to hear how hard her heart was pounding. Why was she feeling so on edge when De'Andrea was the one about to speak?

De'Andrea took a deep breath and began. "Hello, everyone. My name is De'Andrea Whitman. My husband Malik and I moved to Rolling Hills last summer. Our daughter Nina started in kinder-garten this year. I also sent a message to the parent community last night. There's not much more I can say beyond what I shared in my message last night.

"But I would encourage you all to read it again and also ask yourselves this question: Why is it that you believe that engag-ing with current events and academic excellence are mutually exclusive? Or is it that you only feel comfortable with the current events *you* feel are worthwhile?"

As De'Andrea continued to address the group, her voice didn't waver as she talked about how empowering it had been to learn rac-ism was systemic and institutionalized, how it helped her to realize that there was nothing inherently wrong with her or any other Black person. That she wished she'd learned those lessons much sooner—before she reached adulthood, which is why it was so important that her daughter and her classmates learn these lessons now.

"We've been at this school less than a year, and we've already been asked if our daughter's photographs can be added to the school's website and admissions materials." De'Andrea turned her head toward the front of the room and looked directly at Mike Tanner.

"Like many schools, Magnolia Country Day wants to *look* racially diverse, but is that all you care about?" De'Andrea looked around the room at all the parents. "Or do you want to start thinking about diversity as more than a marketing strategy?"

Oh, Jesus. Is this about me? Rebecca didn't just feel dumb, she felt implicated. Like De'Andrea wasn't only talking to all the annoying white dads at the meeting but was, in fact, talking directly to *her*.

"If you want this school to truly become a place that welcomes, celebrates, and advocates for a diverse community, then there needs to be *more* of what Miss Heather organized, not less."

As De'Andrea finished speaking, Rebecca, Harita, Jenny, and several other parents clapped.

Mike—continuing with his disappointing performance—showed no emotion whatsoever when he thanked De'Andrea for her comments and then closed out the meeting with a promise to send a follow-up communication in the coming days.

You're not so hot now, Mike Tanner.

With the meeting adjourned, Jenny and Harita both said they had to race out for other appointments.

"That was amazing, De'Andrea," Rebecca said. "I can't believe how people are reacting to all of this. It's a *toy* protest, for crying out loud."

De'Andrea hesitated in her response and finally said, "Hey, can I ask you a question?"

"Of course!"

"I still don't know you that well, but I do know you're not shy about expressing your opinions, and you're most definitely not nervous about speaking in public. Do I have that right?"

"Yes, that's right," Rebecca said, with caution, bracing herself for wherever De'Andrea was taking this.

"If that's the case, why didn't you say anything contrary to what white man after white man said in that meeting?"

Rebecca was truly at a loss for words. So she did what she always did when she couldn't find the right words. She blurted out a lot of words. "Oh! Gosh. I guess, well, I guess it was just that I wasn't sure exactly what to say. And, well, I mean, you were so amazing in your remarks; there was nothing I could have said that would have been better."

"But I shouldn't have to do that," De'Andrea said. "I was the only Black woman, Black *person*, here this morning. It would have been nice to have some backup, especially from the *head* of the parent diversity committee. You keep trying to be my friend. A friend would have spoken up."

All Rebecca could say was "Oh."

Before she could apologize or say anything further, De'Andrea added, "I'm running late for my next appointment, too. I'll see you later." She bolted from the Letcher Room at a pace that sent out a "no chitchat" alert to anyone she passed.

Rebecca gave De'Andrea a head start before leaving herself. She'd fucked up. *Again.* De'Andrea was right, of course. Rebecca should have said something. But she also knew De'Andrea had said everything better than she would have. What if Rebecca had spoken up, said the wrong thing, and then De'Andrea would have had to get up and talk anyway to correct her?

Walking to her car, she wondered whether it was possible to ever get any of this right. Or at least not go backward.

She got into the car and as she was buckling her seat belt, she received a call from Memory Village.

"Hello?" she answered over the car's Bluetooth.

"Ms. Rebecca."

It was Nana's aide, Joanne. Rebecca's stomach dropped.

"Mrs. Myland is okay." Rebecca forced out the breath she didn't know she was holding.

"But she did fall, and we think she may have broken her hip."

"Oh, dear. Okay, Joanne. I'm on my way. Thanks so much for calling."

"Hey, Siri," Rebecca said, feeling tears welling up. "Call Todd."

TWENTY-ONE

De'Andrea

Malik's head peeked out from behind his computer screen. "You look nice," he said, placing his ballpoint pen on top of a nearby notepad to let De'Andrea know she had his full attention.

"Why, thank you." She twirled in front of the mahogany-framed full-length mirror across from the doorway.

At the last chapter meeting, the support group had discussed what to wear when visiting their loved ones, that certain colors had the power to make their time together more enjoyable. So for today's visit with Mama, De'Andrea had chosen a pale pink long-sleeved dress, a color known to have a calming effect. After defining her curls into tight ringlets, she'd put on the heart-shaped diamond studs Malik recently gifted her for Valentine's Day.

"Are you sure you're fine visiting Mama alone today?" Malik leaned back in his office chair. "I can come. I'll stop working if you want me to." Then, with a bit of uncertainty, he added, "Or if you *need* me to."

"No, I'm fine. I actually like when it's just us sometimes. You know how me and Mama love our girl time." De'Andrea walked over to Malik and leaned in to give him a goodbye kiss, grateful their passion was slowly but surely returning.

After a few weeks of quietly holding each other at night, their intimacy had been somewhat restored. Except their lovemaking was different now. It was the gateway to not only comforting each other but also sharing their truths. Sometimes, they spoke in hushed whispers afterward. Malik seemed more willing to talk about Mama in the darkness and safety of their bedroom. But most times, they lay awake holding each other in silence as they drifted off to sleep.

Malik put his hands on her hips. "You sure, Dee?" He sang out the words as he looked up at her, forcing a smile. She wondered if that lively spark would ever return to his eyes.

"I'm sure, Leek." When she leaned in to give him another kiss, Malik pulled her into his lap. She snuggled into his embrace, and he held her this way for a moment, slowly swiveling his office chair side to side.

"I love you, Dee. I—" Malik paused. "I just . . . I love you and hope you know that."

De'Andrea nodded, her head still nestled in what she liked to call "her spot" between his shoulder and neck where she could savor the smell of his cologne. "I know you do. And same, you know that."

She lifted her head from his shoulder to look him in the eyes and was surprised to see tears streaming down his face. She gently wiped them away with a soft swipe of her fingertips. "Leek, what's wrong?"

"I know I haven't been the best husband lately," he said, his voice cracking. "I know I haven't been the man you need me to be."

De'Andrea interrupted. "Leek, stop it. You don't have to—"

"Let me finish, babe. Please," Malik pleaded.

She wiped away more of his tears and nodded to let him know she was listening.

"I know I work too much. There have been so many nights I've been in this office when I should have been upstairs with you. But it's . . . Look, all I know is to work hard, to provide for my family. That's what I was taught. That's what's supposed to make me a good man, you know? But now I know it takes more than that, that you need more from me. Sometimes, when you look at me, I can just feel it, you know. Like, I can see that you need me. That you need more from me. I just . . . I don't know how to give it to you. I just don't know how to give you what you need and deserve, Dee."

She placed her hands on the sides of Malik's face and kissed him softly. As she guided his head to her chest, he began to sob. His shoulders rising and falling with each release as he hugged her tightly. She rubbed his back in slow circles the same way she did Nina's when trying to comfort her.

There was such truth to Malik's words. His confession was a painful acknowledgment, a regular topic of discussion among many of De'Andrea's confidantes. Their husbands were good men—good partners, fathers, caretakers, siblings, and friends. But they'd be *great* men if they allowed themselves to be vulnerable. If only Black men felt safe to do so. If only they existed in a world where they weren't afraid to be soft, where they didn't feel they had to be stoic.

"I have to tell you something." Malik's deep, raspy voice was laden with guilt. "I . . ." But instead of saying whatever he wanted and needed to say, he hugged her tighter and continued to cry.

De'Andrea's heart began racing. The moment was so familiar,

so eerily similar to the first year of their marriage when Malik had been in deep mourning over the death of his favorite cousin Rashad. His passing had been one of those senseless tragedies, his life taken too soon by a drunk driver who'd struck his car head on, killing him instantly. Rashad's death had rocked the close-knit Whitman family to its core. But no one more so than Malik. The two men had been thick as thieves throughout their childhood and college years, and in the blink of an eye, his best friend was gone. Afraid of appearing weak to his new wife, Malik confided in an old girlfriend, a woman who'd gotten to know Rashad while they were dating. What started as an emotional affair quickly turned into a physical one. De'Andrea knew nothing about the infidelity because on the nights he came home late she'd believed her husband when he said he got caught up "working at the office."

It had been the only time Malik had gone to therapy, and that was because it had been De'Andrea's non-negotiable ultimatum. Still, there was one thing she'd forgiven but hadn't been able to forget: Malik had been able to live two lives, to love two women, without missing a beat. He only confessed when his ex-girlfriend became a liability. The woman began wanting more and threatened to expose him if he didn't leave De'Andrea. And Malik had began his confession with the same words he'd just cried: "I have to tell you something."

Without realizing it, she'd stopped rubbing his back. She felt the urge to stand up. To remove his head from the comfort of her bosom. She felt her body tense in a quiet resolve as she asked, "What is it, Malik? Tell me. Now."

He raised his head, surprised by her bluntness. Then he remembered why. "No, baby. I would never. I promised I'd never hurt you that way again. And I meant that."

De'Andrea breathed in deeply. Now she felt like a child sitting on his lap. Like she'd done something wrong and was waiting to find out her punishment. "Then what is it then? What do you need to tell me?" She hated how she sounded, relieved yet still heartbroken by his betrayal all those years ago.

"Come here, Dee." He pulled her closer. "God, I was so stupid. You're never going to get over that. And honestly, I don't blame you. I was wrong. I was so, so wrong. I just didn't know how to let you in. And I'm sorry. I'm so sorry."

It had taken years to break her own stoicism, to let go of the need to be seen as a strong Black woman and embrace being sensitive about Malik's affair. She was allowed to have this moment, to continue grieving the one plot twist in their fairy tale, the one stain on their otherwise unblemished love story. She knew no one was perfect—that if Malik hadn't been unfaithful, he would have done something else to remind her that he was flawed.

Still.

"That's actually what I want to talk to you about." Malik nervously cleared his throat. He reached into the pocket of his jeans, unfolded a piece of paper, and began reading it silently. "Okay," he whispered. "Okay, I'm ready."

"Malik, what is going on?" De'Andrea demanded. "You're scaring me."

"Sorry. I just—" He refolded the piece of paper and went to put it back in his pocket, but De'Andrea snatched it out of his hand.

"Gimme that!"

Malik hung his head. "Sorry, I just wanted to get it right, to say it right."

The words in blue ink were written in Malik's chicken scratch, each phrase started with a bullet point just like he did his work notes. As De'Andrea began reading the checklist aloud, he buried his face in her curls.

- Be open—let Dee know you have something you want to tell her.
- Be loving—letting her know how much you love and appreciate her.
- Be honest—tell her you don't know how to give her what she needs.
- Be apologetic—let her know you're sorry and that you're willing to do whatever it takes to be better.
- Be vulnerable—when she asks what you're going to do or how she can help (bc she's going to ask), tell her you're in therapy and that it's the first step.
- Be spontaneous—give Dee the gift!

Malik looked at her, somewhat embarrassed as he mumbled, "Well, there it is. Brian told me to read from the paper if I needed to. But I wanted to memorize it, you know? I mean, I thought it would sound better. I don't know why I got so nervous! I just—"

"Oh, Leek!" De'Andrea interrupted. "Babe, first of all, I'm so proud of you. And so happy for you. This isn't just going to help us—it's going to help *you!*"

She'd long since given up on trying to convince him to go to therapy. He'd made it clear early on that it "wasn't his thing." He'd only gone with De'Andrea after his affair because she said it'd be the only way she knew their marriage could be saved. And yet here he was taking the first steps on his overdue journey to healing. *Thank God!*

"Brian? That's your therapist's name?"

"Yup!" Malik smiled. "Brian Quill Yardley, the Third. What a name, right? I reached out to Dr. Jones and she recommended him. Said my therapist needed to be a Black man and that he was the best she knew. He isn't even taking on new clients, but she called in a favor. And she's right. He's great. I mean, I've only had two sessions with the guy, but whew! He's already getting me in line."

She took Malik's face in her hands once again. This time, she kissed his lips, forehead, nose, and cheeks repeatedly as he closed his eyes and playfully moaned. "So *this* is what therapy does? I love therapy. Therapy is the best."

De'Andrea laughed, shaking her head as she continued to kiss him. "Now, before I head out to see Mama, let me see this spontaneous gift you got for me."

As she walked through West End to visit Mama, De'Andrea was ever mindful of the new double heart pendant on her necklace. She reached for Malik's gift, toying with the princess cut diamond surrounded by a diamond rim. The double heart symbolized the next chapter in their love story, tangible evidence of the promises Malik made to her and, more importantly, to himself.

De'Andrea stopped at a stone fountain and tossed a penny in the water, adding her prayers for Mama to other well-wishers' hopes and dreams. She still missed the vibrancy of East End. There were vast differences between the two residential campuses, and the peacefulness of Mama's new community was a reminder she was in the advanced stages of her illness and needed silence more than stimulation.

"This is De'Andrea Whitman." She spoke into the intercom outside the three-story multiunit building. "I'm here to visit Florence Whitman, my mother-in-law." The main door to the residential structure buzzed open, and she walked inside.

Along with her dedicated caretaker, Nurse Marcelle, Mama's new residence was heavily staffed by a team of dedicated medical professionals trained in de-escalating aggressive Alzheimer behaviors. And De'Andrea appreciated the added security measures, too. Although Mama hadn't had another violent outburst, safety was of the utmost importance. Mrs. Marcelle was always nearby, and the nurse's sweet demeanor had a way of making even their heaviest visits seem lighter.

Nurse Marcelle met De'Andrea at Mama's front door. "So good to see you. Florence is having a really good day, adjusting well to her new medications. It's like I said, once doctors find the perfect cocktail, it makes all the difference in patients' quality of life." She winked at De'Andrea before adding, "And yours."

"I'm so happy to hear this. Thank you." She hung her tote bag on the coatrack and slid off her shoes.

"You have a visitor," Nurse Marcelle called out to Mama. "Someone special is here to see you."

"Really? Who is it?" Mama asked, her voice sweet as ever, although her speech was slower.

"It's your daughter-in-law! And look at this pretty pink dress she's wearing."

Nurse Marcelle led De'Andrea over to the kitchenette, where Mama was leaning forward in her chair, peering into her memory chest. Several family heirlooms she'd pulled out were scattered on the table. Because Mama's vision had weakened, De'Andrea stood directly across from her and patiently waited to be acknowledged.

Mama was wearing a pale blue Peter Pan collared pantsuit. De'Andrea smiled as she recalled Heidi surprising her with the dementia-friendly ensemble for her mother-in-law's recent birthday. To get dressed, Mama just slipped her arms in the front of the jacket, and then Nurse Marcelle secured the velcro wrap in the back. The matching culottes had a side zip which made it easier to slip the pants on and off. Mama was so cute pretending to be a model as she tried on Heidi's gift.

De'Andrea had been so emotional that day. She'd cried and thanked Heidi profusely for her thoughtfulness. Soon, both women were crying and later, laughing at themselves as they blamed perimenopause for turning them into big ol' cry babies. But they both knew it was more than that. It was so much more.

"Hi Dee." Mama smiled. "That *is* a pretty dress you've got on there. I like it."

"Thank you, Mama." De'Andrea felt relieved, grateful that Mama recognized her. She pulled out a chair as she asked, "What are you looking at? Can I see?"

"Of course!" Mama said. "Come on over here. Get closer to me."

She slid her chair next to Mama. "Tell me about this." De'Andrea picked up a bottle of Chanel No. 5 perfume and handed it to Mama.

Mama raised the square glass bottle to her nose, closing her eyes as she breathed in the fragrant notes. "My mama gifted this to me on my wedding day. And I felt so fancy dabbing it on my wrists and behind my ears. I loved it so much! It was sad watching it . . ." She paused, trying to find the right word. "Watching it go. But Paul surprised me with a new bottle on my birthday. Wasn't that sweet of him?"

"So sweet," De'Andrea said.

"Have you seen Paul?"

"No, I haven't," De'Andrea answered honestly while making eye contact with Nurse Marcelle.

"I haven't either," Mama said. "He's probably at work. That man loves working, I tell you."

De'Andrea nodded as she thought of Malik. The apple certainly didn't fall far from the tree.

Nurse Marcelle turned on a Billie Holiday playlist and then she went to sit on the couch so she was close enough to help if needed but far away enough to give Mama and De'Andrea some privacy. The Whitman women talked through Mama's memories, sorting through gifts and keepsakes from her past.

"Oh, what's in here?" Mama began pulling photos and newspaper clippings from a tattered envelope.

"Look at you on your wedding day," De'Andrea said, handing Mama a sepia photo in a clear, protective cover.

"Is that me?" Mama giggled as she smiled at the younger version of herself.

As she often did during visits with Mama, De'Andrea found herself thinking about her own mortality. She knew such thoughts were common, and she'd learned to lean into these feelings rather than run from them. What would she and Malik be like in their senior years? They were both in their early forties, at that place in their lives where they had to accept they likely had more years behind them than ahead. She bet Malik would be one of those distinguished-looking older men whom aging makes even more handsome and refined. De'Andrea hoped she would age gracefully, too, that each wrinkle and gray hair would be a testament to wisdom earned and learned.

Piano chords and a lone trumpet echoed in the room as Billie Holiday's "Strange Fruit" began to play. Mama dropped the photograph in her hand, tilting her head to the side as she listened. "Nobody speak, nobody move," she whispered.

De'Andrea had heard the song many times, but there was something about hearing it with Mama—something about how she reacted that made the ballad more sacred than it already was. Tears welled in her eyes; the song always had that effect on her as she took in its meaning. When Billie Holiday crooned, "Then the sudden smell of burnin' flesh," tears streamed down De'Andrea's cheeks, but she heeded Mama's words, staying still instead of wiping them away.

"My folks heard her sing that live." Mama's soft voice broke the heavy silence as the final chords of the song played. "Said it was the last song in her set. That everybody had to be still. Everybody. Even the waiters stopped serving folks. All the lights were turned off so it was pitch black save for one spotlight on Billie Holiday's face. My mama said she sang this song with her eyes closed, that it was like being in the presence of an angel singing a prayer for our people."

Nurse Marcelle took a tissue and dabbed at her eyes before handing the box to De'Andrea.

"Oh, don't you cry now." Mama patted De'Andrea's hand. "Things are better now. Better for you than they were for me. Will be better for Nina than it's been for all of us. Holiday's "Pennies from Heaven" began playing and Mama hummed along, smiling as she rocked to the cheery tune. "Where's Paul? He loves this song."

"Excuse me, Mama. I'll be right back, okay?" De'Andrea motioned for Nurse Marcelle to follow her to the foyer.

"That was incredible," De'Andrea said, still in disbelief at Mama's memory. I know it's only temporary, but it was like . . . like Mama was her old self!"

Nurse Marcelle nodded. "Isn't it amazing how our senses can reawaken memories? Smell is the strongest, but much like today, I've seen the power of music. There are even patients who can no longer speak, but they can sit at a piano and play Beethoven flawlessly. I'm so happy you got to share this moment with Florence today. It's incredibly special, and it was beautiful to watch."

When Mama retired for her afternoon nap, De'Andrea decided to go for a walk. Her visit with Mama *had* been beautiful, and she wanted to savor it a little longer before heading home. She opened the gate that led to the visitors' trails and chose the guided pathway with a sign that read "To the Pond," inscribed below a blue windmill.

Looming sycamores shaded the pebbled pathway making the air cooler. De'Andrea pulled a scarf out of her totebag and wrapped it around her neck as she took in the woodsy scents and sounds around her. Water from a nearby stream trickled softly as it passed through the ravine. Birds chirped and, even though she couldn't see them, De'Andrea could hear squirrels rustling through the fallen leaves. She slowed from a brisk walk to a leisurely stroll and reflected on the wisdom Mama shared as they listened to "Strange Fruit."

Things are better now.

Better for you than they were for me.

Will be better for Nina than it's been for all of us.

It was already true. De'Andrea knew that Mama's life, her own life, and Nina's were beyond her ancestors' wildest dreams. Her own mother had always said, "Our job is to make sure that each generation is better than the one that came before it. Don't matter how much better just so long as it ain't worse." She knew it was the reason her mother had been at peace on her deathbed, because her hard work and sacrifices had been worth it to ensure De'Andrea's life was better than her own.

The pond came into view, and De'Andrea quickened her pace down the pathway, eager to sit by the calming water. As she neared, she noticed a woman sitting on one of the wooden benches in a green hooded sweatshirt, her shoulders slumped over in a familiar posture of defeat. If there was one lesson De'Andrea had learned from the Alzheimer's support group, it was that people caring for loved ones with dementia were a special kind of chosen family. She walked over to see if the woman needed consoling or if she preferred to be left alone.

"Hi," De'Andrea said in a gentle tone. "Are you okay?"

When the woman turned to face her, she was surprised to see who it was.

Becky?

"De'Andrea." She wiped her face with her sleeve. "Hi. I . . . yeah, I'm okay." She paused and reconsidered. "No, I'm not okay, honestly."

She felt a small pang of guilt. She'd been avoiding Becky since the toy protest drama. Her energy had long since been depleted and her patience worn thin by white parents and their "we want to look diverse but not be diverse" foolishness. But that didn't mean she couldn't have checked in with Becky to see how things were going with her mother-in-law.

"Cool if I join you?" De'Andrea asked. Becky nodded.

The women sat in silence for a bit, watching koi circling in the water and causing ripples whenever their flipping tails broke the surface. A koi leaped into the air, its orange and white scales glistening in the sunshine.

"Did you see that?" Becky asked excitedly. "I bet it's a sign of good luck!"

De'Andrea nodded. "Well, I most certainly need it."

"Same." Becky sighed. "Same."

"You know, I'd been trying to manage everything on my own, and it all became too much. Joining the support group has been wonderful. Our discussions help me so much. Have you ever been to the meetings?"

"No." Becky continued to look out at the pond. "I mean, I've thought about going. I want to go. But . . ."

"But what?" De'Andrea asked.

"But if I go, I want Todd to come with me. Like, Nana is *his* mother. Wives always get stuck handling this stuff. I mean, I watched my mom take care of both her mom *and* my dad's mom until the very end. But, if I'm being honest, it's starting to piss me off. Plus, Jack—that's Todd's brother—his wife just left him. She used to help me, but now that things are all weird between them, I'm back to doing everything by myself and . . ." She hesitated. "I don't know . . ."

"It's okay. I understand. Trust me."

"And Todd is always Mr. Sunshine, you know? 'Keep things light!' He says that all the time." Becky rolled her eyes. "You wanna have some fun or laugh? Todd is your guy. And I love that about him. Truly, it's great. Until, it's not. Plus he's got some big stuff going on at work right now, so he's been working all the time. I feel like I'm doing everything alone."

"Yeah, lots of people use work as escapism. Malik sure does. And I mean, I used to do it, too," De'Andrea confessed. "But it can really be annoying when you *know* someone is using work as an out. Malik and I have had plenty of fights about that. Although we had a real breakthrough recently. I finally have hope that he's going to be okay. That *we're* going to be okay."

"Wait, you and Malik have these problems, too?" Becky looked genuinely shocked. "He seems like the perfect husband."

"I don't think there is such a thing."

Becky nodded. "Right. And I guess from the outside looking in, everything always seems perfect."

"Emphasis on 'seem.'"

"Oh my God, I'm so sorry. I've just been *unloading* on you. Gosh, I can't imagine how I must sound. Like, oh poor me—"

"Pause." De'Andrea pulled out her beloved Tiffany & Co. pillbox. "I have something special for moments like these."

"Moments like *these*?" Becky questioned.

"Yeah, girl. Moments that call for medicinal support."

"Oh, I don't do pills." Becky held up her hands as she eyed the case. "And no judgment here, I just—"

"Girl, I don't do pills, either." De'Andrea laughed. "These are medicinals that were made especially for mamas like us."

"Oh, edibles!" Becky peeked at the assortment of gummy bears. "Oh my God! They're so cute!"

"Cute and calming. And potent. Normally, I suggest starting with one-third. But it kinda depends on how the day is going, what you're dealing with—"

"Well, until I ran into you, my day had been pretty awful. And you want to know the worst part? I can't find my goddamn planner! It's my bible! Do you know how much time I spent filling in that damn thing? It's color-coded and everything. And some random person is just going to be like, 'oh look, someone left their little notebook here' and probably throw it away. Without even realizing they're throwing away my *entire life*!"

For some reason, this made De'Andrea laugh. A deep chuckle rose from her belly and seemed to ricochet around them. She leaned over, gave Becky a hug, and then placed a red gummy bear in the palm of her hand. "Here, honey, eat this."

"Should I just eat a little piece? Like, bite off one part of it?"

Oh, Becky! Bless your heart!

"No," De'Andrea instructed. "You, my friend, should eat a whole gummy bear. And you know what? I'm gonna do the same."

Lawd, bless both our hearts!

TWENTY-TWO

Rebecca

R ebecca had spent the first part of the morning by Nana's bedside, watching her mother-in-law sleep, which the nurses said was a good thing. The surgery to repair the hip fractures was successful, but due to a post-op infection, recovery had been rough. It was hard to believe she was on week three of what should have been only a two- to three-day hospital stay. A reminder buzzed on Rebecca's phone: visiting hours were almost over. As she packed up her bag, she reflected on the past few weeks.

It's felt more like three months.

After having a mini-meltdown about Nana's fall, Rebecca had sprung into action like always. She took the lead in communicating with the medical team. She brightened up Nana's room with freshly cut flowers and Isabella's drawings. And she created a rotating family visiting schedule so Nana was never alone for too long.

Not surprisingly, Rebecca had taken on the bulk of visiting time, but it wasn't so bad. Especially with the edibles De'Andrea had given her.

Was that the reason she'd been able to manage so many of her day-to-day responsibilities from the hospital? If so, she needed to get her own medicinal marijuana card. Because during Nana's hospital stay, Rebecca had been able to make more than three dozen phone calls to town council members, local business owners, and other community leaders to convince them that the Longstreet historic landmark initiative needed to go away. And she'd succeeded! Well, it wasn't *only* her. Not by any stretch. Harita had done more than her share by convincing nearly two hundred Magnolia Country Day parents to sign the Drop the Longstreet Landmark Lie petition and lobby their council reps. And to both Harita's and Rebecca's surprise, hundreds more Rolling Hillsians came out of the woodwork to do the same.

The reality was, more people in Rolling Hills wanted Longstreet removed than didn't. The Professor Chucks and the Carl Jensens were nothing more than a way-too-vocal minority. That young woman Rainee from Justice in Parks had been right: the historic landmark petition filed by Supporters United for the Confederate Society had no legs. And even Council Chair Strummond—with all his questionable politics—recognized it and cast the tie-breaking vote to deny the landmark status petition. When the vote finally came up in the council about the statue's removal, it was unanimous: the statue was coming down.

There was still the issue of what would be put up in its place, but the hard part was behind them. Which is why Rebecca and Harita agreed that a celebration was in order. The "Rolling Hills Reconciliation," they were calling it. A chance for residents to come back together, to prove that community was more important than some old, crumbling statue.

Something else big had happened after Nana's surgery. Tina reached out. Finally. Jack had told her about his mom's fall and she sent a beautiful bouquet of white calla lilies—Nana's favorite—

to the hospital. Rebecca had taken a picture and texted it, along with a "thank you," to Tina. She hadn't really expected a response after all this time, so Rebecca was surprised when Tina replied with a somewhat cryptic message telling her there was something she needed to talk with her about and would there be a good time to chat?

Rebecca's first thought was *No, there's literally never a good time to talk. The time to have talked would have been months ago when you left our family.* But then a feeling of major curiosity, laced with an undertone of dread, won out. She agreed to call her later that evening once she and the girls got home from soccer practice. After all this time, Rebecca couldn't believe Tina had the nerve to reach out. Jack had still never told Rebecca and Todd what happened with the marriage. After a while, with their busy schedules, they got used to Tina being gone. At some point, the girls had stopped asking about her, too. Once they made it to a year of legal separation, they'd officially divorce and that would be that.

But now that Rebecca had heard from Tina, she felt anxious to know what all this was about. She simultaneously couldn't wait to talk with her and dreaded the conversation, so she was relieved to be spending the next couple of hours with Harita working on Rolling Hills Reconciliation plans. She gently kissed Nana's forehead goodbye, packed up her things, and texted Jack a reminder to arrive by 5:00 p.m. that evening for visiting hours.

"That SUCS group can suck it," Harita said as she flipped to a new page in her planning notebook. Sure, it was a low-hanging fruit of a joke, but it felt cathartic to hear her say it.

"Amen to that!" Rebecca added.

The reconciliation event would be held in the park in two weeks. Harita had invited committee members and kids over for brunch that Sunday to make signs and plan other decorations for the event. Rebecca offered to help. Looking at a list she had made in the notes app on her phone, she reported on her progress:

"Okay, I've ordered balloons, streamers, poster board, markers, stencils, wooden handles, and glue. It's all getting shipped to your house by Friday at the latest."

"Perfect," Harita said. "Now, menu. What do you think I should serve for beverages? Mimosas or Bloody Marys?"

"Hmmm, let me think." Rebecca scratched her head. "Yes?"

Harita laughed. "Of course. Both it is! Look at us making jokes with each other, Rebecca Myland. Who would have thought?"

"Not me in a million years." Rebecca almost switched back into logistics mode but then thought, *What the hell.* "Why were you always so annoyed with me?"

"Because you were always annoyed with me!" Harita shot back. "Plus, you're such a bossy bitch. No offense. I mean that in a nice way now."

"But you didn't before."

"Uh, no, I did not," Harita replied, smirking. "You *do* know you're a control freak, right?"

"And you're *not*?"

"Okay, I'll give you that. But think about how hard it is for a fellow control freak to not have control of anything! You always made all the decisions and ran all the committees and all the events. It pissed me off. Look, you're good at this stuff, so I get it. But so am I. And I think a woman of color should be in charge of the diversity committee."

What started off as lighthearted banter had suddenly gotten a little more serious. But Harita was genuinely smiling and calm as she said all of this. *She has a point*, Rebecca had to admit to herself. Maybe Rebecca *shouldn't* have been in charge of the diversity committee, but running all these school activities was her thing. Besides, there were barely any moms of color at Magnolia Country Day and, in the wake of the whole Mountain Top tragedy, no one else had taken the lead. Was she really supposed to give this up? Before she could respond, Harita continued.

"Anyway, this statue project was the first time you shared power, so you kinda grew on me. Plus that town hall was such a shit show. I feel a little trauma-bonded to you now."

Rebecca laughed. That had been a turning point for her, too, with Harita.

"Are you sure you don't wanna start doing Stretch and Sip with us on Wednesdays?"

"No, thank you. I do not do yoga with skinny white bitches."

"Oh shit." Rebecca cupped her hand to her mouth. "Are we appropriating Indian culture by doing yoga?"

"Are you fucking serious right now?" Harita asked. "Oh my God, you *are* serious." She laughed again. "Relax, Rebecca. You can keep doing your yoga."

"Remember, girls. It's *Mister* Sean, okay?" Rebecca lectured through the rearview mirror as they approached the main gate. She lowered both the driver's and left-side passenger windows as Sean stepped out of his security booth.

"Welcome home, Miss Rebecca," Sean said with his usual

cheer. "And helloooo, Miss Lyla and Miss Isabella. How was school today?"

Isabella called out from her booster seat, "Hi, Sean—" *Thwap*. "Lyla! Ow!" She rubbed the side of her leg. "Hi, *Mister* Sean."

"Hi, Mister Sean!" Lyla said. "School was good."

Oh, Rebecca liked how that sounded. So respectful. She had felt so bad when she'd googled the whole "mister/miss" thing and learned that Black people thought white kids were so rude when they called adults by their first names. Rebecca hadn't meant it to be disrespectful. Her kids called white adults by their first names, too. It was her own little rebellion against having to use Mr. and Mrs. plus last names during her entire childhood. She never even knew the first names of her friends' parents back home. But no use in stewing over it; best she could do was implement the rule now.

"How's your day, Sean? Good?" Rebecca asked.

"Can't complain," he replied. "Thank God March is finally here. Feels like it's warming up. So that's a good thing!"

"Yes, spring is sprung! Finally."

"Alright, you all enjoy your evening now!"

"Thanks, Sean. You too!"

Driving down the curved street toward home, all Rebecca could think about was the imminent conversation with Tina. She rushed the girls inside and set them up with their tablets, then she picked up the phone.

⌒

Tina answered on the first ring. "Rebecca, hi."

"Hi, Tina, how are you?" she asked reflexively.

"I'm okay," Tina responded. "How's Elaine? How are you and Todd and the girls? How's everyone holding up?"

"We're all fine, Tina." Rebecca clenched her jaw. The months of unanswered calls and texts—of Tina's *total* silence—filled the air between them, and Rebecca refused to do anything else to clear it to make this exchange any less uncomfortable. Maybe Tina was ready to explain herself. Maybe even apologize. Not that it would make any difference at this point. Too much time had passed.

Either way, make her *do the talking.*

Rebecca could hear Tina take a deep breath. "Right," Tina said. "I'm sure you want me to get to it. Thanks for calling. I . . . I don't really know where to start, but there's something I need to tell you about Jack."

"Tina, I won't listen to you bad-mouth Jack. He's never done that with you." Rebecca wagged her finger and shook her head, as if she were talking to Tina face-to-face.

"No, wait. Just listen," Tina pleaded. "What I need to tell you isn't a matter of me complaining about him. I have been sitting on this for a long time. From even before we split up. But my therapist has helped me to understand that I have a responsibility to tell you because, well, maybe you and Todd can get through to him. I sure couldn't. Rebecca, Jack has been getting into some weird stuff."

"What do you mean, weird?" Rebecca asked cautiously. "Like *sexual* stuff? Like a cult?"

"No, not like that. Well, not sexual stuff. But maybe sort of like a cult?"

"What? Stop it. That's ridiculous." This was some next-level bullshit Tina was offering up. What a pathetic way to make an excuse for what she did to Jack. To their entire family. Rebecca debated whether she should hang up.

"No, not like you think. Please, hear me out"—then Tina's

words spilled out more quickly—"I think he's part of a White Nationalist group."

"Tina. What are you even talking about? What the hell is wrong with you? How dare you—"

"Rebecca—*listen*." Tina was very calm. "I found stuff on his computer."

"Okay, I need you to back up because, honestly, you sound crazy right now." Rebecca switched her phone to speaker mode so she could rest it on the kitchen counter while she brought her hands up to her temples.

"So, we'd been struggling for a while. Like a long while. I had gotten so sick of arguing about the whole kids thing that I started to pull away. I spent more time at the gym, logged in way more hours at work, and spent a lot more time with my girlfriends on weekend trips. Rebecca, I *wanted* to want to have kids. And I think Jack *wanted* to be understanding, but it felt like we had reached an impasse. We couldn't enjoy anything together anymore. We stopped bingeing shows, we rarely went out on dates—unless it was with you and Todd—and it always felt like we were faking it. I don't know if you picked up on this or not when we were on the Vineyard, but we could barely stand to be around each other."

Um, yeah, we noticed. Rebecca shook her head but remained silent so Tina would continue.

"Things got even worse when we got back from vacation. He started holing up in his office most nights, spending hours on his computer. When I asked him what he was doing in there, he told me he was working. But something felt off. I started to think he was having an affair. I kind of hoped he was, actually. That way, I could leave him and not feel guilty about it. If he was cheating, then our marriage ending would be *his* fault, not mine for not giving him children."

Tina stopped talking and Rebecca could hear her taking a drink of something. Rebecca thought she could use a drink of something herself right now.

"So, I'm not proud of this. But I started snooping. I remember the first night I did it. He and Todd had gone out for one of their steak dinners. I had finished a second glass of wine and, I can't describe it, I just felt compelled to check his laptop. All I had to do was open it up. No password. He had left all his tabs open."

"And? What did you see?" Rebecca still wasn't sure she believed any of this.

"Well, the first thing I saw was a golf website; it looked like he was shopping for a new set of clubs. But then I clicked on *another* tab and saw he had been watching this YouTube channel called When There's Freedom. I pressed play and saw this twenty-something clean-cut white guy dressed in a suit sitting at what looked like a green screen TV news desk. He said he was reporting from the front lines of the war against patriots."

"He could have been watching it as a joke," Rebecca said, hoping.

"I told myself that, too," Tina replied. "And then I went to *another* tab. That one was a site called Truth News-dot-net. It had headlines about whiny, liberal snowflakes and social justice warriors. I don't remember all the details, except that it was bizarre to think that Jack would be buying into it."

"Did you ask him about it? You could have called me, you know. We could have all talked about it together."

"I didn't do anything that night except click back on the golf website and close his laptop. I didn't ask him about it. I didn't want to tell anyone. I still didn't fully believe it."

"So what, Tina? How are you jumping from some conservative news sites to thinking he's a white nationalist?"

"Well, then I started picking up on other stuff, too. Like when we would have the TV on in the mornings and whenever there'd be a news report that had to do with race, he would make a comment like, 'you can't say anything anymore these days.'"

"Todd says stuff like that sometimes, too. It annoys me, but it's harmless."

"Rebecca, he started saying stuff about you, too," Tina said.

"*Me?* Like what?"

"I mean, not a lot of stuff. Just that anytime he saw one of your social media posts about Black Lives Matter, he would make a joke about you flying the woke flag or whatever."

Todd *also* teased her. Maybe Jack was doing it in that spirit. But then why wouldn't he have teased her to her face?

"After that first night of checking his laptop, I became almost obsessed with doing it whenever I had a chance. And, usually, I'd find the same types of sites I found the first time. Run-of-the-mill, right-wing conspiracy bullshit. But then one morning when he'd left to go for a run, he had his email tab open. I saw a message with a subject line that said something like, 'Welcome and Thank You for Your Contribution.' I opened the email, and it was from some society that was working to save Confederate monuments."

Wait, what? Rebecca felt like she was trying to keep up with what Tina was saying, but her brain couldn't move fast enough. Like in one of those dreams where you try to run, but your legs won't work.

"When I saw the Confederacy thing, I realized I couldn't avoid all of this anymore. Especially because he had donated money. I would never want my money to be associated with something like that. So I sat down in his desk chair and waited for him to get back from his run. He eventually found me sitting there, with his laptop open, and he freaked out. Yelled at me for violating his privacy. Said he couldn't believe I had turned into one of those snooping wives. It was a mess. I asked him what the deal was with this society membership, and he said it wasn't any of my business, that he had paid for it with money from his own account."

"Did you ask him *why* he wanted to be a member of that group? Or why he was visiting all those far-right news sites?"

"Yeah, and he gave me some answer like, 'I don't like where this country is headed and I'm tired of standing by in silence' . . . blah blah blah. I argued with him for a while, but he asked me why I was suddenly paying attention to him . . . said I stopped caring about what he wanted a long time ago. That was the night I realized our marriage was definitely over. Like, how could we come back from that? How could I live with someone who talked like that?"

Jesus. This was un-fucking-believable. It didn't sound like Jack. Not *really*. But on the other hand, a spattering of memories that had previously seemed unrelated were starting to string together in Rebecca's mind. A snarky comment about current events. A jab at Rebecca's volunteering. The comments about the statue removal.

As if Tina was reading Rebecca's mind, she continued. "I knew our splitting up was hard on all of you. But I had to choose myself, Rebecca. And not for nothing, it was hard on me, too. I missed you all. I *miss* you all. But I didn't know how to explain all of this. And I also knew there was so much going on with the girls being back in school and with Elaine. I decided at the time that I shouldn't bring any of this up. But, if I'm being honest, I wanted it all to go away. And I guess part of me hoped it was a phase. But then last month I saw all the stuff on social media about how wild that town council meeting got. And I watched a video clip of a guy being interviewed about why it was important to keep that statue up—which, by the way, what statue are they even talking about?

"Anyway, behind him, I saw a big banner that read Supporters United for the Confederate Society. That's the group from the email, Rebecca. That's who Jack has been making donations to. I looked them up. They are raising money to stir up protests all over the country. They claim it's to preserve history, but they also say some really fucked-up shit about taking back our country by any means necessary. I don't think it's harmless. I know the statue is coming down, so maybe this will all blow over and Jack will back off and move on to something else. But I don't know. What if he doesn't?"

What. The. Fuck? *SUCS?!* How could Jack be involved with SUCS?

Rebecca knew Jack didn't agree with the statue coming down, but to join and give money to SUCS—to support keeping these statues up all over the country? That was shocking enough, but she was also surprised that he had taken steps to join anything. He talked a big game about a lot of things, but like Todd, he didn't really get involved in anything that deep. She'd always considered him kind of apathetic in that regard.

It wasn't making any sense. All those SUCS guys at the town council meeting were . . . she hated thinking it . . . but, well, they were *losers*. Old, redneck-y, losers. They reminded her of a lot of the people she'd grown up with. The ones who peaked in high school, the ones she'd cut off a long time ago. Jack was still sort of a bro, sure, but he was young and attractive and successful. He had so much going for him. Why would he want to be associated with those kinds of people? She thought about Elaine. What would she have said at this moment? "Tacky." That's what she would have said. Of course, this was worse than tacky.

She wanted to hang up with Tina and call Jack right away. But she needed to think. And she needed to talk to Todd. Could he have known about this already? Was he a part of it, too? *No, no.* Todd would never.

"Tina. This is a fucking lot."

"I know. I'm sorry. I needed you to know, though. He still adores you; he will always look up to Todd; and he *really* loves Lyla and Izzy. I think if anyone can pull him out of this, it's you all."

"Thank you—I guess?—for telling me," Rebecca said, unsure of what else to say. "I'll talk to Todd, and we'll figure something out. Do you want me to let you know how everything goes?"

"*No,*" Tina nearly shouted. "Sorry. I mean, no thank you. I felt like I should tell you about this, and now I need to draw a boundary. Jack isn't my problem to fix. I do love you all, though, and I know this is a long shot; I know you probably never want to see me again. And I deserve that. But . . . I would really like to see Lyla and Izzy. Do you think they could forgive me? Could I at least FaceTime with them sometime?"

Rebecca bristled. What she wanted to say was "Seriously?"

But then she thought about Tina's question. It would probably take all of five seconds for Lyla and Isabella to forgive her. Rebecca didn't want to punish them by keeping Tina away. But still . . .

She sighed. "Can I think about it? Elaine gets discharged from the hospital next week. Let me get through that. Plus this whole clusterfuck you've just dropped on me. And then I'll reach out. Okay?"

They hung up. Rebecca felt a sense of dread about the next conversation she had to have: telling Todd that his brother was possibly a white nationalist. That would be a three-finger scotch kind of talk.

She fed the girls an early dinner of spaghetti and meatballs and let them continue watching videos until bedtime. She couldn't muster the energy for anything more. She poured herself a glass of wine, turned on an episode of *Suburban Housewives* from the very backlogged DVR, and waited for Todd, who had texted an ETA of 9:00 p.m. As the beat dropped on the show's opening credits song, Rebecca leaned back into the sofa and closed her eyes.

"Honey, honey." Rebecca could feel a hand on her arm nudging her. "Honey," a voice whispered. "Honey."

She opened her eyes to Todd kneeling next to her. The TV had a black screen with the "Are you still watching?" message. Her wine sat untouched on the coffee table.

"What time is it?" Rebecca pulled herself up to a sitting position. She grasped the side of her neck, which felt locked at a forty-five-degree angle, and tried to massage it.

"It's ten thirty, babe. I'm sorry. I texted you that I was going to be later than I thought, but I guess you had already fallen asleep."

"No, it's fine. I was only resting my eyes."

Oh God. I'm officially my mother. Rebecca rubbed her eyes

and tugged on her top to straighten it out. "Todd, sit down. We *really* need to talk."

While Rebecca filled Todd in on all that Tina had said, he mostly listened. He let Rebecca get all the way through without interrupting, except for a couple of "whats?" and "no ways," which Rebecca expected, given that those had been her initial reactions, too. When she finished, Todd sat still, not saying anything.

"Well?" Rebecca held her hands up. "Has he mentioned any of this to you? Is any of it a surprise?"

Todd leaned forward, resting his elbows on his knees, his head in his hands. He ran his fingers through his hair, his signature thinking move. He took a deep breath. "Look, you know we make jokes about PC culture, and I told you how Jack and I both feel a little under attack these days with all the bias workshops and everything at work. But that doesn't mean he's a neo-Nazi or something."

"What about those news sites and society memberships and making donations—and all that stuff Tina found? You're not into any of that, are you?"

"God, no! Besides, when would I have time?"

"Okay, but what about the Confederate monuments group? Did you know he was supporting them? Do *you* support what they're doing? You did say that taking the statue down was anti-history."

"What? No! I mean, no . . . I'm not supporting what they're doing. I do think some of this stuff has gotten out of hand and there are bigger problems in the world to worry about than monuments that people don't even notice. But I'm not trying to *stop* them from coming down. Babe, you know me. I don't join groups; that's your thing."

"But did you know Jack was?"

Todd scrunched up his face and ran his fingers through his hair again. "Well, I never really thought anything of it, but you know that day he stayed for a bit after we got back from my mom's birthday lunch? You went upstairs, and he was really irritated by the whole statue thing. I kinda agreed with him at first, I guess. But then I remember he talked about it for longer than I had any interest in. I'm pretty sure I made a joke about something else to change the subject."

"Well, we've got to talk to him. I helped get the votes to get the statue removed. And to have someone in my own family who worked against that? What the hell?!"

"Let *me* talk to him. I don't want it to feel like an ambush."

"Okay, but do it soon. We can't let this fester."

"I know. I will. Let me get through the next few days. I'm gonna close this deal soon. I can taste it."

"Don't avoid it, Todd. I'm serious."

TWENTY-THREE

De'Andrea

As De'Andrea walked through the West End to meet up with Heidi, she thought about how much she'd come to enjoy their weekly strolls. They spent time talking through whatever was on their hearts and minds as women, beyond being mothers, wives, and caretakers.

Because as Heidi liked to remind her, women first and foremost belong to themselves.

It wasn't that De'Andrea *didn't* know this. Of course she knew she was her own person, a beautiful and brilliant woman who had so much more to contribute to the world than caring for the Whitman crew. And she knew she couldn't pour from an empty well, and that saying "no" was a form of self-care. It was just that some days—okay, most days—she struggled with tapping into that seemingly selfish place of prioritizing herself.

But Heidi? Not so much. She had mastered the art of compartmentalizing every area of her life so that she didn't lose herself in any of it.

Before getting married, she'd spent her thirty-five years selfishly living multiple lives. De'Andrea loved when she reminisced about her past. She could always count on learning something new about her friend every time they chatted. Like when Heidi told her she'd gotten into tech to impress a man she'd *thought* would be the next Mark Zuckerberg.

"Only much, much hotter," Heidi made sure to emphasize.

Unfortunately, she'd quickly discovered that she was smarter and, more importantly, had a stronger work ethic than the much-hotter-Zuckerberg. So while he and his tech bros spent hours talking about what they were planning to do, she'd made a name for herself in the tech world by creating some of the world's first microsite dot-coms and doing a host of other techie things De'Andrea didn't understand. As a result, she'd spent much of her twenties making a lot of money for herself.

"So, yeah, I have he-who-shall-not-be-named to thank for being able to retire at thirty." Heidi grinned. "And I swear to you, he's right where I left him ten years ago. Still blabbering about how he *almost* invented a social media platform that would have changed the world. You know what else? He's not even hot anymore. He has a dad bod and he's not even a dad!"

It was like getting an inside peek into the secret lives of white women.

Heidi's openness often led to the friends laughing—an always welcome and much-needed release—and her tendency to preface the wildest statements with the caveat "Okay, I'm pretty sure this is a white woman thing but . . ." only made De'Andrea cackle more. Because it *was* usually something only a white woman might do—like dip Froot Loops cereal in milk one by one as a snack. "Oh, that scene in *Get Out* was real, my friend," Heidi confirmed. "Someone definitely did their research!"

Even though De'Andrea had yet to master the art of prioritizing herself, she had to admit that things weren't as challenging as they used to be. Having the Alzheimer's group's support and a dedicated live-in nurse for Mama certainly alleviated some of the stress. And Malik's therapist, the wise counsel he needed to become the best version of himself, remained a godsend. Therapy had helped him become a better son, husband, and father.

Now, if only Calhoun would officially commit to the Whitman Way. Then she'd have something meaningful to fill the time she'd reclaimed.

The last time she'd asked Malik for an update, he'd told her that Calhoun was reviewing it, along with other organizations seeking his support. She thanked Malik and asked him to keep her posted. But what she really wanted to say was "Ain't he a damn billionaire? What's a measly million dollars for a few worthwhile causes?"

As De'Andrea entered the botanical garden, Heidi waved and Charlotte wobbly ran down the sidewalk toward her. She bent down and gave her a big hug. God, children were so innocent and sweet. She grabbed De'Andrea's hand and they walked back over to Heidi, who was excitedly patting the empty space next to her on the wooden bench. Perhaps Heidi might know a way to light a little fire under Calhoun. She always came through with the best "rich white people problems" advice.

"Hey, you!" Heidi stood and gave her a big hug. "Can you believe I was able to get *the* bench today? Winning!"

The bench was the only coveted wooden two-seater that faced the large fountain where visitors tossed in coins and made wishes for their loved ones. Flanked by prize rosebushes and beautiful hydrangeas that thrived in the bright sunny spot, the bench was rarely available because when people snagged it, they rarely sat there for less than an hour.

Their conversation began as always: "Before we talk about all the things, just want to confirm the seniors are good?" Heidi asked.

"Mama is doing great." De'Andrea nodded. "Today's visit was actually really nice."

"Same," Heidi shared. "That man keeps me laughing."

"Like father like daughter!" De'Andrea playfully nudged her shoulder into Heidi's. "So, what's on your plate this week?"

"Eh, not much." Heidi reached into her purse and pulled out her cell phone. "Although I do have something exciting to share. I'm sending the siblings a gift."

"Okay, growth!" De'Andrea clapped. "Look at you being all mature and whatnot. I'm proud of you!"

"Well, wait to see what it is first. I mean, it is growth. It's still a gift. And it's edible."

"Let me see." She leaned over to look at the image on Heidi's screen and screamed. She quickly put her hand over her mouth, which did little to silence her cackling as she stared at the photo of white chocolate butt cheeks.

"'The perfect gift for all the assholes in your life.'" Heidi read the website's description. "'Go with our signature greeting, From One Asshole to Another, or create your own—'"

"Please stop!" De'Andrea begged, as tears streamed down her face. "Please, I'm literally about to choke!"

"It's perfect, right?" Heidi chuckled. "There's the option to send it anonymously, but where's the fun in that? I'll definitely be letting them know this gift is from me."

"It's so perfect." De'Andrea wiped away tears. She couldn't stop laughing. "I mean, right down to it being white chocolate. Like, they can't even eat it!"

Heidi squealed with delight. "I know! White chocolate is the worst!"

God, Dr. Jones was so right. Even though no one could ever replace Simone and Toni, it *was* nice having someone to hang out with in Rolling Hills. Who would have thought that the Make-a-White-Friend challenge would result in De'Andrea finding a confidante and co-conspirator with an equally wicked sense of humor and a propensity for shenanigans? And who lived right across the street!

"What about you?" Heidi asked. "Anything fun on the agenda?"

"Not sure I'd call it fun, but we're going to attend the town's reconciliation party. Are you going?"

"Nah, we'll be away visiting the in-laws, which sucks because I'm *always* looking for a reason to hold hands with strangers and sing kumbaya!"

"Ha ha," De'Andrea said dryly. "I don't think they'll take it that far. I am glad the town did *something*, though. I still can't get over how insane that town hall was."

Heidi agreed. "A helluva start, especially for Rolling Hills. Honestly, I think there are a lot of folks who don't even know they're racist."

"So many well-meaning white folks here." De'Andrea shook her head.

The struggle is real!

"Funny how folks still think living in the suburbs is the dream," De'Andrea continued. "I'll admit, I bought into it, too. Growing up, I didn't even know neighborhoods like this existed, let alone think I'd ever live somewhere like Rolling Hills."

"Well, now you know it isn't all it's cracked up to be." Heidi turned to face De'Andrea. "Listen, I get why people, especially parents, think these little best-neighborhood safe havens are what's best for their kids. And maybe in some ways, they are. But in other ways, they just don't represent the real world.

"When I went off to college, I was absolutely clueless. I literally had never seen a Black person in real life, only on TV!

"The friends I made. The different cultures and foods. Living in a big city opened my eyes to so much. I mean, I don't hate Rolling Hills. It's still beautiful. And aside from that insane town hall, it's still safe and serene. But I'd be lying if I said I wasn't looking forward to going back to New York. Of course, now that we have Charlotte, we're also looking outside of the city. We have friends in Nyack. Have you ever been there? It's so dreamy."

De'Andrea's heart dropped. "Wait, you're . . . you're leaving? You're moving back?"

"I mean, yeah. That was always the plan. When the inevitable happens, of course. So I'm certainly not rushing it."

But you're my white friend! De'Andrea wanted to scream. *You can't leave me!*

Heidi gave her a big hug. "Don't look like that! We'll stay friends and keep in touch. And you'll make more friends here."

No, Heidi. Statistically, the next white woman I try to befriend will likely be a sociopath.

"Plus, I'm pretty sure we have plenty of time," Heidi said. "Dad continues to defy the odds . . . just like he does his doctor's orders."

The women laughed.

"Good," De'Andrea said. "Because I need you here with me in Rolling Hills. Not sure how I'd get through some of these days without you."

"Same, girl. Same."

They sat in silence for a bit, people-watching, while taking in the beauty of the botanical gardens.

"Heidi, since we're friends and all, can I ask you something about rich white people?" De'Andrea questioned. "Specifically, how to get them to donate their coins to the Whitman Way? Because I've got plans."

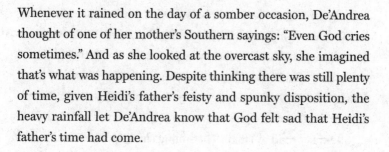

Whenever it rained on the day of a somber occasion, De'Andrea thought of one of her mother's Southern sayings: "Even God cries sometimes." And as she looked at the overcast sky, she imagined that's what was happening. Despite thinking there was still plenty of time, given Heidi's father's feisty and spunky disposition, the heavy rainfall let De'Andrea know that God felt sad that Heidi's father's time had come.

Today, 2:34 PM
Becky
Hey, hey! Do you see this cuteness? 😍

De'Andrea tapped the attached photo of Nina and Isabella wearing matching aprons over their Princess Tiana dresses. She enlarged it with her thumb and forefinger to get a closer look at what was on the large baking sheet in front of them.

Today, 2:35 PM
De'Andrea
Chocolate chip cookies! Save some for me! 🍪 And thank you again for letting Nina hang out today.

Becky

Of course! Anytime. 😊

"Got everything?" Malik asked as he opened the refrigerator to double-check they'd packed all the meal prep containers.

"Yup, I think we're good to go!" De'Andrea had stacked them in a travel cooler even though she was just walking across the street.

She'd done what she did best in helping others during challenging times: cooked and baked with love. Besides making comfort food for Heidi and her family, De'Andrea had also made enough meals for well-wishers who might stop by. Although Heidi had talked a lot of trash about the "other Johnson kids," her heart softened amid their shared grief—so much so that De'Andrea finally learned her brother was named Hunter and sister, Hannah.

She was proud of Heidi. The siblings had their own little town hall of sorts. The confrontation had been ugly, *real ugly*, with lots of hurtful words and accusations that made De'Andrea grateful she didn't have siblings. Of course she sided with Heidi; it had been totally unfair for her to carry the weighted responsibility of caring for their father alone when she had siblings. But what was done was done. There was no way to turn back the hands of time for Hunter and Hannah to do things differently. Their family had two choices: continue to deepen their wounds or forgive and move forward. And somehow, watching them go through the process of ultimately choosing the latter made De'Andrea more optimistic about the town's reconciliation party.

Perhaps there was hope for Rolling Hills after all.

"How are you feeling?" De'Andrea asked Malik after she returned from Heidi's house. "I know work is really busy right now—"

"C'mon, Dee. Be honest." He walked over, grabbed her hand, and smiled. "You can tell me what you're really thinking."

Seriously? Why was everything so much easier for men!

Malik could eat healthy for two days and lose twenty pounds, whereas it took her two years to achieve the same results. And now, he'd only been going to therapy for a hot second, and he was already open to having the hard conversations.

De'Andrea confessed. "Alright, I'll be honest. I know how we both feel about death and dying and funerals and all that stuff. And I know you want to support me. And I appreciate that. It's just that—"

Am I really about to cry? Geez, pull yourself together, woman!

It had been an emotional week with Heidi's father's passing. The finality of it all—and being forced to confront what was inevitable for Mama—made her realize what was awaiting them on the long journey ahead. It was why she'd asked Becky if Nina could have a playdate with Isabella today. Whenever she thought of Mama's fate and Nina was around, it was harder to keep her tears at bay.

"It's just that what, babe?" Malik gently encouraged. "I mean, I think I know, but I want to give you the opportunity to say what's on your mind."

"Alright, Malik, look. I don't want to cause you any additional stress. But the Alzheimer's Association is hosting its annual potluck, and I want you to come, but of course, there will be a lot of conversations about—"

"Conversations about what? Alzheimer's?" Malik deadpanned. "Look, I appreciate you looking out for me, Dee. Seriously. But I've been putting off going to these meetings with you for long enough. And I feel like now is as good a time as any. As my therapist said,

'Avoidance doesn't make anything go away. It just delays how long you wait to deal with the thing.'"

Oh, that's good. De'Andrea pulled out her phone and added the quote to her notes to share with Becky during their next "avoidant husbands" discussion.

"Okay, okay. I'll add both of our names to the potluck list," she said, before adding, "And thank you, Malik. Thank you for everything."

"You're welcome, babe."

⟋

As the weekend neared, all everyone seemed to talk about was the town's reconciliation gathering at the park. What was supposed to be a lighthearted day with friends and neighbors had suddenly become the place to be. It seemed someone had tipped off news crews that Rolling Hills had found a way to "make things right."

De'Andrea had filled the girls in on the latest shenanigans during their Sunday Zoom, and of course everyone had their own suspicions.

"I'm telling you, this is their way to make sure the world knows what's happening this weekend," Simone said, "because that town hall was embarrassing as hell."

"I mean, I get it," Toni said. "But how are y'all supposed to heal with cameras and whatnot all up on the scene?"

"Because it's not about healing!" Simone rolled her eyes. "It's about saving face! *Duh!*"

De'Andrea laughed. "I'm just grateful the hideous Confederate statue that started this whole mess is coming down. It's covered in tarp. Definitely don't want any television cameras getting a close-up of *that* guy!"

She'd tried to get ahead of the shopping rush, but it seemed everyone in town had the same idea. When it came to day-at-park staples like disposable serving ware and prepackaged snacks, the shelves were bare.

"We'll see just how much reconciliation work has been done when it comes time to share!" Simone said jokingly.

But thankfully, Malik had come to the rescue. She'd been surprised to see his arms filled with shopping bags when he came into the house Monday evening, especially because she hadn't asked.

"I overheard you complaining to the girls last night," he said as he placed the purchases on the kitchen island. "Gonna get these last few bags out the car. If I forgot anything, just let me know. I can always grab more things tomorrow on my way home."

God, Malik had been so attentive lately. So generous and kind with his words and actions. She knew firsthand that therapy worked wonders, but she hadn't expected to have the perfect husband—

Hold up. Why is he being so nice?

"Gosh, Leek, I can't even begin to tell you how helpful this is," De'Andrea said as she began unloading the shopping bags. "You got everything I needed and more. Thank you, babe!" She kissed him sweetly, taking his face in her hands, which she knew he loved.

Then she went in for the kill.

"Seriously, so thoughtful. Especially since I know things are so busy and hectic with work." She pretended to be preoccupied with putting perishables in the fridge. "What *is* the latest with Calhoun, by the way? Did he ever get a chance to look at the proposal?"

Now. Let's see if you're being nice for the sake of being nice. Or because you're just trying to soften the blow.

"I was actually gonna talk to you about that tonight." Malik grabbed an orange from the fruit bowl and started peeling the rind.

Hmmmm. As soon as I ask. How convenient.

"Really?" She tried her best not to sound sarcastic. "You have an update?"

"I do." He smiled as he popped an orange wedge into his mouth and started chewing.

"Malik, stop playing with me. What does he think? Is he interested?"

"*Very* interested. He's willing to put up the initial seed money if he can get one or two other investors on board, which certainly won't be a problem. We already have a few prospective calls scheduled this week. This is the perfect philanthropic project. It literally checks all the boxes—"

"Malik!" De'Andrea grabbed the half-eaten orange out of his hands and damn near threw it on the counter. "Are you serious right now? Like, he's in? Calhoun is all the way in?"

"He's in *in*, babe." Malik picked her up and spun her in a circle. "Congratulations. You did it!"

Oh my God, oh my God, oh my God!

Immediately, she went into work mode.

Today, 7:33 PM
De'Andrea
Y'all! Calhoun is IN on The Whitman Way! Malik said he's
just looking for one or two investors to commit funds. But he's
already committed to the seed money. So I'm tapping the
network to see if anyone knows someone who knows someone.

She smiled at the sound of confetti popping and dropping from the top of her screen.

Today, 7:34 PM

Toni

Congratulations! Let me tell Craig. I bet he knows some folks. Prayers going up! 🙏

Simone

Aye! Let's go! 🙌 I'll tap the art world and see what's what.

De'Andrea

Thank you, friends! Let me email the one-pager so y'all can share it. Made a few tweaks since the last version y'all saw.

Pop! Pop! Pop!

Another round of confetti dropped from the top of her screen. This time, De'Andrea let out a little squeal. "It's happening! It's really happening!"

She ran upstairs and hopped onto the bed where her laptop screen was still flipped open. After rubbing her forefinger across the mouse pad to wake up the monitor, she drafted a quick email to Toni and Simone and attached the revised one-pager. Then De'Andrea did something she hadn't done in a long time— allowed herself to unapologetically cry tears of joy.

Rebecca

By her third trip from the house to the car, Rebecca was officially pissed off. So far, she'd packed the picnic basket, blankets, napkins, and cutlery, and the cooler full of string cheese, fruit salad, and everyone's favorite La Croix flavors. Today was supposed to be a celebration but with each trip to the car, her resentment at having to load it all by herself was compounded by the residual anger she was carrying from the night before when Todd told her he would not join them for the celebration.

"What do you mean you're not coming?" Rebecca had already been lying in bed, face regimen complete, sleep mask on, minutes away from falling asleep.

"I've got a lot of work to do, Bec. And besides, this is kind of a moms' thing, isn't it?"

Rebecca sat up in bed and pushed her sleep mask up to her forehead.

"No, Todd, it's not a moms' thing. It's a community thing. And God, could you be any more sexist? Plenty of other dads will be there—including Malik."

"Well, I heard from some of the guys that they aren't going to go."

"Some of the *white* guys? Come on, Todd. Do you really want to be like that? You're telling me you're okay with skipping an event that's about celebrating the removal of a Confederate statue? With leaving Malik—your *new friend*—hanging like that?"

"Listen, Bec. You know I have this huge pitch coming up and I have to kill it. You want to keep saving the world? That's fine. But I actually have to *work*."

She almost felt sorry for Todd after that. *Almost*. What followed for the next twenty minutes could only be described as an exorcism, only she hadn't needed a young priest or an old priest. Once the passageway in her throat was cleared with her initial reaction to Todd's insult, Rebecca felt compelled to free herself of every comment, complaint, fear, and frustration that had settled within her psyche in the past several months, ranging from the subject of Todd's mom:

"What do you think your mother would have said if she had known that someday she'd get Alzheimer's and her sons, who only live fifteen minutes away, couldn't be bothered to see her more than twice a month until she broke a hip!"

To managing the girls' daily lives:

"Do you have any idea how much freaking time it takes up to research and register for all the girls' activities? Let alone getting them to and from everything! And don't even get me started on summer camps."

To the family's health:

"And how about all the doctors' appointments? And the dentist! I bet you like to flash those pearly whites at all your big important client pitches. You know why your teeth look so good, Todd? Because I make sure you get your freaking cleaning every six months! Oh, and did I tell you that Lyla needs braces?"

To household management:

"And how in the hell do we have a house that literally cost millions of dollars and there's always something wrong with it? We have a different type of contractor here every single day. And speaking of contractors, did I tell you I fired Stu? I had to because he came out so hard against the statue removal, and it damn near killed me because I *like* Stu. AND I STILL HAVEN'T GOTTEN MY GODDAMN KOI FISH!"

Todd did nothing but watch, his eyes wide in shock, or maybe fear. He leaned back against the bedroom doorframe, perhaps bracing himself for her head to make a 360. Just when she'd slow down, thinking she'd unleashed it all, something else would reach her throat and need to escape. She would have thought she was having a psychotic break had it not felt so good.

It was way better than meditation. Maybe even better than edibles.

"And another thing! I'm beginning to wonder if you're really all that concerned about Jack and what he's been up to. Thank God those Confederate statue-loving losers didn't win, but we've got a bigger problem here. And if you don't confront him, I will."

Eventually, Rebecca slowed down for good. She probably had more to say, but she'd hit a point of total body and mind exhaustion. Except for Todd promising, again, that he'd talk to Jack, the two went to bed with nothing really resolved. After all of that, she hadn't really wanted Todd to come with them to the park anyway.

But seriously, was he really not coming? In her twenty-plus years of knowing him, she'd always been able to talk him—or at least guilt him—into just about anything. Why was he putting his foot down now? Why didn't he think this was important?

She called upstairs to Lyla and Isabella to finish getting dressed. At least she could make *them* help her. Thirty minutes and a lot of wrangling later, Rebecca and the girls hopped in the car, ready to go. And just as she pushed the ignition button, Todd came jogging out of the house to the car and tapped on the driver's-side window. Rebecca rolled it down.

I changed his mind!

"You forgot your coffee mug, babe," he said with an apologetic smile.

Rebecca wanted to reject the peace offering because it wasn't enough. But she wanted her coffee even more. "Thank you," she said with an air of formality. "Girls, say bye to Dad! We won't be seeing him for the rest of the day."

Because work is more important than his family, apparently.

Rebecca rolled down the back seat window, and both girls yelled, "Bye, Dad!"

~

"Can this day be any more perfect?!" Rebecca said to her girls as they arrived at Rolling Hills Park, coaxing some excitement out of herself. It was an objectively beautiful day. She and Harita had reserved the picnic shelter area between the statue and the playground because of its corrugated iron overhang, but it turned out the cover wasn't needed. No April showers today. Only sunshine and celebration, infused with the scent of cinnamon and clove from the recently bloomed rose-pink rhododendrons and azalea bushes.

As the girls ran off to join the other kids at the playground, Rebecca wheeled her wagon of snacks and drinks over to the group. She greeted Harita, Victoria, Jenny, and the rest of the crew with hugs, including the preschool moms Olivia, Ema, and Maya. Besides Victoria, Rebecca was the only one who came without a husband. When the others asked about Todd, she explained how he was working on a big project while swallowing her jealousy that the other men *were* there.

The signs they made at Harita's were laid out on one of the picnic tables, ready for the group to grab once the festivities began. They were a creative bunch, she thought. Plus, the kids' handwriting was surprisingly good.

"So long, Longstreet!"

"Longstreet Coming Down! A Long Time Coming!"

"Roll Your Way Out of These Hills!"

Rebecca looked over toward James Longstreet, who was covered by a giant black tarp wrapped in ratchet straps. To balance out the eyesore that the monument had become, Harita had the idea to surround it with rainbow bouquets of helium balloons. It helped, but the ugliness loomed.

"I almost feel sorry for the guy," Jenny said, shaking her head.

"I don't!" Victoria said. "Fuck that guy!"

"Vic!" Rebecca admonished. "Language!"

Harita laughed. "I'm with you, Victoria! The kids can't hear us from over there anyway."

"Ninaaaaaaa!" Rebecca looked up and saw Isabella running from the playground over to Nina, De'Andrea, and Malik, who were walking toward the group from the parking lot. De'Andrea nodded to Nina, giving her permission to join her friend at the playground.

"Hello, hello!" Rebecca greeted De'Andrea and Malik. She wasn't sure if they were at the hugging stage yet, so she held back. But Malik went for it, hugging each mom and giving each dad the classic handshake-pull-into-a-quick-hug-and-a-back-clap. Fist closed, of course. Rebecca felt sorry for De'Andrea, who really had no choice but to follow Malik's lead. And then something shifted for Rebecca. She started to believe what she'd half-heartedly declared to Lyla and Isabella when they arrived. Maybe the day wasn't *perfect*, but it would be a good one. She felt satisfied she'd been able to convince De'Andrea to join them. But not because becoming her friend was important. Rebecca did hope they'd become closer but also realized that there was a possibility they wouldn't—even if their daughters were. De'Andrea may never like her all that much, and Rebecca realized she had to stop trying so hard because she was making herself crazy. And, honestly, she'd had other women force friendship on her, and it was annoying as hell. This was a good first step for her, for both of them, actually. They didn't have to be best friends to still be there for each other. Every mom needed other moms.

Aside from how things were going between her and De'Andrea, there was a sense of accomplishment within Rebecca that she hadn't felt before—that felt different from the relief that came with finishing a school event like the auction. The statue was coming down. That was something, wasn't it? Something bigger?

The Jack problem was still nagging at her, but she'd learned enough about the Myland way: Today, she'd put Jack in a compartment and worry about him later. Same with Todd. Besides, the more she thought about Todd, the less angry she felt. He *did* have a big presentation next week. She hadn't worked outside the home in a long time, but she could still remember what all that pressure felt like. And Todd carried their entire livelihood on his shoulders. She needed to tell him how much she appreciated how hard he worked.

"Just in time!" Harita said. "The DJ is here! I need all the dads! Please go help that young man!"

As the dads followed Harita's instructions to meet the college-age boy pulling two dollies across the grass, Malik excused himself. "I swear I'm not trying to skip out on duties, gentlemen! I gotta hit the restroom, and then I'll be right over to help."

Malik jogged over to the public restrooms next to the amphitheater, laughing while the other dads teased him.

"Okay, ladies," De'Andrea said. "Put me to work!"

Surprised, pleasantly, by how upbeat De'Andrea sounded, Rebecca offered her a stack of red and white checkered tablecloths. "Wanna help me cover all the tables with these?"

But before De'Andrea responded, her eyes widened as she focused on something past Rebecca's shoulder and pointed. "Who the hell are they?"

Rebecca turned around and saw a group of twenty or so men dressed in matching khaki pants, white polo shirts, and black combat boots marching side by side toward the amphitheater. The men in the very center of the formation held a parade banner. They were still too far away that Rebecca couldn't make out the words, but she would recognize the colors and logo from any distance. Supporters United for the Confederate Society.

"What the hell are they doing here?" Rebecca shouted as she ran over to the playground to grab her kids, other moms close behind.

The dads dropped what they were doing with the DJ setup and joined their families. The rest of the Rolling Hills residents who had gathered for the event left their respective picnic blankets and coalesced as a crowd, ready to confront the SUCS group.

There's way more of us than them, Rebecca thought. But the number imbalance in her group's favor wasn't all that comforting.

Seeing a group of white men dressed the same, marching toward them, was frightening. What if they had guns? What if *anyone* had guns? *Why the fuck is the world like this?*

They lived in Rolling Hills for a peaceful existence. What was happening? Whatever was about to go down, Rebecca and her crew didn't even need to say it out loud: it was time to go.

She grabbed her phone from the back pocket of her jeans and zoomed in to get a closer shot of the SUCS banner. She texted it to Todd with the message "Look who crashed our party. Packing up now." She didn't wait for a reply.

"Girls," she said to Lyla and Isabella. "Help me pack up the wagon. It's time to go home."

"Mommy! What's going on?" Isabella cried out.

"Mom! Who are those people?" Lyla asked.

"I'll explain in the car," Rebecca responded. She could hear the other parents and kids having the same exact exchanges all around her.

"Where's Daddy?" That was Nina.

Rebecca turned around and saw that Malik hadn't yet returned from the restrooms.

De'Andrea reached for Nina's hand and said, "It's okay, Daddy will be right back."

Oh shit.

The restrooms were right next to the amphitheater, right where the crowd was growing.

"Oh look! How pretty!" Isabella shouted, pointing up to the sky. All the helium balloons had been released, and for a moment Rebecca paused to watch them float away.

Shouting from the groups of people surrounding the statue

immediately called her attention back down to the ground. It was only a matter of time before it escalated. Malik needed to get out of there fast.

Rebecca didn't want to alarm Nina or any of the other kids. In the calmest voice she could muster, she said, "De'Andrea, why don't you text him? Maybe he got turned around? One of the guys could go meet him and we could link up with him in the parking lot."

De'Andrea paused for a moment and held mostly still except for her right hand, which she was tapping on the side of her thigh, concentrating all her nervous energy so the rest of her could remain calm for her daughter.

She locked eyes with Rebecca while addressing Nina. "I think I'll go over and get Daddy. Can you stay here with Miss Rebecca and all the other mommies?"

"Are you sure?" Rebecca asked. When she saw De'Andrea's desperate and silent plea, she added, "That's a good idea. Isabella, honey. You and Nina can help me finish packing up the wagon."

She turned to De'Andrea. "We'll meet you at the parking lot. I'll keep my phone out. You do the same, okay?"

And with that, De'Andrea sprinted in the direction where none of them should have gone: toward the crowd.

Within a few minutes, the whole diversity committee crew was packed up and ready to head toward the parking lot. Rebecca swiped open her phone. No new texts or calls.

Fuck.

"Mom!" Lyla pointed toward the parking lot as the group took a shortcut to the cars. "It's Dad! You said he wasn't coming today!"

Rebecca's shoulders dropped. *Thank God.*

Todd ran up to the group and breathlessly greeted the girls as he put his hand on Rebecca's shoulder.

"What are you doing here?" she asked him, smiling. She was relieved but hadn't expected this.

"I got your text." He grabbed the wagon handle and started pulling. "Let's get the heck out of here, right, girls? Who thinks they can beat me to the car while I'm lugging this thing?"

"I'm obviously going to win!" Lyla ran off with Nina and Isabella already behind.

Rebecca grabbed Todd's wrist. "Babe, De'Andrea and Malik."

"Oh, right," he said, looking around. "Where are they?"

She explained what had happened and Todd said, "Here, you catch up to the girls. I'll go find them."

"No, let me go. I don't want to leave De'Andrea on her own."

"Bec, it's getting crazy over there."

"I'll be fine," Rebecca said. "You take the girls home. Better yet, go for ice cream or something. Keep them entertained and happy. I'll be in touch."

Todd didn't look convinced, and she could tell he was about to insist he go. She didn't have time for the tug-of-war. She took off toward the crowd and called back to him to say, again, "I'll be fine!"

Rebecca's pace quickened with each step. Before she got to the theater, she stopped en route, in shock. The tarp had been torn down to reveal Longstreet, and the cheers in response were deafening. She kept going, and as she got closer, she saw police officers herding what had to be at least a hundred people behind yellow police tape. Nearly every single person had a phone out. Some were snapping photos, others recording demonstrators yelling at one another—all of it a regurgitation of what people had been arguing about ever since the town hall.

As soon as she got close enough for a clear shot, Rebecca took out her phone and got her own photo of Longstreet and texted it to the group chat. She scanned the crowd.

How am I going to find them in the middle of this shit show? And then . . .

She understood what De'Andrea meant about sticking out in this town. There really weren't any other Black people—except for over by the restrooms, where she spotted De'Andrea and Malik.

She headed in their direction, and as she got closer she saw . . . *What?!*

Malik was in handcuffs.

What the fuck?!

"Hey!" Rebecca called out, trying to get the police officers' attention. "What is going on here?!"

De'Andrea appeared to be arguing with two police officers— both white men, one very tall and one very short—plus another tall white man whose back was to Rebecca.

She continued elbowing her way through the crowd to make it to the other side of the statue where the squad cars were parked. She ducked under the police tape.

One officer—the shorter one—held his hand up. "Ma'am, I'm sorry. This is a restricted area."

"Restricted by whom?" she asked, hands on her hips. "This is a public park, and I have every right to go wherever I want!"

The other officer, De'Andrea and Malik, and the other man all turned around at the same time.

Oh, for fuck's sake. Rebecca was stunned. *This is not happening.*

"Jack?"

"Rebecca! Thank God!"

"What are you doing here?" she asked, not wanting to know the answer. Jack's face and arms were scuffed up, and his pants had streaks of dirt all up and down the side of one of his legs. "What happened to you?"

"I lost my phone, and I was working with these officers to get in touch with Todd."

De'Andrea looked at Rebecca, then at Jack, then at Rebecca again. "You know this man?"

Oh, Jesus.

"Yes." Rebecca glared at Jack while answering De'Andrea. "This is my brother-in-law."

Jack pointed his head toward De'Andrea and Malik and asked Rebecca, "Wait. You know these people?"

"Yes, Jack. From school," Rebecca answered. "Remember Izzy talking about her friend Nina?"

Rebecca put her hand on De'Andrea's arm in reassurance. "Don't worry about Nina. Todd's got the girls and is taking them to get ice cream. She can stay at our house as long as you need."

Jack shook his head as if he couldn't believe what was happening, either. Rebecca noticed the right side of his face was bright red, scraped up, and his right eye was starting to swell.

"Jack! What happened to your face?!"

"Why don't you ask your friend here," Jack said, pointing to Malik.

"My husband did not touch this man," De'Andrea said, ignoring Jack and talking only to the officers. "My husband is the one being attacked here!"

"No one is attacking him!" Jack yelled. "I'm the one who has clearly been assaulted!"

"Assaulted? Really?" De'Andrea fired back. "I saw what happened. And you were the one who started all this."

The same police officer who tried to stop Rebecca from crossing the police tape put his hands back up again and addressed De'Andrea. "Okay, okay, calm down. Let's try to get to the bottom of this."

Did he really tell her to calm down?!

"Did you really just tell her to calm down?" Rebecca decided this was worth saying out loud. "Her husband is in handcuffs!"

The thing was, De'Andrea was actually—impressively—holding it together. Rebecca would be screaming if the police had put Todd in handcuffs. And Malik was even *more* calm.

He turned toward the policemen to talk directly to them. "As I was saying, Officers, I was here in the park today with my wife and daughter and a group of families from her school. I left the group to use these restrooms.

"As I was walking out of the restroom, I could tell something was off. We haven't lived here a long time, but I saw a crowd forming and people becoming more agitated. I immediately wanted to get back to my family, but then that group of men over there—"

Malik pointed toward the group of SUCS men who were still holding their banner and shouting in people's faces, only now they'd been joined by a lot more people—mostly men, but some women, too—who Rebecca recognized from the town hall. This was supposed to be a reconciliation! Why were they here? This whole issue had already been settled!

Jack interrupted. "That group of men over there are defending our democracy!"

Rebecca snapped her head toward Jack. "What are you *talking* about?"

Malik took a deep breath and wouldn't even look in Jack's direction.

The taller officer, who appeared to be at least ten years younger than his partner, gestured to his notepad and said, "I'm with you, sir, but please, let him finish so I can file my report."

"You're *with* him?! What is this? A police conspiracy? And what kind of report are you going to file? This is insane! Let me have your badge number!" Rebecca could hear herself and knew she should probably take it down a few notches. But this didn't feel like real life.

The officer with the notepad ignored Rebecca, which pissed her off even more, and motioned to Malik to keep going.

"As I was saying, Officer . . ." Malik had to shout over two distinct chants that had broken out in the crowd. Rebecca tried to make out what they were saying.

With the help of two men, a young woman had climbed atop the statue. *Oh!* Rebecca realized it was Rainee, the girl from Justice in Parks! Shouting into a megaphone, she led half the demonstrators in a call and response.

"The people! United! Will never be defeated!"

Every time they finished, another group of people would answer the chant. "The South! Still rises! We'll never be divided!"

Determined to give his side of the story, Malik spoke even louder. "More and more people kept coming, and I was literally overtaken. All I wanted to do was get back to my wife and little girl. But then all of a sudden, people started getting rough. Shoving in all directions. Somehow I tripped, and as I was falling to the ground, I fell onto this man."

The longer Malik maintained his composure, the more agitated Jack became, until he couldn't wait any longer to jump in. "You mean you *tackled* me!"

He gestured to his face and his pant leg. "Look at me! Does this look like the result of an accidental fall?"

Rebecca couldn't hold herself back any longer, either. "Come on! There is no way that Malik attacked you."

She turned to the officers. "There is no way he attacked him. No way."

This time, the other officer spoke. "Ma'am, please, we need to get a statement from both men and find out whether Mr. Myland here wants to press charges."

"Press charges?! For what?" Rebecca demanded.

And I dare them to tell me *to calm down.*

"This was clearly an accident. Look around! Everyone here is acting insane." Rebecca threw her arms up in the air, pointing toward the chanting crowd. Their voices had settled into the background like the too-loud jukebox music in a bar that everyone ignores and shouts over. "What are you going to do, arrest everyone?"

"No, ma'am, that's not our plan. As long as everyone remains peaceful," said the officer taking notes. "But if there's been an alleged assault, then we may have to make an arrest."

Rebecca turned to Jack. "Look at me. Don't you dare file charges. These are my friends. You need to let this go. It was an *accident.*"

Rebecca was trembling with rage, fear, and sheer disbelief. This was surreal. She'd watched, shared, and commented on viral video after viral video for years. She knew people still wanted their Confederate monuments, their whitewashed history. She knew white people accused Black people of violence and that the police couldn't help but side with the accusers. But all that happened in two-minute videos that could fit in her palm. It happened with someone else, *somewhere else*. Not here. Not in Rolling Hills. How was it that Rebecca was now in one of those videos? And there would most certainly be videos. She looked around and saw at least half a dozen people filming their exchange.

Without even waiting for Jack's response, she turned back to the police officers. "He won't be filing charges. You can uncuff this man and we can all go home. Unless you want to be known for arresting the only Black man here. Do you *really* want to do that? With all these people filming? Is that what you want?"

Rebecca's heart was pounding and she sucked for air, the same way she did after sprinting the last stretch on her long runs. She could see De'Andrea and Malik in her periphery, but she wasn't sure how, exactly, they were reacting to her rant because she refused to turn away from the police and Jack.

"Mr. Myland?" The older officer looked up at Jack.

Jack straightened up, brushed the dirt off his pants, and smoothed out his shirt. He puffed out his chest and gave the officers a nod. "It's okay, fellas, no charges. Let's let this one go."

Rebecca squinted at Jack and shook her head. *You asshole. Who the fuck put you in charge?*

The officers looked at each other. The older one said to his partner, "Go ahead, take 'em off."

Then he turned to Malik as his partner removed the cuffs. "Well, Mr. Whitman, you're free to go. No hard feelings, right? We're just doin' our job. I'm sure you and your wife understand."

Rebecca wanted to yell. *No hard feelings?! Seriously?* But she had already said enough, and more than anything, she wanted an end to this entire shit show. So she remained silent and watched Malik rub his wrists as De'Andrea hugged him tightly and rubbed his back.

Malik cleared his throat. "Thank you, Officers. If it's alright with you, we'll be heading home, then."

He took De'Andrea's hand and nodded toward Rebecca before turning and walking to the parking lot.

Rebecca nodded back, lifted her hand to give them a tiny wave, and exhaled. She didn't know what to do with Jack. But at least the situation had de-escalated. Malik was safe. And the statue *was* coming down. Her head was still spinning, though, and the pit in her stomach growing. Everything had worked out, hadn't it?

Then why didn't it feel over?

TWENTY-FIVE

De'Andrea

Malik followed closely behind De'Andrea as they walked toward the high-rise building on Peachtree Street, and she found herself staring at his reflection in the mirrored glass. His face was still handsome, but thinner. The classic Adidas tracksuit paired with shell tops had become a daily uniform of sorts, even though it no longer hugged his once-toned physique. But it wasn't just Malik's appearance that worried her. It was how he seemed to move through the world, less confident and certain of himself.

Ever the gentleman, he quickly met then passed her stride to hold open the main door. When they stepped inside the building's grand entryway, De'Andrea grabbed Malik's hand and gave it a soft squeeze. It was her silent way of asking the rhetorical question "Are you okay?"

They headed toward the security desk, still hand in hand, their fingers interlocked in a comforting familiarity. She squeezed Malik's hand again and this time his large palm tightened around hers with an answer: No, he wasn't okay. But he was working on it. *They* were working on it.

Day by day.

That was all they *could* do.

"Hi, we're here to see Dr. Jones. Suite 802." De'Andrea reached into her tote to retrieve her wallet as Malik pulled out his trifold and placed his driver's license on the counter.

Brown-skinned and pretty, the guard's long braids were pulled into a simple ponytail that called attention to her youthful face. Even a basic security uniform couldn't hide her enviable shape. As she slid Malik's ID toward her, De'Andrea read her name badge: *Chanté.*

She probably assumed the Whitmans were some B-list celebrity couple. Ever since their lives made national news, De'Andrea and Malik had started doing something they used to joke about, something they'd sworn they'd never do: wear sunglasses inside. Chanté reached for a ballpoint pen to write their names in the visitors log. Now accustomed to the unwelcome recognition, De'Andrea braced herself and waited.

You'll figure out who we are in 5, 4, 3, 2 . . .

As Chanté returned their identification, she looked up at them sympathetically and whispered, "I've been praying for y'all. Like, really praying."

"Thank you. We certainly need it." Malik tried his best to sound upbeat, but it didn't land.

His attempts at being positive rarely landed these days.

De'Andrea forced a smile as she slid her ID back in her wallet and dropped it into her purse. "Yes, thank you so much, Chanté."

Then, because she'd also become accustomed to not making small talk, De'Andrea hooked her elbow with Malik's and turned toward the elevators.

She knew Chanté meant well. That, like most people, she had no idea how De'Andrea felt knowing strangers were interceding with God on the Whitmans' behalf. Nor how odd it was that strangers felt compelled to tell her about their prayers. Likewise, there was no way of knowing when someone's petitions would switch to prying.

"Are you going to press charges, because ain't no way . . ."

"Placing racists on paid administrative leave. Paid? That's a damn shame! Is that even legal?"

"It must be so hard for y'all to even sleep at night. Gotta be having the worst dreams, right?"

"I just know if that happened to me or someone I love . . ."

There was so much public commentary, so many unsolicited thoughts and opinions. If only people knew how stressful rather than soothing their words were.

"I hope y'all have a great day!" Chanté called out as De'Andrea and Malik walked across the lobby. "Remember, God is in control! No racist weapon formed against you shall prosper!"

Heads turned in their direction. Murmurings grew louder as more people either wondered or recognized who they were. Even with sunglasses shielding their eyes, De'Andrea felt exposed.

That day in the park had changed everything.

It had been almost two weeks since they'd escaped Rolling Hills for Atlanta, and De'Andrea must have replayed the town's reconciliation gathering in her mind a million times. Somehow, she'd driven to the Mylands', taken Nina from Todd's arms, and thanked him. She was grateful he'd kept their daughter safe but also angry and confused. How could *he* be the brother of the man who'd accused her husband? Somehow, she'd driven her little family back to 25 Oakview Lane, a place that no longer felt like home.

Even though Nina didn't see or know what happened to her daddy, she knew *something* had happened. Something so terrible it was best to not ask her parents. Instead, she'd insisted on sleeping in their bed that night, a request she hadn't made since her toddler years. Somehow, Nina knew Daddy needed *her* to comfort *him*.

Malik had done his best to console his daughter, saying their normal good night prayers as he tucked them both under the covers. De'Andrea had watched them drift off to sleep quickly, both exhausted and finally safe in each other's arms. She had no idea how long she'd stared at them. But she did remember lying awake for hours thinking of how close they'd come to the unthinkable.

At some point during the night, De'Andrea dozed off, although it was also quite possible she'd passed out from fatigue. Regardless, she'd awakened in a panic from a nightmare even more horrific than the one she was living: watching a black casket being lowered into the ground as she stood alone at a grave site weeping. She'd gone to the bathroom and vomited uncontrollably, as if her body was forcibly trying to release all the emotions she'd been holding in the pit of her belly since she saw Malik in handcuffs.

Even now, two weeks later, that feeling still lingered.

"You alright, babe?" Malik pulled her close to him as the elevator doors closed behind them.

"Yeah," De'Andrea lied. After pressing the button for the eighth floor, she leaned into him and rested her head on his broad chest. "Just glad no one got on here with us."

Common things, like riding in elevators with strangers, now made her anxious.

Because simply being around anyone other than their friends made her anxious.

As the elevator ascended, she thought about the pictures and videos of Malik in handcuffs, how their painful ordeal now lived forever on the internet. Whenever she was out in public, De'Andrea couldn't help but wonder, *Did they see what happened? Do they know that day at the park damn near ruined our entire lives?*

Some folks at the park had shared footage from their cell phones in real time, and in less than twenty-four hours, her husband had become the latest trending tragedy. Seeing his very personal and very painful experience be used for others' agendas was even worse.

Malik Whitman was another reason to abolish the police. Malik Whitman was another person to remind America of its racist past and present. Amateur journalists and internet sleuths dug up information on the entire Whitman family. Pictures of De'Andrea's childhood home in Mississippi to underscore her humble beginnings and rise to an accomplished lawyer. Pictures of Nina from a STEM camp she'd attended last summer to highlight her beauty and brilliance. Pictures of Malik speaking at conferences and stepping off planes with Mr. Calhoun, one of the richest and most successful businessmen in the world. Proof that if something like this could happen to a well-educated and wealthy Black family like the Whitmans, it could happen to anyone.

De'Andrea doom-scrolled and googled "Racism in Rolling Hills" for hours the next morning, unable to pull herself away from reading every headline and social media post about what had happened. Even as each comment section became more torturous than the last. White folks who wished Malik had been lynched. Black folks who insisted that's what Malik deserved for "living out there with white folks." And there were white *and* Black folks who claimed the entire incident was staged.

Between cursing and crying, De'Andrea tried to respond to texts from loved ones and former coworkers expressing concern that their calls were going straight to voicemail.

"Oh my God! I saw what happened. Call me!"

"We're so sorry this keeps happening. Why does this keep happening?!"

"Are y'all alright out there? Just let us know that you're okay."

Within a few hours, De'Andrea had simply given up, overwhelmed by the volume of messages and from copying and pasting the same response over and over:

De'Andrea

Thank you for checking on us! We're okay. We just need some time. Promise to call soon! 🖤

Especially because her replies didn't pacify the senders. Rather, it seemed to only encourage deeper inquiries. The last text she'd read before turning off her phone entirely was from James:

Sunday, April 8 at 9:23 AM
James

Hi Mrs. Whitman. Please accept my sincerest apologies for texting you during this difficult time. Just want to let you know it might be best for y'all to stay in the house. Lots of news crews out here. Of course, I won't let them inside. But seems like they're posting up and planning to stay for a while. They tried to interview me too, ask me questions about y'all. But I declined. I'm so sorry about what happened yesterday. Please give my regards to Malik. If anything changes out here, I'll be sure to let you know. And when I get off work, I can come by the house if you want me to. You know, if y'all don't feel safe. Just say the word and I gotchu! ✊🏾

De'Andrea had felt trapped. She hadn't thought about leaving the house, but there was something terrifying about knowing that she couldn't.

Malik stayed in bed all morning. And although she wanted to lie next to him, her gut told her that he needed to be alone. His rest certainly hadn't been peaceful—throughout the night, she'd watched him toss and turn with Nina in his arms, trying to escape whatever was troubling him.

Besides, what would she even say to him? What *could* she say that she hadn't already said? The only solace she could offer were kisses as she rubbed his back in small circles the way he liked and bringing meals to his bedside that remained uneaten.

When Nina had finally awakened, De'Andrea spent much of the late morning and early afternoon playing pretend with her daughter. It was so much easier than dealing with reality. After lunch, she'd settled Nina in for an afternoon nap—the first nap she'd willingly taken since De'Andrea could remember.

How had *this* happened to *them*?

Somehow, sleep found her in late afternoon, a dreamless slumber that she awakened from upon hearing a vehicle turn into their driveway. Instantly, her heart began pounding, her palms were sweaty and clammy as she ran into the living room and rushed over to the window to peek through the tightly shuttered blinds. When she saw Craig's truck, De'Andrea screamed and ran outside. She was met with Toni's and Simone's loving embraces. The twins hugged her legs as LL barked and ran in circles. All the commotion awakened Malik and Nina, and thankfully the kids believed the adults when they said, "These are good tears. We're crying because we're just so happy to see each other."

God bless James for having the wherewithal to let their friends through security without permission.

Craig had gone to the bedroom with Malik and closed the door. Toni and Simone told De'Andrea that she didn't need to pack, that they'd already taken care of everything. When the twins told Nina to gather her favorite things because they were about to embark on a surprise road trip to Atlanta, she'd squealed. Even though De'Andrea wanted to escape Rolling Hills, she hadn't given much thought to how they'd do it. But, of course, they had to drive. Malik was all over national news and social media. Trying to walk through an airport and board a flight would have been its own harrowing experience.

The friends had hit the road shortly after sunset, foolishly hopeful the darkness would encourage the kids to sleep through the nine-hour drive. The last thing De'Andrea remembered was listening to Nina's and the twins' giggles from the third row. Unlike the children, she'd slept soundly, nearly the entire ride, safely sandwiched between Malik on her left and Simone on her right, grateful that their village had driven all that way just to save them.

Once they were safely tucked away in the comforting familiarity of Atlanta, hunkered down in one of Toni and Craig's guest bedrooms, the last thing De'Andrea wanted was to return to Rolling Hills. She couldn't stop thinking about white folks who'd been at the park. The despicable ones who marched in favor of preserving a Confederate statue. The parents and neighbors who'd stood around and watched and, even worse, filmed, and shared images of Malik being handcuffed and treated like a criminal for simply trying to defend himself. Maybe they thought they were better than the proud bigots, but in De'Andrea's mind, they were equally horrible. How could they take a stand *against* a statue but not take a stand *for* Malik?

Why had there been only one person willing to do that?

Becky had gone well, full Becky on those cops. It reminded De'Andrea of a viral clip she'd seen of a white woman placing herself between a Black man and the police officer attempting to arrest him. Because that white woman *knew* she wouldn't be harmed. Or at least, that she had far less of a chance of being harmed.

Even though Becky had a way of getting on her last nerve sometimes, she'd shown up for her and Malik that day. Shown up and showed out!

As much as she hated to acknowledge the truth, De'Andrea knew they could only hide away in Atlanta for so long. They had to go back to Rolling Hills. At least for the foreseeable future. Mama was there. Malik's job and Nina's school were there. And in an absurd twist of irony, now De'Andrea had roots there, too—she'd signed a year-long lease for the Whitman Way's office space. Do-gooders across the country continued to donate to the nonprofit, and of course, she'd give back every dollar to undo what had happened to Malik. But since she couldn't, she used the money to establish a special endowment to cover dementia care for Black and brown folks. The way she saw it, the influx of donations were like micro-reparations.

Rolling Hills wasn't perfect. Not even close. But it would have to be good enough. For now. Besides, wasn't home wherever Malik and Nina were?

And then there's that other reason we need to stay in Rolling Hills, De'Andrea thought. A big one. And a total surprise. She hadn't yet told Malik, but a tiny hint of a smile appeared on her face as she imagined how she'd reveal the news to him later that day.

"Ready?" Malik interrupted her daydreaming as the elevator stopped and the doors slid open.

"Ready." De'Andrea responded, and she grabbed Malik's hand as they stepped out to head to their last in-person appointment with Dr. Jones.

Craig had offered to drive the Whitmans back to Rolling Hills, but Malik had insisted on renting a car. They'd processed a lot in Atlanta with Dr. Jones and with their friends, but there was something about the road trip that seemed necessary to transition back to their everyday lives. And they wanted time alone during the nine-hour drive. With Nina in the backseat wearing headphones and entranced by something on her tablet, Malik and De'Andrea were able to talk through everything that might come next.

"You know what I keep thinking about?" Malik asked. "What do we need to do to get on with our lives? Like, I don't want to be stuck thinking about this and just feeling like a victim forever. I just want to feel normal again."

But what was normal?

De'Andrea wondered if they would ever feel that seemingly elusive feeling again and also if they'd felt that way in Rolling Hills in the first place.

"I know we've already talked about this and there's no way we can even think about moving right now, but . . . you do want to move at some point, right?" Malik turned his head for a quick glance at De'Andrea before focusing back on the road.

"I mean, I don't know. I don't know . . ." De'Andrea felt her eyes watering up. She blinked and felt tears stream down her face. How long before she would stop crying about all of this?

"You know I'm okay now, baby. I'm safe." Malik put his hand on her knee.

"Are you, though?" De'Andrea challenged. "Am I? And what about Nina? God only knows what's going to happen when she returns to school on Monday. What if her classmates tease her about her daddy getting arrested or something? That apology the police department issued was just some PR bullshit. Maybe there's something more we should do to hold them accountable. I know attorneys who can—"

"It's not worth it, Dee." Malik shook his head. "It's just not worth all the hassle and drama that's going to come with that. It's not going to fix the problem. And it's not going to change—"

"What happened." De'Andrea completed his sentence.

Malik was right. And she knew he was right. They were not the only Black folks something like this had happened to, nor would they be the last.

Still, it just didn't seem fair.

"You know, I'd honestly never given much thought to what happens after this kinda stuff," De'Andrea said. "You know, to the people it actually happened to. But now we know. Like, we know *know*. And it's not easy. But dammit, Malik. I refuse to let this take more from us than it already has."

"That's what I like to hear, Dee. We're going to survive this, babe. We already have."

"You're right, Leek. And I'm so grateful. Like, so grateful." De'Andrea's voice cracked. "I was so afraid of losing you that day. I mean, anything could have happened. Anything! But you're alive, you're still here. *We're* still here. And we have to celebrate that."

"And there's so much more to celebrate." Malik brightened up.

De'Andrea put her index finger to her lips to "shhh" him. She looked back at Nina to make sure she wasn't pretending to watch videos while actually eavesdropping on her parents' conversation. They didn't want to tell Nina the news that she was going to be a big sister until after De'Andrea's twelve-week sonogram.

Nina looked up from her tablet and shouted, "What, Mommy? Why are you looking at me?"

"Nothing, baby. Just making sure you're good. You good?"

Nina gave a thumbs-up and looked back down at her tablet.

De'Andrea laughed and admonished Malik. "Listen, I told you not to get too excited yet."

But she couldn't help but feel excited, too. Nothing was better than the moment she'd showed Malik the three positive pregnancy tests after their last appointment with Dr. Jones. She couldn't believe it. Getting pregnant with Nina had taken a lot of work and money and it hadn't been romantic at all. But this . . . this just happened who knows when. And once she got over the initial shock, there'd been nothing but joy. There was something that felt revolutionary about bringing another Black child into the world. Something that she imagined her ancestors must have felt—determined to keep going, to keep living, in spite of.

As soon as Malik pulled into the left turn lane and the Preserve signage came into view, De'Andrea's hopefulness was overridden by what felt like the onset of a panic attack. While they were away, Heidi had provided updates on the status of things in Rolling Hills. So she knew that even the most persistent journalists had given up on glimpsing the Whitmans and moved on to cover more salacious stories. Still, De'Andrea couldn't shake the memory of the mob of reporters Craig had driven by on their way out of town just a few weeks ago.

Deep breaths, Dee. Deep breaths.

When Malik approached the community's gated entrance and saw James standing at the security booth, they were thrilled.

"What's up, youngblood?" Malik dapped him up. "Man, thank you again for letting our friends in that day. Gettin' away for a while was exactly what we needed."

De'Andrea agreed. "Seriously. That time in Atlanta was so good for us."

"You're so welcome. Happy to help." James peered into the back window and laughed. "Ah, there's my buddy. She is knocked *out*!"

"What??" De'Andrea and Malik said in unison as they turned around to see Nina, her tablet slipping off her lap and neck crooked to the side.

"You know that child stayed awake the entire drive and now, five minutes from home, she finally falls asleep?" De'Andrea shook her head.

James smiled. "Well, I'm glad y'all got away for a while because it got crazy. I'm also really happy you're back!"

Well, at least someone is happy about it! De'Andrea thought.

"What's going on with you?" Malik asked, eager to change the subject. "How's school?"

"Everything's going good," James replied. "Just ready to wrap up this semester."

They'd lingered at the security booth talking to James for a few more minutes, but they could only delay the inevitable for so long.

25 Oakview Lane awaited.

Malik drove along the tree-canopied streets slowly. And De'Andrea knew he had just as much trepidation, if not more, than she did.

Thankfully, Ingrid wasn't tending to her garden. Nor was Heidi outside playing with Charlotte. De'Andrea wasn't ready to see her neighbors just yet. Not even the ones she liked.

"Well, look at that." Malik nodded toward their front door as he pulled into the driveway.

Dozens of flowers, both fresh and wilted, semi-filled helium balloons, and handwritten posters had been placed on their steps and entryway.

"Not sure how I feel about that." De'Andrea heard her sharpness and tried to soften. "I mean, it's a nice gesture and all. Just . . ."

"Nah, I get it," Malik said as he put the car in park and turned off the ignition.

No amount of goodwill could change what had happened or how they felt. Still, maybe it was something. Or the *beginning* of something, at least. Maybe the whole park incident *had* opened more people's eyes. Maybe they'd begun to understand that no amount of "All are welcome here" signs could make a place feel welcoming; that their hospitality came with a set of conditions, the principal one being: We want you here. But only if you'll act like us. *Maybe*. But De'Andrea knew better than to hinge her choices and happiness on waiting for any of that to happen.

They sat in the rental car for a few moments.

"Guess we have to get out at some point, right?" Malik said.

De'Andrea returned his half-hearted smile and said through

clenched teeth, "Do we? I mean, I'm just fine in here. It's kinda cozy."

They left Nina sleeping and got out of the car to survey all the offerings on their front porch. Several of the signs were covered in childlike drawings and propped up by stuffed animals. As soon as she woke up, Nina would be so excited to see all of this. De'Andrea smiled as she thought about her daughter's still innocent and easy-to-forgive heart. She'd appreciate the neighborly kindness even if her parents were conflicted.

It was time to go inside. While Malik gathered Nina into his arms, De'Andrea punched in the coded numbers to turn off the alarm. She wasn't sure what she was expecting to see. It was just their house, after all. And it seemed to be just as they'd left it. But it was surprisingly harder than she thought it would be to muster up the strength to open the door and walk inside.

After Malik took Nina upstairs to her room and laid her in bed, he came back downstairs and joined De'Andrea in the sunroom.

"I can't believe my plants are still alive," she told him. "Simone's little watering hack actually worked."

Malik walked over and took the flowerpot from her hands. "'Be resilient like a snake plant.'" He read the words etched into the ceramic. "What's that even mean?"

"These plants are hard to kill," she explained. "They can go weeks without receiving proper care. They can even grow in the dark."

"Hmmm," Malik said.

Before De'Andrea could respond, she felt her phone buzz in her back pocket. It was James.

"Hi, James. What's up?"

"Sorry to bother you, Mrs. Whitman, but Mrs. Myland is here to see you. She's been by a few times in the past couple of weeks to drop off flowers and such. I've let her through, but since you're back and all, I wanted to make sure it was okay. She told me to tell you she just wants to drop something off, to give you something."

De'Andrea sighed. She really didn't want company. And she most definitely didn't want to rehash what happened in the park or hear a rundown of what had happened while they were away in Atlanta. De'Andrea knew she'd have to face Becky at some point. Nina had asked three times on their drive home if she could have a playdate with Isabella when they got back.

Guess now is as good a time as any!

"Sure, James. You can let her in. Thank you."

Malik raised his eyebrows. "What's up?"

"We have our first vistor," De'Andrea smiled. "Be right back."

De'Andrea opened the front door and stepped outside. A few minutes later, a silver Range Rover turned into their cul-de-sac. After pulling into the driveway, she got out of her car and waved before walking around to the passenger side to retrieve a large insulated bag.

Oh, I know she ain't bring us no white people food! De'Andrea stifled a giggle. She reminded herself it was the thought that counts.

"Hiii! It's so good to see you. When Todd told me he'd gotten a text from Malik that you all were getting back this evening, I thought, you know what? They're going to need some food. So I wanted to drop off a few things—fresh fruit, eggs, milk, coffee pods, and that organic peanut butter puffs cereal Nina always likes to eat when she's at our house. And this," Becky held up a round casserole dish like a trophy. "This is my mom's famous Tater Tot chicken hotdish. I know it sounds weird but it's so good. The ultimate comfort food. Just warm it up in the oven for a bit and voilá! Dinner is served. And don't worry, I know what you're thinking. I added seasoning," Becky said proudly.

De'Andrea laughed. "Well, thank you for that. And it's good to see you too."

"But listen, you all just got home. Get settled! I'll text you in the morning to see when we can get the girls together, okay?"

"Sounds like a plan," De'Andrea said before adding, "Thank you, Rebecca."

"You're so welcome."

De'Andrea waved as Rebecca—her friend, she supposed— drove off.

Then she stopped abruptly and turned back around to face De'Andrea again. With her brow furrowed and tone earnest, she added, "I know there's a lot to talk about. We can do it in your own time. If you want to."

De'Andrea nodded. "Thanks, Rebecca."

De'Andrea went back inside, put away the food, and joined Malik in the sunroom.

"You good?" Malik asked, feet still up, drinking his tea in the sunroom.

"Yup! Matter of fact, I'm great," De'Andrea answered. She rubbed her fingers on the snake plant and sat on Malik's lap.

"You know what?" She wrapped her arms around his neck. "The hell with snake plants. Black people have got to be the most resilient beings on this planet. We go through so much! Too much!"

"Yet here we are. Still surviving."

De'Andrea walked over to the large pictureesque window and looked out into the backyard. Flowers swayed in the greener than green grass as four deer emerged from the woods. Soon, the Whitmans would also be a family of four.

"Not just surviving," De'Andrea smiled as she rubbed her barely noticeable belly. "Surviving and thriving."

ACKNOWLEDGMENTS

Well, here we are. The hardest part of a book for every author to write: the acknowledgments. How is it possible to thank everyone who played a role in getting *Rebecca, Not Becky* into the hands and hearts of readers? From our first editor, Jenn Baker, who trusted and believed in our vision to Tara Parsons who helped us sprint across the editorial finish line, I cannot express enough thanks to the many HarperCollins and Amistad publishing professionals who helped make *Rebecca, Not Becky* a book Catherine and I are proud to be our first co-authored novel. (Also, I *must* thank my dear friend, Catherine, for trusting me when I said, "Let's write a novel together! It'll be so much fun!" Okay, so I might have lied about the 'fun' but um, did you die? Ha!) And of course, a huge shoutout to our literary agents who advocated for us and *Rebecca, Not Becky* every step of this journey: Emily Sylvan Kim of Prospect Agency and my amazing agents at New Leaf Literary & Media, Joanna Volpe and Jordan Hill.

As any author will tell you, writing a book is a daunting task (yes, even when you're doing it with a friend!). Because the time and energy required doesn't just take a toll on authors, our work also impacts the lives of our loved ones. From our partners and children to our closest friends, thank you for supporting this book. Thank you for listening to my every complaint and giving me constructive criticism when I needed it. Thank you for enlightening and enriching De'Andrea's storyline by sharing your personal experiences with racism and encouraging me to be bold in the retelling them. Thank you for understanding the many times I canceled or rescheduled plans . . . because revisions. And a very special thank you to my two very best friends—my mother and my daughter, Nalah—for being my constant cheerleaders and biggest fans.

Lastly, I want to thank you, dear reader. For not only reading *Rebecca, Not Becky* but for committing to 'getting comfortable with being uncomfortable' while doing so. It is my hope that this novel allows you to see yourself and your community through a different lens, one that focuses on learning and growing from the past rather than repeating it. Because we are all here to do more than survive—let's thrive. And let's do so together.

Christine Platt

I think because this is my first novel, I'm tempted to thank every single person who has played any type of significant role in my life from early childhood until now. And in this moment, as Christine and I finish the book, I do feel an overwhelming sense of gratitude, but this isn't the Oscars. So I'm doing my best to be concise.

To Jenn Baker, a passionate editor and advocate, thank you for believing in this book—and in Christine's and my ability to write it—from the very beginning. To our editor Tara Parsons, your enthusiasm for this project was the invitation and inspiration we needed to pull ourselves out of a hole we thought we'd never climb our way out of. You helped us believe in ourselves again and find our way to the other side of this. Thank you.

To my agent Emily Sylvan Kim, I can't believe it took from 1989, when we were classmates at Hill Middle School, until 2020 to finally find each other. But we sure have made up for it. Thank you for inviting me into Rolling Hills and for your seemingly bottomless reserve of kindness and optimism, which sustained me through this project when I felt most challenged.

Christine and I spent nearly three years writing this book which means there have been too many drafts to count. Thank you to Amanda, Barb, Carolina, Emily, and Mary for reading early versions and providing honest feedback to get us closer and closer to the story we wanted to tell. And thank you to Carolina, Colleen, Ed, Joanna, John Taylor, Jess, Kavitha, Lina & Max, Rebecca W., Rick, and Scott R. for spending time helping me get the most random details right. I now know more than I could have ever imagined about home security systems, tequila and gut health, shady real estate practices, multicultural festival dishes, the "flush", fancy wine, fancy scotch, golf jargon, the UVA Comm School, minor league baseball, and the utility of handcuffs over zip-ties.

My work in antiracism and storytelling began in earnest when I answered a job listing for a part-time gig with a documentary film production company called Point Made Films. Taking that job sent me down a trajectory that completely changed my life. I know conventional wisdom tells us we shouldn't call our co-workers family, but Point Made was a family and I'm grateful for our messy, chaotic, boundary-blurred time together. Thank you, Barb, for creating that family and, beyond that, being my friend, mentor, and fairy godmother all these years. So much of what I've accomplished has come about because you pushed me, taught me, and believed in me. And to André, my work husband-turned brother, thank you for your partnership in all things creative and your support as we each continue to "greenlight" ourselves.

Rebecca, Not Becky is ultimately a book about how we show up for one another. And I wouldn't have been able to explore or write about that without all the people in my life who've shown me how to show up. I witnessed my mother care for both her mother and mother-in-law as they succumbed to dementia and I've watched countless friends do the same with their own parents, while also caring for young children—just as De'Andrea and Rebecca try to do.

To my older brothers, thank you for teaching me how to be tough, how to be funny, and how to take care of family through any kind of crisis. To my sister Mary, you've been there for me through *literally* everything. Thank you for showing me what unconditional love looks like.

And to my own little family of Norm, Kayla, Helen, Lizzie, and PJ (I told you I'd include him, Lizzie!), I love you all so much and wake up every day in near-disbelief that you are my family. I don't know how I got so lucky. Thank you, Norm, for holding down the fort when I had to disappear for hours and days on end to go on writing and editing benders. You kept everyone fed, clean, and on time to all the things. Now that I'm done with the book, I'll finally put all those clothes away that have been piling up in the corner.

And finally, to Christine, my co-author but even more importantly, my friend... We did it! I've loved playing around in Rolling Hills with you and can't wait to see where our imaginations take us next. Not only are you a source of light and inspiration and wisdom who gives so much to those you love and to the world, but you're also funny as hell and I can't believe how lucky I am that our paths crossed. The very last line of Charlotte's Web, one of my all-time favorite books, reads: "It is not often that someone comes along who is a true friend and a good writer. Charlotte was both." Thank you, Christine, for being my friend and a good writer. What a gift it has been to do "the work" with you.

Catherine Wigginton Greene